Clinch River Justice

Clinch River Justice

Alfred Patrick

To order additional copies of this book, contact:
Xlibris Corporation
1-888-795-4274
www.Xlibris.com
Orders@Xlibris.com
114564

CHAPTER 1

September 1942

Around midmorning Monday, Sheriff Hargis Fielding, three deputies, and several volunteers divided into two groups; each group would search its assigned side of the river below the Narrows. In the Narrows, Clinch River was forced into a sluice not more than a third of the width of the river above it, with vertical limestone walls on each side, and this dreadful waterway was strewn with boulders up to the size of a railroad car. Water roared, cascaded, churned, sprayed, and whirled in every direction imaginable as it plunged through the gorge to the riverbed at least sixty feet lower than the river channel at the bridge above the Narrows.

The object of the groups' search was the body of Sol Massey. At about 5:00 a.m. this morning, Madeline Massey called Sheriff Fielding to report that her husband had been drinking, left home after midnight, and had not come home yet. She told Harg that Sol had wanted her to go with him down to the river and left by himself when she wouldn't go.

"Where on the river do you think Sol went, Maddie?" the sheriff had asked.

"Years ago, the little beach just above the swinging bridge was a favorite place of ours. If he went to the river, it was probably to that spot."

"Okay, Sol might have gone anywhere after he left home, but I'll check down by the river and then come by your place. He might have come back home by then. Anyway, I'll see you in a while."

Harg had called Deputy Charley Scott and told him he would pick him up in half an hour to go look for Sol Massey. The sheriff pulled up to the Scott house in his black sedan, a 1940 four-door Dodge; Charley got in the car and Harg drove off. The sheriff was proud of the practical and durable car he had owned for two years, and he sometimes boasted of the eighty-seven horses the six-cylinder engine cranked out.

Hargis Fielding was an experienced lawman, having served as a deputy and two elected terms as high sheriff before he was elected again last year. He was thorough and careful and fair as he carried out investigations into any case, whether it involved a minor infraction of the law or a major crime. As he drove, Harg related to Charley what Maddie had told him, and they headed toward River Road and the swinging bridge. As they rode upstream beside the river, they heard the roar of the Narrows. The swinging bridge came into view; a truck sat barely off the road a few yards past the bridge, pointed in the direction from which they came. Harg passed the truck and parked behind it. They got out of the car and walked back to the black Dodge pickup; with its dents, scrapes, and accumulated grime, it looked older than its six years.

"That looks like the Massey truck," Charley said.

"Yep, I believe it is," the sheriff replied.

Harg and Charley inspected the truck; they noted a cracked side mirror, a tail light with no bulb or cover, two missing hubcaps, and a deformed front bumper. The top edge of the tailgate swagged near its midpoint; something round and heavy, like a log or a large pipe, had been dropped on it. The spare tire on a wheel fastened to the truck in front of the passenger-side door had good tread, but it was deflated. The truck's one windshield wiper arm hung from above the windshield without its blade. Sol Massey wasn't known for taking care of anything—not his truck, not his farm, not his family.

Charley looked inside. "The keys are in the truck," he told Harg, "so Sol must be nearby. Since he'd been drinking, he may have passed out somewhere around here."

They walked down to the beach, saw two sets of fairly fresh undisturbed tracks in the damp sand—one set made by man-sized feet and one set by smaller feet.

"Looks like tracks made by a man and a woman," observed Harg.

The tracks came from near the water's edge where indentions and tracks in the sand indicated that two people had sat there. From the river's edge, the tracks led toward the bridge. As they stood near the tracks, they scanned upstream and down for some sign of Sol. The river was running high and fast, and its color reminded Charley of lightly creamed coffee. The river carried small sticks, grass, dried cornstalks, bigger pieces of trees and dead wood, and other debris that had washed in upriver. Charley noticed something on the end of the swinging bridge and pointed it out to Harg. They walked toward the bridge and up the stone steps. Lying on the last step up to the bridge were a pair of black shoes and a folded coat, both of which appeared to fit a man.

Charley said, "These may belong to Sol."

"Could be," Harg agreed, "but we'll ask Maddie. For now, let's see how these shoes match up to the tracks."

He picked up the coat and pair of shoes, strode over to the tracks, and placed the shoes in the larger set of tracks. "A perfect fit," he said, almost to himself.

To Charley, the sheriff said, "We ought to have some sort of record of these smaller tracks. Why don't you get that tape measure from my car. Then draw yourself an outline of one of the tracks, and measure the length of it and the width of the heel and the widest part of the foot."

Charley drew an outline in his notebook, measured, and recorded the length and widths Harg asked for. They checked thoroughly around the bridge area on both sides of the river but found nothing else of interest.

The sheriff said, "Let's go see Maddie. You drive the truck if it'll start, and I'll follow you up to the Massey place." He placed the coat and shoes in his car.

Charley started the truck with no problem, and they drove to Sol and Maddie's house. As they drove up beside the house and got out of the vehicles, Maddie came out on the back porch and said, "Sheriff, you found Sol's truck! Where is Sol? Is he all right?"

"Yeah, we found his truck, but we don't know exactly where Sol is. We also found something else we need you to look at."

As Maddie walked toward the car, Harg pulled the coat and shoes out of his car and asked, "Do these belong to Sol?"

Maddie stopped abruptly when she saw the coat and shoes, and a hand flew to cover her mouth. Then she reached for the coat, inspected it and said, "This is Sol's coat, and those shoes are his too." After a short silence, she asked, "Where did you find them?"

"Layin' on this end of the bridge," the sheriff said.

"Oh, no! No. Don't tell me Sol went into the river!" Maddie wailed.

"We're not sure where Sol is or what happened to him. Why don't you tell me everything that happened last night from the time Sol got home until he left here."

Madeline related an account of what happened. Sunday night Sol wandered home after midnight and after several days' absence.

"I was in bed but hadn't gone to sleep, and I heard his truck pull up near the house," Maddie said, "and I heard the truck door slam shut. As he came up on the porch, he was singing, or trying to sing, 'Clementine' at the top of his lungs.

"He always loved that song," she said. "He sang it, he whistled it. Sometimes he sang it and put my name in it in place of Clementine. You know, 'Oh my darlin', oh my darlin', oh my darlin' Mad-uh-linc.' Cecilia and Lucas heard the song so much that they often whistled or sang it too."

Charley nodded; he knew her two children, Cecilia and Luke.

Maddie said that as Sol stumbled through the kitchen door, he had stopped singing and yelled, "Maddie! Maddie, where are you?" From her bedroom, Maddie answered, "I'm here, Sol. I'm coming."

She quickly slipped into a housedress and bedroom shoes and hurried into the kitchen. In a drunken stupor, Sol could barely stay upright as he walked. His hair was dirty and disheveled, he had three or four days growth of beard, and his white shirt was stained and dirty.

Maddie asked, "Where have you been, Sol?'

His quick retort as he swayed on his feet was, "None o' yer business. I don't answer tuh you."

Maddie put a hand behind Sol's elbow and said, "Why don't you sit down by the table, and I'll find you something to eat."

Sol slapped her hand away and swung at her with his fist. Maddie stepped back, his fist missed, and he almost fell. "I don't want tuh eat. I don't want nothin' from you, you naggin' witch!"

He flailed at Maddie with his left fist, and she dodged it again. She wasn't expecting him to swing again immediately, but he struck with his right arm. His fist caught her on her left cheekbone and staggered her back against the wall.

"That's how I got this bruise," Maddie said as she gingerly touched her bruised face.

Maddie continued, saying that even though Cecilia and Luke were now teenagers, they were afraid of their father and didn't want to be around him. Maddie was thankful that they were asleep in their rooms at the other end of the house. She said that after hitting her, Sol had plopped down in a kitchen chair and stared vacantly at Maddie. She began talking soothingly to him, saying they used to have lots of good times and that they should start doing some things together that they used to enjoy so much.

She said, "Friday or Saturday, let's go to Bristol and look around in some nice stores. Or, better yet, let's go to Abingdon and have a special meal at Martha Washington Inn, and then we could go see a Barter Theater play."

Sol said, "Don't want tuh go tuh Bristol, and don't like tuh eat at them fancy places like Martha Warshin'ton. Anyway, drivin' that far would use too much gas, and I'm 'bout out of gas ration stamps for this month."

"Out of ration stamps for the month already? Well, we could go to Norton and see a picture show."

Sol didn't respond but sat quietly for two or three minutes. Then he said, "Let's go down tuh the river, like we use ta. Way back, we had some good times by the river."

Maddie said, "Sol, you and I both need some rest. It's too late to be out gallivanting around by the river and howling at the moon. Let's go to bed, and tomorrow or tomorrow night we can go down by the river."

Maddie told them that Sol then lurched up out of the chair and said, "You go tuh bed. I'm goin' down tuh the river." Then he wobbled to the door and shuffled out on the porch and on toward his truck.

Maddie said she yelled, "Sol, you shouldn't be driving now. You're not sober enough. Come on back, I'll make coffee, and we can go to the river later."

Sol kept walking and weaving, got in the truck, started it, and drove off. Maddie said that was the last she saw of Sol.

"What time did you say Sol left the house?" Harg asked Maddie.

"Around two or two fifteen this morning, maybe later than that. I know it wasn't any earlier."

Harg told Maddie that Sol might still be somewhere else but that he thought they should begin looking for a body in the river. Charley and the sheriff left Maddie standing in the yard looking distraught. They wondered what she would tell Cecilia and Luke.

When Cecilia had heard the car and truck pull up by the house, she got out of bed, padded down the hall to the kitchen, and looked out the window. She saw the sheriff's car and Sol's truck, and her mother was talking to the sheriff and Charley Scott. Cecilia crept to the door and eased it open enough to hear the conversation between her mother and the lawman. As she listened to her mother tell the officers what happened last night, she closed her eyes and put her hands over her face as if she was trying to block or wipe something from her memory.

As they drove away from the Massey house, Charley asked the sheriff, "Do you really think Sol went into the river?"

"I believe he did," was the reply. "If Sol had gone somewhere else, why did he leave his coat and shoes? Would you go somewhere else barefooted?"

"I don't think I would. Sol was drunk, though. Hard to tell what a drunk man might do." Charley was silent a few seconds, then said, "But there's something else that bothers me about this."

"What's that?"

"The tracks in the sand," Charley said. "One set must have been made by Sol. His shoes fit the tracks just perfect. But who made the other set of tracks, the smaller tracks?"

Harg said, "That bothers me too. I'm glad you're thinkin'. I'm afraid there's more to this story than we know right now. We'll just have to keep diggin'. But for now, I think we need to round up men for search parties and try to find out if Sol's body is in Clinch River."

CHAPTER 2

September 1942

Now at the river, some of the men in the search parties believed that Sol had just walked away, but they were willing to be part of the search effort. Of those who thought Sol might have gone into the river at the bridge, nobody expected to find him alive; the Narrows was deadly. They just hoped that if Sol went in the river, they would find his body.

The sheriff asked Charley's search group to cover the south bank of the river, so they headed toward the swinging bridge to cross the stream. The bridge had always been an appealing structure to Charley that provided him access to the other river bank and to his grandparents' farm. He remembered that even as a preschooler he had been attracted to and fascinated by the swinging bridge. To his young mind, the bridge had resembled a gigantic, upside-down tent caterpillar stretching across the river, holding on to two strands of webs spun across the stream.

On each side of the river, two strong locust logs were embedded deeply into the earth several feet back from the river's usual flood tide. These two creosoted posts on each side of the river stood about four feet apart and supported two thick steel cables. The cables were anchored to large metal eyelets embedded in concrete on each side of the river, and the cables spanned the stream. The four posts and two large steel cables carry the load of the other bridge components and of whoever or whatever crosses the bridge.

The large cables stretched across the river supported smaller vertical steel cables whose bottom ends were fastened to oak crosspieces. These vertical cables and crosspieces supported the bridge's board walkway from one end of the bridge to the other. On each end of the bridge, cemented stone steps led from the embankment up to the beginning of the bridge flooring. The floor of the bridge, about forty inches wide, was higher above the river than the highest flood level ever seen in the area. The bridge had never been damaged by floods. Walking across the bridge causes an undulating up-and-down motion of the floor, and the floor can be made to sway from side to side by heavy-footed walkers or by rambunctious, mischievous lads.

Normally, as he tramped across the bridge on such a pleasant sunny fall day, Charley paused to feast on the unique sights, sounds, and smells of the river he treasured. Today, however, the deputy couldn't stop to enjoy this ancient stream.

Charley led the search group in his charge across the swinging bridge, and as they lurched across the swaying span, Charley noticed how badly the old bridge had deteriorated. Some of the rough, weathered oak floorboards had wide cracks in them. In several places, pieces of boards had broken away completely, leaving potentially dangerous gaps in the walkway. Around one gap in the floor near the center of the river, where Charley figured a five-gallon lard bucket could fall through without scraping its sides, he noticed that the boards were springy and probably wouldn't bear much weight.

The deputy stopped and said, "You boys better watch your step here. We've got some weak-looking floorboards. If you step anywhere near this hole, we might be trying to fish you out of the Clinch too."

Everyone crossed the bridge safely. The men climbed up the hill over the tall limestone escarpment and back down to the river's edge at the lower end of the most treacherous portion of the Narrows—about

150 yards below the bridge they crossed. The sheriff didn't want any of the men out in the stream unless they spied something they thought might be Sol's body. Harg didn't want to lose a searcher to the river. So Charley and his group began searching from the shore.

The searchers spread out down the riverbank with about ten yards separating each man from the next, and each man was charged to search carefully and thoroughly the small section of the bank and river assigned to him. Charley had told his men to search their assigned sections until they heard his whistle, at which time they were to move downstream and begin scouring another segment of the water and shore. The river still ran higher, faster, and muddier than normal; if Sol's body had lodged underwater on a snag, tree limb, or rock, it would be almost impossible to see.

Search team members saw kingfishers, wood ducks, and killdeers but found no sign of Sol during the morning. Each man searched his assigned areas until Charley whistled them together. As the afternoon began, Charley sent Tommy Reynolds, a capable eighteen-year-old, back up to the bridge where Charley's mother, Belle Scott, would deliver a lunch and cool tea for the men searching on Charley's side of the river.

Tommy trekked back to the bridge to fetch the food and drink from Mrs. Scott. Belle poured Tommy a large full glass of cool, sweet tea, and he downed it thirstily. As he drank his tea, the heavenly aroma of ham biscuits mingled with the equally enticing scent of fried apple pies caused Tommy's mouth to water and his belly to growl. The growl did not go undetected.

Mrs. Scott handed Tommy a ham biscuit and a fried apple pie, saying, "Since you've had all this extra walking from the search party and back to them, you eat this here. Then when you get back to the others, you can have the same portion each of them gets. A hardworking young man needs to eat to keep his strength up, don't you reckon?"

Tommy reached for the extra treats; he grinned and agreed, "Yes, ma'am, I reckon I do, at that. And I thank you kindly, Mrs. Scott."

Belle wrapped the meat and biscuits in a dish towel and the fried pies in another towel; she stowed both bundles in a clean white feedsack. In a three-gallon bucket with a tight-fitting lid, the type many farm wives used to take their cream to a creamery to sell, Tommy carried tea for the men awaiting his return.

Tommy hastened back to where Charley and the others waited. Charley doled out to each man two freshly baked biscuits, one with fried pork shoulder meat on it and one with fried country ham, plus cool, refreshing sweet tea. Charley's mother had also prepared enough fried pies for each searcher to have one made with dried apples or dried peaches. After they ate and rested, the men resumed the search and kept at it throughout the afternoon without finding a body.

While the river was still running full and fast because of heavy rains upstream in Russell and Tazewell counties to the northeast, it began decreasing in flow and depth by midafternoon. In some places, giant trees spread their branches from both banks toward the middle of the stream, reducing the field of vision for the searchers. Shortly before sundown and about a mile below the bridge, Luther Owens spotted something white floating in an eddy above a large rock jutting out into the river. He found a long stick in a pile of driftwood and used it to snag and retrieve the floating item. It was a white, lacy piece of cloth—a handkerchief, he thought. Luther yelled for Charley, and Charley was at his side in a few minutes.

Taking the wet cloth in hand, Charley muttered, "Looks like a handkerchief."

"That's what I thought," Luther said.

"It has two letters on it—MM. Looks like they're embroidered on."

Luther asked, "Could it be Sol's?"

"I doubt it. It more likely belongs to Sol's wife. MM. Madeline Massey."

"Hmm, would Sol have been carrying one of Maddie's handkerchiefs?" Luther asked.

Charley responded, "From what Maddie told us about what happened last night, it just doesn't seem to me that he would have had one of her hankies."

Since darkness would soon be upon them, Charley whistled his men together, and they began their hike back to the bridge and to their homes for the night. Six of the ten men who helped search agreed to gather again the next morning to continue looking for Sol's body. The group searching the other side of the river under Harg Fielding's direction had found no body, no clothing, nothing; some of them would be back tomorrow to search again for their lost neighbor.

Charley showed Harg the handkerchief Luther found. Harg pondered the lacy cloth for a few moments, then sighed. "If this is Maddie's handkerchief, why would Sol have had it last night?"

Charley responded, "That's what I can't understand either."

"Oh well, who can tell what a man might do, sober or drunk?"

The September sun had been up more than an hour the next morning when Charley led his group of searchers across the bridge, and he noticed that the water level had fallen almost two feet below its level yesterday morning. Maybe the lower water would reveal what had been hidden yesterday. After his group crossed the rocky dome and got back down to the river's edge, Charley asked the men to spread out along the bank and walk slowly downstream with every man checking everything he could to try to find Sol Massey's body.

The group moved slowly downriver all morning, and by noon they were as far downstream as they had searched yesterday. In places along the river, the deputy had noted familiar outposts of rocky bluffs from which hard-muscled hickory, walnut, and oak trees stood as vigilant guards over the river and its denizens.

Charley called a halt for the group to rest. While the other men rested, he walked on down the river and around a curve. Not far below the curve, he saw on their side of the river giant palisades standing like sentinels hovering over gentle rapids and small cascades that sang their lullabies to the drooping sycamores and silver maples on the opposite bank. Charley whistled softly to himself as he thought, *No way around that cliff face. We'll have to climb up that steep hill and come back to the river below the cliff.* He turned and walked back to the men, dreading to tell them of the hard climb and steep descent facing them around the river curve.

As the deputy neared the group of men, Tommy Reynolds was standing on the riverbank near a small mass of tangled driftwood that had lodged near the shore against a dead fallen tree trunk with a few broken limbs protruding above the water. As Tommy peered out along the skeletal tree trunk, an area in the water near the tip of the tree caught his eye. Something just under the surface appeared to be white. He called out, "Hey, Charley, come look at something?"

Charley came over to him and asked, "What? Where?"

"Right there at the end of that tree, twenty-five feet or so out," Tommy said as he pointed to the spot.

"Looks like something white. Maddie said Sol was wearing a white shirt."

"But how do we get out there to see if that is Sol?" Tommy asked. "It's way too deep to wade out there."

"How cold is the water?" Charley asked.

As Tommy dipped a hand in the river, he said, "It don't feel too cold on my hand, but it would feel a lot colder if you're thinking about swimming out there."

Charley said, "Actually, I was thinking about *you* doing the swimming."

"Me?" Tommy gasped. "I can't swim much, and in this water, I'm afraid I'd cramp up and get drownded."

"Well, I don't see any other way to find out if that's Sol," Charley replied as he began removing his shoes and socks, then his denim jacket and blue chambray shirt, and finally his faded denim pants. He piled his clothes on a slab of limestone near the river's edge and stood in the autumn sun clad only in boxer shorts.

He strained to focus his eyes more sharply on the spot Tommy had pointed to; because of the sun's glare on the water, however, Charley couldn't be certain there was something white below the water's surface.

With reluctant, careful steps, he eased into the river and waded out about ten feet where the water came above his waist and rose higher with each step; he had to lean upstream a bit to offset the force of the river current. "Brr," he growled, "this water is cold." Then he swam quickly toward the object they wanted to know more about.

As Charley neared the last protruding broken tree limb, he saw a white object a few inches below the river surface that appeared to be white cloth, probably a shirt. With his left hand, he anchored himself to the tree limb and felt the submerged object with his other hand. He felt what he assumed was the back of a torso under the white cloth. Charley also felt what must be a belt in belt loops of pants.

"I think this is Sol," he called to the men gathered on the bank.

The body had snagged on the tree limb. The legs and feet hung deeper into the water on one side of the snag, and the chest, shoulders, arms and head dangled down on the other side of the limb. Charley couldn't see more than six or seven inches down through the murky water. He released his hold on the tree limb and swam and waded back to the bank; there he wiped off some of the water on his body with his shirt. He shivered as he donned his clothes, socks, and shoes; he wondered if Harg or any of the men with him across the river were anywhere close by.

Charley began calling out, "Harg! Hey, Harg! Anybody over there?"

He stopped to listen. Nobody answered his calls, so he tried again.

"Harg! Anybody over there? Hey, Harg!"

Charley paused again to listen, and he thought he heard a faint reply from downstream. It sounded as if someone might have yelled "Charley."

He called again and heard someone reply, "Yeah, we're here, down below you. We hear you."

It sounded like Harg. Then the voice said, "We're comin' upstream."

In three or four minutes, Charley saw movement downstream on the opposite bank, and then he saw that a few men were moving upstream. In another five minutes, Harg and three others were opposite Charley's position.

Harg hollered, "What've you got?"

"We've got a body," Charley replied. "It must be Sol, but we need a boat to get the body loose from where it's stuck on a snag."

Harg yelled back, "Alvin Fletcher's place is just below here, and he has a boat. I'll send a man to see if we can borry it. Just hang on over there until I get back."

About half an hour later, four men lugged a flat-bottomed wooden boat to the water's edge about twenty-five yards upstream from where Charley and his party waited and slid it into the river. Another county deputy sheriff, Rufus Wallace, got in the boat and was handed a long slender pole. The boatman stood in the rear section of the craft and poled it across the river. The current carried the boat downstream as Rufus pushed toward the shore, and he nosed the boat into relatively calm water near the bank just above the tree on which the body was caught.

Rufus said, "Charley, Harg said for me and you to get the body in the boat and bring it back over to where he is. He has a truck over on the road nearby. So hop in."

Charley did, and with Charley sitting on the front of the boat, Rufus carefully poled the boat toward the limb pointed out to him. When they reached the snag on the tree, Charley grabbed it. He used a piece of rope attached to the boat and tied the boat to the snag. The body was still below the surface, but by this time the level of the river was a few inches lower and noticeably clearer than it had been when Charley swam out to the corpse earlier.

Rufus saw that the current stirred the object back and forth slightly, and he said, "Yep, that's a body for sure."

The current swung the boat around enough that Charlie could reach the body.

Charley looked at Rufus with a "how do I do this?" look.

Rufus said, "See if you can pull the body around beside the boat. It'll probably take both of us to get it into the boat."

Charley responded, "I was afraid you was going to say that." After a long pause, he said, "Well, here goes."

He reached into the water, felt the body, and a shiver ran through his body. Charley had never touched a corpse before, much less try to haul one into a boat. He moved his hand until he felt a belt. He grasped the belt and pulled; the body moved a bit, but something held it and kept Charley from moving it away from the snag.

"Great, it's stuck," he said murmured. Then, "Let me try again."

He took hold of the belt again, braced himself on the side of the boat with his other arm, and heaved hard. He heard a cracking, wood-splintering sound and the body moved away from the tree limb.

"It's loose now," Charley quietly told Rufus.

"Okay," Rufus said, "now move 'im on back alongside of the boat so I can get ahold of 'im, and we'll lift 'im into the boat."

Rufus grabbed a leg and Charley the belt and they pulled the body up over the side of the boat. One leg was in the boat, then one arm and part of the torso were over the side, then the other leg, then the entire body was lying in the boat. Both men stared at the ravaged body. The body, especially the face, hands, and feet, had been severely torn, scraped, and lacerated as it had been hurled through the Narrows, scraping against boulders and snagged driftwood.

"Oh, Lord," Charley murmured, "is that Sol Massey?"

"Can't tell for sure, but who else could it be? It has to be Sol."

"Yeah, I guess so. Let's get the body across the river so Harg can do whatever has to be done." Rufus began poling them toward the opposite riverbank.

CHAPTER 3

September 1942

His picture in an eighty-by-ten frame sat atop his shiny oak casket. The handiwork of the town's mortician was not in evidence because the casket was closed. The black-and-white picture had been made a decade earlier and showed a smiling, attractive man with straight white teeth and thick dark hair. The bright, trusting, inviting eyes in the picture were not the eyes Charley remembered. Throughout the last several years, the eyes he recalled had taken on some quality that reminded him of the eyes of ferrets and weasels he had seen pictured in *National Geographic*.

Most of the people in the room either whispered to someone beside them or thought to themselves that it had been several years since they had seen Sol Massey as happy and healthy as he looked in that picture. Solomon Massey was dead at the age of forty-six. His body had been pulled from Clinch River three days earlier, so marred and disfigured that an open-casket funeral was not an option.

Solomon was more than two decades older than Charley Scott, and Charley had known him for as long back as he could remember. Charley called him Sol, as did almost everyone who knew him. Some had derisively called him King Solomon because he had been a pampered, spoiled mama's boy who avoided work and responsibility whenever possible. Those who had known his mother, Martha, judged that she was too protective and overly indulgent with her only child.

As he stood beside Sol's casket, Charley wondered about the circumstances of Sol's death. Organ music signaled the beginning of the funeral service. Charley looked around the chapel room in the funeral home and saw only familiar faces—Masseys, their friends and neighbors, local townspeople, and folks from outlying farms and communities who had known Sol or his parents or his wife or his children. Both of Sol's parents were dead, and Charley thought it was a blessing that they had not lived to see this day.

When Charley arrived at the funeral home a few minutes earlier, he wasn't surprised to see fewer than a dozen parked cars and pickups. He knew that, because of gasoline and tire rationing as part of the war effort against Japan, Germany, and Italy, many who attended funerals in Creedy walked to them—some from three or four miles out in the county. He parked beside the newest car in sight—a fancy dark blue 1942 Packard 180 Sedan that Brewster McGraw had bought eight months earlier. Charley admired the car's polished finish and its abundant exterior chrome, and its grey-blue broadcloth upholstery was accented with rich wood trimmings.

He headed toward the chapel room and noticed two saddled bay horses, one with a side saddle, in the shade of a huge ash tree. The bays stamped feet and switched tails and ears to discourage pestering flies; their reins were tied to iron rings fastened to the tree. The horses belonged to Chester and Maude Barton, who lived at least seven miles from town on Sandy Ridge Road.

Dressed in his crisply pressed county deputy sheriff uniform, Charley moved toward the front bench on the right side of the aisle where pallbearers were being seated by Delbert Kent, mortician and funeral director. At the request of Sol's wife, Madeline, Delbert had asked Charley if he would serve as a pallbearer. Charley nodded to the other five pallbearers and shook hands with the two nearest him, saying, "Howdy, Jeff, howdy, Phillip," and took his seat.

He looked to his left and saw on the front pew Sol's wife and their two children, Cecilia and Luke, aged fifteen and thirteen. Madeline looked worn, haggard, worried, detached; a large bruise on her left cheekbone wasn't completely hidden by makeup. The children appeared to be stunned, as if they didn't fully comprehend what had happened to their father. None of the three was crying at the time. Luke glanced furtively from side to side but seemed not to want to make eye contact with anyone.

The organ music stopped as Reverend Harley Davenport, pastor of Clinch Missionary Baptist Church, moved to the podium. Mr. Davenport also served his community as its postmaster. The preacher said, "We've gathered here today to say our good-byes and pay our last respects to Solomon Massey. To some of you, Sol was a neighbor, to some an acquaintance, to others a friend. He was also a son and a father and a husband. And we come to share the grief of his children, Cecilia and Lucas, and of his wife, Madeline."

Charley's mind drifted back the few days to when he helped search for and recover Sol's body from Clinch River. He remembered how upset, how emotionally drained, how sick in soul he was as he shared a borrowed boat with the torn, lifeless body of a man he had known all his life. Charley was roused from his traumatic reverie as the man seated next to him rose to his feet. The organ was playing again, and the preacher said the congregation would sing "There's a Land That Is Fairer Than Day." As Charley had relived his part in the search for Sol Massey's body, he had not consciously heard the preacher try to comfort the family of a man whom many in the community thought had few redeeming virtues. But in spite of feeling as they did about Sol, they attended the service for him to show their respect, compassion, and support for his family.

Preacher Davenport led in singing all three verses of the old familiar hymn. Charley glanced at the people behind him. Two rows back were his mother and father, Nannie Belle and James Robert Scott; just about everyone who knew his father, except Belle, called him J. R. Beside his parents were his girlfriend, Bonnie, with her parents, Eleanor and Brewster McGraw. As happened every time he saw Bonnie, Charley's heart leaped and thumped faster for a few seconds.

Charley's favorite aunt, Lucille Thacker, and her husband, Verle, were also behind him. His Aunt Luce was his mother's younger sister. Luce was so close and dear to Charley that she seemed almost like a second mother to him; to Lucille, Charley helped fill the place of the son she never had. Belle, Lucille, and most of the other women in the room wore dark dresses made by their own hands, dresses that matched their solemn demeanor and the somber occasion. The greater portion of these clothes had seen many days of service, but they were clean and crisply pressed.

On one side of Verle was his mother, Clarissa Thacker, known to some friends and neighbors as Clare and to some as just the Herb Woman. Beside his aunt and uncle were his grandparents, Estella and Jesse Musick, parents of his mother and Aunt Luce. The Musicks' son, Charley's uncle Woodrow, also stood with them. Several men in the room, including Charley's father and grandfather, wore black or navy blue suits, white shirts, and ties. Others, like his uncles Woodrow and Verle, wore a white shirt and dark suit but no tie. Whether they wore ties or not, many of the men in suits seemed to be stiff and ill at ease. Some of the men had never owned a suit, but they wore the best clothes they had, most of which were clean and without wrinkles.

Charley's grandparents lived on their farm up in the Chestnut Ridge area of River Mountain. Estella and Jesse were barely into their seventies, but they were in good health and still led active lives. Up until the past year or so, they had walked from their farm to Creedy when they needed to come to town; now Woody owned a car and could drive them where they needed to go. Charley had spent many happy, carefree days and nights at the Musick homeplace.

The hymn ended and the preacher prayed the closing prayer, asking the Lord to comfort, bless, and guide Sol's wife, Madeline, and his children, Cecilia and Lucas. As Delbert Kent and his staff prepared to move the casket to the hearse for transport to the cemetery, Charley moved over to stand near Sol's widow and children as a man and woman expressed their condolences.

As the couple walked away, Charley said, "Mrs. Massey, I'm so sorry for what's happened to you and your children. If there's anything I can ever do for you all, be sure to let me know."

"Thank you," she whispered.

He shook hands with the widow and looked at the children. Instead of looking at Charley, Cecilia and Luke kept their eyes on the floor or on their hands. Charley grasped each of them gently on a shoulder, said "Take care," moved a few steps away, and watched as Sol's casket was wheeled down the aisle toward the door.

Charley noticed that a teenager, Rafe Hawkins, came tentatively over to Cecilia, put his hand on her elbow, and said, "Cecilia, Luke, I'm so sorry about your papa."

Cecilia forced a wan smile and nodded; Rafe turned and strode toward the door. Charley was needed to help carry the casket down the steps and to the hearse, so he joined the other pallbearers, three on each side of the casket. They carried the coffin to the hearse and slid it inside.

As Charley started toward his car, Bonnie McGraw intercepted him and put a hand on his arm; Charley was again captivated by the beautiful green, hazel-flecked eyes he gazed into. Charley was always pleased to have this pretty, smiling, auburn-haired schoolteacher near him.

She said, "Charley, I'm not going to the cemetery for the burial. Your mother, Aunt Luce, and I will help get food arranged for family and friends to have a meal over at the church after the burial. There really aren't many family members."

"Okay," Charley said. Then he added, "I can take you to the church before I go to the cemetery."

"No, Daddy is going to drop me off there and pick me up later. You go on to the burial."

Bonnie continued, "Enough food has been brought in to feed an army, so come back over there and eat. And bring Harg with you. Oh, why don't you try to get as many as you can of the men who helped search the riverbanks for Sol to come back for a meal too."

"I will," Charley said with a smile as he patted the hand resting on his arm. "See you at the church soon."

Bonnie turned away from Charley and headed toward her father's Packard sedan where her parents waited. Bonnie, as always, looked dazzling to Charley. She wore a stylish navy blue suit with padded shoulders and knee-length skirt; Charley guessed it came from Parks-Belk in Bristol. Bonnie's jaunty tilted hat matched her suit, as did the gloves and purse she carried in one hand. As she walked away from Charley, his eyes followed her lovely figure, including her shapely legs, which he noted were not covered by hose. Because the need for nylon and silk was so great for the war, especially for making parachutes, these fabrics were in extremely short supply. Ladies' hose were now almost impossible to find.

The small funeral procession wended its way toward the country cemetery about three miles from the funeral home. As Charley drove along in the procession, his mind returned to its task of trying to figure out what led up to Sol Massey's death. He recalled Sheriff Hargis Fielding's call to him four mornings earlier at about 6:00 a.m. Charley was still living with his parents on their small acreage about a half mile out of town, and he had a telephone installed when he became deputy sheriff because the high sheriff had felt strongly that he should be able to reach Charley at home by phone when needed. While telephones were not rare in town, only the Masseys and a few other prosperous farmers outside of Creedy had telephone service.

The town was named after Isaac Creed, a survivor of revolutionary war battles in the Carolinas. He migrated to the area after the war and claimed a grant of over two thousand acres of bottomland and forested hollows and mountains. The town grew up on the northwest side of Clinch River and downstream less than half a mile from the mouth of Drowning Creek. Farther to the northeast, the saw-toothed crest of Powell Mountain rose like the undulating spine of a giant prehistoric monster. The town's enterprises included a grocery, hardware and farm supply, clothing, and furniture stores as well as a bank, drugstore, barbershop, and post office. In one corner of the grocery store, Eula White ran her café, the only public eating place in town.

The town's once bustling blacksmith shop was now Charles Garage and Repair and did welding and equipment repairs for farmers. Bruce Charles, the owner, also catered to automobile owners with a mechanic and a gasoline pump. Mandy Charles, Bruce's wife, operated the Charles Boarding House where she provided lodging, breakfast, and supper for her small clientele of Norfolk and Western Railroad section hands, drummers, a few miners who worked too far from home to travel back and forth every day, an occasional visitor or government official, and anyone else who needed a place to stay for a few days or weeks. The community boasted three churches. In addition to Clinch Missionary Baptist, there was Mt. Zion Primitive Baptist and Powell Methodist.

The Norfolk and Western train depot was a hub of activity as passenger trains made regular stops to take on their riders and freight shipments, and huge locomotives steamed past pulling long strings of coal-laden cars. Most of the coal was headed for Norfolk, Virginia over 450 miles away where it would be exported to other countries to fuel many of the world's navies and steel mills and electric power plants.

Creedy perched high enough above Clinch River that it, unlike many towns along the river, had never flooded. Named for an explorer whose name is remembered only by the river's name, Clinch River originates near Tazewell, Virginia. Numerous creeks, branches, and rivulets empty into it before its waters unite with the Tennessee River about thirty-five miles west of Knoxville.

When Charley was in the sixth grade at Drowning Creek Elementary School, he traced on a large wall map the route of the Clinch waters.

The Tennessee makes its meandering, tortuous, roundabout journey southwesterly through Tennessee by Chattanooga and into Alabama. Near Guntersville, the river turns northwesterly back into Tennessee and northward from there into Kentucky and joins the flow of the Ohio near Paducah, Kentucky. The waters of the Clinch soon mix into the Mississippi and finally become part of the Gulf of Mexico.

Charley loved Clinch River. To him and to most people in and around Creedy, it was simply "the river." Before the river was dammed in the mid-1930s, Charley had heard of its bountiful production of freshwater mussels and pearls. Mussels were an important food for Native Americans and were used by settlers as fish bait and hog feed.

As a youngster, Charley had gathered mussels several times and pried them open with his pocket knife and a screwdriver he had brought from home; he was looking for pearls. Chewing on his tongue as he worked intently to get the mussels open, he usually wound up with skinned fingers, broken fingernails, and no sign of a pearl. His main motivation for trying to find a pearl was his daddy.

As a young man, J. R. Scott found a beautiful, unblemished pearl in a Clinch River mussel. It was the size of a large pea, and J. R. gave it to his sweetheart, Belle Musick, telling her that some day he would have it set in a ring. After he came home from World War I and got a job as a mechanic with the Norfolk and Western Railroad, he had the pearl set in a solitaire ring by a jeweler in Bristol. Belle told her husband it was the most beautiful ring she had ever seen, and she was careful not to wear it when she was working around the house or in her garden. She usually wore it only to church and on special occasions.

At the cemetery, Reverend Davenport conducted a brief burial ceremony under a clear blue sky as fall colors were beginning to show on burning bush shrubs and sumac bushes. Golden leaves of scattered sassafras, poplars, and hickories shimmered brightly just outside the cemetery; maples flaunted their bright yellow and red covers.

CHAPTER 4

September 1942

After the burial, Charley invited Harg and others to come to the Clinch Missionary Baptist Church for a meal. Harg and several men and their wives accepted the invitation. On his way to the church after the burial ceremony, Charley was looking forward to being with Bonnie. He was a lucky man. He didn't know what Bonnie saw in him that made her choose to date him and nobody else. Many local boys and some from other counties had tried to woo her, but she never encouraged any of them.

Bonnie grew up in a family where money was not scarce, even in the depression. Her father, Brewster McGraw, owned the grocery store and the hardware store in Creedy. The McGraws lived in a large comfortable house that had conveniences Charley and his neighbors couldn't afford: electricity, a central-heating coal furnace, hot and cold running water, an indoor bathroom, and a telephone. Brewster also owned commercial buildings and rental houses in town, and he had a large profitable farm plus a small coal mining operation.

In spite of having been brought up in a well-to-do family, Bonnie was as down-to-earth as a sharecropper's daughter. She had simple tastes and cared more about the welfare of others than about her own. Charley thought this caring for and wanting to help others was the reason Bonnie saw teaching as a *calling*, not just a job.

Public schools in Southwest Virginia offered grades one through seven for elementary school and eight through eleven for high school. Bonnie and Charley attended Drowning Creek Elementary school for grades one through seven. Charley was a year older than Bonnie and started school one year before Bonnie did; but when he was in the sixth grade, he came down with a severe case of measles, was quite ill, and developed complications. So he missed several weeks of school and had to repeat sixth grade in 1932, and that year Bonnie was in the same grade as Charley. The young pair of students went to Creedy High School, beginning in the eighth grade.

Bonnie's brother, Donald, was a year behind his sister and his friend Charley in school. The three of them spent much of their out-of-school time together, whether it was at Saturday matinee movies in Creedy in the small theater above the Clifton Shoe and Clothing Store, picnics or Sunday dinners with one of their families, or church activities. Charley and Donald also loved to fish for bass, red eyes, and catfish in Clinch River and Drowning Creek. They liked to gig frogs and to hunt surrounding fields and forested mountains for small game—groundhogs, rabbits, squirrels, quail, and grouse. Whatever wild creatures they caught or killed—whether finned, feathered, or furred—their families ate. Bonnie joined them on some of their fishing outings, but she had no interest in tramping through water, grass, brush, and trees in search of some animal or bird to gig or shoot.

As their high school years sped by, Charley and Donald became close steadfast friends. Charley and Bonnie became more than just good friends. By the time they were high school juniors, they weren't officially dating, but they were together at every opportunity and they were not dating anyone else. By the middle of their senior year, they were sweethearts. The two were together as much as they could be at school, usually had a date on Saturday, and saw each other again at Sunday School and church on Sunday mornings and on Sunday evenings at BTU—Baptist Training Union—and worship services. By now, in 1942, Charley and Bonnie had known each other for almost a dozen years—five years as good friends and more than six as sweethearts.

At the church after the burial, Charley and Harg walked together to the spacious basement room furnished with tables and chairs where food would be served buffet style. When they entered the room, the deputy paused as he savored a mixture of enticing aromas that permeated the room: fried chicken, baked country ham, corn pudding, baked bread, spicy stewed apples, and pumpkin pie. He knew that several other toothsome vegetables and desserts also awaited the diners.

Charley saw that his parents and grandparents were seated at a long table. J. R. saw his son and the sheriff come in. He got Charley's eye and motioned for the two lawmen to come to their table as he pointed to empty chairs. Before he sat, Charley went to his grandparents, whom he called Pa Jess and Ma Jess. He hugged each of them, said "It's so good to see you," and asked how they were doing.

"We're doin' just fine, honey. How are you handlin' all this drownin' business?" Ma Jess replied.

Charley smiled and said, "I'm okay. It's not something I like to deal with, but it has to be done."

Pa Jess was a wiry, tireless man of medium height with a full, thick, salt-and-pepper mane. He could outwork most men who were two decades younger. Aside from a "little rheumatiz" when the weather changed, he was in remarkably good health, especially for a man who was a couple of years past his seventieth birthday. He still had most of his teeth and wore spectacles only for reading his Bible, newspapers, monthly issues of *The Progressive Farmer*, or perhaps the latest Zane Grey novel that one of his children or grandchildren gave him.

Ma Jess always seemed to have a pleasant half-smile on her face. She loved people and would do anything to help a neighbor, or even a stranger, in need. She had been a beautiful young woman and was a beautiful older woman. She was happiest when she was busy, and she loved to be with her children and grandson.

Charley's mother, Belle, seldom failed to speak what was on her mind, and she quickly asked, "Well, Charley, have you and Harg found out anything more about how poor ole Sol ended up in Clinch River?"

Charley looked at Harg but said nothing. The sheriff stared at the tabletop in front of him, then turned slowly toward Belle and said, "Miz Belle, we don't know much for sure. We're still investigatin'. As of now, the coroner has ruled the death a accidental drownin'. Right now, I don't know of anything that is likely to change that rulin'."

Belle responded, "Still, Sol has been around the river all his life. He knows what the Narrows is like. Even if he had been drinking too much, I can't picture him falling into the water. And I just can't imagine Sol intentionally going into the river near the Narrows."

"So," Harg surmised, "you don't think it was an accident? And you don't think Sol would drown hisself? Then what else might've happened to cause his death?"

Belle threw up her hands and said, "Oh, I don't know. I don't know what it is, but something just doesn't seem right."

"I agree with that, Miz Belle," Harg said.

"And it was such a shame that Sol's body was so tore up that family and neighbors couldn't even see him when they paid their last respects."

The sheriff nodded in agreement but added nothing.

J. R. said, "Mama, let's talk no more about Sol right now. Let the sheriff and his men do their job. I'm sure they'll get to the bottom of it all. At least Sol's funeral wasn't anything like the one for Aunt Rachael Lukens." He looked at Charley and said, "Did I ever tell you about her funeral?"

Charley said, "No, I don't think so, Pop. To tell the truth, I don't believe I knew you had an Aunt Rachael."

"Oh, no, she wasn't really my aunt. Wasn't no kin atall. Ever'body in our family and lots of other people referred to the old couple as Aunt Rachael and Uncle Pierce Lukens. Well, it was a scarifyin' thing that happened with her."

Belle interrupted, "Oh, James, this is no time for one of your big tales! We've just come from a funeral service."

J. R. grinned as he patted his wife on the arm and said, "Now, Mama. This is no big tale. I'm just tellin' what happened. Aunt Rachael and Uncle Pierce lived way up in the River Mountain area, up near the head of Laurel Branch. This was in early fall of 1901. My mother and daddy rode horses up to the Lukens place for the funeral, but I didn't want to go, so they let me stay home. Rachael died, or she seemed to be dead. In them days, bodies was kept in their homes until burial, and most people who died wasn't embalmed. No doctor or official had examined Rachael to officially announce her dead, but Pierce made a casket for her, plans was made for a funeral and burial, and friends and neighbors was notified.

"On the day of the funeral, a neighbor woman come to pay her respects to the dead woman's family and laid her hand on Rachael's face as she laid there in her coffin in the front room. Rachael's face didn't feel cold. The neighbor come out on the porch and said, 'Uncle Pierce, Rachael's face is warm. I don't believe she's dead, and I don't think you ort to bury her today.' Uncle Pierce looked around at the gathered friends and neighbors and glanced up at the clear, sunny sky. He thought a few seconds and then said, 'Well, it's a purty day, and ever'body's hyere. We might as well go ahead with the burial.' And they did."

Belle said, "I've heard that story before, but is it really true?"

"My ma and pa told it to me for the truth! Are you sayin' they would lie about somethin' like that?" J. R. responded.

"Oh, James, don't get snippy! I'm not saying any such thing. Let's just get in line for some of that good food on the serving tables."

Charley noticed that Bonnie, now without her hat and gloves, was looking his way; and he motioned for her to join them as he and his family headed for the lineup of fried chicken, country ham, casseroles and dishes of vegetables, cornbread and biscuits, and a grand array of desserts. Bonnie's father and mother couldn't come for the meal, and she was happy to have the chance to share a meal with Charley. After the men and women filled their plates and returned to their table, talk centered around Sol's wife and children.

Bonnie worried about the children, Cecilia and Lucas. Two years earlier, Bonnie graduated from East Tennessee State Teachers College in Johnson City with a bachelor's degree in science and math, and she returned to her hometown to teach at Creedy High School. In the past two years, Bonnie taught Cecilia general math, geometry, general science, and biology. Bonnie taught each of the Massey children this school year—Cecilia a junior, Lucas a freshman. Cecilia excelled in algebra; its inherent ordered structure and consistency appealed to her because she seldom found these elements in her unpredictable, volatile home life. She also studied chemistry independently under Bonnie's tutelage. Lucas sat in Bonnie's general math class this year, but she had no notion yet of whether he shared the topnotch scholastic potential of his sister. Some of Luke's elementary teachers rated him as bright but felt he studied just enough to be an average student.

Bonnie took a special interest in Cecilia. A pretty, intelligent girl with the ability to become anything she wanted to be, she applied herself to her studies. Cecilia was a happy, outgoing, straight *A* student popular with both girls and boys. Sometime around the middle of the past school year, however, Bonnie noticed that Cecilia grew more introverted and withdrawn, slower to smile, and her grades dropped enough to concern Bonnie. Cecilia neglected her studies. She obviously didn't study at home as much as previously; in class, she became inattentive and indifferent, and her mind sometimes appeared to be in a faraway place. Bonnie tried to befriend Cecilia as much as possible without being obvious about it with other students and teachers around.

Bonnie also had Rafacl Hawkins in a class, but she had good reason to remember him from an encounter almost three years earlier. Rafe, as he liked to be called, was one grade ahead of Cecilia, but he seemed so taken, almost obsessed, with her. Rafael took every opportunity he could find to get near Cecilia. Cecilia was never rude to him, but she did nothing to warrant or encourage his attentions. That didn't stop Rafael from trying to develop a closer relationship with her.

Bonnie said, "I feel so sorry for those two children. Well, I feel sorry for Maddie too, but I think she will probably be able to cope with Sol's death better than the kids."

Charley responded, "I think Maddie must be a pretty strong woman. You know, she hasn't had an easy time the last few years, seein' as how Sol wasn't much help on the farm even when he was *on* the farm. Maybe she can be a strong support for Cecilia and Luke."

"Oh, I agree Maddie's strong, but the kids concern me. Cecilia has changed over the last several months, and I'm afraid her father's death may make her worse."

"How do you mean 'she's changed'?"

"Well, she's no longer the happy, outgoing girl she had been. She doesn't seem to be as interested in school. She seems to have drawn back into a shell. Two years ago she was looking forward to going to college—to East Tennessee, or Berea College, or Lincoln Memorial. Lately, she seems not to be thinking much about college."

Belle asked, "Honey, what do you think might have caused such a change in Cecilia?"

Bonnie sighed and said, "I really don't know. But I wonder if something at home is affecting her."

"Like what?" Charley asked.

"I don't know what, Charley! I'm just worried about her. Something must be gnawing at her. I've talked with her and given her chances to let me know what is bothering her, but she hasn't seen fit to tell me. I just feel that something has happened or is happening that has changed her attitude and outlook."

The conversation topic changed, and Charley concentrated on enjoying the remainder of his fried chicken and fixin's and good-sized samples of apple *and* chocolate pie.

As the sheriff cleaned the last chocolate morsel from his plate, he said, "I'm full as a tick, and I sure enjoyed eatin' with y'all."

Patting his ample girth with both hands, Harg observed, "I'm a purty good judge of food, and as you can tell, I've had lots of practice in developin' that judgin' ability. And my verdict is that was a mighty good dinner." Then with a broad smile he said, "And now, if you folks will excuse Charley and me, we need to get busy and try to earn the big salaries the county is payin' us."

Charley waved good-bye to his family at the table, touched Bonnie on the shoulder, and said, "Bye, Bonnie."

Harg and Charley walked out to the sheriff's car and got in. He turned to Charley and said, "What time did Maddie say Sol left the house Sunday night when she saw him for the last time?"

"About two o'clock or later. She was sure he didn't leave any earlier than that."

"That's what I remembered," replied Harg. Then he went on, "Rufus Wallace told me this mornin' that a young man he knows said him and his girlfriend stopped at the beach area near the swingin' bridge last Sunday night. But they found that somebody was already at their favorite beach spot, so they drove on downriver. Know who else was there?"

"Who?"

"Well, they didn't actually see anybody there. But a truck was parked there. His description fits Sol's truck exactly. Where the young man said the truck was parked was right where we found Sol's truck."

"We already knew Sol's truck was there. What's new about that?"

"Charley, he said they saw that truck at the river just a minute or so after one thirty. And he said he was certain about the time. He had looked at his watch wonderin' who was out that late if they had to work Monday."

"So-o-o-o," Charley said, as he raised his eyebrows.

"So, is right. That's earlier than the time Maddie said Sol left their house."

"What does that mean, Harg?"

"I don't know if it means anything, but it makes me wonder. Why would Maddie tell us Sol left the house later than he really did? I want to talk to this young man. If he sticks to his story, we may need to talk to Maddie again."

Harg decided that he would talk to the young man, Dennis Elkins, about what he had told Rufus. He told Charley to go on home but to be on call in case they needed to talk to Maddie again.

About two hours later, the sheriff drove up to the Scott house, tooted his horn, and Charley came out. "Hop in," Harg said, "we better go see Maddie. The Elkins boy repeated what he told Rufus, and he said he was sure about what time they saw the truck by the river—right at one thirty Monday mornin'."

"Hmm," was Charley's response as his boss headed toward the Massey place.

Harg said, "There's one other thing we haven't talked to the widow about."

"What's that?"

"Think, Charley. What evidence do we have related to Sol's death?"

Charley thought for a moment, then said, "Well, we have Sol's coat and shoes. And we saw two sets of tracks in the sand. That's it, I guess." He was silent, thinking for a few moments, then sat up straighter and said, "Wait! There's one other thing!"

"Yeah," the sheriff said, "the bit of evidence you and your boys found in the river before you found Sol. The double-M handkerchief." He tapped his left shirt pocket from which about a third of an envelope protruded and said, "We need to ask Maddie about this too. But before we get to the Massey place, I want to stop for another look around on the beach where we found Sol's truck."

The sheriff pulled off the road at the beach, and he and Charley made a careful search of the entire area. They found nothing helpful. The two sets of tracks they had seen in the sand were no longer discernible. Apparently several people had a campfire party a night or two back; many tracks had obliterated the ones the officers had seen there when they found Sol's truck.

"That pair of tracks we saw here still bothers you, don't it?" Charley said to his boss.

"You're mighty right they bother me."

"Bothers me too. Who could have been here with Sol?"

The men left the beach not knowing any more than before, and that was precious little. As Harg pulled his car away fron the beach area, he asked, "Charley, what do you think we're after here?"

Charley responded, "What do you mean? I'm not sure what you're asking."

"Oh, I know that right now we're lookin' into the cause of Sol Massey's death. But lookin' at a broader picture of what the sheriff's office does, what are we after? What should the people of Powell County expect from us?"

Charley thought while he looked out the car window. Finally he turned toward the sheriff and said, "Well, Harg, I'm not much for highfalutin words and ideas, but I think what we have to be after is justice."

"Oh?"

"When I was in school, elementary and high school, we pledged allegiance to the flag almost every day. In our pledge we say that we are one nation under God with liberty and justice for all." Charley paused again, seeming to struggle with his emotions. Then he continued, "I reckon we've had young men from Powell County die recently protecting our liberty, and I . . . uh . . ."

The sheriff interrupted, reached over, patted his deputy on the thigh, and said, "I think I know who you're talkin' about, Charley. Go on."

Charley cleared his throat and said, "I think the job of the sheriff's office is to work for justice for the people here in this county—justice, pure and simple."

Sheriff Fielding looked at Charley and nodded approval, saying, "That's a good answer. But I have to say this—in my experience, justice is hardly ever simplc, and almost never is it pure. Keep to that line of thinkin', though, and you'll serve Powell County well, Charley."

After a few minutes of riding in silence, they arrived at the house that had been Sol's. They exited the car, went up the steps to the front porch, and Charley rapped lightly on the door. He heard a voice inside, saw movement, and the door slowly opened. Lucas Massey peered at them with dull questioning eyes—maybe even resentful eyes.

Harg said, "Howdy, Luke. Is your mama home?"

"Yes."

Harg heard Maddie's voice, "Who is it Lucas? What do they want?"

"It's the sheriff, Mama, and I don't . . ."

Maddie cut him off in midsentence, saying, "Well, tell him to come in. I'll be right there."

Wordlessly, Luke pulled the door back, and the two men walked in with hats in hand. Maddie came out of the kitchen into the front room drying her hands on a towel with an exasperated look on her face.

"Sheriff Fielding, I'm surprised to see you again so soon. Have you learned more about how Sol died?"

"No, Miz Massey, we haven't, but I need to ask you about the time Sol left the house Sunday night."

"Why, I told you that already," Maddie said.

"Yes, ma'am, you did, but I just wanted to verify the time again now that you've had a chance to get over the shock some and get yourself settled a bit."

"Well, I told you he left no earlier than two o'clock and that it was probably two fifteen or so. That's what I'm telling you again. The time hasn't changed. Is the time Sol left here of some great importance?"

"That's all right, Miz Massey, I just wanted to verify the time. I'll let you know if we come up with anything more."

Then, seemingly as an afterthought, the sheriff said, "Oh, I almost forgot. There's just one more little thing." He pulled the envelope from his shirt pocket and gently extracted the white handkerchief found in the river. Harg held it out to Maddie and asked, "Can you tell me whose handkerchief this is?"

Maddie took the hankie by one corner and with her other hand held an opposite corner as it unfolded. Her face showed a fleeting reaction of surprise or worry, the men couldn't tell which. Then she said, "Why, this is mine. How do you come to have it?"

"We found it in the river the day before we found Sol," Charley replied.

Harg said, "We figured it must be yours because of the initials on it. Do you know how it got in the river?"

Maddie responded, "I surely don't. But Sol must have had it in a pocket when he went into the river."

"Did Sol often carry one of your embroidered handkerchiefs?"

Maddie said, "No, he didn't. He certainly didn't pick it up when he came into the house Sunday night. He must have had it with him while he had been away from home for those several days. Maybe he cared more for me than he showed if he was carrying around one of my hankies."

"Just seems kinda odd that a man like Sol would be carryin' around a woman's fancy handkerchief, even his wife's," Harg posed.

"Sheriff, I really can't tell you any more about it. Do you want to keep the hankie?"

"Well, I reckon we might keep it for now."

Maddie handed the hankie to Harg, and he returned it to the envelope and stuffed it in his shirt pocket.

The sheriff heard movement in the kitchen and assumed it was Lucas or Cecilia or both, and he continued, "Do you need Charley or me to do anything for you or your children? We'd be happy to help in any way we can."

"No, thank you, sheriff, we'll be fine."

"Good night to you then," the sheriff said as he and Charley turned to leave. Back in the car, the two men looked at each other with puzzled expressions.

"So, what now?" Charley asked. "Who do we believe about the time?"

"Don't know," Harg sighed, "but we got two people who seem certain about two different times that Sol could have been at the river. And we don't even know if the time is of any importance anyway."

Charley added, "And we saw that smaller set of tracks in the sand beside Sol's. They seemed to have been made at the same time Sol's tracks were made."

"Did you happen to notice the size of Maddie's feet, Charley?"

"Yes, I did."

"What size shoes do you think made them tracks?" Harg asked.

Charley pondered the question for several seconds and responded, "Well, I think a female made the tracks, and I believe that female wore about a size seven or seven-and-a-half shoe. I also believe that's about the size shoe Maddie Massey wears and that her shoes would have fit right into those smaller tracks."

The sheriff replied, "I agree, Charley, but we have to remember something else about that size. That's a mighty common shoe size for women, which means any one of a whole host of women could have made the tracks. So what other women might have been with Sol that Sunday night?"

As he patted the envelope in his shirt pocket, Harg continued, "And how does this fancy handkerchief fit into the picture? I just can't imagine Sol carryin' a handkerchief like that. We'll just keep thinkin', and we'll keep our eyes and ears and minds open."

Charley wondered aloud, "Are we ruling out suicide then?"

"We're not rulin' nothin' out. But most of us who knowed old Sol would likely agree that he loved hisself too much to even think about suicide."

"That's for sure," agreed Charley.

Harg ended their conversation with, "This may be an accidental drownin'. And it may not be. I just hope to the Lord we can find out which it is."

CHAPTER 5

Cecilia Massey heard the conversation between her mother and the sheriff; and as soon as he and the deputy pulled away in his car, she hurried to her room to change into her nightgown. Even though darkness had not quite settled, she didn't want to be with her mother now. Cecilia left the bedroom door ajar several inches because she wanted fresh air to circulate from the open window near her bed. She pulled off her blouse, slacks, and underclothes and got into her gown. As the gown fell down to drape her from neck to midcalf, she turned toward her dresser, caught her breath, and almost screamed. With a hand over her mouth, she stared at the reflection of Luke in her dresser mirror. Luke was enjoying the mirrored view through the partly open door.

As she ran to the door, Cecilia hissed, "You little rat, I'll brain you! You Peeping Tom. You, you . . ."

But Luke had already scampered down the hall to his room, and she heard the thumb latch click as he locked his door.

Cecilia's mother called from the kitchen, "What's going on with you two?"

"Nothing," was the reply. Cecilia thought, *what's the use to say anything*?

She went back into her room, closed the door, flipped the latch, and fell onto her bed, staring at the ceiling. Tonight wasn't the first time she had caught Luke looking at her when he shouldn't have been. *Telling*

Mother hasn't made any difference in the past, except that she gets mad at me and blames me instead of Luke. Luke has probably spied on me other times without me realizing he was around.

Cecilia remembered several times in the past two years when she had been aware that Luke had been at the right place to watch her in various stages of undress or exposure of her body. Once was behind the barn when she had a sudden urge to empty a full bladder, and instead of going to the outhouse, she dropped her pants and panties and relieved herself. As she straightened and pulled up her clothes, she saw Luke at a corner of the barn looking at her with unabashed attention and satisfaction.

And on a hot, humid afternoon last summer, she had walked down to the river. As it ran clear, cool, and inviting, she decided she would take a quick skinny-dip. She moved over behind a clump of willows, pulled off her clothes, and waded out into the refreshing stream until the water was up to her waist. She submerged and quickly came back up. *Oh this feels so good!* She went under the surface once more, came up, wiped water from her face and eyes, and started walking toward her clothes on the bank. As she moved into shallow water, a twig broke, and Cecilia looked up. On the bank just to the left of her clothes stood Luke, big eyed and unashamed. She screamed, "Luke Massey, get out of here! I'm telling Mother!"

Luke said, "Hah! Make me," as he continued to enjoy the view of his sister's nude, curvaceous body. Then he had turned and sauntered away.

Angry and embarrassed, Cecilia had hurried back home. As she came inside the house, her mother saw her and said, "Child, how'd your hair get so wet?"

Cecilia said, "I was hot and sweaty, so I took a dip in the river."

"Your clothes are dry, so you must have taken them off."

"Yes, I did," Cecilia said.

"All of them, even your underclothes?"

"Yes, all of them. And when I walked out of the river to get my clothes, there stood Luke watching me. And with me stark naked!"

"Girl, what do you expect? Lucas is thirteen. He's at the age to be inquisitive."

"Inquisitive? Is that what you call it? I've caught him watching me other times when he shouldn't be."

"You're just going to have to be more careful where you undress, aren't you?"

"Mother! Luke is a Peeping Tom! It's not natural for a brother to want to watch his sister like that and to always be looking for the chance, and even making the chance, to watch."

"Cecilia, he'll grow out of it," Maddie snapped. "You just take care about exposing yourself when you shouldn't. No telling who might be watching you besides Lucas."

As Cecilia lay in her bed with darkness just beginning to descend, she heard the familiar "who, who, who cooks for you" call of a great horned owl from out past the barn. She shivered. She was sad. She was worried. She was confused. *My father is dead, my brother is a pervert, and my mother never has a kind word for me. Mother never shows me any love or concern. She has plenty of good words, smiles, and hugs for her darling Lucas, but none for me. What kind of a life can I have?*

Cecilia's thoughts drifted back to happier times. Her earliest childhood memories were happy, carefree ones. Her daddy paid lots of attention to her, taking her places with him, taking her horseback riding, or on trips to town in the truck, or to fields as he supervised the tenant farmer and seasonal farm hands as they worked in tobacco, corn, and hay fields. Sol had done very little of the actual farm work, and Cecilia realized now that he had thought he was too good to have to do the hard, back-breaking work that had to be done on a farm. Sol had given her piggy-back rides, tickled her, and pushed her in the rope-and-board swing attached to a strong limb of the huge white oak tree in their backyard. He often read Aesop's fables to her, and sometimes he told bedtime stories.

Her father liked to sing and whistle. Songs like "Camptown Races," "Great Speckled Bird," and "Wabash Cannonball." But the tune he favored most was "Clementine." He sang it, he whistled it. He especially liked to sing it to Cecilia's mother, Maddie. And by the time Cecilia was five, she could whistle the Clementine tune, and she often whistled it when she was with her daddy.

Her mother had told her that her grandfather Massey died several years before Cecilia was born. Cecilia could remember her grandmother Massey, her father's mother, but she didn't remember a lot about her. She did remember that her grandmother had seemed to have a perpetual sour look on her face and few kind words for her two grandchildren. And she recalled one particular instance when her grandmother talked to her. One day Cecilia whistled "Clementine" as she played in the front yard while her grandmother sat in her rocker on the front porch.

Her grandmother said, "Cecilia, come here, child." As she walked toward the porch, Mrs. Massey said, "Young'un, do you know the old sayin' about whistlin'?"

"No, Grammaw, I don't reckon I ever heard of it."

"The sayin' is, 'A whistlin' woman and a crowin' hen, both will come to no good end.' Now, mebbee you should try to remember that, Cecilia."

Later the child told her mother what Grammaw had said and asked, "Is it a bad thing for a girl to whistle?"

Her mother responded, "Oh, I guess it bothers your grandmother, but I don't think there's any reason for you not to whistle if you want to."

Cecilia remembered that her grandmother got sick. Some woman, whom she now knew to be Mrs. Clarissa Thacker, had come to the house to doctor her grandmother, but Grammaw Massey died.

Her little brother was two years younger than Cecilia. Most everybody, including Cecilia, called him Luke, but his mother always called him Lucas, his given name. Cecilia loved her brother, and he liked for her to play with him. Luke called his sister Ceecee. Their mother took good care of them and showered them with love and affection.

At around the age of ten, Cecilia had become aware that her daddy wasn't acting the way he used to act. He didn't give as much time and attention to Luke and her as he used to. She also realized that he was drinking whiskey enough that it affected the way he acted and looked. Her daddy had been a handsome man, almost six feet tall with brown eyes and black hair. He had always been particular, even finicky, about how he looked and dressed. But he had started neglecting his grooming and appearance, as well as his clothes. Sometimes now, he looked dirty and unkempt, and he didn't smell good like he almost always did before. Most of the time now, she could smell whiskey on her daddy's breath.

By the time Cecilia finished elementary school, her parents were having trouble getting along with each other, arguing and fussing in the children's presence. Whether or not Maddie's problems with Sol were the reason, Cecilia realized that her mother changed; she grew less interested, less caring, and less loving toward her. Her father stayed away from his family for days at a time, leaving her mother responsible for running the farm operation. When he came home after these absences, Sol was usually either still drunk or looked as if he was getting over one.

For the past two years, Cecilia's home life had grown much worse; verbal battles between her parents became commonplace. Sol threatened Maddie physically, but as far as Cecilia knew, he had never struck her. Sol practically ignored his children, although he occasionally had a good word for Luke or spent a few minutes with him; he hardly ever had time for his daughter. Her father drank even more than before and was away from home as much as he was there. Her mother took over practically all the farm decision making and relied more and more on their sharecropper, Demus Ferguson, to oversee the day-to-day farm activities. If it was possible, Cecilia now got less and less attention and support from her mother.

In her first two years in high school, Cecilia enjoyed her science and biology classes under Ms. McGraw, and she earned solid *A*'s in them.

Her teacher told her she should think about going to college to study in some area of science or in a science-related field. Cecilia asked Ms. McGraw what might be such a field.

Ms. McGraw had responded, "One area would be medicine. Most all areas in the country need more doctors and nurses, and that's especially true for the mountains here in Virginia. We need many more medical people here."

"I might learn to be a nurse, but I couldn't be a doctor."

"Why not? You're a bright girl. If you set your mind to it, you can be a nurse or a doctor."

With a puzzled look on her face, Cecilia asked, "But aren't all doctors men? I've never seen a woman doctor."

Ms. McGraw smiled and placed her hand on the girl's arm as she said, "Cecilia, honey, there are women doctors. There just aren't any around here. When I was in college, a well-known doctor—a woman *and* a surgeon—came to Johnson City and talked to students at convocation about her experiences in becoming a physician and practicing medicine. She did it, and you can too if you set your cap to it."

Since that conversation with her math and science teacher, Cecilia learned she could probably become a registered nurse with two years of study after high school, and that three or four or five or more years of study might be required for her to become a doctor. The possibilities excited her. *Nurse Massey. Nurse Cecilia Massey. Or even better, Dr. Cecilia Massey*!

Cecilia's thoughts returned to what was going on in her life now. She recalled the conversation she heard earlier tonight between the sheriff and her mother, as well as the one between them the day after her daddy left that Sunday night. For some reason she couldn't, she wouldn't, let her mind take her back a few days to that late night when her daddy left home for the last time. Something was blocking any memories of that night, and a dark, foreboding feeling caused her to want to get her mind focused on other matters as quickly as possible.

As Cecilia lay on her bed with light from a bright half moon streaming through her window, she pondered how and why her life had become so complicated and unhappy. *Well, let me see. I can list some reasons.*

One, my daddy drank too much and practically abandoned us. He and Mother fussed, sniped, or quarreled constantly. Now he's dead.

Two, my little brother loves to look at me when I'm naked.

Three, my mother acts as if I don't exist except when she finds some reason to criticize or scold me.

Four, I probably won't be allowed to go to college because my mother didn't get to go.

And, let's see, what else? Oh, yeah. A senior boy at school is making my life miserable there. Rafe Hawkins bugs me constantly. He wants to be my boyfriend in the worst way. I can't keep him away, and he won't take "no" for an answer. He wants to sit by me on the school bus. He wants to take me to a movie. He wants us to go for a walk on Sunday afternoons. When he's around and thinks I don't see him, he examines me from head to toe. I know what's going on in his one-track mind. I know exactly what he wants from me.

Is there any reason to hope that my situation at home or school will get any better? There's nobody I can turn to for advice—certainly not Mother. Cecilia was getting drowsy; she yawned. She slid under her quilt and was fading toward dreamland when a thought came to her that held a glimmer of hope. *Ms. McGraw, my favorite teacher! She has told me more than once she would like to help me any way she could. Maybe I'll talk to her tomorrow. Yes, I will.* She relaxed and was soon asleep.

CHAPTER 6

Early October 1942

Following Sol's death and burial, Maddie tried to carry on with her life as best she could, knowing that she now had full responsibility for her own future, for her own happiness, and for her children. She was sure she could do a better job of managing the farm and finances than Sol had done. At least the money he had poured into whiskey, gambling, and carousing would no longer be wasted. Even so, making a decent living on a farm was not easy, and Madeline Walls Massey wasn't willing to settle just for decent any longer.

A daughter of sharecropper and coal miner Conley Walls, Maddie was the oldest of five children—three girls and two boys. Life had not been easy in her home. Her daddy had toiled night shifts in a coal mine for meager wages, and he tried to raise crops on a neighbor's farm throughout most of his summers. In spite of his hard labor, his scant income was barely enough to keep his family fed and clothed, especially during the Depression years. Most of Maddie's clothes had either been made by her mother or passed down to her from two aunts who tried to help her as much as they could.

Brutish labor, inadequate rest, wet mining conditions, and inhalation of coal dust over the years brought about an early death for her father. He died two years after she married; he was not yet fifty years old, and he didn't live long enough to see grandchildren. Maddie, now a widow at thirty-six, wanted to be able to live a good life with some of the fine things of life that she had never been able to have. Before their marriage and for a few of their first married years, Sol had made grand promises to her about what they would do, what she could buy, places they would go; none of his promises came to pass.

Maddie had heard stories about Sol even before she was in high school. He made friends easily, he was a good looking lad, and many local girls hoped to have a chance to go out with him. Sol was happy to fulfill that hope for as many girls as possible. As an older teenager, he began to drink—homebrew, beer, or whiskey—whatever was available, and he ran around with almost any willing girl or woman, single or married. By the time Maddie was a high school junior, Sol had set his cap for her even though she was ten years younger than he. She welcomed Sol's attentions, the attentions of a good-looking older man whose family was wealthy, compared to her own.

While Maddie and Sol dated, she learned that his mother, Martha Webber Massey, adamantly opposed her son marrying Madeline Walls. Sol's father had died several years before his son married. In versions of the stories Maddie heard, Mrs. Massey saw the girl her son was wooing as a gold-digging tart, just poor white trash. According to these stories, his mother had pleaded, cajoled, ranted, and raved trying to convince Sol not to marry Maddie, but Sol was enamored of the girl and vowed that he would never marry if he couldn't marry Madeline Walls. Despite his mother's objections, Sol married Maddie in 1924, shortly after she finished high school.

Maddie got pregnant three times during the first five years of their marriage. After one miscarriage, their beautiful little Cecilia was born in 1927, followed by son Lucas in 1929. Even though he had a wife and children, Sol didn't like to work or accept the responsibilities of a husband, father, or family breadwinner. Gradually he lost the fervent love or obsession or whatever strong feelings he first felt for Maddie; she seldom saw or heard any expression of his love. He did love to drink and gamble and, not infrequently, to share his illustrious self with women other than his wife.

When Sol's father, Thaddeus, died, his will stipulated that the large farm and even larger forested mountain tracts were to be jointly owned by his wife, Martha, and Sol until Martha's death when the farm would then be owned by Sol and his wife if he was married. During the winter following Cecilia's sixth birthday, Martha Massey took to her bed with a severe case of influenza. The flu progressed into pneumonia, and Sol's mother's condition worsened slowly.

When Maddie learned her mother-in-law had influenza, she had suffered an almost numbing fear. What if Maddie or her children came down with the flu? She was terrified because she remembered that in 1918 and 1919, most families in Powell County lost one or more members to that deadly strain called Spanish influenza. That vicious flu bug had attacked her family when she was twelve years old. Of her immediate family, only Maddie and her father did not fall ill. Nobody could explain why some members of a family didn't get the disease while others died from it. Maddie helped care for the sick ones.

Clarissa Thacker was called Clare by some of her family and friends. Some of the folks scattered around the surrounding mountains and hollers pronounced her name as *clare-uh-see*, but many of them knew her as the Herb Woman. Clare came to help care for Maddie's sick mother, brothers, and sisters. She couldn't spend much time with the Walls because she needed to help tend to so many other people stricken with the flu, but she left medicines and instructions for using them.

Maddie still carried a mental image of her stricken sister whose sickness seemed to be ordinary flu, but it quickly turned into a horrible type of pneumonia. Along with a terrible cough that produced viscous greenish sputum, Eilene's fever spiked so high that Clare said she had never seen anyone with such a burning fever. The other sick family members never got as bad as Eilene had. A neighbor took Maddie to the drugstore in Creedy to get medicine Clare asked that they try. As she walked from the neighbor's car toward the drugstore, she noticed three little girls jumping rope. The rhyme they recited as two girls turned the rope and the other skipped was:

> *I had a little bird, its name is Enza.*
> *I opened the window, and in-flu-Enza.*

Maddie knew she would never forget that rhyme.

Eilene's lips and fingers turned purple, and she struggled to clear her airways of blood-tinged froth that sometimes gushed from her nose and mouth. She became delirious and struggled pitifully for air until she suffocated. Four days after first showing flu symptoms, Eilene was dead. While his daughter suffered, Conley Walls, as well as many other Powell County parents of children with influenza, wished they lived near more doctors, nurses, and good hospitals. What they didn't know was that all over the world, well-trained doctors were helpless against this strain of influenza.

The Herb Woman treated Martha Massey, but none of her remedies seemed to help. Clarissa Thacker said that this type of flu didn't seem to be anything like the 1918 strain, but she recommended that Doc Easton be brought in at once.

Martha would not agree to that, saying, "If Clare can't help me, a doctor won't do me no good. If it's my time to go, all the doctors in the country can't keep me here."

She died less than two weeks after she got sick. Sol and Maddie became owners of the Massey land.

Martha Massey had invested a little of their hard-earned money in insurance coverage for her son. When Sol was in the fourth grade, she took out an insurance policy on him with Jefferson Standard Life

Insurance and made small monthly payments on it until it was paid up in 1930. No more premiums had to be paid, but the policy remained in effect, and $5,000 would be paid to the named beneficiary when Sol died. After Sol married, Martha changed the beneficiary from herself to his wife, Madeline.

Friends and family asked Martha how she could afford to pay insurance premiums all those years, and her response had always been "I can't afford not to for the sake of whatever children Sol may have."

In early 1933, a young man representing a company in Bristol, Virginia called Huff-Cook Burial Insurance Company made his rounds through Southwest Virginia urging families to buy insurance to cover burial expenses. Martha was in her late fifties then, and she thought the cost of a policy on herself was too high. She decided to buy a burial policy on Sol, who was thirty-seven then. The persuasive insurance agent convinced her to take out a policy on Sol and one on herself, even though she fretted over committing that much money each month for the insurance. Martha agreed to pay a total of $1.05 each month in premiums—70 cents for herself and 35 cents for Sol. She had given copies of the policies to Madeline and made her promise to continue to pay the premiums on Sol's policy after Martha died.

Maddie had kept her promise even though she often questioned the wisdom of paying the 35 cents when the Huff-Cook agent came to collect each month. Martha died after paying only two months' premiums, so all of her burial expenses were paid. What a great investment that $1.40 had been. And now that Sol had died, Huff-Cook would pay his burial expenses.

Sol had not been a good farmer. He had not been a good manager, not a good provider for his family. In spite of pleading appeals, even threats, from Maddie about his laziness and neglect of the farm operation, Sol became less and less concerned with his family and with all aspects of farming. He drank and gambled more, he was with Maddie and the children less; when he was at home, he was usually drinking or verbally abusive to Maddie, or both.

Over the past two years, Sol and Maddie's lovemaking dwindled to nothing. Maddie knew that Sol's frequent prolonged absences from home included trysts with other women. Sometimes between those trysts, Sol demanded that Maddie provide him sexual release, but that wasn't lovemaking. There was no love involved in their brief physical couplings, and they brought her no pleasure.

Two weeks after Sol's burial, Maddie sat in her living room. With a long sigh, she rose from her chair, walked to a window, and stood looking out with hands in her slacks' hip pockets. Huff-Cook will pay Sol's burial expenses, and Jefferson Standard will send her $5,000 as life insurance proceeds. That will enable her to hire workers to make needed repairs on farm buildings, replace fences, buy tools and a couple of pieces of equipment, buy a few more head of Hereford cattle, and still have a good portion of that money left. Without really discerning specific objects or details in her field of vision, Maddie stared out over part of the farm *she* now owned and thought, *Well, I won't have to put up with that sorry Sol anymore. It's up to me to make a better life for myself. I do what has to be done, and I'll take on whatever or whoever I must to get out of this hand-to-mouth, dirt-poor-farmer living I've known all my life. Don't know yet exactly what I'll do, but I don't intend to keep on living the way I have been.*

CHAPTER 7

1923 to 1930

Charley Scott remembered incidents of his early childhood, starting when he was four or five years old. Mixed in with all the good memories of time with his grandparents' on their farm, Charley had a couple of unpleasant, scary recollections. He recalled being with his Pa Jess one bright, warm summer day when he was about eight years old. His grandpa was pulling locust logs out to the top of a knoll from where he had cut them; later he would cut them into seven-foot lengths for fence posts. The hard locust wood was slow to rot away, and most farmers used them in their fences.

While Pa Jess used Bird, his sorrel mare, to pull out one log at a time, Charley had followed his grandpa and Bird as they pulled three or four logs out; then he got bored and tired of just walking back and forth. So Charley stretched out on his back in soft green grass near a summer Rambo apple tree that was heavy with ripening, red-striped apples. Chewing on a sweet, juicy apple and with one hand behind his head, he watched a red-tailed hawk and heard its cries—two- or three-second hoarse, raspy screams—as it made lazy circles in the clear blue sky above. Some neighbors called the bird a chicken hawk because they believed small chickens were one of its favorite foods.

The boy wondered what it would be like to be up so high and what he would be able to see. *I could probably see all of Ma and Pa Jess's farm,* he thought. *Bet I could even see Clinch River and Drowning Creek and Creedy. I might even be able to see Mom and Pop's place—my home. Could I see the ocean? Could I see China?* Charley's wool gathering was interrupted by a call from Pa Jess. "Sonny, would you like to ride Bird as we pull in more of these logs?"

"Really?" Charley chirped as he hopped to his feet beaming. "You know I would!"

Pa Jess lifted Charley up on Bird's back; holding the hames in front of him, the boy rode the horse, looking as proud and happy as a knight of old would have looked on his favorite steed. The horse worked up a lather as she pulled the logs, and her sweat began to get Charley's pants and legs damp.

His grandpa noticed what was happening and said, "Charley, Bird is gettin' mighty hot. Don't you think it might be better for Bird and you if you got off her?"

The grandson looked disappointed but said, "Yeah, I guess so," as he slid down over Bird's side to the ground.

Pa Jess drove the mare back for another log. He brought that log out to the knoll and started back for another. Bird stopped suddenly. After standing still for just a few seconds, she reared up on her hind legs; with flared nostrils and blazing, frightened eyes, she thrashed the air wildly with her front legs. Then she whinnied pitifully, fell backward, and was still. She was dead.

Charley stared wide-eyed at the splendid horse he had just been riding. With surprise and disbelief etched on his face, Pa Jess gazed on the inert form. He dragged his worn and faded red bandana from the hip pocket of his bib overalls, took his hat off, and wiped his sweaty brow. In such a low voice that Charley barely heard him, he said, "Lordy, lordy. Look at that! She just rared up and keeled over."

After several seconds of silence, Pa Jess continued, "I sure hate to see her like this. She was a mighty good mare, and I'll miss her."

Charley saw a sadness in his grandpa's eyes that he had never seen before. Charley's eyes seemed glued on the large, unmoving animal that just minutes earlier had been so strong in body and striking in appearance.

Pa Jess exclaimed, "Charley! What would've happened if you'd still been on Bird? Looks to me like the Good Lord was watching out for you today, boy."

The shaken lad focused on Bird's sweaty, glistening body and her big beautiful, unseeing brown eyes. He slowly nodded his head, not fully grasping what had happened. Then he realized he would never ride Bird again.

Pa Jess said, "I guess the old girl must've had a stroke or heart attack."

Even after all these years, Charley occasionally recalled that day with a mixture of sorrow and fear.

Charley was born in September 1919 at home where his mother, Belle, had been attended to by Clarissa Thacker and young doctor Franklin Easton. Charley was J. R. and Belle's third child. Reagan had been born seven years before Charley but died one year before Charley's birth. Edwin was five years older than Charley. After baby Charley was a few weeks old, his eleven-year-old aunt Lucille (Aunt Luce to him) began spending three or four nights a week with his parents, looking after her "little Charley." In her mind, she adopted him as her baby. After she reached high school age, Lucille spent most weeknights with the Scotts so she could attend Creedy High School. The bond between Lucille and her nephew continued to strengthen.

As he grew older, Charley spent considerable time with his aunt Luce and uncle Verle and with his Musick grandparents. His mother commented many times, "You'd think that boy doesn't have parents or a home, he stays away from both so much," but she was pleased to see evidence of love between her son and his aunt and between him and her own dear parents.

At about age ten, Charley began helping his uncle Verle on his and Luce's farm; he worked in corn and tobacco, put up hay, and cut off pastures with a small scythe his grandfather made for him. By this time, his brother, Edwin, had left home in search of adventure and, he hoped, a better job than he had been able to find in Powell County. In addition to the happy life he had with his parents and Aunt Luce, Charley treasured remembrances of time spent with his Musick grandparents. Jesse and Estella Musick lived in the Chestnut Ridge area of River Mountain, not far from the Clinch River swinging bridge. To get to his grandparents' farm by county roads meant a trip of twelve to fourteen miles, since no road bridges crossed the Clinch closer than six or seven miles above and below the swinging bridge. But Charley could walk from his house to the swinging bridge, over it, and about a half mile more to the Musick farm. His mother, Belle, had always cautioned him to be careful crossing over the bridge but trusted that he would get to her parents safely.

When Charley first started talking, the family had tried to teach him to say "Grandpa Jesse." The best the boy could get out was "Pa Jess," so that became his name for his grandpa. It was easy for him to transfer this speech achievement to Grandma Estella, except that she became Ma Jess. Pa Jess and Ma Jess would always be Charley's name for his grandparents.

Ma and Pa Jess's house had painted poplar weatherboarding on the outside with a metal roof. The original part of the house had been built by Pa Jess's father, and he had built well. The house was nestled snuggly at the narrow end of a valley where two low ridges met to form a wide angle. A pair of towering white oaks stood as sentinels in the front yard. An expanse of level to slightly rolling fields spread out in front of the house; pastures, a small orchard, and woodland claimed the surrounding ridges and additional ridges farther back. Other structures encompassed the house—a large barn, corn crib, hog pen, chicken house, smokehouse, dairy, combination workshop and blacksmith shop, and toilet. The Musicks carried their water from a fast-flowing, icy-cold spring that rushed from under a limestone outcropping near the house and ran through their springhouse.

Charley learned many lessons from his grandparents, especially from Pa Jess. Some of the lessons were about farming, such as how to use a hillside plow or that the time to plant corn in the spring was when oak leaves were the size of a squirrel's ear. Charlie learned about gardening and tending cattle and sheep by being with Pa Jess and paying attention to what he did as he went about his daily routines of farm work. The boy learned you can't breed mules and why. He learned that horses and mules are mounted on their left or nearside, not on the offside. But cows are milked from the right side. With a grin and twinkling eyes, Pa Jess had said, "All of our cows are right handed." Charley learned why chickens stood in running water below the springhouse during cold winter days. Why did they? Because as cold as the water from the spring was, it was warmer than the ground and air.

The Musicks' outdoor toilet was in the opposite direction from the spring, out near the barn and crib. Old newspapers and catalogs stored in the outhouse served as their toilet paper. One day Pa Jess told Charley that they now also had red and white corncobs in the toilet. Charley asked, "Why'd you put corncobs in the toilet?"

"Why, to wipe with, son! What else could they be for?" his grandpa had replied with mock seriousness.

"Ouch! That would hurt. But why have two colors?"

Pa Jess said, "Well, Charley, first you use a red cob, then you use a white one to see if you need to use another red one," and then he laughed with gusto.

No electric power lines came into the River Mountain hollows, so the Musicks used kerosene lamps for lighting inside the house; in the front room, Ma Jess had an "Aladdin Lamp." She used this lamp to sew by at night; both she and Pa Jess used this lamp to read by. This lamp burned kerosene, but it had a wick and a mantle that was part of the chimney or globe. The Aladdin Lamp provided an amazingly brighter light than did regular kerosene lamps. Pa Jess said it gave as much light as a 50-watt electric light bulb in houses in Creedy. The house had two stoves that burned both coal and wood—a heating stove in the front room and a cooking range in the kitchen.

The Musicks milked three or four Jersey cows year round. After the milk sat in a container for a few hours in the chilly spring water running through the springhouse, cream in the rich Jersey milk rose to the top. Ma Jess skimmed off the cream, churned it to make butter, and took butter they didn't use, plus any excess eggs from their white leghorn hens, to Amos Baldwin, manager of Creedy Grocery. There she traded them for food staples they needed but couldn't produce on the farm, or Amos would keep a running credit tab that she could use later.

Immediately behind the grandparents' house and dug into the side of a hill was the dairy, or what some people called a root cellar; it was one of Charley's favorite spots on the Musick farm. In the dairy, board shelves and bins held apples and potatoes through the winters as well as canned berries, fruit, vegetables, and meat. Ma Jess kept a big crock of sauerkraut in the dairy. Charley relished the musky smells of the dairy tinged with the aroma of apples. Temperatures inside the dairy were always cooler than they were outside on hot summer days and warmer than outside in the cold of winter. A little farther up the hill from the dairy was the smokehouse where salted pork shoulders, hams, and side meat were cured and stored.

During summers and on weekends during the school year, Charley spent time with his aunt Luce and as much time with his grandparents as his mom and pop permitted. Pa Jess taught Charley to fish in Clinch River and took him squirrel hunting and rabbit hunting before he was old enough to carry a gun. He showed his grandson how to set rabbit boxes to trap rabbits when they came out of holes. He showed Charley how to make a "gravel shooter" using the Y fork of a small tree limb, strips of rubber cut from a discarded red rubber inner tube, and a leather tongue from an old shoe. With this little homemade weapon and smooth marble-size gravels for ammunition, Charley practiced his marksmanship on tin cans, crows, and sparrows. Occasionally his aim was good enough to bag a rabbit that sat still thinking it was hidden from hunters' eyes.

Jesse Musick was a good farmer, a good carpenter, and a good woodworker. His father had been skilled at the same crafts and had passed them, as well as his excellent tool collection, along to Jesse. When Jesse's father died, Jesse and Estella moved to the farm; when his mother died, it belonged to Estella and him. The farm needed a lot of work because Jesse's father had not been able to do much to keep the farm up because of his age. Over several years, Jesse had toiled long days trying to bring the farm back to its once good state of repair and production. One Sunday after church, Reverend Davenport came home with them for one of Ma Jess's famous chicken and dumplin's Sunday dinners.

After the sumptuous meal, Jesse and the reverend were looking around the farm, and the preacher commented, "Well, Jesse, you and the Lord sure have done wonders with this farm." With a wry smile, Jesse's response was, "Yes, Preacher, but you ortta seen it when the Lord had it all to hisself."

As a young man, Jesse had helped his father and other men build the swinging bridge over the river which he, his children, and grandchildren trod so often between Creedy and Chestnut Ridge. In earlier years, the bridge had been a vital connection between the communities across the river and the town of Creedy—the only way of crossing the river for miles upstream or down. As more people owned automobiles, fewer of them depended on the bridge, but a few families south of Clinch River who didn't own a car or truck still had to rely on and use the bridge. And the bridge was Charley's gateway to happy times with Ma and Pa Jess.

CHAPTER 8

1931 to 1936

From his birth, Charley's aunt Luce helped care for him, feed, and dress him. Most of all, she loved him, and Charley returned that love. Although Lucille was married and had a home of her own to tend to, when Charley came down with a severe case of measles, she insisted on sitting by his side throughout the nights so his mother could get much-needed rest. As Charley began to be affected by the illness, he developed a dry cough and watery, bloodshot eyes. His eyes became painfully sensitive to light, so his mother pinned a blanket over the window in his room. He had pain in his muscles, and three or four days after first feeling bad, a skin rash appeared as discolored areas and solid, red, raised splotches. Charley itched, wiped a runny nose, and complained of a sore throat.

Clarissa Thacker, Aunt Luce's mother-in-law, had come by to look at Charley. She left garlic and valerian root to help combat infection and to help the boy rest, and she recommended sponge baths in warm water. She learned that since Charley had become ill, he had eaten very little and didn't want to take much liquid, so she told his mother to try to get him to eat oranges and drink orange juice if they could find oranges. She said the fruit ought to cause him to eat and take in more water.

Two days later, Mrs. Thacker came back to check on Charley and was concerned that he seemed to be no better, and he had a high fever. She gave him lemon balm tea to reduce his fever and left additional treatments. One was dried tumeric root powder mixed with lemon juice and honey. She also made up another mixture for Charley comprised of equal parts of hyssop, marshmallow, catmint, and ribwort plantain sweetened with honey to sooth his cough and to lubricate his dry mouth and airways.

Luce and Belle noticed tiny white spots in his mouth and decided it was time to bring in Doc Easton. J. R. went to the doctor's office in town and asked him to come take a look at his boy. By the time the doctor arrived, Charley had become delirious and was seeing things and talking out of his head. Doc Easton was alarmed by his hallucinations but tried to reassure the parents that their son was strong, had no other health problems, and should be all right. His unspoken worry was that the boy might develop pneumonia, bronchitis, or infections. He said he knew nothing else to do but let Charley's system work to overcome the disease.

After two days of delirium, Charley started showing signs of improving. His temperature dropped to near normal, but his persistent cough remained. Charley drank more fluid and ate a little better. He sat up in bed a bit and, with help, moved around a little to try to reduce his chance of getting pneumonia. He gradually grew stronger but was still too weak to do much for himself.

One morning Charley awoke realizing he was hungry as a horse. His aunt was sitting near his bed, and he said, "Aunt Luce, I'm hungry. I want some good fried streak-id meat for breakfast."

"Little man," Luce replied, "I'll see that you get all the streak-id meat you can eat." And he did.

Doc Easton told the Scotts that their son had developed bronchitis and that it might be something Charley would always have to some extent. By this time, Charley had missed more than two weeks of school; and because of the cold, snowy, blustery winter weather they were having that year, Doc said Charlie should not be out in it, even to get to and from school. So Charley didn't attend school the remainder of that school year. His aunt Luce wanted to wait on him hand and foot and did much more hovering over him than he would have preferred, but he didn't say or do anything that might cause her to think he didn't appreciate all the care and attention she had showered on him while he was down sick and as he got better.

Over the next few months, Charley gradually regained strength and vigor. Even though he occasionally had coughing spells and difficulty getting enough air into his lungs, his chronic bronchitis didn't usually bother him enough to slow him down.

The following fall Charley went back to school and was in the sixth grade again. He was glad to be in sixth grade this year because a pretty little girl named Bonnie McGraw was also a sixth grader, and they often worked together on their lessons in school and after school. Bonnie's brother, Donald, was in the fifth grade at Drowning Creek School, and Charley liked him too. Bonnie called her brother Donnie; Charley called him Don. So Donald, Bonnie, and Charley became good friends and spent as much time together as they could. All three of them did well in school, but Bonnie outpaced the two boys; she was exceptionally bright, and she applied herself to her studies.

When Charley came to his grandparents' home for weekends, he often brought his best friend, Donald. Bonnie would have loved to join Charley and her brother for weekends with Ma and Pa Jess, but her mother wouldn't permit it.

She said, "It's not proper that a girl your age go with the boys, even though Mr. and Mrs. Musick would probably be happy to have you there."

On a blistering, humid July Saturday, Charley and Donald helped Pa Jess and Woody stack hay. At the end of the day, all of the hay was secure in two stacks, and all four of the workers were tired and dirty. When they came home from the field, Ma Jess met them in the yard and suggested they take turns getting a quick washcloth bath using a dishpan-sized basin she brought from the house.

Charley volunteered to go first, and as he started back behind the house where they could wash in a bit of privacy, his grandmother said, "Now wash off good, Charley."

Pa Jess added, "Yeah, Charley. You be sure to wash up as far as possible, then wash down as far as possible," and after a short pause, he continued with, "and then wash possible!"

The second scary experience Charley remembered of his time with his grandparents, in addition to the day the sorrel mare died, began on an early frosty Saturday in mid-November when Charley was in the sixth grade. He walked from his parents' home to the river. As always, he enjoyed crossing the river on the swinging bridge, and about halfway across, he paused to look upstream and down. He saw a kingfisher perched on a tree limb a few feet above the water. Suddenly the pretty, crested blue and white bird dived into the water and came back up with a small wriggling fish in its beak. *Breakfast time,* Charley thought. *Poor little fish.* The carefree boy hurried on toward his grandparents' place.

The sun was shining brightly, but it didn't have the strength to warm the day very much. Charley's breath puffed out in small clouds as he walked with his chilled hands in his pockets. He had looked forward all week to going rabbit hunting with Pa Jess and Uncle Woody. Woodrow Musick was the younger son of Jesse and Estella Musick, the younger brother of Charley's mother and Aunt Luce. The Musick's older son, Jacob, had been a casualty of the terrible Spanish flu epidemic and died in 1918, as had other family members and many friends and neighbors.

Shortly after Charley got to the Musick house, he was on his way rabbit hunting with Pa Jess and Woody. His grandpa carried a double barrel, 12-gauge shotgun, and Woody had a 20-gauge single barrel. Charley carried his grandpa's old single-shot .22 rifle. The .22 was accurate, and Charley was an excellent marksman with it, but he yearned for his own rifle. The .22 was good for rabbit hunting only if the hunter could spot a rabbit before it left its hiding place and took off running. Charley had a good eye for game. He often spied sitting rabbits and usually added them to the game bag. Charley and all members of his family liked fried rabbit, rabbit hash, and stewed rabbit with gravy.

As the trio of hunters tramped along, Pa Jess and Woody talked about the skunk they had seen in the barnyard the day before. The critter had roamed around aimlessly, seemingly unafraid of anyone or anything while twisting parts of its body as if it might be in pain. At his father's direction, Woody had got his shotgun and killed the skunk.

As they had examined the body, turning it over with a stick, Pa Jess said, "That's what I was afraid we might find," as he pointed to the froth around the edges of the skunk's mouth.

"It's mad. Got the rabies."

His grandpa's concern was that when you see one rabid animal, more that you don't see are sure to be around and that some of these rabid ones could bite and infect dogs, cats, and other farm animals.

After about three hours of hunting, Pa Jess suggested that they had had good luck hunting and maybe should head home. Charley had spied a rabbit sitting in the edge of a little brush pile, betting that the hunters wouldn't see him if he sat perfectly still, but Charley's sharp eye located him. Charley bagged him, and Woody and Pa Jess had gotten two rabbits each. They headed back down the holler toward the house.

With help from Charley, his grandpa skinned the rabbits, cut them into pieces, and washed them. They would provide two or three tasty meals for the family. After they had turned the rabbit pieces over to Ma Jess, Charley and his grandpa went to the barn to clean out accumulated manure in the horses' stalls. Pa Jess picked up a pitchfork he would use to fork manure onto the big sled.

Charley reached to get a fork also, but his grandpa said, "Before we start, I need another drink of water. That huntin' made me thirstier than I realized. Would you fetch us a little bucket of water from the spring?"

"Sure will," Charley answered and headed toward the house to get a bucket as his grandpa began forking manure mixed with hay and straw onto the sled. The man had transferred only a few forkfuls when he heard an urgent shout, "Pa Jess!"

He turned in the direction of the sound and saw Charley running toward him, leaving a spilled bucket of water behind; behind the bucket was a large dog running toward Charley. Pa Jess recognized the short-haired, brindle dog as one of Lem Puckett's. The dog's snarling muzzle revealed bared fangs and a foamy mouth as it charged growling toward the fleeing boy. Jesse thought, *Dear Lord, that's a mad dog, and he's after Charley.*

Charley's only thought was to get to the barn and his Pa Jess.

"Run for the barn, Charley," Jesse yelled as he ran toward the scared boy and the vicious dog.

Charley passed his grandpa and had a fleeting thought, *I didn't know Pa Jess could move that fast*! As he neared the barn, he heard a sharp yelp, a screeching howl, and whimpers behind him. Looking over his shoulder, he saw that the dog was no longer chasing him. He stopped, turned around, and saw his grandpa standing beside the dog.

He ran back to Pa Jess. Looking at the unmoving form of the dog, the man was still holding the handle of the pitchfork with its tines embedded in the front ribcage of the lifeless animal. The dog's bloodshot, unseeing eyes glared as froth and blood oozed out of its mouth and nose; a dark wet splotch grew larger in the barnyard dust where the animal bled around the pitchfork tines.

Jesse took his hat off and wiped his forehead and eyes with his bandana and commented wearily, "Talk about a close call, boy! That was real close. You come mighty near to gettin' bit by a mad dog. Seems like the Lord has to put in a lot of time takin' care of you when you're here on the farm. You might want to give him some extra words of thanks tonight, son."

Charley nodded solemnly.

By the time they graduated from high school, Bonnie McGraw and Charley Scott were serious sweethearts, and Donald was still Charley's best friend. Bonnie already knew she would go to East Tennessee State College; she wanted to be a high school teacher. She tried to interest Charley in going to college, but he knew his family couldn't afford to send him. Anyway, he didn't know what he would want to study; he just couldn't see himself as a college boy.

CHAPTER 9

1937 to Mid 1939

For most of the first year out of high school, Charley had helped Pa Jess and Uncle Verle with their farm work, as well as helping his father on their small acreage. Bonnie was away at college, and Charley sorely missed being with her.

By the fall of '38, Charley decided he wanted to do something other than farm. His grandpa had tried to interest him in carpentry and woodworking. Based on some work that Charley had done under his supervision, Pa Jess felt the boy had a natural talent for the crafts. Realistically, though, with the effects of the Great Depression still lingering, there was little local demand for that talent.

A job became available at a small sawmill on Drowning Creek a considerable distance upstream from the school. Charley asked for the job and got it. When he began his job, he liked it. He enjoyed the shrill whine of the big circular saw blade as its sharp teeth chewed their way through huge hemlock, oak, and poplar logs, transforming them into strong lumber to be used in building projects, large and small. Charley savored the woodsy fragrance of sawdust and newly cut lumber. After a few days' work at the mill, however, he began to regret getting the job.

Sawmill work bored Charley, as he did the same thing over and over, hour after hour, day in and day out. Hard lifting and carrying heavy loads of slabs, boards, and beams made up most of his duties, so Charley was dog-tired at the end of his work days. His shoulders broadened, and his chest and arms grew. He became a strong young man. Except in the coldest weather, the chronic bronchitis that resulted from his bout with measles affected him only slightly.

Charley looked forward to weekends away from the sawmill—weekends he often spent with his friend Donald and, about once a month, with Bonnie when she came home from college or he went to Johnson City. He missed Bonnie every day he wasn't with her, and she told him that she missed him too. He told her half jokingly but also with some genuine worry that, since she now had "all those smart, cultured college boys" around her, she would soon be ready to give up on a plain country boy who couldn't provide her all the comforts most of them could give her. Bonnie had pooh-poohed that idea and told Charley that he was the only man she was interested in.

She had also scolded him, saying, "I don't want to ever hear you put yourself down again. You're as smart as any of those college *boys*, and you're a whole lot smarter than the great majority of them. You're also a good *man*. I'm going to keep you."

After their high school graduation, they had talked about marriage. Charley had never asked Bonnie to marry him, but they both assumed they would marry. But Bonnie wanted go to college and get a teaching job before she married, and Charley felt he should have a job that held some promise for the future before he would feel worthy of asking Bonnie to marry him. He was thinking now that his sawmill job sure didn't hold much promise. By early summer of 1939, Charley decided he couldn't take the boring, repetitive sawmill work any longer, so he quit and spent most of his summer back in the fields with his Pa Jess and uncle Verle.

Charley cherished a memory of one weekend that summer when Bonnie was home, and he replayed it over and over in his mind. But something else had happened then that he tried not to think about at all. He, Donald, and Bonnie had gone to Clinch River for a combined picnic and fishing trip. Bonnie fixed a picnic lunch; Donald and Charley seined minnows for bait and gathered their fishing equipment. They set out to a secluded fishing hole, one that most anglers thought required too much walking to get to. The three had a long, hot tramp through woods, stinging nettles and biting buck flies, but they were treated to nature's colorful displays as cardinals, gold finches, and red-wing blackbirds flitted and fluttered from one perch to another. They listened to multiple melodies of mocking birds and incessant scoldings of blue jays, crows, and gray squirrels. Twice Bonnie stopped their march to study steep rock walls above the river with their cool, moist nooks and crannies where delicate ferns thrived in the shade of trees or jutting rock overhangs.

Finally they were at their fishing spot. Donald hurried to get on with his fishing, but Bonnie and Charley sat beside a narrow, clear mountain stream that emptied its cool, nourishing waters into the river just below their fishing hole. The two enjoyed the solitude as they sampled Bonnie's fried chicken, sweet tea, and apple pie. They listened to the gurgling, happy song of the little waterway, and the only other sounds encroaching on its tune were the distant hammering of a red-headed woodpecker, the buzz of honeybees on flowering river weed blossoms, and a splash in the river as a bass or a red eye captured a floating morsel for its noon meal. With their snack finished, Bonnie and Charley walked over to where Donald was fishing. Bonnie said she was going upstream to a secluded little beach to refresh herself in the cool water and that she would be back in a few minutes.

Several minutes and two rock bass later, the young men began wondering why Bonnie wasn't back yet.

More minutes passed, and Charley finally said, "I'm worried about Bonnie. I'll go make sure she's okay."

He quickly hurried upriver, praying that nothing was wrong. As he came out of the willows at the edge of a sandy area, there was Bonnie bending over to pick up the old blue chambray shirt of Donald's she wore that day. The late morning sun bathed her smooth, cream-colored skin. She was bare from her waist up, and her wet slacks clung to the alluring curves they covered. Charley was transfixed as he drank in the beauty of her glistening auburn hair and emerald eyes, her full red lips, and her perfect, generous breasts.

Bonnie lifted the shirt no higher and uttered a quiet, "Charley!"

Charley couldn't force his gaze away from his sweetheart's stunningly beautiful body. Finally he stammered, "Bonnie . . . I, uh . . . I," and she interrupted, "Charley, just turn around so I can get my shirt on."

Red faced and embarrassed, but aroused, he turned away. In a few seconds, Bonnie's hands were on his shoulders, and Charley turned to face her. He put his hands on her hips and she put hers against his chest.

He said, "Bonnie, you're so beautiful, and what I just saw makes me almost mad to see more of you. And to do more with you."

"I know, Charley," she said as she laid her head against his chest, and his arms went around her, pulling her tight against him. "I want to too. But we're going to wait until we're married."

"Aw, I know, I know. Your mother and daddy have welcomed me into their house as Don's friend and as your beau. They've entrusted me with their only daughter, and your father has let me know more than once that I had better never break that trust. But it's hard!"

"Yes, it is, isn't it? I can tell," Bonnie said as she wiggled her body against his. With an impish grin, she added, "Oh, you meant the waiting . . ." Then, laughing as she raised her head, she pulled his head down and looked into his eyes.

"You little she-cat!" Charley hissed. "You know what I meant."

"Yes, I do, but your words also described something else." Then she gave him a long, passionate kiss and he responded with equal fervor.

As Bonnie finally pulled away from his lips, Charley was smiling broadly as he said, "Whew, this sure beats fishing!"

With her hands holding his face, Bonnie said, "Charley, honey, before we know it, I'll be through school and we can begin talking seriously about marriage. In the meantime, just remember what you saw today and remember that there's a lot more to see and a whole lot for us to do that will be incredibly wonderful and beautiful."

"Oh, I'm sure of that, woman. But I don't know if I'd be better off remembering it or trying to keep it all out of my mind."

Charley gave a long sigh and continued, "But no matter what, I'd wait for you 'til I was a tottering old codger if I had to." He took her by the hand and said, "C'mon, we'd better get back to Don. He's probably already wondering what's keeping me up here so long."

As Bonnie and Charley started to move away, they were startled to hear, "Aw, don't you'ns be runnin' off so soon now."

A dirty, beardy man with shaggy, greasy hair faced them. His filthy bib overalls were worn and patched. Beady, bloodshot eyes stared at the couple, and a leering grin showed his tobacco-stained, rotting teeth. The man was not tall, but he was sturdily built, with big arms and thick chest and neck. Charley realized who this repulsive man was—Gabe Hawkins, one of a family of three brothers and their parents. The youngest brother was probably about to finish elementary school, or maybe just starting high school. The two older brothers and their father worked a little now and then but spent most of their time and effort tending moonshine stills, and they were known to be bullying troublemakers who were quick to fight. Now here one of them stood; was he up to no good today?

"What're you doing here, Gabe?" Charley asked.

Without taking his eyes off Bonnie, the man responded, "Right now I'm enjoyin' what I see. I liked what I was lookin' at even better afore you got hyere. Them willer bushes got in my line of sight somewhat, but even so, I saw a great show."

Bonnie's hands flew up to her now beet-red face as she gasped, "You were watching me?"

"Shore wuz, and a mighty purty sight it wuz. Pyert nigh the purtiest I ever seen. And I don't see any reason tuh stop the show now." Giving his full attention to Bonnie now, Gabe continued, "Missy, why don't you just take off that blue shirt so's I kin git a up close look at what's under it."

Charley stepped in front of Bonnie and said, "Gabe, we don't want any trouble, so you just leave and we'll all go on about our business."

"I don't b'lieve so. I'm just thinkin' like you said you wuz a few minutes ago. I want to see more of what this purty little gal has, and I'm a mind tuh do more with it than you 'pear tuh want tuh do."

By now the high color in Bonnie's face and neck was not from embarrassment; she was furious. She said, "Why, you vile, filthy . . ." and Charley stopped her with a touch on her arm as he glared at Gabe. As he took a step toward the man, he started to speak, but all he got out was "Gabe," when a fist hit him hard on his left jaw. Charley saw stars and bright lights and stumbled back. He caught his heel on a root and fell into the edge of the beach sand.

"I'm goin' tuh teach you tuh respect yore elders, sonny," Gabe rasped as he started toward Charley, who was up on one elbow shaking his head, trying to get rid of cobwebs that seemed to be blurring his vision. Bonnie flew at the attacker, hitting him with her shoulder. She pounded at his face with her fists and scratched at his face and neck. Gabe was momentarily taken aback by her attack, but he grasped her wrists, held them in one large, strong hand, and slapped her with his other hand. Then he pushed her hard, and she fell into a patch of river weeds.

By this time, Charley was up and coming in behind Gabe; and as the smelly brute turned toward him, Charley landed a hard, crunching punch on his nose. Gabe went down with a startled, surprised look on his ugly face. He wiped the back of his hand under his nose. His blood-covered hand and the pain told him that this young squirt had busted his nose.

Charley then turned to look at Bonnie, who was getting on her feet as Gabe came charging toward him with his head lowered. Bonnie screamed, "Look out, Charley!" Charley realized too late that his attacker was upon him. Gabe's shoulder hit him hard in the side, and he was on the ground again. As Charley scrambled to his feet, Gabe threw another roundhouse punch. Charley managed to dodge enough that the big fist only grazed his head and had little effect; before he could react, another fist slammed hard into his belly, doubling him up as he gasped for air and fell to the ground. He saw a worn, muddy work shoe and an overalled leg above it coming at his head, so he rolled to his left. The big shoe missed its mark, but Charley was still on the ground on his back. Gabe leaped astride Charley and sat on him as he closed his rough hands around Charley's throat. Now Bonnie was beating and clawing at the man to no avail. Charley felt the big hands tightening around his throat; using all his strength, he tried to pull an arm or a hand away from his throat. He could not. He wondered, *Is this the end for me . . . where Bonnie will be violated and disgraced?* If he could just get a piece of driftwood or something to hit Gabe with, maybe he could get those hands off his throat. As he thrashed and felt around beside them in the weedy patch they had landed in, his fingers brushed against something hard. He moved his hand back and realized it was a loose river rock, probably a little larger than his fist. He clutched the smooth rock. By this time Charley was beginning to feel weak and woozy. He knew that if anything was to be done to get those hands away from his throat, it had to be done now. So with all of the fading strength he could muster, he swung the rock into the side of Gabe's head. The man tumbled over into the weeds beside Charley and lay still. As Charley gasped for breath and eased the burning in his lungs, Bonnie was beside him.

"Charley, are you all right? Are you okay, honey?" she asked as she stroked his face, panic showing clearly in her face and voice.

Finally Charley responded, "Yeah, I reckon I'm still alive. For a little bit there, I thought I was a goner." Then, with a worried look, he sat up and hugged Bonnie to him. "Are you all right, Bonnie?"

"Other than being scared half to death and fearing that I was seeing you die right before my eyes, I'm fine." After a pause, she said, "No, I'm not fine! I'm mad. I'm mad as H-E-double L! Mad that some brute like that passes for a man and has no regard for another human being."

The two of them looked at the still form lying in the weeds. They could see blood seeping through the stringy, matted hair just above his left ear and drying blood around his nose and on his lips and chin. Obviously worried, Charley looked closer at where the rock had struck Gabe and said, "I've never done that to a living thing in all my life!"

"Charley Scott," his sweetheart said, "if you hadn't hit him with the rock, you wouldn't be alive now! And I can't stand to even think what would have happened to me." Then, as if just remembering something, she asked, "Say, how did you find that rock, anyway? I didn't see any others lying around here."

Charley answered, "My fingers just brushed against it as I was flailing my arms around hoping there might be a stick of wood within my reach."

"Honey, I believe that rock was just where it was supposed to be."

"What do you mean?"

"I mean, I believe the Good Lord had that rock there in just that spot for you to use to save your life and probably mine too."

"I think I agree with that. This must be about the third time the Lord has taken care of me when I was in a fix that could have been the end of me. He must be getting pretty tired of saving my bacon."

Bonnie observed, "He must have something good, something important in mind for you then, don't you think?"

"Maybe so, but I sure don't know what it is."

Bonnie's mind came back to their attacker. She pointed at the unmoving man and asked, "Is he dead?"

"I don't think so."

"Good. I'm glad you hit him, but I hope he's not dead."

Charley moved to the man's side, watched him carefully for several seconds, and then put his fingers to the man's throat. "His heart's still beating, and I'm pretty sure he's breathing." After a short pause, Charley added, "Let's go get Don and get out of here. When we get back home, we'll let the sheriff know what happened. Gabe has brothers, and I've heard that one of them is just about as mean as this one."

As the two young people stood up to leave, they heard from behind them, "Yep, Gabe does have two brothers, and one of them is right here."

Startled, they whirled around and saw before them a tall, reedy young lad, probably in his lower to mid teens. He looked like he wasn't shaving yet. He had curly straw-colored hair and piercing blue eyes. The boy held a rifle in his left hand with its muzzle pointed to the ground instead of at Charley and Bonnie. *At least, that's a good sign,* Charley thought. *But here we go again with another Hawkins facing us.*

"Hello," Bonnie said and, pointing to the man on the ground, asked, "this is your brother?"

"Yes, ma'am, he is. That's Gabe and I'm Rafe."

Charley said, "I'm Charley Scott and this is Bonnie McGraw."

Rafe replied, "I've seen you both before. Usually see you together, but I didn't know your names."

Bonnie asked, "How did you come to be here?"

"Well, Gabe and me was fishin' up around that bend," Rafe said as he pointed upstream with the rifle barrel. "Fishin' was pretty slow, so Gabe said he wanted to look around a little and headed off down thisaway. I waited a good spell and finally decided I'd better come along for 'im. Looks like I found 'im, all right."

Charley asked Rafe, "You always fish with a rifle?"

"Nah, I never fish with a gun. I just brought my .22 along to see if I could bag us a good turtle. There's lotsa good meat in a big turtle, ya know. Especially a big soft shell turtle. Didn't see any sunnin' on rocks or logs 'cept little bitty ones. Not worth shootin'."

Charley said, "I don't know what you're thinking, but you have my word that we didn't want any trouble with your brother. He surprised us and said some things about Bonnie he ought not have said and was trying to make her undress. I tried to protect her, and Gabe attacked me."

Bonnie interceded, "That's true, Rafe. And that man"—pointing to the man on the ground—"almost killed Charley."

"It sure looks like brother Gabe come out on the short end of the stick this time," the young brother said with a wistful half smile, almost as if he was pleased. Then he continued, "Sometimes Gabe don't use what little bit of sense he has. He's one of them fellers that has a black outlook on most ever'thing anyway, and a few drinks of likker makes his mood even nastier. Pap tries to keep 'im away from likker as much as he can, but that's a right hard job." Looking Charley in the eye, he said, "I guess you know what I mean by that."

"Yes, I think I do."

Rafe continued, "Gabe's had a few drinks today, and he's been edgy and cranky. I guess he's been spoilin' for a fight for a while. Maybe it'll do 'im good to get a whuppin'."

Gabe was starting to stir a little and moaned softly. His brother said, "You all go on about your business, and I'll look after Gabe. Seein' as how he has such a hard head, he'll likely be up and around in a little bit."

Bonnie said, "Young man, we're sorry your brother is hurt, but he deserved worse than he got."

"I'm sure that's a fact, ma'am," the boy replied, and he continued, "but I think I should tell you fair that a Hawkins is not one to forgive or forget. Gabe's goin' to always be lookin' to get back at y'all. So watch yer backs."

"Thanks for the warning, Rafe. We'll be on our way then," Charlie told him. He and Bonnie headed downriver.

When Donald saw them coming toward him, he was putting another minnow on his hook and, without looking up, said, "It's about time. I've caught another good red eye. But I also hooked a grampus—what some people call a hellbender salamander. He was a foot long and the ugliest thing you've ever . . . seen." By now he was looking at his sister and his best friend. He noted Bonnie's still damp slacks, weed stains and dirt on their clothes, their disheveled hair, and on Charley's jaw a lump that was starting to show a big bruise. Puzzled, he glanced back and forth between them and with raised eyebrows asked, "Hey, what've you two been up to?"

"Oh, be quiet, Donnie!'" his sister snapped.

Then they told her brother about Gabe Hawkins without including the details of what had preceded Gabe's appearing. As they made their way toward home, Bonnie asked what all three of them had been thinking, "How much of this horrible tale do we tell, and to whom do we tell it?"

Donald's answer to his sister was, "I don't think we should tell Mother and Dad. Knowing how Dad is so protective of you, I don't think he would be satisfied with just telling the sheriff about Gabe Hawkins. I think he might do something to the man, something he would later regret."

"I think you're probably right," Bonnie replied, "but why not tell Mother?"

"Bonnie, you know Mother can't keep a secret from Dad even if she wanted to, and most likely she wouldn't want to keep this one from him if she knew. Also, I'm afraid Charley might be blamed for what happened today, even though all he did was to protect you."

After a thoughtful pause, Bonnie agreed, "Okay, we won't tell my parents."

Considerable further discussion followed, and the decision was that they wouldn't tell anybody. Not the sheriff. Not Charley's parents. To explain the large bruise developing on Charley's jaw, he would tell his parents that he slipped and fell at the river and banged his face against a rock. If any bruising should develop from the slap Gabe gave Bonnie, she could cover it with makeup. Charley hated the idea of lying to his parents, but he told himself he was protecting them from needless worry about him. So that was the plan they would follow.

As they continued their long walk back home, they became quiet, leaving each to his or her own thoughts and memories. Charley's thoughts returned to his fight with Gabe and how he had been no match for the bigger man. As a result of farm work Charley had done over the years and the months of hard labor at the sawmill, he had developed wide shoulders and strong muscles, but he realized how little he knew about how to fight. Gabe had taught him that lesson.

Charley's last fight had been in sixth grade, but the bout with Gabe had been no sixth-grade pushing, wrestling, flailing tussle. He remembered Rafe's warning about Gabe getting even and decided that he needed to learn how to protect himself, how to fight. Or, to make it sound a little less barbaric, he needed to learn to box.

CHAPTER 10

Mid 1939 to 1940

Donald McGraw had spent the past year as a college student at Lincoln Memorial in Harrogate, Tennessee. His father, Brewster, assumed his son would someday own half and be in charge of all the McGraw businesses, and he wanted the son to be educated. He had asked Donald to take as many business courses as he could get at LMU. Bonnie had taken heavy class loads at East Tennessee State each college term and also went to school during summers, so she expected to finish her degree requirements by the end of the summer term of 1940.

Charley still loved to hunt and fish and took advantage of every opportunity he had to do so. He now owned a .22 caliber rifle as well as a single-shot 12-gauge shotgun he had ordered from Montgomery Ward, and he had been an excellent marksman since he was ten years old. Beginning when he was in the seventh grade, Charley had enjoyed target practice with his uncle, shooting Verle Thacker's .38 Smith & Wesson revolver. Both Verle and his nephew were excellent pistol shots.

Charley was learning that getting a job that paid a decent wage was no easy matter. Jobs with Norfolk and Western Railroad paid fairly well, but the railroad was hiring only skilled mechanics, boilermakers, or steamfitters. His father, J. R., was hired by N & W a few years after Charley's birth because of the mechanic training he got in the army to repair tanks, and he had worked at the Norton N & W locomotive maintenance yard the past two decades. Every workday, J. R. rode a Mining and Railroad Bus about fifteen miles each way to and from work.

Charley didn't want the hardware store clerk job Bonnie's father had offered him. Although he enjoyed farm work, he didn't have money to buy a farm, and he didn't want to be a sharecropper. He began considering the kind of work that several men in and around Creedy did. Maybe he should become a coal miner. He mentioned to Bonnie the possibility of becoming a miner, but Bonnie was adamantly opposed to it. Charley talked to Bonnie's father about working in one of his mines, and Brewster tried to talk the young man out of the notion of working in a mine.

When Charley's parents, Belle and J. R., learned he was considering going to work in a coal mine, they counseled against the idea; his mother pleaded with him not to "go back in one of those dark, dangerous places to work." Mining, dangerous and backbreaking though it was, seemed to Charley to be the only work he could get that paid enough for him to be able to ask his sweetheart to marry him in a few years. So in spite of his family and Bonnie's opposition, Charley decided he had to give mining a try, and he asked Brewster for a job.

Brewster finally agreed that he would check with the bosses at his two mines to see if they could use Charley, and the answer he got from one of them was yes. When Bonnie learned that her future husband was going to mine coal, she let both him and her father know just how upset she was with them.

In early November of 1939, Charley began a totally new kind of work—mining coal. When Bonnie was home from college for a long Thanksgiving holiday weekend and then for a two-week Christmas break, she wasn't with her boyfriend nearly as much as he would have liked. When they were together, Charlie thought Bonnie was a tad distant and aloof toward him. But during their last few hours together before she had to go back to Johnson City, Bonnie told him they needed to talk about his work.

"Have you decided that maybe you don't want to be married to a coal miner?" Charley asked her.

"Charley, I'll marry you if you ask me, no matter what your job is. You're the only man I've loved, probably the only man I ever can love. My concern about your being a miner is not what the job *is*—it's what I'm afraid the job may *do* to you. It's dangerous work. It makes young men old before their time. I know my father operates mines, but over the last several years, I've seen what many miners have become, how so many of them develop lung and joint problems and other health problems. And you with bronchitis problems sometimes, how will your lungs be affected?"

Charley started to respond, but Bonnie held up her hand and said, "Shhh, Charley. Let me have my say. And the last thing I want to say is, if you're set on mining coal, go ahead and do it. I want you to be happy, and I will never mention coal mining again unless you want to talk about it. So there! That's my say. Now let's enjoy the last couple of hours before I go back to Johnson City." And they did.

The new miner began his job working with an experienced miner, Jake Ashton. Jake tried to teach the newcomer as much about mining and mine safety as he could and as quickly as he could, and Charley was a good learner. Conditions in the mine where Charley worked were much better than in many other mines Jake had been in. There was no standing water in the shaft, and plenty of timbers were provided to shore up the roof as the coal was dug out deeper and deeper into the mountain. While the seam of coal they worked was usually thick enough that a miner could stand erect when he wanted to, at times it thinned down to four feet or less, making the task of removing coal a more difficult and tiring process.

Charley and his partner had to bore holes into the coal face with a long auger, which the miner pressed against with his chest as he used his hands and arms to turn the auger. After boring holes four or five feet back into the coal, they then put blasting powder containers in the holes, tamped them gently with a tamp stick, and put a blasting cap against the powder. Attached to each blasting cap was a fuse, the length of which was determined by how long they wanted the fuse to burn before it reached the blasting cap and set off the powder charge. Into each hole after the fuse and cap were in place, "dummies" were tamped to keep the force of the exploding powder from just shooting out of the hole rather than breaking the coal seam apart.

These dummies usually consisted of rolled-up newspaper sleeves containing dirt or mud. When the fuses were lit, Charley and Jake ran back down the shaft and around a corner to get away from effects from the blast. After the powder charges exploded, the miners had to wait for the coal dust to settle before they went back to the coal face and began shoveling the blasted coal into coal cars. The loaded cars were then hauled on the steel tram tracks to the mouth of the mine where the coal was dumped into a chute to the tipple.

About seven months after starting in the mine, Charley and Jake were working as usual and were getting ready to put up more roof timbers and props when their day became far from routine. Jake had been inspecting a suspicious looking section of the roof they were working under. He heard a cracking, tearing sound above them, and he grabbed Charley's arm and screamed, "Jump back!" as he lunged backward, pulling Charley with him. With a thunderous, jarring crash, a huge chunk of stone fell from the roof.

They had barely missed being crushed under a "kettle bottom" roof fall, and both of them were still alive only because Jake knew mines and mining. He had been alert for danger and reacted quickly enough to get himself and his partner out of the way of the deadly piece of rock that separated from the roof. The three- or four-ton rockfall with a rounded, domed top missed the two miners only by inches; but as it fell onto the tram track, a hand-sized shard of rock busted loose and ricochetcd. The sharp, pointed fragment partially embedded itself in the calf of Charley's left leg.

Other miners had heard the noise and came running to help if they could. A foreman had a first-aid kit. Charley's leg wasn't bleeding badly, so the foreman decided not to remove the piece of rock from his leg for fear that it might cause worse bleeding. The man wrapped Charley's leg loosely with strips of gauze, leaving the piece of rock in place, and four men carried him out of the mine on a stretcher to a waiting car in which he was hurried to Doc Easton's office in town. Doc looked at the leg and said Charley should be taken to the hospital in Bristol where he could get good treatment from trained surgeons. By that time Charley was in much pain and in a beginning stage of shock, so Doc gave him a morphine shot and said, "Charley, you're going to be fine. This shot is going to relieve your pain, and you will get sleepy. Don't fight it."

The next thing Charley was aware of was somebody holding his hand, and he felt a cool hand on his brow. He opened his eyes to blinding light. As his eyes gradually became accustomed to the light, he saw a beautiful angel. The angel was standing over him, looking at him. He knew this angel. Bonnie had been the first to be at his bedside after the doctors said he could have a visitor.

She whispered, "Thank the Lord, Charley. I was petrified when I heard you had been in a mining accident. I was afraid I had lost you already."

Soon Charley's mom and pop and Donald and Brewster McGraw were in the room, all looking and saying how relieved they were that the doctors had determined that the rock fragment had done little, if any, permanent damage to his leg. After several minutes a motherly nurse came to the room and said, "Our patient needs to rest now. So say your good-byes. You can come back tomorrow, and he should be feeling much better by then."

Each of the visitors bid him good-bye and said they would be back. Bonnie lingered until the others had left the room. She clasped one of his hands and kissed his lips tenderly but longingly. "Bye, honey," she whispered, "I'll see you tomorrow. I love you." She started to move away, but Charley held on to her hand.

"I have something to tell you," he murmured.

"You do? What is it?"

"Jake Ashton is going to have to train a new partner."

"Why's that?"

"I've worked my last day in a mine. I don't want any more of this kind of stuff."

In less than a week after injuring his leg, Charley was at home—his parents' home—and was getting around well using a crutch and trying not to put too much weight on his left leg. The leg was healing well and was only slightly painful, but Charley was getting restless doing nothing but resting, napping, eating, and reading.

After another week he ditched the crutch and, with Doc Easton's blessing, began to walk more and more, trying to regain strength in his injured leg. His mother, his aunt Luce, and Bonnie all worried that he was doing too much too soon; but his leg continued to heal, and his pain lessened to the point that he scarcely noticed any discomfort in it. After recovering from his accident, he again began helping his grandpa Musick and uncle Verle with their farm work.

Bonnie McGraw had started her career at Creedy High School where she taught math and science classes. She was eagerly looking forward to helping teenage boys and girls understand, and perhaps even enjoy, mathematics. She wanted to expose them to the fascinating world of science and help them appreciate how everyone is affected by science and scientific principles.

On the first day of classes, Ms. McGraw went into her sophomore science class, told them her name, and began calling names on the roll and associating faces with names. She came to a name that she wasn't likely to forget: Rafe Hawkins. She hadn't seen this student recently; at least, she hadn't recognized him. She called the name, and a voice from a back corner of the room responded, "Here."

She looked where the voice came from but couldn't see a face. She said, "Rafe, would you please raise your hand."

A hand went up slowly, and now she saw the face. "Thank you," Ms. McGraw said.

He was the boy she remembered from that scary day at the river when his brother Gabe had insulted her and fought Charley.

Rafe had not changed a lot, but he was a bit more mature, taller, more muscled. He was a good-looking young man. He wouldn't have problems getting girlfriends. She finished calling the roll, took care of some routine classroom and housekeeping procedures, explained in general terms what she wanted the students to learn in her class, and talked about a few basic scientific principles that affected everyone in the room. She gave her students their first assignment for study in their textbooks, told them she would see them tomorrow, and dismissed them. As they started to file out of the room, Bonnie said, "Rafe Hawkins, I need for you to wait a moment, please."

Rafe looked surprised and puzzled, but he waited as other students left the room. He sat back down in his seat with downcast eyes as his teacher came toward him. When she neared him, Rafe looked up and said, "Is something wrong, Ms. McGraw?"

"No, nothing is wrong, Rafe. I just want to say something about the only other time we've met."

Before she could continue with her thought, Rafe blurted out, "But, Ms. Mc—"

With hand held up, she said, "Wait, Rafe. I'm not upset with you. I wanted to thank you for the way you acted that day by the river. And I want you to know that I don't have any ill feeling toward you because of what your brother did that day. I'm looking forward to having you in my class. I know you can learn much about science. So I'll see you in class tomorrow."

Rafe rose from his seat, said "Yes, ma'am," and left the room.

CHAPTER 11

Late 1940

Charley had sworn off mining, and here he was once again, in August of 1940, racking his brain trying to come up with some notion of what kind of permanent work he could find. He and Donald had talked recently, and his friend said he wasn't going back to LMU to finish a degree. Donald said he hadn't been a very good college student anyway. His father tried to convince Donald to start working for him to learn as much as he could about his business, mining, and farming operations, but the son had too much of an itch to see and experience things he had never seen or done before.

Donald wanted to see more of this country and more of the world, if possible. He had suggested to Charley that they go to some large city up north where jobs were supposed to be available. But Southwest Virginia was Charley's home. He realized he was just beginning to appreciate the beauty of the forested mountains and the small fertile valleys, of Clinch River and its many small tumbling tributaries, of the beautiful landscapes painted each fall in bright colors by poplar, hickory, maple, blackgum, dogwood, and other trees and shrubs. His family would never leave here. His sweetheart would not leave because she wanted to continue teaching at Creedy High School to help local boys and girls prepare themselves for better lives than many of them now had. Whatever Charley might end up doing for a living, he wanted to do it here in Powell County.

On a late Saturday afternoon near the end of August, Charley and his father sat on their front porch, enjoying the quiet and the cooling of the day, when a car marked Powell County Sheriff on its sides pulled to the side of the road and stopped in front of their house. Sheriff Hargis Fielding climbed out of the car, moving his considerable girth with remarkable ease. The sheriff stood about five foot ten, and he was a strong, muscular specimen with thick chest and neck and large muscled arms and legs, plus more fat than he needed here and there. His full head of hair was gray at the temples with more gray salted through the rest of it.

Hargis, whom everyone called Harg, wore a Police Model .38 caliber Smith & Wesson revolver in a holster on his belt, but nobody in the county could remember when he had used that weapon in his profession other than to try to maintain his marksmanship with regular target practice. Harg's bulk and obvious strength were enough to convince whatever lawbreakers he had encountered that they would suffer less if they just did whatever the sheriff instructed them to do.

As he walked toward the porch, the sheriff said, "Howdy, J. R., Charley. How're things goin' for you?"

"Can't complain," J. R. responded, "and it wouldn't do any good if we did."

Harg came up the steps and onto the porch. The two men stood and shook Harg's hand, and Charley asked, "How's the sheriffin' business?"

Harg smiled and shrugged his big shoulders, saying, "Well, that all depends on who you ask. My opponent in this election, Mr. Calvin Hess, says the sheriffin' in Powell County is lower'n a lizard's belly. I happen to have some disagreement with that. But that's why I'm here. I sure would appreciate your vote in the November election. You all know me, and I reckon you know whatever kind of job I've done as a deputy one term and sheriff for the past two terms. I don't have any big ideas to make changes in the way I carry out my duties, but if you've a mind to ask me about anything dealin' with my job, fire away. I'll tell you what I know."

Charley's father said, "Now, Harg, you've always got my vote and Belle's. We think you're the best man for the job. This is Charley's first year to be able to vote, but I think you might persuade him to vote for you too."

"I hope so, J. R. And, Charley, I heard about your minin' accident. Sounds like you and your buddy are mighty lucky to be alive."

"We are, for a fact."

Harg continued, "Brewster McGraw told me that your leg must be better now because you've been helpin' your grandpa and uncle with their farm work. Is that the case?"

"Yep, that's right. My leg is fine."

"You got any plans for what you're goin' to do after their crops are in this fall?"

"Not a one," Charley replied, "but I need to find something as soon as I can."

"Charley, if I win this election, and I b'lieve I will, I may have somethin' for you if you don't have a job by then that you want to stick with. You just keep that in the back of your mind and under your hat."

"I'll do that, sheriff."

After the sheriff's car was down the road a ways, Charley looked at this dad and asked, "What do you think that was all about? What would the sheriff have that would have anything to do with me getting a job?"

"Don't know, son. You'll just have to wait and see."

What Charley and his dad didn't know—in fact, nobody except the sheriff and Bonnie's father knew—was that Brewster McGraw had talked to Harg Fielding about a possible replacement for one of Harg's deputies who would retire at the end of December. Brewster McGraw suggested that Charley Scott would make a fine deputy. The young man was intelligent and learned quickly, he was a hard worker, he was strong and healthy, and he was a good man—he would always try to do the right thing and could be trusted to do whatever he said he would do. Since Brewster had been a strong supporter and a contributor to his meager campaign finances, Harg took seriously the businessman's suggestion about Charley.

Two days after the sheriff had visited with Charley and his dad, another visitor showed up at the Scott front porch. Donald McGraw came to talk with Charley about joining the armed forces. The two young men discussed the war in Europe and in Asia based on what they had read in newspapers, heard on the radio, and seen in news reels at movie theaters. Donald also talked about the war based on what he had learned in the past two years at LMU and on what some of his professors believed would happen.

He told Charley, "Two of my professors, one in history and one in economics, told their classes that they believe war for the United States is sure to come. They think that since Hitler and the Japanese are running roughshod over countries, we will have to join the Allies to keep the Axis from reaching their goal of world domination."

Donald pointed out that early this year, President Roosevelt had included almost two billion dollars in defense spending in his budget. He also pointed out that the president's advisors had recommended that the US begin drafting men into the armed services and that congress was now considering such a bill. Experts were speculating that the bill would pass with little opposition.

Charley interrupted his friend. "Don, war is a terrible thing. Pop doesn't like to talk about what he saw and went through in the Great War, but I've heard enough and read enough to know that no sane man would've wanted to be in it."

Charley went on to tell about how his father was inducted into the US Army in early 1918 and had his basic training at Fort Benning, Georgia. That summer and fall, over 1.5 million US soldiers were sent to fight. J. R. was shipped to England and trained as a Mark V tank mechanic, and from there he was sent to the front in France to help maintain tanks under the command of Col. George S. Patton in the Meuse-Argonne offensive.

J. R. Scott had been at the front less than two months when the war finally ended November 11, 1918, but the devastation and carnage caused by trench warfare, machine guns, artillery, poison gas, and tanks were terrible. Some of it he had observed personally, some of it he had heard about from survivors of earlier battles. Charley had read accounts of World War I and had been horrified to learn that more than nine million combatants died on the battlefields. In addition, nearly that many people on the home fronts died because of food shortages, genocide, ground combat, and bombing from the air.

By the time J. R. was in England and France, Spanish influenza was raging around the globe and the armies on neither side were spared the horrors of the deadly disease. Worldwide, somewhere between twenty million and forty million people died from influenza. About 675,000 Americans died of influenza, ten times as many as in the Great War. Of the US soldiers who died in Europe, half of them fell to influenza, not to the Germans and their cohorts.

In some American units, the Spanish flu killed 80 percent of the soldiers. Of the US servicemen mobilized for the World War, more than sixty-two thousand had died of disease, and over two-thirds of those had died of the flu, while almost thirty-seven thousand were killed in action and nearly fourteen thousand more died of their wounds. J. R.'s family considered it a miracle that he had escaped injury and the Spanish flu and had come home without being "shell shocked" as so many of the war's survivors had been.

Charley concluded his recounting of some of what he knew about the war's terrible events and outcomes and said, "So I'm not in a big rush to get involved in a war if I don't have to."

Donald said, "Charley, I want to do something with my life that matters, something that makes a difference somewhere. And I believe the best way I can do that now is to join one of the armed services and do my small part to keep Hitler and Tojo from taking over the world, including us right here in Powell County."

"What are you saying, Don?" Charley asked with obvious surprise.

"I'm saying I want to join the navy, and I want you to join up too. Now, before you start giving me all the reasons we ought not to join, think about this. If the proposed draft law passes, we could be drafted into the army. But as I serve my country, I would rather be able to see new ports and new parts of the world as I serve. So I want to join the navy."

Charley asked, "Does your family know about this?"

"Yes, they know. They're not happy about it, but they say if I feel so strongly about serving the country, they won't interfere. It's my choice."

"Oh boy, Don. You've dropped a hot potato in my lap. I'll have to do some thinking and talk with my parents, but most of all, I have to talk it over with Bonnie before I make a decision."

As Donald left his chair and started for the porch steps, he said, "Okay, old friend. Just don't take too long. I'll see you again soon."

Charley felt no urgent drive to enlist in some branch of the armed forces, but he did feel obligated to do his part as an American to fight for the country. He explained to his mom and pop what Donald was asking him to do and asked for their advice. They both told him that they didn't want him to put himself into a situation where his life would be in great danger, but they hastened to add if that was what he thought was the honorable and patriotic thing to do and he decided to do it, he would have their blessings and their continuing prayers for his safe return home.

Bonnie was aware of what Donald wanted to do, so she was not greatly surprised when Charley talked to her about volunteering for service. She told him essentially what his parents had. With tears in her eyes and quiver in her voice, she added that she would miss him horribly every day he was away and that she would count the days until he returned to her. Then she kissed him, whispered "I love you," and retreated to her room. Charley left with an aching heart and a troubled mind. *What should I do? Should I leave my parents and the girl I hope to make my wife?*

About a week later, Charley had made his decision. He would volunteer. He told his parents, and he told Bonnie; they were not surprised at his decision. Charley had a surprise for Donald, however; he would join the army instead of the navy, telling Donald, "I don't like the idea of being a sitting duck out in the ocean, so I'm going to the army."

On September 14, 1940, the two of them rode in Donald's Ford coupe to the induction center in Bristol. At the center, the boys filled out paperwork and indicated the branch of the armed services they wished to join. Donald listed navy and Charley army. They completed the mental and aptitude tests and submitted to the sometimes embarrassing physical exams required. They were told they would be notified within a week about whether they met requirements for the branches they chose. Two days after they were at the induction center, Congress passed a law instituting military conscription; military draft was now the law of the land.

The next week, the two friends went together to the post office to get their notifications from the induction center. They opened their letters at the same time. Donald had been accepted into the navy. Charley had been classified as 4-F, not acceptable for service. A short note explained that he was not accepted because of his medical history, including the severe case of measles that, officially at least, had left him with chronic bronchitis. Another factor of concern was his leg injury in the coal mine. Charley was disappointed and thought that, as active as he had been after those incidents, neither of them should hinder him as a soldier. But the decision had been made. He would not become a U.S. soldier.

In the November election, Hargis Fielding was re-elected to his third term as high sheriff of Powell County; and a little more than two weeks after the election, he paid another visit to the Scott family. After he had been invited into the living room out of the blustery, cold afternoon,

Harg was sipping a cup of hot coffee Charley's mother served him, along with a cup each for Charley and herself. J. R. was not home from work yet. After passing a few pleasantries and emptying his coffee cup, Harg set the cup on a table by the couch and said, "Charley, remember when I told you a couple of months ago that I might have something for you if I was re-elected?"

"I remember that, sheriff."

"What's your work situation now, Charley? Do you have a full-time job? Somethin' that you think you would want to stick with for a good while?"

"No, no full-time job. Just planning to help my grandpa and Uncle Verle get their tobacco crops ready for market." Charley wondered what the sheriff was getting around to.

"No need for me to keep beatin' around the bush, Charley. How would you like to be one of my deputies? Lester Miller is retirin' at the end of December, and I need to fill that position with somebody who can think and is willin' to work hard and is strong enough to handle a rowdy drunk or an upset husband if he has to. Most of all, I want somebody I can trust in whatever kind of situation we might find ourselves. Now, that's a longwinded speech for me, but what I'm sayin', Charley, is that I'd like to have you as a deputy."

"Well, I sure didn't see that one coming, sheriff."

"You know that we've never had much crime here in the county. Drunks, husband and wife problems, moonshinin' and bootleggin' here and there, a few thieves, and such. Now, I don't think you or me or any of my other deputies are goin' to be in life-threatenin' situations. But I can't say that will never happen. We just never know when somethin' like that will pop up."

After a pause, Charley replied, "I'm flattered and most appreciative that you've confidence in me being able to be a deputy. I know what I'd like to tell you right now about your offer, but could you give me a day or two to think about it and to talk to Mom and Pop about it, and maybe one or two others?"

"I sure can. Let's make it a week. If I don't happen to see you somewhere during the next week, I'll drop by here, and you can tell me what you've decided. I want you to know, Charley, I hope you'll be my deputy."

As Harg rose and started toward the door, he said, "So long, Charley. Good-bye, Miz Belle. You all take care." With that he opened the door, went out, closed it quietly behind himself, and headed to his car.

With concern obvious on her face and in her voice, Charley's mother said, "A deputy, Charley? Have you known Harg might offer you a deputy job?"

"No, Mom. Today's the first I've heard anything about being a deputy. Back in August, Harg came by and talked with Pop and me for a few minutes. He said he might have something for me if he won the election. I didn't know what he was thinking about, and I don't believe Pop did either."

After his father got home from work, Charley talked with his parents about the deputy job. His mother expressed her fear for his safety as a deputy. His father pointed out that a man could get hurt or even killed in many kinds of work—farming, mining, fixing a broken truck or train or railroad track, or almost any other job. After a considerable time of discussion, Belle and J. R. told their son that, as was the case when he was considering joining the army, only he could make the decision on whether he should become a law enforcement officer.

Donald was away in the navy, so Charley couldn't bounce off him ideas and questions about the deputy job, but he could discuss the job with the most important McGraw in his life. At her family home, Bonnie had listened quietly as Charley told her about Harg's offer. Charley told her that the job wouldn't pay a lot, but it was a job in which he felt he would be contributing to his community. His work hours might be erratic, with long days at times. He would get an expense allowance for his car, if he had one.

Bonnie wasn't sure she wanted Charley to be a deputy; the job could be dangerous. She hadn't wanted him to be a miner either. *I'm not sure*

I have the right to object to his taking a job if he wants it, she mused. It seemed to her that Charley really wanted this job.

Finally she told him, "I can't tell you to take or not take the deputy job. I *can* tell you that I will support you in whatever you decide. It's your decision to make." Then she rose from her chair, kissed him, said "I love you," and went to her room. The same thing she had said when Charley had told her that he wanted to join the army, with one difference: she had no tears in her eyes this time.

CHAPTER 12

1941

Charley told the sheriff he wanted to be his deputy. Charley was sworn in for his new position a few minutes after midnight on January 1, 1941. The next morning he was fitted for his new uniforms and picked up his badge, .38 Smith & Wesson with holster and belt, a pair of handcuffs, and a billy stick. He hoped he would never have to use the stick or the revolver, but in the back of his mind, he knew he might. If the inexperienced young man could have had any inkling of the rash of deaths he would investigate in the Creedy area during the next four years, would he have declined Sheriff Fielding's invitation to become a deputy?

After he got his driver's license during his sixteenth year, Charley had always driven his dad's pickup truck. But now he needed a car of his own. His dad had heard about a widow near Norton who wanted to sell a car. Her husband had taken ill soon after he bought the car and had died back in the summer; she couldn't drive, so she was eager to get rid of the car. The 1939 Ford V-8 sedan had been driven less than a thousand miles, and Charley bought it for $375. It took a chunk out of the money he had saved over the last six or seven years, but the car was a bargain, and now he had his own official deputy vehicle.

For the next two months, the deputy was immersed in learning some of the basics of his new job. The first half of January he spent at the State Police Division Headquarters in Wytheville where he spent long days, with assigned reading material at night, learning various facets of law enforcement—studying areas ranging from criminal laws to investigative methods, from first aid to fingerprinting and photographing, from obtaining confessions to jujitsu. The martial arts instructor offered extra optional evening sessions for trainees interested in learning and practicing more jujitsu moves, and Charley was one of half a dozen who participated. He learned one additional move, not martial arts, but an effective hold—a chokehold called a sleeper hold. The instructor demonstrated the hold on each of the participants and had each of them practice it, getting their arms placed correctly around their opponent's neck but not applying the pressure that would quickly render the opponent unconscious. The one area Charley was already familiar with and proficient in was shooting his .38 on the firing range. He was easily the best revolver marksman in the group and enjoyed the practice.

After one of his jujitsu lessons, Charley had asked the instructor if he knew anyone near Creedy who could give him more training in self-defense, preferably in boxing. The instructor recommended a man he knew who had boxed in college at the University of Virginia and did some competitive boxing in the U.S. Army. He had made a name for himself as he boxed army, navy, and marine opponents. The man left the army with the rank of captain, graduated from law school, and was now a lawyer and businessman in Big Stone Gap. The instructor gave Charlie the office address of Lloyd Anderson.

At the first opportunity he had, Charley drove to Big Stone Gap, found Anderson's office, and talked with him about wanting to learn to box. He welcomed Charley to the small gym he owned and said he could give him instruction on Thursday nights. The deputy could also spar with others who came to the gym.

In response to Charley's question about cost, the lawyer said, "No charge. I'm just doing this to try to provide an opportunity for local young men to develop an interest in something they've never done before. And maybe they will develop a skill that will give them confidence in themselves and that just might enable them to better protect themselves or their families if the need should ever arise. So as a law enforcement officer, you're welcome to come."

Thus began Charley's process of learning to box.

After about three months of getting instruction from Lloyd Anderson and sparring with him and others at the gym, Charley rigged up a punching bag at home to practice on between his visits to the gym. The contrived bag consisted of more than a bushel of cornmeal in a heavy cloth sack with a strong burlap bag over that and a heavy canvass army duffel bag over the burlap. He hung the bag by a rope from a beam in their barn hallway.

With strips of cloth wound around his hands to protect his knuckles, Charley practiced at least a half hour three or four days each week. He moved and danced around on quick feet as Lloyd had demonstrated as he threw jabs, hooks, crosses, and uppercuts at the improvised bag while trying to remember to dodge or protect his face and body from the fists of an imaginary opponent.

Charley often had long days on the job as he carried out the usual routine, mundane tasks of providing court security, serving various civil process papers, and patrolling his assigned areas. Occasionally he had to intervene in a quarrel between two neighbors or between two spouses, or escort a drunk and disorderly chap to the county jail.

Once in a while something happened that brought the deputy a smile, or even a hearty laugh. One such occurrence involved Monroe Bowman, the taxi operator and one of "the characters" in Creedy. In addition to, but often in conjunction with, his taxi service, Monroe had provided another service for several years that was important to a certain clientele in the town and surrounding countryside. He bootlegged whiskey. If Monroe was convinced that a person was not trying to set him up so the law could nab him, that person could buy either moonshine or "bottled in bond" whiskey from him. In addition to selling his wares, he also frequently consumed them—not the best of proclivities for a taxi driver!

Sometimes Monroe drank to excess. One afternoon, as Charley and his dad sat on their front porch, Monroe pulled to the side of the road in front of their house and motioned for them to come down to the car. J. R. joined Monroe at his car, but Charley remained seated on the porch. It was soon obvious to J. R. that the man had been drinking, and after talking with him a few minutes, J. R. concluded that Monroe had consumed enough whiskey that he should not be driving.

J. R. said, "Monroe, I think maybe you've had a little too much to drink, so just to be safe, I'm going to drive your car and take you home. I'll go tell Charley to follow us in his car so he can bring me back."

Monroe said, "Oh, J. R., just get in and we'll go. I'll bring you back home."

Bonnie and Charley were with each other as much as their busy schedules allowed. In addition to teaching her classes, Bonnie was busy trying to get a minimal science laboratory set up, equipped, and stocked at the high school. Her father had donated a generous amount to the school with the understanding that it would be used to provide needed equipment that the school had no funds to purchase.

The hot, dry summer passed, and the welcome days of fall and Indian summer brought pleasant, sunny days and cool nights. Donald McGraw usually wrote his family about once a week and Charley once a month or so. He seemed to still be enjoying his duty in the navy and wrote about his activities only in general terms. He couldn't divulge the name of the ship he was on or where it was. Each letter from Donald seemed to have taken a few days longer to get to the little town of Creedy than the previous one. Thanksgiving came and went.

On December 8, 1941, at 12:30 p.m., President Franklin Roosevelt made a speech to a joint session of congress that was broadcast by radio to Americans throughout the country. Charley and his family did not get to hear the original broadcast of the president's speech, but that evening they listened to one of their favorite newscasters, Lowell Thomas. They, as did almost everyone who heard his reassuring voice of authority, knew that between his opening line of "Good evening, everybody" and his sign-off of "So long until tomorrow," they would hear accurate news.

On this night, the news they heard was astounding, horrendous. Japanese planes had bombed the U.S. Pacific naval fleet in Pearl Harbor, at the island of Oahu in Hawaii, the previous day. To their horror and sorrow, families learned of the great damage done to American ships in the harbor and of the high death toll of American sailors. President Roosevelt said that December 7, 1941 "is a date that will live in infamy" as he decried the underhanded, malicious attack. Less than an hour after his speech to congress and the American people ended, Congress passed a formal declaration of war and the president announced that on December 8 the United States had declared war on the Empire of Japan.

Many ships were damaged badly in the Pearl Harbor attack, and the battleship *USS Arizona* sank, going down quickly with all hands aboard. Charley and his family and the McGraw family worried about Donald; they didn't know where he was or how much danger he was in. Three days later, on December 11, Adolph Hitler declared war on the United States. Our country was now at war with the Axis—Germany, Italy, *and* Japan.

Three more days later, in the waning afternoon, Mr. and Mrs. McGraw sat in their living room. They didn't hear the car that pulled up before their house and stopped. A knock sounded at their door, and the McGraws wondered who might be coming to visit. They were not expecting anyone. Brewster opened the door and faced a man wearing a uniform—white shirt, black boots and dark blue pants, coat, tie, and cap. Emblazoned on the cap and on the upper sleeves of the coat were the words "Western Union," and in one hand the solemn man held a small yellow envelope. Brewster's heart leaped to his throat. He knew what he was going to learn. The uniformed man asked, "Sir, are you Mr. Brewster McGraw?"

"I am."

"This is for you, sir," the man said as he handed the envelope to the obviously distressed man before him. The McGraws had hoped and prayed they would never receive the message in that telegram. *The U.S. Navy regrets to inform you that your son, Petty Officer Third Class, Donald B. McGraw, is missing in action and presumed dead.* Donald had been an anti-aircraft gunner on the *Arizona*.

CHAPTER 13

January to November 1942

CHRISTMAS AND NEW YEAR holidays passed. Charley, Bonnie, and her parents struggled emotionally as they continued to deal with the loss of Donald. They busied themselves, trying to displace their pain; but nights for all of them brought sleepless hours of remembering and reliving their good times with Donald, with grief always rising to their consciousness, renewing their deep sorrow.

Charley grew more confident and at ease in his deputy role, and he and Bonnie had a bit more time to spend together, though not nearly enough to suit him. He had continued with rigorous regular workouts on his punching bag in the barn and his once weekly sparring bouts at the Big Stone Gap gym. Lloyd Anderson said he couldn't teach Charley anything else about boxing, that now the deputy just needed to work on honing to sharper levels his offensive and defensive boxing skills.

Infrequently, Sheriff Fielding rode with his newest deputy as they patrolled or responded to official calls. On one such ride, he told Charley he had heard rumblings that could mean trouble for miners, mine owners, and especially for law enforcement personnel in Powell

County. The sheriff talked about what happened in Wise, Russell, and Lee counties in the early 1930s when miner rebellions brought state police troopers in to deal with rowdy miners who were upset by what they deemed to be unsafe working conditions and unfair pay. And in the spring of 1939, about forty state troopers were sent to Clinchco in Dickenson County to keep the peace for six weeks by prohibiting "unlawful parades" of thousands of miners. Things got hot and dangerous. Big boulders were rolled off the sides of mountains, and vehicles of troopers and civilians were hit by snipers' rifle fire. There may have been injuries in some of those confrontations, but the sheriff didn't believe anybody had been killed.

"I hope nothing that serious comes up around here," Charley said.

"I think the miners and owners around here can work out their differences without it comin' to violence. Too bad more of the owners don't operate the way Brewster McGraw does. He pays his miners as good or better than union miners gets paid, and he is a stickler for safety in his mines. But who knows what may finally happen. We just have to be ready to do what we can to head off real trouble."

Early on a frosty November morning, Charley was on his way to see two farmers about five miles up Drowning Creek Road. He drove through Creedy and then passed farm houses. At some of the houses, mostly in town, dark smoke from chimneys and a slightly sulfurous odor indicated the homeowners heated with coal. Where the telltale bluish white of wood smoke spiraled up from chimneys and stovepipes, Charley inhaled its pleasant aroma.

Charley passed the Massey house before he turned off of River Road, and he thought back on Sol Massey's drowning two months earlier. A search party had found Sol's torn and battered body in Clinch River. Sheriff Fielding and Charley heard Maddie Massey's account of when she last saw her husband alive, and they investigated the death but found nothing relating to how or why Sol's body came to be in the river.

Word circulated through the community that Maddie had collected a right tidy sum of life insurance on Sol, and those who had known Sol felt that whatever amount she got from the insurance company probably was not enough, considering how he had treated his wife and children. Charley and the sheriff continued to talk and think about Sol's death. Though they still had reservations about the final ruling that Sol's death was accidental drowning, they had no evidence to prove otherwise. The accidental death ruling, however, did not mean Sheriff Fielding closed the case. The case remained open because the sheriff and Charley could not explain some of the facts of the case, and the deputy often found himself wondering, *Who made the set of small tracks in the sand beside Sol's tracks? How had Maddie's handkerchief come to be in the river? Why was there a discrepancy between the time Maddie said Sol left their house that night and the time a witness was sure he saw Sol's truck at the beach?*

As Charley passed Drowning Creek School, where he had gone to elementary school, he remembered the story Clarissa Thacker, his uncle Verle's mother, had told him when, as a third grader, he had asked her how that creek got its name.

At a homestead by the creek in 1773, a young mother who thought her husband had been killed by marauding Shawnees or Cherokees had hidden herself, a four-month-old baby, and two other young children under sagging tree branches in the edge of a deep pool of the creek. To keep the baby from crying or making other noise as Indians drew closer to where she hid with her little ones, the mother clamped her hand tightly over his mouth and unconsciously lowered herself farther down in the water as she held the child against her.

The Indians passed the scared woman and children without discovering them, and a while after they had passed, the mother and two older children stood up. They were safe. Then she looked at her baby: his lips were blue, his pale hands and arms dangled loosely, his cheeks were no longer rosy, and his eyes were closed. Her baby was dead. She realized she had held his head under water while they were hiding. Her husband and the oldest son also escaped detection by the Indians, and when he found her, she was sobbing and moaning, sitting on the creek bank rocking her upper body to and fro. She held one hand tightly over her mouth to keep from screaming, and with the other arm she cradled her lifeless baby boy. The husband and father led his grieving family back to their cabin and told his wife and children they would bury baby Matthew the next morning, and they all went to bed.

Morning came, but the mother was not in the house, nor was Matthew's tiny body. Her husband finally found his wife, back at the same deep pool where her baby died. During the night, she had walked up the creek from their cabin; cradling the baby tightly against her body, she had waded into the pool, sat down in the water, and drowned herself. Creek currents had moved her body to the shallow, rocky, lower end of the pool, and even in death she still clutched her baby to her breast.

Charley shook his head as if to clear the sad story from his memory, and his mind came back to the reason he was going up Drowning Creek Road. A farmer had accused a neighbor of cutting poplar trees that were on his land, not on the neighbor's; the neighbor contended he owned the land. After meeting with the two men, Charley suggested a way to settle their disagreement that seemed fair to both, and they agreed that they wanted no hard feelings over the matter. Charley left the two men and wished all disputes that involved him could be settled so amicably, but he knew that most would not be.

As the deputy started back toward Creedy, he decided he would drop by the Thacker farm to visit his aunt Luce and Verle. He turned off of

Drowning Creek Road, and after a few minutes on a narrow graveled lane, he reached the house and outbuildings. The once simple but attractive two-story house with a long front porch across its front now needed new paint on the peeling and weathered weatherboard exterior. As he walked from his car toward the house, Charley noticed that the barn needed roof repairs and boards were missing on the wall facing the road. A small, neat board-and-batten cottage sat in a back corner of the large yard, glistening in the weak autumn sun, obviously showing off its recently applied new white paint. Verle's mother, Clarissa Thacker, lived in this small house.

Charley climbed the steps to the front porch as the door opened, and a short, hefty, smiling lady greeted him with outstretched arms. His aunt Luce hugged her nephew, saying, "Charley, honey. Look at you! You're a sight for sore eyes. And these eyes tell me you look better every time I see you. My, my, that police uniform sure does become you."

"How are you, Aunt Luce?"

"Now that you're here, I'm real fine. Seems like I hardly ever get to see you anymore. Too busy as a deputy, I guess."

In the doorway stood a little short-haired, black-and-brown-spotted white feist dog with wedge-shaped ears tilted forward and with small dark eyes that were bright and perceptive. He probably weighed twelve to fourteen pounds, and he wagged his tail and whined eagerly as he pranced and twisted in front of Charley. Charley reached down and scratched the little mutt behind its ears, saying, "Little Handsome, it's good to see you too."

Little Handsome was Aunt Luce's pride and joy; she absolutely adored him. She gave the little dog more love and attention than many children Charley knew got from their parents. Charley's father, J. R., had reflected what many people knew about how Lucille treated her Little Handsome. He said, "If I could come back to earth again after I die, and could pick what or who I wanted to be, I'd choose to be Lucille's Little Handsome."

As Luce led her dear nephew through the door into the front room, she said, "Well, come on in and sit down, Charley, and we can talk."

"Can't stay long, Aunt Luce. I have to get on back to town."

"You can stay long enough for a cup of coffee, I know. Now sit, and I'll bring it out for you."

Charley sat in a rocker that had a soft, cushioned seat. Little Handsome hopped up on the settee, settled on a folded fuzzy blanket, and sighed contentedly as he stretched out with his head resting between his front legs, clearly at ease and satisfied in his domain. As Charley looked around the familiar, comfortable room with its polished dark pine floor and brightly patterned papered walls, he saw family pictures on those walls and on tables. He saw pictures of his aunt's parents, of Luce and her sister—his mother—Belle, and their two brothers. Luce also had pictures of Charley's family—his father and mother, two brothers, and himself.

Two pictures in his aunt's display always caught his eye and brought sadness. In one picture, Ma Jess was holding a boy, her son, Jacob, who was about four years old when the picture was made. The other picture was of Charley's mother sitting beside a boy who was less than five years old. Both boys had died in their childhood. Charley's brother Reagan, at the age of six had contracted Spanish influenza and died in August of 1918 while his father, J. R., was on or near a French battlefield. Uncle Jacob Musick had also got the deadly strain of flu and died not long before his tenth birthday, two months after Reagan's death. Edwin, Charley's older surviving brother, contracted the flu but survived, as did his grandmother Ma Jess.

Charley's mother and aunt had told the horrid story of the boys' deaths. They had suffered the classic, agonizing symptoms of Spanish flu. Both strapping boys had been strong, healthy, and active. In a matter of a few hours after their first symptoms appeared, they became so feeble they couldn't walk. The flu rapidly turned into a terrible form of pneumonia. The boys complained of severe aches in their muscles, backs, joints, and heads and developed high fevers followed by bouts of delirium. Their coughs produced thick, greenish sputum accompanied by nosebleeds.

Their fingers, extremities, and mucous membranes took on a blue tint because they could not get enough oxygen into their lungs. Four or five days after their first symptoms, the boys died of suffocation.

Charley was roused from his woeful reverie by Aunt Luce returning from the kitchen as she asked, "Charley, what's wrong? You look sad, or upset, or something."

"All of those, I guess, Aunt Luce. I was just remembering how Jacob and Reagan died. Let's talk about something more pleasant."

Aunt Luce knew that it was hard to find anything more pleasant to think about than a molassy cake with either apple butter or blackberry jam between each of its many layers. So she said, "Well, I've got something that always perks you up. Here's a nice big slice of stacked molassy cake, your favorite. And a cup of good hot coffee with cream and sugar, just the way you like it."

Charley chewed and swallowed a generous forkful of cake and said, "Umm, umm, Aunt Luce, you still make the best cake I ever tasted."

Lucille sat quietly, just enjoying having her nephew near her. Then she asked, "Charley, honey, have you and the sheriff learned any more about how poor ole Sol Massey went into the river?"

"No, Aunt Luce, we sure haven't. We have some unanswered questions but no real facts. We're still looking for answers."

Charley changed the topic of conversation by inquiring about his Uncle Verle. Luce replied, "Oh, Verle is over across the hill patching a fence. Two of our cows got over in Johnny Deskins's winter wheat field. Johnny was kinda riled up over it. Verle needs to be getting the rest of his tobacco crop graded and tied up so he can take it to market. Farmers are saying the price is good for burley this year. It's sure about time."

Pa Jess had talked about growing burley tobacco in 1930 and '31 to try to raise much-needed cash. The 1930 crop sold for an average of $12 per hundred pounds, and the next year the tobacco brought just a little over $8 per hundred. He had little profit the first year for his hard labor, and he didn't get enough in '31 to even meet his out-of-pocket costs for the crop.

Charley knew about marketing quotas and price supports congress established in response to the Great Depression. After burley prices rose, tobacco became an important cash crop for Appalachian farmers, including those in Powell County. Evidence now abounded of burley tobacco's importance to the survival of farmers, large and small, in hilly Southwest Virginia. Tobacco patches could be seen in valley bottoms, on upland slopes, even in steep mountain fields; and owners of most farms—even small ones—now raised burley tobacco.

Burley provided an important economic supplement, and income from it often meant the difference between financial survival and abject poverty for many Appalachian families, including Charley's grandparents and his aunt Luce and uncle Verle Thacker. Charley heard good news from farmers who had already sold their tobacco this fall of 1942. Prices for all grades of burley combined were averaging $42 per hundred, making it a profitable crop for Powell County farmers this year. He made a mental note to check with Verle to see if he needed help in getting his tobacco graded, tied, and hauled to market.

The nephew also asked Lucille about Verle's mother, Clarissa, whom he referred to as Aunt Clarissa. Lucille responded, "Mama Thacker? Well, she's just Mama Thacker. She's about the same as usual, no major health problems that I know of. But she's no spring chicken. I've never known exactly how old she is, but she has to be at least way up in her eighties."

Clarissa Thacker's grandmother had been half Indian, a medicine woman respected and revered by her tribe of the Cherokee Nation. The grandmother had passed down to her daughter, who passed on to her daughter, Clarissa, a vast store of knowledge about finding, collecting, and using herbs, wild plants, roots, berries, and tree barks to treat many common ailments. Clarissa gathered these natural medicines in their seasons and dispensed them to cure or alleviate symptoms of various ailments. She assisted women during childbirth. She was an unofficial medical provider for residents of the surrounding area—herb doctor and midwife. When asked by a patient or patient's family how much they owed for her services and medicines, Clarissa's response was always, "Oh, I can't charge you." But most patients pressed some amount of money on her, and she always said, "Thank you, I appreciate it."

According to mountain folklore, Clarissa also had another gift. Because she had never seen her father (who had been killed by lightning as he stood under the shelter of a tree in a thunderstorm downpour), she had the power to cure thrush in babies by blowing into their mouths. Thrush was an eruption of small creamy-white lesions on babies' tongues, inner cheeks, roof of their mouths, and gums. Many afflicted little ones were brought to Clarissa's home for a quick treatment. She was also reputed to be able to remove warts by rubbing them with her fingers and telling the afflicted person, "Just don't think about the warts. One morning, you'll wake up and they'll be gone." Many people she treated swore that what she said would happen to the warts really did happen.

Charley finished the last morsel of his molasses cake, drained his coffee cup, and rose to leave. He kissed his aunt's cheek and said, "Give my regards to Uncle Verle and Aunt Clarissa."

Lucille responded, "I'll do that, honey, but I wish you didn't have to leave so soon."

"I do too, Aunt Luce, but I need to get back to work."

As Charley walked across the porch and down the steps, he left her standing at the door. He glanced back and waved as his aunt watched him with tears glistening in her eyes and a forced, thin-lipped smile on her face that he knew conveyed more loneliness and regret than happiness. As the nephew drove away, he was worried about his aunt. She was too heavy. She seemed to have put on more weight since he had last seen her about a month ago.

Lucille Musick had been a beauty with long dark hair and large, laughing grayish green eyes. Her beautiful, oval, dimpled face caused most men, upon first seeing her, to take a second look. She had the figure of a beauty queen—she was a beauty queen. Luce, as she was called by almost everyone except her parents and her sister, was Creedy High School queen as a junior; she won the Miss Powell County title in her senior year. She graduated from Creedy High School with honors; as salutatorian of her graduating class of '22, she delivered an address at the baccalaureate ceremony on the Sunday prior to commencement exercises. In her address, she exhorted her classmates to live up to the potential each of them possessed. She assumed she would certainly practice what she preached.

Some of Luce's teachers urged her to go to college, and one even had a verbal commitment from the dean at Lincoln Memorial University in Harrogate, Tennessee that Luce could get a scholarship to cover almost all of her tuition, room, and meals. Luce had her heart set on going to college and getting a nursing degree, and at her graduation she still hoped she could convince her father to allow her to enroll at LMU. But Jesse Musick didn't see the wisdom of sending his daughter away to college. He thought his daughter should become a housewife and mother, and she didn't need to go to college for that. Lucille graduated in the spring and married Verle Thacker in October 1926, a few days after her eighteenth birthday.

Verle was seven years older than Lucille. Charley's mother, Belle, had surmised that Verle had always fancied himself as being the Lord's gift to the ladies—to any or all of them. Belle was convinced that her sister's marriage to Verle was a mistake. After the marriage, she commented to her mother, "I'm afraid Lucille will regret marrying Verle. But she's made her bed, now she'll have to lay in it."

Even after he married Luce, Verle admired pretty women and imagined ways he might be able to get better acquainted with them. And he had done more than imagine with a few of them, but his brief flings had been carefully executed and were not fodder for the local gossips. Lucille had no inkling of Verle's straying escapades, and he had no thought of lasting relationships with anyone but his wife—at least, not until he began to get better acquainted with a neighbor, widow Madeline Massey.

Luce and her husband owned a 120-acre parcel of land his parents had owned. Shortly after Verle's father died, Clarissa Thacker deeded the farm to her son and daughter-in-law with the stipulation that she would live in the cottage behind the main house for her remaining days and would get 25 percent of the farm profits each year. The farm lay beside the Clinch River with Drowning Creek forming the western boundary of the property. About seventy acres of the land could be farmed or grazed. Verle and his wife always seemed to have money problems, whether it was due to poor management, unnecessary spending, bad crops, low prices for whatever they sold, or sick and dying sheep or cattle.

Luce had always loved children and wanted to have a houseful of her own; she and Verle tried to have them. A year passed, two years—no babies. She became despondent, lethargic. One response to her depressed state was to eat. In addition to eating full meals three times a day, she ate between meals and before bed at night. Luce loved bread—cornbread, biscuits, yeast rolls. Her snacks might be a ham biscuit left from breakfast, cornbread and soup beans in the middle of the afternoon, jellies or preserves on buttered biscuits and rolls, or desserts at any time of the day or between supper and bedtime. She loved chocolate cake with peaches, baked or fried apple pies, and bread pudding. Lucille ate at the kitchen table, and she ate as she lounged on the couch in her front room. Not only did she eat too much, she moved too little. She walked out of the house only once or twice a day, plodding the short distances from the house to the toilet or to the mailbox. Lucille gained weight—about sixty pounds.

Then Lucille learned she was pregnant in the third year of her marriage. But after two months, she miscarried. Sad, difficult times again. Luce continued to gain weight. Two years after her miscarriage, Luce's prayers were answered; she gave birth to a baby girl, Rebecca. The birth was difficult, and Dr. Easton told her that most likely she would never have another child.

Rebecca was a beautiful baby and little girl, with her mother's sparkling eyes and her father's golden hair. Rebecca became Lucille's reason for living; the mother was happiest when she was doing something for or with her baby. But the child was sickly; she suffered from asthma and had strong reactions to some foods, including cow's milk, cream, cheese, and ice cream. When the little girl was three years old, she contracted a bad cold or influenza which, coupled with her asthmatic condition, quickly progressed to pneumonia. In spite of the ministrations of Clarissa Thacker and Doc Easton, Rebecca died eight days after beginning to run a fever.

Luce was devastated and depressed. She withdrew emotionally, shut herself off from her family and her husband, and spent most of her time in bed or on her couch. She refused to leave the house to visit her sister, Belle, or to go to church or to buy groceries. When her sister came to Luce's house, Belle had to initiate all conversation and usually got no more than a one- or two-word response to questions. Luce was uninterested in anything Verle tried to discuss with her about the farm, crops, or livestock. She had little interest in sexual intimacy with Verle, and during their infrequent couplings, she showed almost no evidence of passion or pleasure.

About three months after Rebecca's death, Luce appeared to begin to get better, laughing occasionally, more like her old self; inside she still grieved and suffered pangs of depression and loss. Luce tried to focus on her husband and on pleasing him, but she was still eating too much. She ate even when she wasn't hungry. By eating, Luce seemed to be trying to satisfy some yearning, to fill some deep void other than hunger. After she finished a meal, cleaned the kitchen, and washed dishes, Luce often ate leftovers instead of keeping them for the next day or throwing them in the bucket for hog slop. She might eat two or three heaping serving spoons of mashed potatoes or half a buttered biscuit or a deviled egg.

Luce grew heavier and heavier, now weighing almost twice as much as she did when she married. As she put on more weight, Luce became less appealing to Verle, and his inattention to her revealed his lack of desire for her. Luce became more depressed as months and years dragged by, even as she tried to project a jolly image to her parents and siblings and especially to her beloved nephew, Charley Scott. Little Handsome became the focus of her love. She treated him royally, loving and pampering him. She talked to the little dog as if he were a child, and she caressed him as he lay beside her on her bed or the couch. When she slept, he was always beside her. She fed him choice morsels of chicken, ham, and leftover gravy that she warmed on the stove and ladled over biscuits or cornbread.

CHAPTER 14

November, December 1942

As Charley drove from Aunt Luce's house back to town, he saw evidence of the effect the war was having back here on the home front. He saw a number of cars and trucks parked with tireless wheel rims resting on the ground or on wood blocks. Owners of these vehicles were unable to buy tires and inner tubes to replace the ones that had worn out or blown out. Rubber was in extremely short supply. Because of the need for food and materiel to support Americans fighting in the war, rationing of many consumer products began this year, 1942; tires and tubes were especially scarce.

Foods, including sugar, coffee, refined flour, meats, canned fish, canned milk, chocolate, and butter, were rationed; every family received stamps for rationed products, with the size of the family determining how much of each rationed item was allowed per family. By the end of the war, consumption of almost every food product except eggs and dairy products was limited by rationing. Of course, buyers of these foods had to have the money to pay for them, but they could not buy them without ration stamps no matter how much money they had. Farmers were considered "soldiers in uniforms" and could get deferments from military service because they were needed to produce food for the nation and its armed forces.

Nonfood rationed products included automobile tires and parts, gasoline, bicycles, fuel oil and kerosene, stoves, typewriters, leather, rubber goods, and nylon. Silk virtually disappeared, because silk and nylon were used to make parachutes instead of stockings. Practically everything made of metal or rubber was rationed. According to radio broadcasts and newspaper reports, no new cars would be produced for civilians after this year until the war ended. Studebaker was making trucks for the fighting men. Ford was building Jeeps and ships. To conserve rubber and gasoline, but mainly rubber, thirty-five miles per hour was established as the national victory speed. In the small Creedy theater, Daffy Duck advised the audience to "keep it under forty" in Warner Brothers cartoons.

Liquor distilleries had converted to producing industrial alcohol, and the U.S. government banned the manufacture of whiskey, so it was disappearing from liquor store shelves. How that development would affect Charley's job was on his mind occasionally. More men who had to have their whiskey in some form would probably be wanting moonshine whiskey. Moonshine and moonshiners were not new or rare in Powell County, but Sheriff Fielding had taken a hands-off policy unless some danger or problem arose concerning specific moonshiners, and no federal "revenuers" had descended on the county.

The sheriff and his deputies knew of most, if not all, of the moonshiners in the county. Some of them the sheriff knew personally and talked with occasionally. A few were even considered friends—not close bosom buddies, but at least casual friends, certainly not enemies. An increase of bootleggers was also likely as enterprising individuals sought to line their pockets by providing whiskey smuggled from Canada or rum from the Caribbean.

Charley recalled an observation he had read about that had gained quite a lot of press during the Prohibition Era, and he heard locals say essentially the same thing. The saying was that, in favoring prohibition, "bootleggers and Baptists are in bed together." Preachers favored prohibition because they assumed alcohol would be unavailable if it was illegal, but bootleggers also wanted it to be illegal. If whiskey could not be bought legally, bootleggers' illegal alcohol would be the only kind available, and they could prosper.

A large sign posted by the road caught Charley's eye as he drove into Creedy. Huge letters on the sign proclaimed "JUNK RALLY." Smaller letters said, "Pick-up date, December 7. Remember Pearl Harbor!" *A week from today,* Charley mused, *the day when one year earlier Don was lost to the Japanese attack. And so were hundreds, maybe thousands, of other sailors.* Junk rallies were held to collect scrap rubber and metal. The poster told civilians that junk helped make ships, tanks, and guns for U.S. fighting men. The remainder of the poster listed many of the types of scrap needed: irons, rakes, bed rails, lawn mowers, farm machinery, stoves, rubber goods, and used toothpaste tubes. The deputy had seen local boys and girls helping in the war effort by pulling their little red wagons from house to house collecting scrap. Trucks came around through towns and communities to pick up the collected scrap.

To people in Powell County, shortages caused by the war were not too bad. They had lived through the Great Depression; compared to the depression, life was not so bad now. People all around the country were learning what Southwest Virginians had long known and practiced—not to waste. Not to waste food, clothing, rubber, gasoline, or kerosene. Now they realized it was important not to waste anything that might help provide for friends and neighbors, for sons and brothers and husbands, who were risking their lives every day in distant lands on the other side of the oceans.

Most Powell Countians and most Virginians were glad to have some way to help in the war effort. They collected scrap metal and rubber. They did without various consumer goods with little complaining. Most in Powell County were already in the habit of making everything go as far as they could. They accepted rationing. Homemakers had to be careful with their stamps. They had to have a stamp for a certain product and a different stamp for something else. Dealing with ration stamps was bothersome but bearable; it was no sacrifice compared to what thousands of young men and women faced on European and Pacific battlefields.

When the national call came asking everyone who possibly could to raise Victory Gardens, most families in and around Creedy were already accustomed to raising large gardens every year. They grew and stored or preserved as much as they could from their garden and backyard harvests—fruits, vegetables, potatoes, dried beans, and more. Most farmers and many who lived on the edge of town raised and butchered their own hogs for a large portion of the meat they would consume throughout the year, supplemented in many cases by chickens, turkeys, ducks, sheep, or beef they raised. Though butter was rationed, virtually anyone in Powell County who wanted butter either made it by churning cream from their own cow's milk or bought fresh homemade butter from nearby farmers or from a grocer who bought it from farmers.

Newspaper accounts and newsreel stories at the theater made Charley aware of multitudes of people who were displaced, homeless, and starving in areas where battles had raged or were still raging. He wished he could do something to ease their hunger and pain but knew that all he could do was to do his small part in supporting U.S. fighting forces and pray that the war would end soon. He was thankful that he and his loved ones had plenty of plain, simple fare and had never known pangs of real hunger. He was glad people in this area were so self-sufficient.

Charley's parents, with whom he still lived and took many of his meals, lived on a small tract of about twenty-five acres, about half of which was woodland. The other portion of the tract was made up of pasture land and tillable fields. The Scotts raised a large garden from which Belle fed them during growing seasons and canned surpluses for the winter. They also planted pole beans, or cornfield beans, in some of their corn rows so the bean vines could run up the corn stalks for support; they grew cushaws, winter squash, or pumpkins in corn rows that got more sun near the ends and upper and lower edges of corn fields.

A small orchard of apple, cherry, and peach trees provided ample fruit to enjoy fresh and for Belle to can and dry for the harsh, cold, snowy months. So they ate a lot of his mom's canned food—beans, sauerkraut, apples, corn, pickles, tomatoes, berries, etc.—plus their home-grown sweet potatoes, onions, squash, pumpkins, dried beans, and dried apples. They also grew potatoes, cabbage, turnips, and parsnips—vegetables they stored in holes dug into the ground to keep them from freezing in cold weather.

The family killed two or three hogs each fall—either Durocs or Poland Chinas, breeds J. R. insisted on. Belle canned some of the hog meat, especially ribs, backbones, sausage, and sometimes tenderloin. The Scotts had salt-cured hams, shoulders, and side meat from the hogs. They kept chickens for eggs and dinners. They also had a cow or two that provided milk and butter. A neighbor was glad to lend J. R. his horses to do what plowing had to be done and for other occasional jobs where horses were needed, so J. R. raised enough corn and hay in his fields to feed his own animals through the winters. Charley and his father amply repaid the neighbor for the use of his horses by helping him harvest hay and tobacco.

After the Japanese attack on Pearl Harbor in December 1941, the first three months of the war brought bad news. Southwest Virginians learned of the war events—some by newspaper reports, a few by magazine articles and movie news reels; most of them heard radio broadcasts of Gabriel Heatter, Lowell Thomas, or Edward R. Murrow. In January, German U-boats inflicted massive damage on U.S. shipping. Japan captured Manilla in the Phillipines, and after fierce battles, American defense of that nation collapsed. So President Roosevelt ordered General MacArthur out of the Phillipines.

In April, though, with bombers taking off from the carrier *USS Hornet* in the Pacific, Lieutenant Colonel James Doolittle carried out a raid on Japanese cities—the first U.S. air attack on Japanese home islands. This raid gave a much-needed boost to the morale of Virginians and to all Americans who had been receiving mostly bad news about the war.

In June, American planes sank four Japanese carriers at the Battle of Midway; but in the same month, Japanese forces invaded the islands of Attu and Kiska in Alaska. While these islands were far away in the North Pacific, many Americans worried; the enemy had now attacked U.S. soil on the North American continent. In November of 1942, the U.S. Navy suffered heavy losses in the Battle of Guadalcanal but still retained control of the sea there.

As the seventh day of December edged closer this year, Charley and the McGraws thought more about what had happened a year ago. Donald McGraw lost his life as the Japanese bombed Pearl Harbor; they sank the battleship on which Donald served. Charley, Bonnie, and her parents had supper together at her parents' house on the evening of December 7, 1942. They talked a few minutes about Donald and recounted some of his funny little escapades. Even though Donald's life had ended too soon, snuffed out by the madness of war, each of the four was thankful that he had been in their lives.

When they were seated at the supper table, an extra place setting was on the table. Eleanor McGraw had set a place for Donald where her son had always eaten at their table. Eleanor said, "Now, eat up. You know Donald wouldn't want us to mope around with long, sad faces. Let's try to enjoy this fried chicken. It was one of his favorites."

CHAPTER 15

December 1942-February 1943

Madeline Massey stood in her kitchen and looked out at the swirling snow, fine pellets driven by a brisk wind. She had sold almost three thousand pounds of burley tobacco for about $1,300. And the calves and yearling steers she marketed brought an additional $350. Since she had been running the farm operation for more than two years before Sol died, she was pleased with how her work and planning were now beginning to pay off. *I've earned every penny I've got,* she thought. *We're making more money on the farm now that Sol's gone.* At the thought of Sol, she wondered, *Will the sheriff ever learn what really happened to Sol? I doubt it.* With some of the life insurance money she received after Sol's death, she had paid for much-needed repairs on the barn and on replacing and repairing fences. She paid to have a new coat of white paint put on the peeling wood exterior of her house.

Sol's old pickup truck was on its last legs, so she bought a 1938 Chevrolet truck for Demus Ferguson, the sharecropper/hired hand, to use for farm-related work as well as for some of his personal transportation. For herself she bought a 1939 Ford sedan. Both vehicles had good tires, so she wouldn't have to worry about finding replacement tires any time soon.

Maddie had thought often of what her mother-in-law, Martha Massey, told her about their property. According to Martha, the Thacker farm that Verle and Lucille now own had deposits of coal in its mountains, and her source of information about the deposits said the Thackers were unaware their land held such deposits.

The Massey farm also had seams of coal on it, Martha had said, but they didn't own the mineral rights to them. Before Verle Thacker was born, Sol's aging father, Thaddeus, sold the mineral rights of their property to Verle's father for money to buy a small sawmill and logging outfit. Mr. Massey's logging and sawmill operation was profitable for about five years, at which time getting to enough timber of adequate size and quality became increasingly difficult and less profitable. So Thaddeus sold his sawmill and lumbering equipment at a price far less than he paid for it.

Martha and Solomon Massey felt the Thackers had taken advantage of Thaddeus by acquiring their mineral rights for a small amount of money, even though Mr. Massey was the one who made the proposal to sell Mr. Thacker the rights. The Masseys became bitter enemies of the Thackers, and the enmity persisted even after Verle and his mother were the only surviving Thackers.

The Thacker farm, though only about a fourth as large as the Massey property, lay between the Massey holdings and the branch line of the Norfolk & Western that roughly paralleled the Clinch River through Powell County. Massey land was bounded on two other sides by the Jefferson National Forest. On the fourth side lay extensive holdings of Brewster McGraw, including farming land, timberland, and a small coal mining operation. The Masseys had long wanted to own property that would give them access to the railway line. They reasoned that, if they were ever able to mine their coal, having the rail line through their property would reduce the cost of getting their coal into railroad cars, thus increasing their coal revenues.

Madeline Massey decided she would get control of Verle Thacker's farm and the mineral rights that belonged to the Masseys before Verle's father cheated them out of the rights. She would make Verle want to marry her. Then she would have property through which the railroad ran, and she would own, at least partially, rights to Massey property coal deposits.

Now in mid-December, Maddie was in Creedy buying groceries and a few extra things for Christmas. She was a slender, attractive, strawberry blond just a few years shy of forty. She had alluring curves—a body that beckoned to men and made most women jealous. Maddie was paying and handing food ration stamps to Amos Baldwin, manager and operator of the grocery store, when she saw Verle Thacker enter the store and start to gather items and place them on a counter. He hadn't noticed Maddie yet, so she ambled in his direction. As he placed a can of baking powder near his other items, he looked up and saw his widow neighbor. Maddie gave him a bright smile and said, "Verle Thacker! It's been a long time since I've seen you."

"Yes, I guess it has."

"Actually," Maddie said, "it's been a long time since I've seen much of anything, with all the things I've had going on the past few months." She eyed the strong, good-looking man and added, "Verle, you sure are looking good."

Verle dropped his head for a few seconds and looked back up at Maddie. He appeared to be blushing a bit under the tan on his face and neck. Maddie was thinking, *Oh my. From comments I've heard over the past several years about this man, I wouldn't have believed him to be the type to blush easily in the presence of a woman.*

Verle was thinking, *Madeline Massey sure is a looker, with her bright smile and inquiring eyes on such a pretty face. And what a figure! That plain dress she has on and the jacket over it don't do much to hide her ample female assets.*

Finally, Verle replied, "Howdy, Miz Massey."

"Miz Massey my foot! I'm Maddie to my friends. Call me Maddie."

"All right, Mi . . . uh, Maddie. How are you and the children doing now?"

"I think we're getting along better than most folks around here expected us to."

"Well, I don't know. Most everybody I know thinks you're an independent, strong-minded woman who can do just about whatever she sets her mind to."

"Is that what you think, Verle?" Maddie asked, looking him boldly in the eye.

"I reckon I do, Maddie, knowing how you kept the farm going during some hard times."

"Thank you, Verle, but it's a hard, sometimes thankless, job for a woman to have to try to keep everything running smooth on a farm and in a family without a man around."

"I'm sure it is. Is there anything in particular right now that you need help with?"

"Oh, there is, but you've got your wife and your own farm to look after."

Verle said, "I've got my tobacco ready for market. Will probably take it off tomorrow or maybe the next day. After that I won't have anything pressing to be done at the farm.

Nothing that can't wait a few days."

"If you're sure you have the time to spare, there's a problem with the truck that you might be able to fix."

"I'm not a very good mechanic, but what kind of problem is it?"

"It's something I should be able to fix myself, but I can't."

"Well, what is it?"

"Now that our tobacco crop has sold, Demus and his wife have gone to spend a couple of weeks with her family over at Gate City. Demus will help them grade the rest of their tobacco crop and take it to market. He left the truck at my house in case I need it on the farm, and his son took him and Emaline to Gate City. But to finally answer your question, the right front tire is flat, and Lucas says the spare tire won't hold air either."

"Well, I sure enough can fix a flat," Verle responded.

"Verle, if you could do that, I would be most grateful. I need to haul some cattle feed and salt blocks and several bags of oats for the horses."

"Why don't we plan for me to come by your place on Friday then?"

"Great!" Maddie replied. "Then I can haul my stuff on Saturday."

"Friday it is. I should be able to get there around midmorning."

"Thank you, Verle," Maddie said as she started to pick up the box of groceries she had bought.

"That box looks heavy," Verle said, "let me take it to your car." He picked up the box and walked out of the store, down the steps, and across the street to her car as Maddie followed behind him, smiling to herself.

At the car, Maddie opened a front door and pointed to the passenger seat, saying, "Just set it there."

Verle placed the box in the seat and turned around. Maddie was standing so close to him. She smiled and placed a hand on his arm as she said, "You're so thoughtful, Verle. Thank you again for everything. I'll see you Friday."

Maddie then went around the car, got in the driver's seat, started the car, and drove off with another smile and a cheery wave at Verle. Verle stood watching as the car went out of sight. *Mrs. Massey is a very nice lady and oh so easy on the eyes. I think I'll enjoy helping a neighbor.* Then Verle realized his heart was beating faster than normal. He had a bit of sweat on his forehead, even though the crisp morning air was quite chilling.

A lighthearted Verle drove toward home with his groceries, humming a tune without realizing what the tune was. He stopped humming and thought, *What's the name of that tune?* After playing the melody in his mind a few moments, he recalled some of the words. *See her walking down that street. Yes, I ask you very confidentially . . .* Then he got it. *Aha! It's "Ain't She Sweet." But why that tune? Why now?* If he had been willing to admit it, he knew why.

At home Verle took his groceries to the kitchen and called for his wife. He heard a faint reply from the bedroom. He walked quickly to the room where he found Lucille in bed, nestled down into a feather tick and covered by at least two colorful handmade quilts. Little Handsome was stretched out on his side near Lucille, and his tail thumped the quilt as he greeted Verle.

"What are you doing in bed in the middle of the day?" Verle asked. "Are you sick, Lucille?"

"I'm not feeling well again, Verle," his wife said, "I'm just going to rest. I don't think I can do any cooking today. Can you make out with the pot of beans I cooked yesterday? And there's about half a pone of cornbread left. It should still be good."

Verle thought, *Not feeling well again. Going to have to rest. What has she done lately except eat and sleep?*

Then he said, "Yeah, I can warm up the soup beans and cornbread."

That night as Verle sat alone at the kitchen table, he ate his beans and bread and washed it down with a glass of buttermilk. He didn't know what was going to happen to Lucille. She still ate too much, and she moved around too little, spending most of her time in bed or on the front-room sofa. She had continued to gain weight and at age thirty-four was already grossly overweight; she probably weighed twice as much as she did when they married.

In addition to her size, Lucille didn't clean and groom herself as she should, and she wore a faded, threadbare housecoat more often than a dress. She seldom put on makeup or lipstick, and her hair was often an uncombed, frizzy mess that needed soap or shampoo. Lucille was no longer an attractive woman. Verle remembered what a happy, beautiful bride she had been. He had loved her and had been sure he would never want any woman but her. After the miscarriage, and especially after Rebecca died, his bride began to change. She grew more despondent, unhappy, and depressed, all the while feeding her sorrowing body excessive amounts of food.

Early in their marriage, Verle thought himself quite a lucky man to have such a good woman, such a pretty and desirable wife who shared the excitement and pleasures of their marriage bed. Over the last few years, their intimacy declined, partly because Lucille was less interested in sex and apparently got less and less pleasure from it, but also because Verle's desire for her had decreased as she became more and more obese. They still slept in the same bed, but there had been no marital pleasure during the past six months. Verle occasionally tried to initiate sex, but his wife's response was always some sort of excuse or pretense, such as, "Honey, I don't feel like it tonight," or "I've had this bad pain in my back for the last several days," or "Not tonight, Verle. Maybe in a few days." And Verle, barely into his forties, still had a strong sex drive. He didn't want to spend the rest of his prime years without a wife who was also a willing and eager conjugal partner.

Then Verle's thoughts went back to Maddie Massey. She was pretty. She was enticing. He had heard catty remarks about Mrs. Massey, about her being a cold and hard woman. He didn't agree. She had been dealt a bad hand in marrying the man that Sol turned out to be. For the last few years, she was the one who had to manage the farm while putting up with her carousing, and often drunk, husband.

Friday morning, Verle was up bright and early, left his wife in bed, and made breakfast of oatmeal and fried bread. After eating, he came to the bedroom door and said, "Lucille, I've got some things to do. I'll be back by supper time." Without opening her eyes, she lifted a hand and wagged it slightly. Verle did his usual morning farm chores and drove toward the Massey place.

When he reached the Massey house, Verle pulled up beside the truck, got out, looked at the front tire on the Massey truck that was flat, and began working right away. He jacked up the truck and removed the wheel. He found a bright, shiny nail in the tire. The previous evening just before dark, Maddie had slipped out of the house to the truck. Using a hammer, she pounded the nail into the tire and wiggled it around until the air spewed out. Then she pushed the nail deeper into the tire until the head was against the tread. With that tire taken care of, she loosened the valve in the stem of the spare tire enough that all its air seeped out during the night. Now Verle had found the two tires just as she had described them three days earlier.

Before he began working to repair the nail hole in the inner tube, Verle checked the spare and quickly found that the valve was loose. After tightening the valve, he pumped up the spare with the tire pump he kept in his truck. As Verle worked, he noticed two different faces peering out a window at him, and neither of the faces was Maddie's. He assumed they were Cecilia and Lucas, Maddie's children.

Just as Verle put the wheel with the tire and its repaired inner tube, now full of air, back on the wheel lugs, Maddie came out to him.

She greeted him with, "Hello, Verle. I'm sorry you have to work out here in the cold, but I sure appreciate what you're doing for me."

He gave a small grunt as he twisted the lug wrench to tighten a nut and said, "The cold's not bad now. I'm used to working outside in weather lots worse than this. Anyway, I'm just about finished here."

Maddie watched as Verle tightened the final lug nut and started to lower the jack. She said, "It seems pretty cold to me, so I'm going back in the house. As soon as you finish, come to the kitchen. I've got coffee perking. That should warm you up, and I made a pie. Hope you like apple pie."

"One of my favorites. I'll be finished here in a few minutes."

Mrs. Massey headed for the house as Verle appreciated the view of her shapely rear in close-fitting pants. He lowered the jack, and the repaired tire rested on the ground, then he stowed his tools back in his truck and headed for the kitchen, coffee, and pie.

Verle relished the huge slice of apple pie; it tasted so good! Lucille hadn't made any kind of dessert for months. He lingered over a refill of his coffee cup as he and Maddie made small talk. A face peering out from under a bushy, unruly mop of blond hair looked around the door frame and said, "Mother."

"Lucas," Maddie said, "this is Mr. Thacker. He came by to fix the tires on the truck."

"Oh?" was the boy's response. Lucas knew about the truck tires. He had been outside when his mother came out and worked her magic on the truck tires. Last evening he hadn't been able to understand why she let the air out. Now maybe he was beginning to see why.

"Hello, Mr. Thacker," Lucas responded and continued with, "Mother, can I have a piece of pie?"

"Of course you can. Cut yourself a piece, and cut one for Cecilia."

"I'll get mine," Lucas said, thinking, *Ceecee can get her own if she wants it.* He quickly got himself a slice of pie and went down the hall to his room.

Verle said, "I must be on my way home. Thanks for the hot coffee and that mighty fine pie. It sure was tasty."

"I'm glad you liked it, and I thank you more than you can know for your kindness in coming to help a damsel in distress, as they said in those stories about knights on white horses ages ago."

Maddie followed Verle out onto the kitchen porch. She put a hand on his arm again and, looking at him with intense, knowing eyes, said, "I really am glad you came today, Verle."

He looked at her and put one hand on top of hers. Smiling, she covered his hand with her other hand. They looked at each other intently for a few seconds. Verle finally said, "I'd better go."

Before he could pull away, Maddie squeezed his hand firmly and said, "I hope I'll see you again soon. So bye for now, Verle Thacker."

When Verle was beside his truck, he looked back toward the porch. Maddie was still there smiling, and a different face was peering out through the kitchen window. *That's Cecilia, I suppose,* thought Verle. Maddie waved to him as the started to move out, and he gave her a nod.

CHAPTER 16

December 1942 to 1943

As he drove toward home, Verle realized he had been a little surprised at Maddie's obvious interest in him, but he quickly acknowledged that he was a good-looking man that many women would be interested in if he weren't already married. He also realized that he was interested in widow Massey. Verle thought about how different his wife and the widow were. Both had been beautiful young women. Because of heartaches, one had grown depressed, despondent, and careless about her appearance. The other remained a beautiful older, but not old, woman who had survived heartaches and hardships but had maintained a positive outlook and kept her beauty.

Over the next weeks, Maddie created opportunities to "run into" Verle. She managed to be in places where Verle came—grocery store, feed store, post office. She let him know, and not in subtle or timid ways, that she was attracted to him. The widow enticed Verle in numerous ways. She was always clean and well groomed. She looked great, even dazzling at times, in the clothes she wore—clothes that accentuated her curves or complimented her complexion and hair color. Verle was captivated by the alluring fragrance of her perfume. Maddie's easy, radiant smile, her bright, frank eyes, and her gentle, seemingly spontaneous touches drew Verle to her and seemed to hold promise of fun and pleasure. She played the poor, helpless widow so well, and Verle contrived reasons to justify visits to her farm or house.

Christmas holidays passed, and 1943 began with Verle making more frequent visits to Maddie's house. Most of the times when Verle was there, Cecilia and Lucas were at school, but occasionally he would be there after school hours or on weekends. Verle always made a point of trying to talk with the teenagers. Cecilia was an observant, sharp-witted sixteen-year-old. She was always polite to him, but she seemed nervous or tense in his presence. Luke, as the boy preferred to be called, was either gruff or nonresponsive when Verle tried to engage him in conversation. *Typical teenager,* Verle thought. But he wondered what made the fourteen-year-old boy appear to be so different from his sister. Verle had observed that the children's mother seemed to dote on the boy and forego any kind of discipline, even when the lad richly deserved it. On the other hand, Maddie was quick to criticize, berate, or belittle her daughter for any minor slip.

As weeks passed and Verle was at the Massey house more, a feeling of respect, maybe even fondness or friendship, seemed to be developing between the teenage girl and him. Just the opposite was happening with Luke. The boy took every opportunity he could to disagree with Verle, to criticize statements he made, or to interrupt Verle when he was talking with Cecilia or Maddie. Luke delighted in pointing out a flaw or inaccuracy in something Verle said, and the more people to witness his trying to belittle Verle, the better the boy liked it. Sometimes Luke pointedly ignored Verle's direct comments or questions to him.

Verle saw Cecilia as an attractive, intelligent, compassionate young woman who displayed clear, logical thinking and sound judgment at levels much higher than girls or boys her age usually showed. He believed she could do or become almost anything she set her mind to. Based on a few brief chats with the girl, he knew that Cecilia wanted to go to college—maybe at Berea in Kentucky or Virginia Intermont in Bristol or East Tennessee State in Johnson City. Maddie Massie had always been stricter on Cecilia than on her brother. Their mother had pampered Luke, overlooked his many shortcomings and transgressions, but she cut Cecilia no slack and was often critical and harsh without cause. Maddie came to resent her daughter's obvious interest in and friendship with Verle, and she sometimes wondered if that was the only attraction the girl felt toward him.

Luke, though, was becoming jealous and resentful of his mother's new friend because that friend was taking some of the attention his mother had previously showered on him. Maybe the boy just needed the influence and guidance of a father figure who could also set boundaries on some of Luke's improper behaviors. Verle didn't know about some of Luke's reasons for acting the way he did. Luke really had little respect for the feelings of anyone other than himself. He also felt an antagonism toward females, including his sister and mother. The boy still had vivid memories of some of his father's actions over the last five or six years of his life. These actions conveyed to Luke the impression that people should be treated as Sol had treated his mother, sister, and himself. His father had threatened and physically abused their mother; he had threatened his children but never actually physically hurt them.

Luke also felt changes, stirrings, and desires caused by increasing levels of hormones as his body began its transition from boyhood to manhood, but he let these stirrings and desires take him in unhealthy directions. Luke was a Peeping Tom, and he worked hard at that activity. He peeped at his sister whenever he could spy on her in states of partial or complete nudity. Cecilia had caught Luke more than once as he gazed at her partially or completely unclothed body. Luke didn't care that she knew he was ogling her. She had told her mother about some of these incidents, but her mother had twisted the situations around to try to make Cecilia feel it was her own fault that her brother was watching her. Luke also looked for opportunities to see other women, even his mother, when they were only partially clothed or, even better, stark naked. The boy had another deviant behavior that caused consternation and anger among females on nearby farms and in Creedy, but they didn't know Luke Massey was the culprit. He pilfered girls' and women's bras and panties from their clotheslines.

Sometimes another boy, an older teenager, was at the Massey house. At eighteen, Rafe Hawkins was a good-looking young man—above-average height with curly blond hair and blue eyes—but there seemed to be something hard, maybe even cruel, that showed in his eyes when things didn't go his way. A few people knew Rafe could be quick-tempered, sometimes showing a mean, sadistic streak. Several young ladies longed to be his girlfriend, but he set his heart on Cecilia Massey. A senior at Creedy High School, Rafe was two years older than Cecilia but only one grade ahead of her because his mother wouldn't let him start school until he was seven. He pestered and pursued Cecilia constantly and relentlessly.

Rafe's father and two older brothers were occasional coal miners. The family lived on a little hardscrabble hill farm up near the head of Horse Pen Holler. Their farm bumped up against Jefferson National Forest, and their nearest neighbors were three ridges distant—more than a mile away as the crow flies, but almost ten miles by narrow, bumpy roads that snaked through rutted gullies or rocky stream beds. They supplemented their meager incomes with a small business endeavor—they made moonshine whiskey.

When Nettie Bascomb agreed to marry Willard Hawkins, she knew what kind of man he had been. She was sure that, with her love and prayers, she could change him, tame him, and turn his wild, reckless streak into productive energy and devotion to a family. Change came, but most of it came to Nettie. A hopeful, cheerful, radiant young woman had, over the years, become worn, haggard, dejected, hopeless. But Willard *had* changed some; he drank more whiskey, worked less in mines and on the farm, and punched Nettie more as her years ebbed by.

Over the first ten years of her marriage, Nettie gave birth to three sons. She saw herself as a righteous Christian woman and hoped, as the biblical Hebrews had, that her sons would live up to the names she gave them. Willard didn't care what she named the boys. Nettie named her firstborn Gabriel, and three years later, she called her second son Michael. She knew these were the names of two archangels who led the army of angels that expelled Satan from heaven. Four years following Michael's birth, and with complications that meant her third son would be the last child she could conceive, Rafael was born. He too was named after an angel in the Holy Bible. To her sorrow, neither of her two older boys displayed angelic qualities from their early teenage years and into adulthood. They only added to their mother's disappointment, sorrow, and despair. The youngest son, Rafael, had not yet caused her the heartache his brothers had; she prayed he would grow up to be a much better man than Gabriel and Michael were. The sons' names were shortened by friends, acquaintances, and most of the family to Gabe, Mike, and Rafe. Their mother always called them by the names she gave them.

Willard and his two older sons, starting as young teenagers, partook heartily of their business product, and they cared little for the welfare of the family. If not for the hard work of Nettie in her garden and on the farm, they would have starved long ago.

Belle Scott had heard at church one Sunday evening that Nettie Hawkins, her husband, and one son were all sick with the flu. Rafe Hawkins had told Cecilia, and she told Bonnie McGraw and Belle. Around 4:00 p.m. the next day, Bonnie drove Belle and herself up to the Hawkins place, taking with them a pot of soup beans cooked with a ham bone in them, a big round and thick pone of cornbread, a gallon of sweet milk, and a nice beef roast cooked with onions, potatoes, and carrots. They also took a beautiful yellow cake with white icing.

When the two women arrived at the Hawkins house, they found that the sick had improved but were a long way from being well. Nettie was up and around beginning to try to fix something for supper. When she saw all the delicious-looking food Belle and Bonnie had brought, she almost wept. She kept going on about how they shouldn't have done so much but also how much she appreciated their doing it. They assured Nettie they were happy to help.

Belle said, "What are neighbors for if they can't lend a hand to somebody who needs help?"

Nettie said her son, Michael, and husband, Willard, were also "feelin' a tad better," were out of the house now, but would be back wanting supper around dark. She eyed the cake and said, "That's a mighty purty cake, and I know it'll taste just as good as it looks. I'm goin' to open some peaches to have with it."

She went into an adjoining pantry and came back carrying a jar of peaches she had canned last fall.

Belle said, "Here, Nettie, let me open that jar for you." She twisted the lid loose and took it off. In doing so, she splashed some of the liquid in the jar onto her fingers and quickly used her tongue to get it off.

This caused Belle to say, "Nettie, I believe these peaches have spoiled."

Nettie got a spoon, tasted the peach syrup, screwed up her face, and said, "They've spiled, aw right."

She quietly twisted the lid back on the jar, set it on a shelf near the table, and said with a mischievous grin, "I'll save these, an' when Willard comes home drunk some night an' wants somethin' to eat, I'll feed them peaches to 'im."

A few minutes later, Bonnie and Belle were getting ready to leave when two men, one older and one younger, came into the kitchen from the porch. Both were dirty and badly in need of baths, shaves, and clean clothes. The sparse horseshoe band of mostly gray hair around the bald pate of the older man was filthy and stringy, as was the dark, bushy mane of the younger one. Both men just nodded to the ladies, saying, "How do," and tramped on into the front room.

As she watched her son slouch slowly into the next room, Nettie shook her head and said, as if to herself, "I vow. That boy is so slow he acts like dead lice is fallin' off of 'im."

Then to her guests she said, "That's Willard and Michael. Hope you'll s'cuse their bad manners and messy looks."

The visitors bade Nettie good-bye, and she thanked them again for the food. She said she should be able to cook for the family in a day or so. As she rode back toward Creedy, Belle voiced how sorry she felt for Nettie Hawkins, for the hard life she had, and for the men she had to put up with.

Belle then asked, "Did you ever see anybody look as dirty and scroungy as those two men did? 'Pon my word 'n honor, they both smelled like kyarn."

Bonnie smiled and agreed with Belle.

Then Belle added, "I know they're poor as Job's turkey, but that's no reason for them to be so filthy!"

From the time Raphael Hawkins was old enough to be in school, his mother had pleaded with him to get an education and not to follow in the footsteps of his two older brothers by quitting before they finished elementary school. Rafael had apparently taken his mother's pleas to heart, because he finished seventh grade and entered high school. By this time, Rafael appreciated the taste of, and resulting good feelings caused by, the family's moonshine; he had also seen how it had affected his father and two brothers. He decided he would never let himself be controlled by moonshine or any other form of alcohol.

Rafael, who preferred to be called Rafe, had gone to a different elementary school than Cecilia Massey had; but in town one Saturday with his mother and father, he first saw her. He was twelve then and Cecilia was ten. Rafe thought then that she was the prettiest girl he had ever laid eyes on. To use one of his pap's expressions, she was "as purty as a speckled pup." Rafe had seen Cecilia several times over the next four years, saying "Howdy," or having all too brief exchanges with her until his second year in high school. That was the year Cecilia was a Creedy High freshman, and Rafe was thrilled that he could see her and be near her every school day. He had become enthralled with Cecilia.

Rafe seized on every opportunity he had and created as many more as he could to be near her. He was jealous and overly possessive of Cecilia.

Cecilia was an outgoing, kindhearted young lady, and she didn't want to hurt Rafe's feelings. And even though she and many of the other students at the high school knew about his family and about the illegal "stills" they operated, Cecilia was not rude to the smitten lad. In a way, she felt sorry for Rafe because of the family situation he was in. She talked with him, let him join in as groups of boys and girls, enjoyed various school and church activities. Even though Rafe asked for dates or asked that just the two of them go to a show at the theater or to this gathering or that meeting, Cecilia always turned him down as tactfully and painlessly as she could. She had never been rude to him, but she didn't ever agree to be alone with him. But Rafe didn't give up.

In the fall of the current school year, Cecilia's brother, Luke, entered Creedy High School as a freshman. Rafe noticed that Luke seemed to be a loner; he appeared not to have friends at school and acted as though he felt left out or not accepted there. Luke's lack of friends gave Rafe an idea of how he might get to be around Cecilia more. He befriended Luke and went out of his way to get Luke to feel indebted to him. He praised Luke, fed his ego, and convinced the boy that he was Luke's best friend. The ruse worked, and quickly Luke saw Rafe as his best friend and was especially pleased about this because his new friend was a senior while Luke was a lowly freshman.

The upshot of this new friendship was that Rafe was often at the Massey house after school and on weekends. Luke often brought Rafe to their house before or after a picture show, to eat a meal, to go fishing or hunting, or to play rook or checkers. Occasionally he even spent a night with the Masseys. This was just what Rafe had hoped would happen. He now had opportunities to be around Cecilia much more than he ever had prior to taking Luke under his wing. Cecilia was not pleased with this new development, but she would not do or say anything unkind to hurt Rafe's feelings.

At first Cecilia had complained to her mother about Rafe being at their house so much, but Maddie said, "Oh, Cecilia, don't be such a crab. Luke enjoys having Rafe here, and from what I've heard about his family, Rafe probably needs to be exposed more to how other people live. He's not going to bother you. He's Luke's friend."

So Cecilia had stopped complaining to her mother about Rafe. Now she tried to be in her own bedroom most of the time when Rafe was around.

It was no accident that Maddie had "bumped into" Verle in town one day and told him she needed help in repairing a pasture fence that crossed a creek on her property—a watergap, she called it. She asked if he could help her. Verle was eager to accept her invitation, and on the following Saturday, he arrived at the Massey farm in the middle of an uncommonly warm afternoon under a sullen, threatening sky. Maddie came out to meet him, but she wasn't dressed in the work clothes he expected to see her in. She wore a pale blue, form-fitting dress that set off her blue eyes and blond hair with a sweater over the dress. *She looks lovely,* Verle thought, but his words were, "You don't look like you're dressed to work on that watergap you mentioned a couple of days ago."

Maddie replied, "We'll get around to that in good time. Let's go have some coffee before we get to work."

With that she took Verle by the hand and led him into the kitchen where the aroma of perking coffee filled the room. She removed her sweater, giving Verle an even better perspective of her full, rounded breasts.

Maddie said, "You go on into the front room and rest on the sofa while I get our coffee ready." Verle did as she suggested. Then she came into the room with two steaming cups of coffee, handed one to Verle, and sat down close beside him on the couch. *Dang, she smells as good as she looks today,* Verle thought as the coffee cup tremored slightly in his hand.

The two sipped coffee and tried to make small talk. Then rumblings of winter thunder came rolling in from the west, and rain started pattering on the metal roof, softly at first, but quickly increasing to a steady, heavy rain. "Well, no outside farm work today, Mr. Thacker," Maddie said, seemingly pleased.

"Maybe there are some chores or something I can do in the barn, since we can't work outside," Verle replied as he placed his empty cup on a table.

Maddie set her half-drained cup beside his and said in a low, sultry voice, "I think we can find something to do without going to the barn."

As she ended her comment, she took his hand in both of hers and slid her body over against his. She looked at him with widened eyes and said, "There's something I've been wanting you to do for me for quite a while, and this seems like the perfect time for it."

Now, with his eyes wide and not quite believing what he was hearing, Verle said, "You mean you want to . . . you want us to . . ."

"Yes, Verle, honey. I want you to make love to me."

"Here? Now? What about Cecilia and Luke?"

"They've gone to the afternoon shows in town, and they won't be back here until after dark. We've got the place to ourselves, so let's not waste this opportunity with any more talk."

With that she leaned against him with her breasts rubbing his chest as she wrapped her arms around his neck and placed a long, deep, passionate kiss on his eager and accommodating lips.

When the kiss ended, Maddie stood and tugged at Verle. He stood also, and she realized that the man was as excited and aroused as she was. Taking him by the hand, she said, "Follow me," and led him down the hall to her bedroom.

Verle closed the door as he entered the room.

CHAPTER 17

Early 1943

When Verle left Maddie's house, the rain had stopped; that fact hadn't registered on him until now. Chilly blue skies held only scattered wispy clouds, and the weak February sun hung two fingers above the horizon as he drove slowly toward his home. *What happened back there?* he thought. Oh, he knew what he and Maddie had done; who could forget that? He would probably never forget it, but what did it mean? Was his life going to change? How would this affect the woman he had vowed to love and cherish "until death do us part"?

Verle arrived at home and was surprised when he entered the kitchen. Lucille was busy, apparently preparing a meal—something she had done little of in recent weeks. With a forced smile at her husband, she asked, "Where've you been? I didn't know you were going to be away today."

Seating himself in a table chair, he said, "Just went to help a neighbor a while."

"Johnny Deskins? Or Harold Kegley?"

"No, Lucille, neither of them."

"Well, who then, Verle? Why the mystery?" Lucille demanded as she stopped stirring in a pot and looked at him with a puzzled, questioning expression, perhaps fearing to hear his answer.

After a pause, Verle lifted his eyes from the floor to face her and said, "I went over to help Mrs. Massey with a couple of small jobs."

"Widow Massey! Oh, I see."

She knows, Verle thought. Not wanting to talk more right now, Verle asked, "What's for supper?"

Lucille didn't respond as she continued to stir the simmering pot on the cook stove. She finished preparing their meal and put it on the table. They ate without conversation.

After Lucille finished her meal, she said, "I don't feel too good, so I'm going to have to lay down. Can you clean up here in the kitchen?"

And without waiting for a response from her husband, she turned and walked slowly to her bedroom as her eyes seemed vacant, unseeing.

A day passed. Two days. Three days. Verle had been sleeping on the couch in the front room, and he hadn't seen Lucille out of her bed. He had scraped together a couple of meals and had eaten some with his mother in her cottage behind the house. He told Clarissa that Lucille was in a bad state again and didn't feel up to cooking.

Lucille was deeply despondent. She must be eating when he was out of the house, because Verle found dirty dishes left on the table and cook pots with leftovers still in them. When he came into the bedroom and spoke to her, she just gazed at the wall, seeing nothing and saying nothing. Little Handsome was always at her side. Verle tried to remember each day to put out food for the dog and to let it out of the house for a few minutes each morning and night.

Verle felt bad about the way Lucille was taking what she had correctly assumed was going on between him and Maddie. He was sad about a lot that had happened to Lucille and him. He regretted that their child had died as a tot. He regretted that they were unable to have more children. He regretted that Lucille grew so unhappy and despondent, and he regretted that his beautiful young wife became such an overweight woman that he felt no physical desire for her. Verle thought, *But I have many years ahead of me, and I don't want to spend them like a monk. And Madeline Massey is an attractive, enticing woman who seems to enjoy lovemaking as much as I do. I'm not sure I could stop seeing her if I wanted to, and right now I don't want to.*

Over the next couple of months, Verle paid more visits to Maddie. If Cecilia or Luke was at home when Verle was there, he and Maddie always tried to make the visit appear to be just one of a neighbor helping a neighbor with some farm task. When he saw Cecilia, she usually gave him a cheery smile, but Luke continued to be sour and disrespectful with him. Maddie suspected, though, that her son and daughter had at least an inkling of what was really going on between her and her helpful farmer neighbor.

Rafe Hawkins had been at the Massey house once or twice when Verle had been there, and he also might have guessed what the relationship really was between the two neighbors. And in the few times he had seen Rafe around Luke and Cecilia, Verle had seen enough to assume that the main reason—perhaps the only reason—Rafe tried to act as Luke's good friend was so that he could be at the Massey house, near Cecilia. To Verle, it was obvious that Rafe wanted desperately to be her boyfriend.

Verle decided that he loved Maddie, but he could not bring himself to leave Lucille. What would she do if he left her? Maddie was enjoying her intimate physical relationship with Verle, and she wanted it to continue, but her primary interest in him was in getting access to his property and especially to coal on Thacker property and the mineral rights he held to coal on her property. In one of their most recent trysts, Maddie had mentioned to her lover how wonderful it would be if they could be together all the time. Verle had responded that he couldn't abandon his wife. She had never intentionally done anything to betray him or give him cause to put her aside.

March 1943 went out like a lion, with piercing winds and small bits of snow that stung whatever man or creature had to be outside. Now, on April Fool's day, Verle was in the kitchen of his widow, merry Maddie Massey. Today, though, she wasn't especially merry. She and Verle had been talking about their future, and she had questioned whether they actually could have a future together. She had pointed out to Verle that she didn't like an arrangement where she got to be with him only when he sneaked away from his wife, even though Verle said he was sure Lucille knew about his ongoing escapades with Maddie.

She asked, "Verle, how can we be happy living like this, having a little time together once in a while?"

Verle answered, "Maddie, honey, I know this isn't the best way for us to enjoy being together, but it's better than not being with each other at all, isn't it?"

"Sure, it's better than that. But it's not near as good as it could be. Not as good as it would be if we got Lucille out of our lives."

"Well, I think she's going to be in our lives a long time. She's not a healthy woman, being so overweight and all, but I don't think she'll be leaving this earth anytime soon."

"You never can tell, though," Maddie replied. "You say she is unhappy and despondent and feels she doesn't have anything to live for. Why not help her end her misery?"

"What are you sayin', Maddie?"

"I'm saying just think about how good it would be for you and me if Lucille wasn't in the picture anymore. Plus, our two farms would support us well, and you wouldn't have to be concerned about money all the time the way you are now."

"Is this your cruel idea of an April Fool's joke?"

"No, it's not a joke, but you may turn out to be the fool if you stick by your wife."

"I can't believe you're saying we should do away with Lucille. That's just plain wrong, Maddie, that's all wrong. How could I ever do that to the woman I married and made vows to?"

"Verle, Lucille now isn't the same Lucille you married. Can you honestly tell me she's the same pretty, desirable young woman you married?"

Staring at the floor, Verle could only shake his head. Whether in disbelief at what Maddie said or in response to her question, Maddie couldn't tell, but she said, "Of course, you can't."

Abruptly, Verle came to his feet and said, "I've got to go home. I'll see you soon."

Maddie stepped in front of him, put her arms around his neck, and kissed him. "You think about what I said, Verle."

Verle left her without replying. As he made his way toward home, he couldn't get out of his mind the unthinkable solution that Maddie had proposed to solve the problem that kept them apart.

Cecilia had known perfectly well for some time what was going on between her mother and Verle Thacker. While she didn't think it was right, her mother seemed to be happier than she had been for a long time; and Mr. Thacker seemed to be a nice man, though a married one. Cecilia had heard a truck pull up near the house and stop, and she thought it might be Mr. Thacker. She read a few more pages in the book on her lap and decided she would go say hello to the neighbor if he was the one visiting.

Cecilia had opened her door and started down the hall toward the kitchen when she heard part of Verle and Maddie's conversation. She stopped dead still in the hallway. She heard her mother say something about *helping her out of her misery* and something about Lucille *not being in the picture anymore.* Verle had said something, including *doing away with Lucille* and then *wrong, wrong.* Cecilia heard clearly her mother's last statement asking Verle to think about what she had said. The girl turned and hurried back to her bedroom and closed the door. She thought, *What have I just overheard? Is Mother trying to convince Verle to kill his wife? Surely not. I must have missed the main point of their conversation.* Then she remembered her daddy being in that kitchen the last time she had heard or seen him, and her memory of him stopped there. Although something more seemed to be trying to push into her consciousness, it couldn't or she wouldn't allow it to emerge.

Two days after her conversation with Verle about his wife, Maddie drove out the lane toward the Thacker place to see if Verle was working near the house. Before she got near the dwelling, she noted that his truck was gone, so she turned around and headed on toward Creedy to pick up groceries and a few items needed for the farm. As she drove into town, she was pleased to see Verle loading onto his truck the last sack of what appeared to be fertilizer.

She stopped beside his truck and waited until he turned around and saw her. She smiled at him and he walked over, bent with his hands on the car door, and looked at her with eager eyes but no hint of anything more on his expressionless, handsome face.

Maddie said, "Verle, we need to talk. I've got to buy a few groceries and some nails and steeples at the hardware store. Please drive out to my place. Cecilia and Lucas are in school now, so we won't have to be concerned about them hearing what we talk about. Will you do that?"

"Yes."

"Good. I'll see you in a few minutes."

About fifteen minutes after Verle pulled his truck in at Maddie's, the widow pulled in also. She got out of the car with a box of groceries in her arms and said, "Come on in, honey."

They hung their coats on pegs near the kitchen door and went into the front room. Before Verle could sit, Maddie was in front of him, holding his face and kissing him. His arms went around her and drew her to him. What happened next was what had happened for the last several times they had come into this room. When their happening ended, they came back to the front room couch and sat with Maddie snuggled against Verle and his arm around her. She looked at him and asked, "How was that?"

"You know very well how it was, Mrs. Massey."

"If we were married, that could be part of our enjoyment every day."

"Now, Maddie! You know I'm not free to marry you. I still have a wife. And what would Lucille do if I left her?"

Maddie jumped up with fire shooting from her eyes and fury in her face. She said, "In spite of the good times we've had together, I must not mean very much to you. I'm purely tired of us sneaking around to be with each other. If you're not man enough to do what must be done, I don't want you around this place ever again."

Verle was completely taken aback, and he sputtered, "Maddie, I love you, and I thought you—" but Maddie cut him off in midsentence.

"I do love you, Verle, but it seems like you're not willing to do what we both know has to be done so we can be together all the time. Please, just leave now."

"But . . . but, Maddie, I . . ."

"Just go, Verle."

Verle slouched out of the room looking like a cowering, whipped dog with its tail between its legs. He got his coat and left the kitchen. Maddie watched her dejected lover leave, and she cracked a smile as he climbed into his old Ford truck and pulled away from the house. *Well, Verle,* she thought, *it's up to you now*.

As Verle drove slowly toward home, he was thinking, or at least coming as close to thinking as he could come, given his agitated and discouraged state of mind. *Lucille or Maddie? How can I betray Lucille? But how can I live without Maddie?* By the time he reached his house, he had decided what he must do. "May the Lord have mercy on my soul," he breathed. Then he thought, *But it's not likely he will.*

CHAPTER 18

April, May 1943

Verle and some of his neighbors who raised sheep were losing lambs, and occasionally a ewe, to what seemed to be a pack of five or six feral dogs that apparently hid out somewhere in the woods, probably in one of the laurel thickets scattered among the many coves and hollows in nearby mountains. Verle had talked with Harold Kegley and Calvin Hess, and they had decided the dogs had to be destroyed some way.

The problem was that the dogs almost always raided the sheep at night and usually at a different farm each night. Even though some farmers had waited with rifles or shotguns, the dogs didn't cooperate by visiting their flocks. The three men decided they should try to poison the dogs if they could locate where the dogs bedded down at night or what paths they traveled most, and Verle said he would look around to see if he could find where the dogs holed up. Beyond that, they made no specific plans.

Clarissa Thacker fed her son a small, simple supper, and as they ate, Verle told her about the lambs he and other farmers were losing to the pack of dogs and about maybe trying to poison them. As he was finishing his coffee, he said, "Ma, what kinds of herbs or plants could be used to poison the dogs?"

Clarissa thought for several long seconds before she answered, "There are several plants or seeds that would do what you want if you could get the dogs to eat them. Jimson weed, foxglove, and monkshood plants could kill dogs, and seeds from castor bean plants would also work. But it's too early in the season to find most of these plants. If you didn't already know where jimson weed grows, it would be mighty hard to find this early."

She paused, pursed her lips, and seemed to be in deep thought. Then she continued, "I can't remember ever seeing the deadly nightshade or monkshood growing anywhere in these mountains and fields. Castor beans can't be harvested until late summer or fall, and the few I have for planting this spring wouldn't be enough to do what you need. But even if you could find what you need, how could you get dogs to eat these poison plants? That's a big problem."

Verle asked, "So you don't think we can get the dogs with plants or herbs or seeds?"

"I doubt that you can, but there's another way that might work."

"What's that, Ma?"

"It might be better to use poison toadstools. You can probably find them now or real soon. Then you could cook them in butter or lard. That would make the dogs want to eat the toadstools, or mushrooms, as many folks call them, and you could combine them with some other kind of food the dogs would like to eat."

"Do you know what these poisonous mushrooms look like?"

"I do, and I think I know where some of them grow. They're called death caps. If I'm not mistaken, I've seen some growing in a place I've been to several times."

"Good, we need to get rid of the dogs as soon as we can. None of us can afford to have more lambs or ewes killed. How soon can we gather the toadstools?"

"Let's see, this is the last week of April. Unless we have some cold nights, the stools ought to be up within another week, by the tenth of next month at the latest."

The Thacker farm was in the approximate middle of the farms where the dogs had killed stock, so Verle thought maybe the dogs holed up in some secluded spot on his acreage and roamed out from there to do their damage to the sheep flocks. He decided to spend two or three days looking for some sign of where the dogs bedded down to rest during daylight hours between raids. Carrying his rifle, he rode out one morning on his chestnut gelding to search for places he thought the dogs might frequent. He looked in hollers, coves, blackberry briar patches, and laurel thickets. He looked under cliff overhangs, what some folks called rock houses. An hour before sundown, he had found nothing to indicate where dogs or any other animals had made their beds, so he made his way back home.

The next morning, Verle rode out on his horse again, searching for signs of the dog pack. After riding and searching almost four hours, Verle neared another thick growth of mountain laurel in a cove near the edge of the National Forest boundary. The dark green leaves shone as if they had been waxed, and fat buds would turn into pretty white and red "peppermint" blossoms in a month or less. He still carried his rifle but knew if one of the dogs spotted him, the pack would disappear into the dense thicket before he could get off a shot. As the horse walked slowly toward the laurel, he perked his ears forward, responding to some sound his rider hadn't heard. Verle stopped the horse with a brief tug on the reins, dismounted, and walked silently toward the edge of the dense growth about twenty yards away.

He heard movement against brush, leaves, something. He stopped, examining the edges of the growth for the two or three feet he could see back into it. In one spot he saw something move. He lifted his rifle, ready to fire. Then he could make out in shadows the head and shoulders of a dog, apparently sleeping while rustling sounds behind it continued. Verle could shoot the dog, probably kill it, but the others would disappear and might not return to the place where one of their pack had been shot. So he lowered his rifle and backed noiselessly away. He led his horse back down the sloping glen. He knew where the dogs were now, where they felt safe enough to nestle down in the leaves to sleep and rest. Now he knew where to bring the mushrooms.

Lucille's mental and physical states didn't improve much. She looked forlorn and dejected. Her skin was pale and pasty, she had large dark bags under her eyes, and her uncombed hair was frizzed and unwashed. She was, however, getting out of bed and coming to the table for supper, but only occasionally did she do any cooking. Little Handsome accompanied his mistress everywhere she went, and she patted and caressed him lovingly. Verle did most of the cooking; Lucille did most of the eating.

The nights remained warm, and by the end of the first week of May, Verle and his mother were on their way to look for mushrooms. Clarissa was not able to walk the distance they had to go to reach the place she had in mind, so Verle took his mother on a small sled pulled by one of their horses to a secluded timbered cove where she had found mushrooms in past years. There she found an abundance of mushrooms—most were the tasty and distinctive edible morels. They found a few immature puffballs, also edible. They also found poisonous death caps.

Clarissa pointed out to her son distinctive features of the poison mushrooms by which he could identify them. Verle had decided, though, that he wouldn't get any of the poisonous mushrooms while his mother was with him, but he wanted to know what they looked like; he could come back by himself and get them. He said, "Ma, I'm not sure yet whether I should try to poison the dogs or not. Some of them might belong to neighbors. So let's just get morels today."

Clarissa agreed but cautioned her son, "Now if you ever get any of these death caps, you be certain to take care with them. A cupful would probably kill several dogs."

She thought for several seconds and continued, "According to tales about people who have eaten the caps, they were quite tasty. Unfortunately, the people who ate 'em died. After symptoms of the poison start, it's too late to treat 'em."

She told Verle she had read about men who were murdered with death caps ages ago. "One of 'em," she said, "was a Roman emperor, one named Claudius, if I recollect right. Another one was a Catholic pope, and the story mentioned others, but I can't remember any other names."

Verle asked, "Ma, is 'death cap' the only name these toadstools go by?"

"No, they have some scientific name too. Let's see. I don't remember exactly, but it was something like 'amnita phallid' or something close to that. Don't matter what they're called, they surely can kill. So you treat 'em like the poison they are."

Suddenly Verle had a thought but was immediately horrified at his thought. Then he remembered his last words with Maddie, and especially her last words to him. He had not been with her since that day. Verle couldn't bear to think about his future without her, and he remembered what he had determined he had to do as he drove home that day.

He had tried to ease his conscience by telling himself that Lucille would be better off not living in the state she was now in, that she really would not have a life knowing Verle and Maddie spent so much time together. To Verle, eating mushrooms seemed to be the easiest, most painless way for Lucille to leave this earth. Since the poison in mushrooms was a natural substance, it shouldn't cause his wife any great discomfort or pain. Also, he reasoned, with mushroom poisoning, the cause of death would most likely not be determined. Verle now knew what he would do, and he had to do it in the next day or two. The two Thackers gathered more than a quart of morels and headed home.

After Clarissa was back in her cottage, Verle returned to the barn, unharnessed the horse that had pulled the sled, put a saddle on him, and rode again to where he and his mother had seen the death cap mushrooms. He gathered almost two pints of them.

On the morning after he and his mother had gathered mushrooms, Verle was in his kitchen preparing mushrooms for the wild dogs. He sliced and sautéed in lard more than a pint of the death caps. Then he mixed them thoroughly into two large pones of cornbread he had crumbled up. He rode his horse over the hill from his house and to the glen where he had found the dogs' lair. When he was about fifty yards away from the laurel thicket, he stopped his horse, dismounted, and carried the panful of cornbread and mushrooms.

Verle saw a large flat rock barely inside the thicket that must be the dogs' home ground, and there he spread the mixture. He threw a handful of it into the thicket to more quickly attract the dogs to the poisoned bait. Quietly he retraced his steps to his waiting horse and climbed into the saddle. Then a color that didn't fit in with the wooded area caught his eye. There sat a large dog with a brindle coat watching him. When it realized it had been spotted, the dog was off like a flash. "One of Harold Kegley's dogs, if I'm not mistaken," Verle said to himself. And he thought, *Harold's dogs must be part of the pack.* He hurried his horse back to his house where he had another cooking task facing him.

Verle knew Lucille liked fried mushrooms. He prepared her supper—buttermilk, a golden pone of cornbread, fried slices of cured pork shoulder meat, mashed potatoes, canned green beans, tender green onions from the garden, and a large serving of sautéed mushroom slices, at least a third of which were not morels. More cooked mushrooms were still in a skillet on the stove.

Lucille asked him if he wasn't going to eat supper, and he told her he had eaten a late dinner with his mother and wasn't hungry right now. "I might get me a biscuit with preserves before I go to bed," he told her.

Lucille loved the mushrooms but asked Verle about a slice that didn't look like a morel. Verle told her it was a slice from a couple of immature puffballs he found, and she said she liked them really well. She even asked for the skillet so she could pick out more of the puffball slices. She had no inkling that Verle had not gathered any puffballs.

Three days later, on Saturday, Lucille began having pain in her abdomen, diarrhea, and vomiting. She said, "Verle, I don't know what could have made me so sick. I guess I've just caught some kind of stomach ailment."

"Maybe Ma should come and check on you. She probably can give you something to make you feel better," Verle said.

"No, I don't want to bother her. She's not been feeling too good herself. Whatever I've got will pass soon, and I'll be okay."

As Lucille began to suffer the effects of the poison mushrooms, Verle was horrified. He had thought she would die quickly and painlessly. Instead she was wracked with flashes of pain in her belly. That afternoon he drove over to the Scotts' place and told them that Lucille was sick. When he got back from his trip, Verle could tell that Lucille was worse, so he brought Clarissa to see his wife. His mother made tea from dried goldenseal roots and leaves she had gathered last year, but Lucille drank only two or three swallows of it. Clarissa also managed to get some oak bark tea down the sick woman as well as a small amount of finely ground slippery elm bark powder in buttermilk. Lucille worried about Little Handsome, but Verle told her they would take good care of the little dog.

Within an hour after Verle got back home, Lucille's sister, Belle, and Charley, with his girlfriend, Bonnie McGraw, came to see Lucille. She was sick, but she knew them and tried to smile when she saw them at her bedside; she was propped up in bed with three or four pillows behind her head and shoulders. She hugged each of the three but clung tightly to Charley as she murmured, "My little Charley, my sweet little Charley. I'm so glad to see you."

When he straightened up after his aunt Luce released her bear hug, he saw that her eyes were brimming with tears and one or more had rolled down each cheek. His vision blurred from tears in his own eyes. Charley slipped quietly from the bedroom into the kitchen. He could hardly believe how bad his aunt Luce looked.

Belle was seated by the bedside holding one of Lucille's hands, hoping to comfort her. After a sharp, stabbing pain brought another moan from Lucille, she looked at her older sister with pleading eyes and asked, "Belle, honey, what's wrong with me? I've never felt like this before."

Belle didn't know what to tell her, so she patted her hand and said, "Shhh, just try to rest."

Lucille appeared to drift off to sleep, and after a few more minutes in the bedroom, Belle said they probably should leave; maybe Lucille could rest better without company.

By the next day, Lucille began to show jaundice—yellowing of her eyes, skin, and especially the roof of her mouth. Belle was back helping tend her sister, and she and Clarissa tried to get liquids into her; but she wouldn't or couldn't swallow them.

Later in the morning, Lucille's parents, Jesse and Estella Musick, and her brother, Woodrow, came to the house. After seeing Lucille and noting how bad she looked, her father and brother came out to join Charley and his dad on the front porch, all of them feeling helpless but wanting to be near Lucille. Ma Jess stayed inside. She wanted to do anything she could to help her daughter, but she also just wanted to be near her.

After initial small talk about weather and war and rationing dried up, Pa Jess said, "Charley, I reckon you know your aunt Luce sure sets a lot of store by you. You're just like a son to her, the son she never had."

"I know, Pa Jess."

"And she loved to tell about funny little things you did and said growin' up."

"Yep."

"I mind one she told about chickens. You remember that one?"

"No," Charley replied, "I remember some of the stories she told on me, but I don't recall one about chickens."

"Well, this one happened when she was still in high school, and you must have been about six. She was settin' on the porch with you and a chicken that was about half growed walked in front of the porch. It had lost most of its tail feathers, and Lucille said, 'Well, that's a pretty lookin' aspect.' The chicken walked out of the yard, and you didn't say anything then. But in a few minutes, another chicken came along, and it looked about as bad as the first one, with missin' tail feathers and all.

Before Lucille could comment about it, you said, 'Aunt Luce, there's another one with its ass pecked.' Lucille always got the biggest kick out of tellin' that story."

They were silent for a while, and then Pa Jess said, "Lucille also cried when you cried. Remember that little duck you had?"

"Yes, I do remember Paddle and what happened to him," Charley responded.

"Aunt Luce cried as much as I did, I think. I was about seven years old then."

"Yeah, that was his name. Paddle. And she did cry over that little duck."

Charley had a vivid memory of the little duck named Paddle. Verle and Aunt Luce had ducks, and this little duckling's mother had died or got killed. So one weekend at Aunt Luce's, Charley had it in the house while it was still a small, fluffy, yellow ball—no feathers on it yet, just downy fuzz. Sometimes he took Paddle out of its box and let it waddle around in the kitchen. That Saturday his aunt and uncle went to town and left him at home. Charley got the duckling out of the box and turned it loose in the kitchen.

As Charley moved around in the kitchen, and, being unaware that Paddle was near him, he stepped on it and killed it! He was heartbroken. Charley was keeping the fire going in the cook stove because the weather was cold. He decided he had to do something with the duck's body right away, so he cremated it in the cook stove fire. In his mind, Charley could still smell the sharp, acrid odor of the burning fuzz and flesh of the little bird. The four men continued to remember other episodes—some happy, some sad—involving Lucille and her family.

Another night and day passed, and Belle and Clarissa Thacker decided they needed to have Dr. Easton there to treat Lucille as soon as possible. Charley told them that Doc had been called to treat an injured miner at Spring City. Belle knew her sister needed more than the Herb Woman could do for her, so she asked Verle if he would drive over to the little clinic in Spring City and tell Doc they needed him here with Lucille. Verle was glad to do something to get away for a while.

Lucille's diarrhea continued, and by the time Doc arrived, she was producing no urine. She began having seizures. Doc arranged a saline drip into her arm to try to rehydrate her. What medications the doctor managed to get down Lucille had no effect. Doc was afraid that whatever was afflicting the woman had already damaged, or maybe even shut down, her kidneys and liver.

When Verle got back to his house with Doc Easton, he went outside through the kitchen door so those gathered on the front porch wouldn't see him. He hurried to the barn. There he saddled his chestnut and rode quietly away, going where he had left the poisoned cornbread for the dogs. All of the mixture had been eaten by something. He heard noise a little ways back in the laurel growth and went to check on it. He found two dogs that were apparently dying; they were obviously in great pain—whining, writhing, whimpering, trying to vomit but had nothing more to bring up. And there was much evidence of vomiting and bloody diarrhea in leaves around the two dogs. Other dogs must have been sick here but had moved farther back into the thicket to die.

When Verle had arrived, another dog bolted from the thicket, showing no apparent signs of sickness. He thought it was the same brindle dog he had seen the day he left the poisoned cornbread. The other dogs apparently had eaten all or most of the cornbread before this dog got its share. Verle couldn't stand to watch the dying dogs any longer, so he left quickly. He was horrified that the dogs apparently had suffered so much, and he was even more distraught over what he had done to his wife. Lucille must be going through the same kind of agony. He thought, *What have I done? I have to talk to Maddie about this.*

Verle waited until darkness fell before he came back to his house; instead of going inside, he hopped in his truck and drove away. To Maddie Massey's house. He had not been near Maddie since the night she had asked him to leave, but he had to talk to her now. As he arrived, a face peered out the kitchen window briefly and was gone. Looked like Cecilia. Verle knocked on the kitchen door, it opened, and there stood Maddie looking fresh and vibrant. On this visit, though, he was in the mood for nothing more than talking with her. His first words were, "Maddie, we've got to talk."

Maddie's response was to kiss him lightly on the lips and with exaggerated pique said, "Well, I'm happy to see you too, Verle."

When Cecilia had looked out the window, she saw Verle pulling to a stop at their house, so she walked quickly to her room. She heard Verle and her mother's first words to each other. She also knew she had heard interesting, maybe important, conversations between the two on past occasions. In bare feet, she moved silently along the hall and stopped near the kitchen. She heard the conversation clearly.

Verle hadn't reacted at all to Maddie's kiss, so she was puzzled. "What's bothering you tonight, Verle? No hug? No kiss?"

Ignoring her questions, he asked, "Remember what you told me the last time I was here, Maddie?"

"Yes, I do, honey."

"And I did what you said I had to do."

"Like you got rid of the sheep-killing dogs?"

"What do you know about the dogs?"

"I stopped by the Kegley's house today to visit with Betsy a few minutes, and one of Harold's dogs was in really bad shape. Harold said you all had talked about trying to get rid of dogs that had been killing lambs and sheep and that you discussed using poison. He said you may have put out poison and his dog may have got some of it. Harold said she had seemed to be in great pain, had diarrhea, and had been vomiting, then the dog began having some sort of attack, like seizures. He said soon she was lying stretched out on her side with her tongue lolled out and seemed more dead than alive. She was a big dog with a brindle coat, and I'm sure she was dead when I saw her. Harold has another dog that seems to be fine, though."

Verle thought, *The dog I saw today that ran away from where I left the cornbread must have eaten a smaller amount of bait and took longer to die.*

At that point, Cecilia changed her position slightly, and a floorboard made a small creak. Maddie and Verle's conversation stopped, and Cecilia scurried quietly back to her room but left her door open. She heard the kitchen conversation begin again but could understand only snatches of what was said. Part of what she heard Verle say was, "I did . . . doing away with her . . . and . . . will kill her."

Maddie said something, but Cecilia could make out only phrases. "Be better off" and "we'll be rid of her." Cecilia assumed they were still talking about Harold Kegley's dog, which Verle must have poisoned. Then she heard the kitchen door open, and both of them must have gone out on the porch because she couldn't hear any more of their conversation.

On the porch, Verle said to Maddie, "Lucille is going to be out of our lives. But now I wonder what kind of life I can have after what I've done."

"Buck up, Verle," Maddie responded, "just give yourself a little time and you'll be fine. After we marry, we'll have a good life together. Of course, we must wait a decent period of time after Lucille's death to marry. Betsy Kegley said your wife is bad off sick, so you better go on home now, you don't want someone to see you here tonight when your wife is ill."

With a good-bye peck on his cheek, Maddie turned and left Verle standing on the porch.

As Verle drove toward home, he realized Maddie had said "after we marry . . ." He thought, *I've not asked her to marry me, but it seems like she has it all planned.* When he got back home and went in the house, nobody asked where he had been. Everyone was worried about Lucille. Lucille looked terrible.

Verle asked how she was doing now. Belle told him, "She's real bad, but the seizures have stopped, at least for now."

Little Handsome wanted to be beside Lucille on the bed. He whined pitifully and nuzzled her unmoving hand and arm, wanting to be petted.

"Pore little feller," Pa Jess said once when he came in the room and saw the dog, "he knows there's somethin' not right with his mistress."

Charley had been appalled at how bad his aunt Luce was within so few days after she first got sick. He wanted to be near her as much as he could, but the next day he would have to be in court in Norton, probably all day, to testify in a libel case brought against an area newspaper, the *Norton Post*. He told his mother he would be back to see them late tomorrow if he could get away; otherwise, he would come by to check on his aunt sometime the next day.

Doc Easton was back by Lucille's bedside early the next morning. Lucille was delirious. Her blood pressure was dangerously low, and her heartbeat was erratic. The doctor said she needed to be in a good hospital, but as weak as she was, he didn't want to risk moving her to Bristol.

Late in the afternoon of the next day, Wednesday, Lucille went into a coma. Doc feared that fluid, possibly blood, had accumulated around her brain and was putting increasing pressure on it. Doc napped on a cot beside Lucille's bed and checked on her every few minutes, able to do little for her and feeling that whatever he did would have scant effect. At 4:20 a.m., Thursday morning, he checked the patient's pulse—she was dead. She had lived six days after the onset of symptoms. The doctor listed her cause of death as liver and kidney failure brought on by some undetermined condition or cause.

When Doc Easton stopped by the deputy's tiny office nook in the Town Hall building around nine o'clock that morning and told him that Lucille had died, Charley just couldn't believe it. *Not Aunt Luce! My second mother. She can't be gone. She's much too young to die.* The family grieved—Charley and his parents, his grandparents, his uncle Woodrow, they all mourned.

Little Handsome was obviously grieving for his mistress. With his tail drooping, he often traipsed listlessly from room to room in the Thacker house as if he was searching for Lucille. The little dog spent most of his days on Lucille's bed and his nights beside it, as he had done when she was alive. Lying with his head resting on his outstretched front legs, he usually moved only his eyes and occasionally whined when Verle came into the room. He now ate little and moved around only to go outside briefly morning and night and to pad from room to room in his search for Lucille.

By his body language, facial expressions, and unkempt appearance, Verle also seemed to be beaten, despondent, and downtrodden. His mother and his in-laws were concerned about him because of the apparent deep grief he was going through. Verle was grieving, but what was affecting him most was not grief: it was guilt. How had he ever come to the place where he could take a life—the life of one who had loved him and whom he had once loved and made sacred vows to love and cherish? His wife's death had been such a horrible, agonizing death; and he remembered again and again witnessing the suffering of two poisoned dogs. His wife had suffered the same dreadful torture. He had done this awful deed just to be able to have another woman, a more desirable woman.

After Cecilia Massey heard of Lucille's death and that Doc Easton wasn't sure what had killed her, she was alarmed and worried about the bits and pieces of her mother and Verle's conversation she had picked up the night before Lucille died. Had they been talking about a dying dog, as she had assumed, or were they talking about something or somebody else? *Do I dare mention this to anyone? But what do I really know? What can I do?*

CHAPTER 19

June to September 1943

Charley tried to stay busy, more to keep his mind occupied with something other than the death of his aunt Luce than the official need to do something. Many friends and neighbors attended Lucille's funeral service at Clinch Missionary Baptist Church. Burial followed in the small cemetery beside the church. Charley's parents, grandparents, and Bonnie tried to ease his sorrow and feeling of loss, but they knew this would be something only he could work out for himself.

What was so hard for Charley to accept was that his aunt died so soon after becoming sick and that Doc Easton didn't really know what caused her death. Doc had suggested that they have an autopsy done to determine cause of death, and Charley agreed it should be done. His mother, grandparents, and Uncle Woodrow hated the idea of having an autopsy done, but they realized that was the only way they might know what killed Lucille. So they too wanted the autopsy. Verle, however, would not agree to the procedure. He said Lucille was gone; having an autopsy couldn't help her, and he didn't want to even think about what would be done to her body if there was one. Belle wondered, *Is there some other reason Verle doesn't want an autopsy?* Charley, the doctor, even Verle's mother tried to convince him to agree to an autopsy but to no avail.

Charley talked with Sheriff Fielding about his aunt's death, telling him her death didn't feel right, didn't seem to be logical. Harg asked, "Charley, are you sayin' you think your aunt didn't die from natural causes?"

"Harg, I don't know if that's what I think or feel or not. It's just that something doesn't seem right. And this is the second mysterious death we've had in eight months." Charley had an additional thought that he didn't want to share with the sheriff yet. *Could there be any kind of a connection between Sol Massey's death and Aunt Luce's? Surely not, but I have to keep that in mind as a possibility.*

"I think I know somethin' about your feelin's for Lucille and how she felt about you. And I know her death is hard for you and your family to come to grips with, but I've talked to Verle, to his mother, to your parents and grandparents, and to Doc Easton. From what they've all told me, there's nothin' to point to as probable cause of death other than natural causes."

In another talk with Doc, Charley heard nothing that he and the sheriff didn't already know. Clarissa Thacker was still visibly shaken and emotional about Lucille's death, and she expressed to Charley her deep regret that she had been unable to help his aunt. Clarissa didn't tell him any more than he already knew about Lucille's sickness and death.

When the deputy asked Verle if he could tell him anything else about his wife's sickness, Verle said, "Charley, I understand that you and Lucille were very close, much closer than most aunts and nephews. But I don't know anything else to tell you. She was my wife, but she's gone. And all the talking in the world won't change that. So let's just stop talking about why and what. That don't matter now. I don't want to talk about what made her sick, what killed her. So just drop it. For my sake. Please."

But the nephew couldn't just drop it. A talk with Delbert Kent, the mortician, regarding what he had observed about Lucille's body gave Charley nothing new. Of course he and Bonnie discussed the symptoms he had observed in his aunt as well as additional ones Doc had mentioned. Since Bonnie had a college degree in science and math, he hoped she might have some insight into what caused the symptoms. He told Bonnie the symptoms had included abdominal pain, vomiting, diarrhea, jaundice, seizures, delirium, and coma. Bonnie could offer no ideas of what might have produced these symptoms.

Several days after the funeral, Charley found a folded piece of lined writing paper lying in the front seat of his car. On the paper, in small, block, penciled letters, were the words "Lucille didn't die natural." He was excited. Maybe this was a break in the solid wall he had run into about the cause of his aunt's death. Charley showed the message to the sheriff, to his parents, to Doc Easton, and to Bonnie. None of them recognized the printing or had any notion of who might have left the message.

Charley thought, *Another dead end? Is this just a cruel prank by someone with a sick mind? No, I think this message has to mean something. Somebody knows something about my aunt's death, and they want me to know that they know. And it's my job to find out who. This makes me wonder all the more if Aunt Luce and Sol's deaths are connected in some way.* Over the next three months, he searched for anything that might be related to Lucille's death and the printed message and for any inkling of her death being related to Sol's, but he learned nothing more of value.

Little Handsome seemed to be in mourning too. He was listless, uninterested in anything, ate only a few bites each day, and lapped in his water bowl occasionally. Verle left the dog in the house while he was away; when he returned to the house, he always found the little dog stretched out on the bed or the couch, just beside the spots Lucille had lain in her bedroom or sat in her front room.

While the little pet used to greet Charley happily, he seemed to not even notice the deputy now. Only when women came to the house did he show any kind of interest or activity. He responded to Charley's mother, Belle, to Mrs. Kegley, and to Ma Jess; but for some reason, he responded most vigorously and happily to Bonnie McGraw when she came with Charley for a visit with Verle or Clarissa.

On one of Bonnie's visits, Little Handsome came from the bedroom into the front room where Verle, Clarissa, Belle, Charley, and Bonnie sat.

Verle said, "I don't know what to do for the little mutt. He has no interest in me, and he barely eats and drinks enough to keep hisself alive."

The dog walked past Belle and Clarissa without seeming to notice them or to care they were in the room; he stopped in front of Bonnie, looked at her, wagged his tail half-heartedly, and gave a low, pleading whine. Bonnie reached down, patted his head, scratched behind his ears, and said, "Good boy," as she listened to Belle speaking.

Little Handsome jumped up on the couch beside Bonnie and whined again. As he nuzzled against her arm, he tried to get his head under that arm. Bonnie lifted her arm, and the little dog moved his head under it and rested his head on her lap as he gave a sigh of what might have been satisfaction.

Charley said, "Bonnie, I believe you have a friend there."

"Maybe so, poor little creature," Bonnie replied.

The little dog's head remained on Bonnie's lap until the time came for them to leave, when she gently moved his head and slipped out from under it. The pet whimpered and looked at Bonnie with a plea in his eyes, and they left the room with him still looking at her as if he was trying to get her to stay.

As Charley drove away with his mother and Bonnie in the car, he said to his girlfriend, "Aunt Lucille's little dog sure seems to have taken a shine to you."

Bonnie replied, "Yes, I feel so sorry for him. He seems lost without Lucille. I wish I could do something for the little critter."

"Maybe you can."

"What can I do, Charley?"

"You could take him home."

"Take him home? And do what with him?"

"Keep him. Make him your dog. I think that's what the dog wants. For whatever reason, he seems to have picked you as his next mistress."

"Do you really think I should?"

"Only if you want him."

"I'll think about it. But I would do it only if Mother and Daddy have no objections to having a dog in the house."

Belle interjected a comment, "Bonnie, if you want the little dog and do take him, it would be the best thing that could happen to him. He's so unhappy and forlorn now."

The next day Bonnie broached the subject of Little Handsome with her mother. Eleanor had no objections to bringing the little dog to live with them. She had seen the pitiful little animal after Lucille's death and felt sorry for him. She said she would talk with Bonnie's father about it too. If Brewster agreed, and if Verle wanted Bonnie to take the dog, she could bring it to their home. The upshot was that Brewster McGraw thought it was a fine idea for Bonnie to have the dog, and Verle was relieved to pass the responsibility for the pet to Bonnie. So Bonnie brought Little Handsome to live with the McGraws. It was obvious that, from the little dog's point of view, Bonnie was his mistress, and he seemed much happier now that she was.

The weeks passed into September with cool, sunny days and great temperatures at night for sleeping. But Clarissa Thacker was not sleeping well at all. She had slept well only a few nights since her daughter-in-law died, and her health was declining. Her Kegley neighbors heard that she was ailing, in addition to still having a hard time dealing with Lucille's death, so Betsy Kegley came over for a visit. Verle brought Betsy into the front room where his mother rocked slowly in her favorite chair, an old rocker that was a few years older than her eighty-nine years. He left so they could have their women talk. After a few minutes of talking about Lucille and her death, Clarissa asked Betsy about how she and Harold were getting along, and they chatted a few minutes more.

Then Clarissa asked her neighbor if they were still losing lambs and sheep to dogs. Betsy told her there had been no evidence of dogs getting into their sheep for more than three months. "But," Mrs. Kegley said, "one of our own dogs died, and that was more than three months ago too."

"What killed your dog?"

"We don't know. Harold thought it might have been some kind of poison, but he's not sure. He and Verle had talked about putting out poison to try to get rid of the dog pack killing sheep on farms around here, but Verle told Harold he hadn't bought any poison."

"Did you find your dog dead somewhere?"

"No, she came home bad sick and soon died there."

"How did the dog act before she died?"

"I didn't see her, but Harold said she was pitiful. She seemed to be hurting real bad. Then she had runny, bloody bowels and vomited. After that she had some kind of fits or seizures. Finally she passed out and was unconscious a while before she died."

"I'm sorry for your dog. Sounds like a terrible way for a dog to die."

"Yes, it was a terrible way for anything to die."

Betsy Kegley saw that Clarissa seemed to grow wearier as they talked, so she bade her neighbor good-bye and urged her to rest. After her visitor left, Clarissa sat in her stilled rocker with a worried look on her face, pondering what she had heard.

Within two days after Betsy's visit, Clarissa suddenly become quite ill. None of her home remedies helped, and when she finally agreed to have Doc Easton examine her, he couldn't do anything but try to alleviate the severe pain she was having in her distended abdomen. Belle Scott helped Verle take care of his mother. After a few more days, Doc told them that he believed Clarissa had a cancerous tumor and that it was in a greatly advanced stage. He said the cancer had probably spread to other organs. Then he told Clarissa. She said she had already decided the same thing and that she would just have to accept that it was the Lord's will to take her this way. Doc suggested surgery, but she was opposed and said it would do no good. The doctor tended to agree. Clarissa continued to worsen and weaken while the tumor in her belly grew.

Late one afternoon, Clarissa asked to talk with Verle alone. The others left the room, and Verle took a seat at her bedside. She mentioned the mushrooms they had found last spring and asked him if he had gathered any of the poisonous ones. Verle stared at his hands clasped in front of him, thinking, *Do I lie to her to protect her, to keep her from suspecting me, and to protect myself, or do I tell her the truth? She probably can't live much longer. She's always trusted me, and I've never lied to her about anything that matters. This is not the time to lie.* Verle raised his head, and his eyes met his mother's as he said, "Yes, Ma, I did."

"Did you feed them to the sheep-killing dogs?"

"I did."

"Did any of them die?"

"All or most of them must have died. There's been no more sheep killed since."

"Betsy told me one of their dogs died."

"Yes, it must've been running with the pack."

"From what she told me, it must have died a terribly painful death."

"Yes, Ma, it most likely did."

Clarissa reached out and patted her son's hand gently, nodded her head slightly, and closed her eyes. Verle sat for a few minutes before he left his mother's bed wondering what had gone on or was going on in her mind.

The next day Clarissa asked that her favorite young couple be brought to visit with her. Bonnie McGraw and Charley Scott arrived together in his car. They visited a few minutes, and after saying good-bye to Bonnie, Clarissa asked to talk to Charley in private. She asked if he had learned any more about his aunt's death, and he said, "No." Bonnie and Charley left.

Clarissa couldn't get out of her mind the fact that Lucille had got sick shortly after she and Verle had gathered morel mushrooms and when she had shown him the poisonous ones. She didn't know what symptoms would be caused by the bad mushrooms. But she couldn't forget the symptoms Betsy Kegley said their dog showed. She couldn't forget that Lucille showed many of the same symptons.

The next day, September 22, 1943, Doc Easton was with Clarissa, and she seemed to be nearing the end, taking short, rapid breaths, barely able to open her eyes. She whispered, "Doc."

The doctor said, "What is it, Clarissa?"

"Closer."

He bent close to her lips and listened intently as she whispered in his ear. Verle, Belle, and Betsy were in the room but couldn't hear what she said.

What only Doc heard was, "Verle . . . amnitas . . . caps . . . wild dogs . . . Harold's dog . . . tell Charley." Then she grew still, stopped breathing, and was burdened with the cares of this world no more.

The next day Doc Easton told the deputy what Clarissa had whispered to him as she was dying. Charley didn't know what to make of it. He mused, *Another puzzle? Or is this a piece of a puzzle? What do these words mean? Why were they so important to Clarissa Thacker that, with her last breaths, she left this message for me?*

The only Harold in the community that Charley knew was Harold Kegley, and he seemed to be the starting point in trying to figure out what Clarissa meant. He drove to the Kegley farm and found Harold working in a shed, putting a new handle in an axe head. They chatted about the war, about rationing, and about what prices might be for tobacco this year. Finally Charley asked, "What can you tell me about wild dogs?"

"Wild dogs?" Harold asked with a quizzical look.

"Yeah, I know this may sound like an odd question, but I have my reasons."

"Well, I'll take your word for it. More than four months ago, I and three of the neighborin' farmers started losin' sheep and lambs to what we had reason to believe was a pack of dogs. We thought they were probably wild dogs. I talked with Verle Thacker and Calvin Hess about how we could get rid of 'em. We discussed poisonin' 'em but never got around to decidin' for sure what we ought to do."

"Why didn't you decide to do something? Didn't the sheep killing just go on if you did nothing to the dogs?"

"No, we stopped losin' sheep no more than a couple of weeks after the three of us talked about it."

"Why do you think the killing stopped?"

"I just thought the dogs must've moved on to another area. For whatever reason, I was glad not to be losin' any more sheep."

"Do you have dogs?"

"I don't have dogs. But I do have one dog. I had two until almost four months ago. One of 'em died."

"When did your dog die? Was it before or after you were having sheep killed?"

"Let's see, I guess it was after the sheep killin'. I don't think any of us lost any more sheep after my dog's death."

"Do you think your dog might have been part of the pack?"

"I can't hardly believe she would've been. She was around our sheep and lambs a lot and never offered to hurt 'em. But I've heard that dogs runnin' with a pack will do things they wouldn't do by theirselves."

"Harold, your dog that died—what killed her?"

"That's somethin' we never learned. She just come in one day really sick, and after a while she was dead."

"How did she act before she died? While she was sick, I mean?"

Harold described the symptoms his dog had shown before she died. Charley got back in his car and made a few notes in a small writing pad, the same pad in which he had recorded Clarissa's whispered last words to Doc Easton. *What a riddle,* Charley thought as he looked at his notes. *How are wild dogs and Harold's dog connected to anything else that's important?*

CHAPTER 20

October to November 1943

Rafe hawkins was not living with his parents and two brothers after he got a job at the sawmill—a job doing much the same work Charley had done there a few years earlier. He lived in a room that adjoined the small office space beside the sawmill. The room was sparsely furnished; it had a cot, a tiny table, two straight-back oak chairs, a small stove, some wooden crates, and a few eating and cooking utensils. The mill owner let him stay in the room without charge, and it saved Rafe from having to travel to and from his parents' house each day. The owner liked having Rafe near the mill at night; he stored tools there. Even though the job was hard labor, Rafe's mother was proud of him. Proud that he was working full time; most of all, she was proud that he wasn't letting whiskey rule his life as his father and two brothers had. Nettie had great hopes that her youngest son would be a fine, honest man who would become a good husband and father.

For years, Rafe's father, Willard, had slapped and punched Nettie, his wife. He thought that proved his manhood and his control of the family. Nettie had no family she could go to if she left her husband; she had no way to live if she left the farm. For long years, Nettie had prayed that Willard would change, that he would stop beating her and treat her as a wife should be treated. And she had believed her prayers would be answered. Instead the abuses became more severe, and they came more often.

On a raw, windy day in early November, Willard Hawkins came home after again partaking of the fruit of his and two older sons' labors at their moonshine still. The severe beating he gave Nettie for no apparent reason that day left her with an eye swollen shut, bruised lips, a tooth knocked loose, and a deep gash on her cheekbone. Gabriel and Michael had not come home that night. The next morning Nettie dragged herself around trying to get breakfast for Willard. She walked over to the table and poured his cup of coffee. Holding the hot coffeepot with a tattered rag wrapped around the handle, she stood beside him and muttered through swollen, hurting lips, "Wonder how it'd feel if I jist dumped this coffee out on yer slick, bald head?"

Willard looked up at his wife. He saw no fear in her, just flint-hard determination. After a long look at her, he said, "Nettie, ya know better'n to pour coffee on me. Ya know what I'd do to ya."

With her one open eye, she looked directly into his bloodshot, shifty eyes and said, "Willard, hit's a pity. You've beat me fer years. There was a time I felt love fer you. I birthed yer sons. I've prayed fer you—prayed that you'd change and stop treatin' me worse'n most people treat a good-fer-nothin' dog or a stubborn mule. But fer some reason, the Lord haint answered my prayers. Now it's time fer me to do more than pray. I've decided I'm goin' to have to hep the Lord take care of me an' of you. So if you ever raise yer hand to me agin, I'll kill you."

Without blinking, she held his gaze and finally walked away. He waved a dismissive hand at her, poured steaming coffee from his cup into the saucer, and slurped it noisily.

Less than a week later, Willard climbed the porch steps and lurched through the front door; he was drunk and in a belligerent mood. As he staggered into the kitchen, Nettie was seated, peeling potatoes for supper.

"Why ain't supper on the table?" Willard yelled.

"Because it's not suppertime yet."

"Don't smart mouth me, woman," Willard screeched as he backhanded her across the face.

Nettie went sprawling, along with her overturned chair; potatoes, peelings, pan, and paring knife flew across the floor. As she began picking herself up from the floor, she wiped a hand across her bleeding lip, looked at her hand, and stared with cold fury at the man who had vowed to "love, honor, and cherish" her in a time that now seemed an eternity ago.

In a low, calm voice, Nettie said, "Remember what I told you the last time you beat me?"

Her husband hissed, "Shut up, woman. Don't give me none uh yer sass, er I'll fix ya worse'n I did last time. Now git my supper on the table. I'm hongry." Then he sat down at the end of the table.

Nettie walked out of the room, and as she left, Willard yelled, "Nettie, git back hyere."

With no emotion, she answered, "I'll be right back."

She was gone only a minute or so. Willard heard her footsteps coming back toward the kitchen, and he grinned an evil, triumphant leer as he said, "Hurry it up! I want my supper."

When he looked up, Nettie was standing less than ten feet away from him. His eyes bulged; his mouth flew open. She was holding his double barrel, 12-gauge shotgun. Both hammers were pulled back, and the black holes of the muzzle were trained squarely on him—staring at him like cold eyes of death.

Sputtering and stammering, Willard said, "Wha . . . what's wrong with . . . what do ya think yer doin'?"

"This," Nettie said as she pulled both triggers. The recoil of the gun almost knocked her down, and she dropped it. The blast tore a large, gaping hole in her husband's chest and knocked him and his chair backward. He was dead before his head bounced on the floor. She stared blankly at his body, showing no fright, no anger, no regret.

Nettie took off her apron, folded it neatly, and placed it on the kitchen table. She walked to the kitchen door, looked back at her dead husband, and murmured, "I told you."

She looked carefully around her kitchen, noting potatoes and peelings on the floor beside her overturned chair, the pot of soup beans on the stove, and in a cold skillet, pieces of streaked meat she had sliced to fry for supper. As she stepped out into the sunny but cool and windy November late afternoon, she wore no coat—just her plain, faded everyday dress and the frayed sweater she wore in the house. Stoically but purposefully, Nettie followed a steep path up a hill toward the ridge crest from which she would be able to see Drowning Creek.

At the top of the ridge, she stopped, held her wind-tossed hair out of her eyes with one hand, and looked around at the familiar mountains to the north, reassuring in their permanence, beauty, and serenity. To the south she let her eyes wander slowly over ordered, fenced farmlands where the railroad and Clinch River ran close together beside green pastures and harvested fields.

Nettie could see high stone palisades across the river; though she couldn't see the swinging bridge, she knew it crossed over the stream near that point. She imagined the roar of the Narrows just slightly downstream from the bridge. In happier times, before they married, she and Willard enjoyed the beach near the bridge and the sounds and sights of the river tearing through that narrow, boulder-choked water sluice. She saw Drowning Creek threading its way toward the river with rays of the setting sun glinting golden off its inviting waters. She could see the place she wanted. With a sigh of resignation mixed with relief, she began her descent from the ridge.

The following morning, Nettie's body was found at the end of a deep Drowning Creek pool. Her pale, bluish face revealed what had brought her to this place—a bruised and split lip, a cut on her cheekbone, and an eye still swollen with green and purple bruises around it. The blotch of a more recent bruise had started to show on one side of her face.

Late in the night—actually, in the wee hours of the morning—Michael Hawkins had come home. The kitchen door stood open, but it hadn't registered in his whiskey-deadened mind that this was unusual. He had gone directly to the bedroom where he and his two brothers slept when they were at home and fell onto his bed to sleep off his drunk, and he didn't stir from his bed until almost ten o'clock that morning. Neither of his brothers was in bed; Rafe was working and staying close to where he worked, and no telling where Gabe spent the night.

Mike lay in his bed several minutes, hoping his pounding headache would subside. He thought it odd that neither Pap nor Mam had roused him from bed much earlier. He decided he needed a cup of strong, hot coffee, so he sat up in bed and kept still for a while, trying not to make his raging headache worse. He was dirty. His long, unruly hair was greasy and stringy, and a razor hadn't touched his face the past week. Finally, with his eyes barely open, Mike lurched to his feet and headed to the kitchen for the coffeepot.

As he entered the kitchen, he noticed potatoes and peelings on the floor, then he saw the pan and overturned chair. *What has Mam done? Made a mess and left it on the floor?* Next he noticed another chair turned over at the head of the table; as he moved two more steps toward that end of the table, he saw his pappy. Pap was lying on his back with dark, dried blood on the floor around him and an area as large as a big plate torn deep into his chest.

Mike croaked, "Pap? Pap?" but he knew he wouldn't get an answer. He said to himself, "Who done Pap in?" and, "Where's Mam?"

Then he saw the shotgun on the floor. It was Pap's gun. He stumbled over to the gun, picked it up, opened it at the breech, and checked the shells in it. Both had been fired. He let the gun fall to the floor as he thought, *That's what killed Pap. But who?* He called out, "Mam!" He went to the door and yelled for his mother several times but got no answer.

Mike was still trying to find his mother when Gabe drove up in his battered old truck looking as filthy, unkempt, and repulsive as his brother. Mike hastily told Gabe what he had found inside. Gabe went into the kitchen and hurried back out, ashen faced and shaken. The two brothers couldn't agree on whether to notify the sheriff's office about their dead father and missing mother.

While they were trying to decide what to do next, Charley Scott pulled his car in behind Gabe's truck. Charley didn't relish the idea of being here alone with the two Hawkins brothers; he remembered the fight he had with Gabe on the riverbank about four years earlier and hoped he wouldn't have to fight either or both of the brothers today. This day wasn't for fighting.

The deputy got out of his car, and without moving closer to the brothers sitting in the yard, he said, "Mike, Gabe, I've got some really bad news for you and your daddy."

The only response he got from Mike was a sullen, disconnected stare. Gabe said nothing for several seconds then sneered, "Mr. Dep-uh-dee, ya may have some bad news fer me and Mike, but ya ain't got any kind uh news fer Pap. And whatever news ya have fer us ain't likely tuh be as bad as what we just seed."

"What do you mean, Gabe?"

"I mean my Pap's daid as a doornail. Blowed to kingdom come with a shotgun. Now, you got any news worse'n that?"

As Charley walked toward the brothers, he said, "Well, I'm afraid I do. Your mother is dead too."

After the Hawkins sons' surprised and uncomprehending reactions to Charley's news, he told them what he knew. Two boys, who had planned to spend their Saturday roaming along the banks of Drowning Creek and nearby hills, found the body of a woman in the creek not long after daybreak.

Charley said, "Sheriff Fielding and I came to where the body was and pulled it out of the creek. It was your mother. It's pretty clear that she drowned, but she had cuts and bruises on her face, and one eye was bruised and swollen. She had what appeared to be a more recent bruise on one side of her face."

As he had looked at the drowned woman at the creek, Charley mused, *Could this be the same pool where the woman and her baby died a century and a half ago? The tragedy that gave the creek its name. I wonder if Nettie knew the story of how the creek got its name.*

"Pore Mam, I shore hate tuh hyear of her crossin' over," Mike mumbled.

Charley continued, "Now what's this about your pap being dead?"

Gabe growled, "Pap's daid. Mam's daid. We'll take care of 'em, we take care of our own. The law don't have no bidness in the matter."

"I'm afraid it is business of the sheriff's office, Gabe. From what you've told me, two people are dead, and we'll have to try to learn how they died and why."

"You look hyere, Charley Scott, if ya think yer agoin' tuh come onta our land and inta our house agin our wishes, ya better think some more. Yer hyere all by yersef, and there's two of us. It won't be like it was on the river that day when ya coldcocked me with a rock. So ya just git in yer po-leece car and hightail it . . ." and his sentence faded out as Harg Fielding's car came to a stop behind Charley's.

Gabe thought, *Yer saved again, Charley Scott. But I'll have my chance. One of these days, I'll have ya with nobody tuh hep ya out. I'll fix ya then. I'll beat ya to a pulp. Might be nice too if that pyert little woman of yourn could be with ya. After I'm finished with ya, I could take my time and really enjoy 'er compney.*

Catching the glaring looks coming from the Hawkins brothers, the sheriff asked, "How are things here?"

The deputy responded, "We're doing fine, sheriff, but we've got more bad news. The boys say their pap is dead too."

"Oh, Charley, no! When did this happen?"

Gabe said, "Don't know. We just fount 'im a few minutes ago. He's in the kitchen."

The sheriff said, "We'll have to check this out. Gabe, you and Mike just stay out here while Charley and I go in and look around."

"Now, sheriff, me and Mike don't want y'all . . ."

Harg interrupted with, "Gabe, we've got two deaths in your family this mornin'. You don't have a choice. We're goin' to check this out. You two stay here."

The sheriff and deputy entered the kitchen, saw potatoes and peels and a small knife on the floor, two overturned chairs, the shotgun, and the body. They also noted a folded apron on the table and beans and frying meat on the cold stove; they examined the shotgun.

As they checked the body, Charley said, "He was probably no more than eight or ten feet from the shotgun muzzle when he was shot. And seeing how the blood has dried so much, he must've been shot several hours ago."

Harg nodded in agreement and said, "Looks like Nettie was fixin' supper when this happened."

He walked to the door and asked, "Do you all know who this shotgun belongs to?" The brothers looked at each other with blank expressions, but Mike finally said, "Yeah, it's Pap's."

Harg and Charley each made notes on what they saw and heard, and Charley retrieved a camera from his car and took pictures of the death scene. This was the first occasion for him to use one of the cameras the sheriff's department bought recently.

Gabe groused, "Ya got no right tuh take pitchers of my daid Pap for all the world tuh see. It ain't right!"

Sheriff Fielding said, "Gabe, these pictures will be used only in the investigation and as evidence if a trial is held. Otherwise nobody is goin' to see pictures of your dead daddy."

Still grumbling, Gabe walked away. After they finished their examination of the scene, the lawmen came outside to talk more with the brothers.

Harg asked, "Do either of you have any notion of who might have killed your daddy?"

Neither of them responded.

The sheriff said, "I b'lieve that if my parents had been killed, I'd want the law to do everything it possibly could to catch whoever was responsible. Unless—" Harg paused a few seconds, then continued "—unless I was the one that did the killin'."

Mike's drooping head popped up, and he asked, "What're ya sayin', sheriff? That one of us kilt Pap?"

"Just look at what we know. Willard was killed in his own house with a gun he owned. The only ones around when we got here are you two. Ever'body knows that the two of you drink too much and that you get mean when you're drunk. That makes both of you suspects. And I'm as sure as I'm standin' here that you boys know more about the killin' than you've told us."

Harg's words prompted the Hawkins brothers to tell him where they were last night and this morning, how Mike had found their daddy and the gun in the kitchen, and how Gabe had arrived at the house just a few minutes before Charley drove up. Both men said they hadn't moved anything, except that Mike had picked up the shotgun then dropped it on the floor where he had found it.

The sheriff said, "So I'll ask my question again. Do you have any idea of who might've shot Willard?"

Gabe sneered, "I ain't no highly trained po-leece man, but I think I alredy have a purty good idee who done the killin'.

"Who do you think did it?" Charley asked.

Without looking up from the ground in front of where he sat, Gabe queried, "Ya said Mam had cuts an' bruises an' a eye swoled up?"

"Yes, she did."

"I 'spect that Mam shot Pap an' then walked over tuh the creek an' drownded herse'f."

Charley gasped, "Good Lord, Gabe! Do you mean that?"

"Course I mean it. Wouldna said it iffen I didn' mean it."

"Why do you think that's what happened?" asked the sheriff.

Mike seemed to be becoming more aware of what was happening, and he said, "I'll tell ya what I think."

Gabe threatened, "You keep your mouth shut, Mike. What goes on in this family ain't no bidness of the law."

"Oh, Gabe. Mam and Pap's both daid, an' we're right smack dab in the middle of a mess. I reckon it's law bidness now, an' I reckon they need tuh know what I think happened." Gabe just sulked.

Sheriff Fielding urged, "So, go on, Mike. What do you think happened?"

Mike told them Pap beat Mam about a week ago, the worst beating he ever gave her. And he concluded his story to them with, "So I reckon he must've hit 'er again last night. That might be what caused the latest bruise you said you saw on Mam. Mam took Pap's beatin's fer yers, an' she prayed he'd stop doin' it. She pleaded with 'im not to hit 'er. But the beatin's only got worse. I b'lieve she just finely snapped. Couldn't let 'im beat on 'er no more. So she got the shotgun an' kilt 'im. I think that was the only way she could get 'im to stop beatin' 'er. Then she was in such a low state of mind that she drownded hersef."

Charley and Harg looked at each other solemnly, and each of them thought Mike might be right about what happened.

Then Harg raised a question. "Mike, why did you and Gabe and Rafe allow your daddy to beat your mother?"

The two brothers looked at him as if he had asked the stupidest of questions. Gabe said, "Why, he's our . . . he wuz our pappy. He wuz head of the house. We couldn't innerfere with what went on 'tween him an' Mam." The lawmen looked at each other and shook their heads in disbelief and consternation.

Charley asked the brothers, "Where's Rafe? He has to be told."

Mike replied, "I don't know 'zactly where he is, but he usually spends some of his Satadees over on the Massey farm. He's still tryin' to get that little gal to take to 'im."

The sheriff told them that he or Charley would get the bad news to Rafe and that the coroner would have to examine the bodies before they could be moved. He promised that the coroner would get to his parents as soon as possible and that the coroner, who was also the mortician, would take the bodies to the funeral home to prepare them for burial.

Belle and J. R. Scott believed in hard work, but they also enjoyed life and laughter when they had opportunities. Such an occasion arose when J. R. came home one Saturday afternoon after getting a haircut at Peg Honagger's barbershop in Creedy. Most of his customers didn't know his given name—everyone called him "Peg" even when they were talking to him. Peg had lost part of one leg; nobody knew how. He had a wooden peg strapped to his thigh. His wooden leg was just a plain piece of wood that was the approximate diameter of his leg below the knee, and it tapered down to about two inches in diameter at the end with a rubber tip on it. The wooden peg was not covered by his pants leg.

J. R. came into the kitchen to get a drink of water, and Belle asked him if there was anything new going on in town.

Her husband replied, "Ever'body at the barbershop was talkin' about Peg Honagger. He's been takin' that tonic we've heard about so much in the radio ads and newspapers. What's the name of it?"

"That N-Vigor?" Belle asked.

An over-the-counter tonic, N-Vigor, was being heavily marketed with claims that it was good for all kinds of problems and would do wonders for anyone who took the concoction.

"Yeah, that's it," J. R. said. "You know, they advertise that it has lots of different herbs in it and that it will do great things to make you feel better and younger. I guess it must be powerful stuff."

"Why do you say that?"

"Well, Peg has been takin' it, and now he has to keep a hatchet handy all the time to keep the sprouts knocked off his wooden leg!" They both had a hearty laugh.

J. R. also had a story about Belle that he enjoyed telling to anyone who hadn't heard it and sometimes to people he knew had heard it. One of Verle Thacker's cows developed a condition called "hollow tail." The home remedy for hollow tail was to split the cow's tail with a knife and rub salt in it. At the same time, a neighbor woman was sick. J. R. asked Belle what was being done to treat the ill woman. Belle misunderstood who her husband was asking about; she thought he was asking about

Verle's cow. So her reply was, "Oh, she should get better soon, they split her tail and put salt in it." J. R. got a good laugh from the story each time he told it, and Belle just shook her head.

Charley's parents, Belle and J. R., had always worked hard, served as workers and leaders in their church, and wanted to help anyone sick or down on their luck. They believed and tried to follow the Scriptures, including passages where Jesus said, "It is better to give than to receive" and "Inasmuch as ye did it not to one of the least of these, ye did it not to me" and "Thou shalt love thy neighbor as thyself."

The Scotts helped neighbors, friends, family, as well as strangers. Their help might be food for a family whose breadwinner was injured at work or a warm coat in winter for a child whose parents didn't have the money to buy one. They helped harvest corn and tobacco crops for a neighbor whose appendix had ruptured and who spent several weeks in a hospital in Bristol but survived in spite of his doctors believing he could not.

After Sol Massey's death, Belle and J. R. had offered to help Mrs. Massey and her two children with anything she wanted or needed, yet they never got an opportunity to help. They volunteered to harvest and shuck corn. They offered to help care for cattle, to fence, to cut winter firewood, and to do other farm tasks; they were always told, "Thank you, but we're doing fine. We'll get along."

J. R., Belle, and her parents tried to help Verle after the deaths of his wife and then his mother, but Verle seemed aloof, preoccupied. He conveyed to them the message that he would rather just be left alone. They never understood why neither Maddie Massey nor Verle would allow them to help in any way.

By words and deeds, Charley's parents passed along to him their commitment to serve and help others. Charley learned much from his parents and grandparents about how to treat people, and he tried to reflect his concern and compassion in the way he carried out his law enforcement duties. He could be understanding and helpful when the situation warranted, but he was firm and forceful when necessary, and he had an uncanny knack for knowing which approach to take in situations he faced as a deputy.

On his way to find Rafe and tell him his parents were dead, Charley wondered how the deaths would affect Rafe. Rafe was a Hawkins, but he seemed to be different from his two older brothers. And Charley knew that Nettie Hawkins had fervently hoped and prayed that her youngest son would be a much better man than his father and older brothers. He had no idea what Rafe's feelings might be for his mother.

When he arrived at the Massey house, Charley climbed the steps to the front porch and knocked on the door. Cecilia opened the door, and her eyes lighted up as she saw who was there. She had seen him often with her favorite teacher, Ms. McGraw.

"Hello, Mr. Scott, it's nice to see you," she said, smiling. Then a dark thought came to mind, and her look became one of apprehension. "Is anything wrong?"

"Yes, Cecilia. I'm afraid there is. Is Rafe Hawkins here now?"

"He and Luke just got back from fishing over at the mouth of Drowning Creek. Fishing wasn't very good, and the damp, chilly weather got to them. They're inside trying to get warmed up now. Won't you come in."

"Thank you, but it might be better if Rafe and I talked in private, at least at first. Would you tell him I need to talk to him."

"Sure, I'll tell him," she replied as she turned and walked back through the house.

After a minute or so, Rafe came to the door and out on the porch. "You wanted to talk to me, Mr. Scott?"

"Yes, Rafe. I've got some bad news for you."

"What have my brothers done now?" he asked, irritation showing in his voice.

"Let's sit, Rafe," Charley said, pointing to a chair as he pulled another close. Then he continued, "It's not about your brothers. It's your parents. Son, I sure hate to tell you this, but they're both dead."

The boy shot up out of his chair and exclaimed, "Dead? Both of them? How?"

"Yes," Charley replied, and he told Rafe where they found his mother and how she had been bruised and battered. Then he told the shocked boy how they found his father. As Rafe asked questions, the deputy filled in more details of what he knew about the deaths. Rafe had been leaning against a porch column most of the time with his head down and shoulders drooping.

After a minute or so passed with no words spoken, Rafe gave a long sigh, looked over at Charley, and said, "I should have killed that sonofabitch myself. A long time ago."

"I'm glad you didn't, Rafe. But why do you say that?"

"Because I knew Pap must've been beating Mam. All the bruises and cuts she had couldn't have been because she was just awkward or careless. She told me that's what caused them."

After another lull in talking, Rafe spoke as if he were talking to the floor he was staring at, "Mam was really the only family I had, the only one that ever cared a whit for me. Pap and Gabe and Mike were so wrapped up in themselves and their moonshine that they hardly knew I existed and didn't care what happened to me. Mam was all I had, and I let her down. I got her killed." Tears rolled down his cheeks and splattered on the porch floor.

"Rafe, don't be so hard on yourself. If you had tried to do something about the way your pap treated your mother, you might be one of the dead now. Or if you had killed him, you would probably spend most, if not all, of your life in prison."

"But if I had done something, Mam might be alive now. That 'might' will hant me as long as I live."

"Rafe, what do you think caused your mother to be in the water of Drowning Creek, and who do you think killed your daddy?"

The boy thought so long that Charley began to think he didn't want to talk about the deaths anymore or that he had just tuned the question out. But Rafe finally looked earnestly at Charley and said, "My guess is that Mam took so many beatings for so long that she just couldn't take any more. Maybe her mind just snapped. Maybe she knew Pap would beat her as long as the two of them were alive. Whatever her reasoning was, she had good cause to kill him. Then, I think, she drowned herself. I'm just sorry that after she killed Pap she thought there was no other way for her but to kill herself."

Charley talked with Rafe a few minutes longer, then called for Cecilia to come out, and she did with Luke following her. Their mother was not home then, Cecilia told him. Charley told the two Massey children that Rafe's parents were dead. He left it up to Rafe to fill in as many of the details he knew if he wanted the two to know more. Charley drove away from the house troubled in his mind about how the death of Rafe's parents, especially his mother, might affect the youngest Hawkins brother.

The Creedy community was shocked and saddened by the Hawkins deaths. The women, especially, felt sorry that Nettie had drowned herself, and they were sorry that the youngest boy now had no parents. But most of the people who had known Willard Hawkins couldn't bring themselves to feel much sorrow or sense of loss because of his death.

Belle Scott and her mother talked about time they had spent with Nettie and having seen her husband and sons. Ma Jess said she had visited Nettie several times and that her house was sparsely furnished but clean. On one of her visits, Mr. Hawkins and the oldest son had been at home that day. Ma Jess echoed the sentiment about Hawkins men that her daughter had expressed to Bonnie McGraw about a year earlier. She said, "They both looked and smelled kyarny, like they lived in a pig pen."

CHAPTER 21

November 1943

Charley had kept up his sparring in the boxing ring once a week at Big Stone Gap, as well as regular workouts on his punching bag. He replaced his homemade bag with one Lloyd Anderson ordered for him. The boxing and bag workouts increased Charley's agility and added strength to his arms and breadth to his shoulders as his muscles grew.

As he and Deputy Elwood Sykes headed toward McGraw Mine No. 1, Charley recalled the conversation he and Sheriff Fielding had a few months earlier about possible miner disturbances and how he hoped that such troubles wouldn't come to Powell County. The sheriff received a tip yesterday that trouble was brewing for Brewster McGraw at one of his two nonunion mining operations where fifteen to eighteen miners were usually employed. Most of the miners who worked at the two mines did not dispute McGraw's claims that he treated them fairly and paid as much or more than they could get at a union mine. He insisted that his mine supers did everything possible to make the mines as safe as they could be made.

Some of McGraw's miners, probably fewer than a third of them, had listened to a union representative tell them how they were being taken advantage of, cheated out of rightful wages, and subjected to unsafe mining conditions. A few of that group decided that now was the time to show that miners could have some say in their destiny, at least as far as pay and working conditions were concerned.

Word went out from the union rep to miners in surrounding counties that McGraw miners needed help from their brethren. The union promoted a gathering to show support for McGraw miners; the prounion miners were to meet at McGraw Mine No. 1. Brewster McGraw and Sheriff Fielding expected that the gathered men would try to prevent any of the No. 1 miners from going into the mines for their shifts. The sheriff told his friend McGraw that he was sending two deputies to the mine just in case any kind of trouble should be in the making. The mine owner said he didn't believe the law would be needed and that he would talk to the men in person to see if they had legitimate gripes about his mining operation. He felt he could defuse the situation before it actually became a problem. The sheriff, though, stood by his decision to have deputies at the mine; he sent Charley and Elwood to the mine.

Fielding gave his deputies instructions to stay in the background if possible, just see and be seen by all the miners there, and to take action only if the situation became volatile enough to threaten anyone's safety. Charley and Elwood were now on their way to the mine and planned to follow the sheriff's instructions.

As the two deputies neared Mine No. 1, they saw many more cars and trucks than were usually at the mine. Charley parked beside the road a considerable distance from the mine entrance, and he and Elwood walked toward the mine. As they drew closer to the mine opening about an hour before time for the shift to begin, they found thirty to thirty-five men already there.

Charley knew a few of the men who worked at the mine, and he identified others as McGraw No. 1 miners. He knew these men came to the mine today to work, because each of them wore a cloth cap with a thick leather piece in front that held a carbide lamp—their light source in the mine's inky darkness. On their belts they carried a tin flask of carbide to fuel their lamps. No. 1 miners also carried, or stood near, tin dinner buckets that held their mid-day meal. With their food in an upper compartment of the bucket, the men stored in the lower portion of the bucket something to drink during their work shift—water for most, tea for some.

Most of the gathered men were not McGraw miners; they were from outside the county. Charley couldn't determine who the union representative was or even if he was present. As more of the men who worked in the mine arrived for work, small groups of visitors descended on them and began conversations which at times became heated.

Just before 8:00 a.m., when No. 1 miners were supposed to begin their shift, a car arrived—Brewster McGraw's. The men watched as the owner exited his Packard sedan and came toward them. The talking stopped, and all eyes were on McGraw as he strode purposefully toward them. Supervisors from mines No. 1 and No. 2 met their boss and exchanged a few words with him. Then Brewster hustled up a bank near the mine entrance, where he was above the men and where all of them could see him.

He moved to the top of the bank with grace and ease that surprised Charley and said, "Men, those of you who work for me know me, and for those of you who don't know me, I'm Brewster McGraw, owner of this mine and McGraw Mine No. 2. I hope all of you who work or have worked for me know that I believe in paying a man a fair dollar for his work, and I think I've done that. I also want to operate the safest mines to be found in Virginia or in any other state. Now, I'm not sure why we have this gathering here today, but if any of you men who work for me have anything to say about what's wrong or about the way I treat you, now's the time to let me know."

As Brewster started speaking, Charley noticed a small huddle of men, about half a dozen, who looked at and listened to a large, bareheaded man who was talking. This speaker showed fiery passion as he moved his hands, changed body positions, emphasized what he said with head shakes, and pounded a fist into the palm of his other hand. Charley couldn't tell what Gabe Hawkins was saying, but it was plain to see that he was upset, or was acting upset.

The deputy knew that Hawkins didn't work for McGraw, because he had been fired permanently after working intermittently over a period of five or six years—fired because he often didn't show up for his shift. And at times when he did show for work, he was either half drunk or feeling so bad after a bender that he couldn't work. His condition at those times endangered him as well as his co-workers in the mine. So Gabe had been fired and told never to come back asking for a job in a McGraw mine, and Gabe never forgot that.

Also, Gabe Hawkins never forgot his encounter with Bonnie McGraw, the mine owner's daughter, and her boyfriend, Charley Scott, beside Clinch River about four years ago. That clash left Gabe unconscious after a fight with Charley. Then more recently, the sheriff and his deputy had, according to Gabe, "lorded over me and my brother, Mike" when their parents died, "stickin' their noses into what should've been Hawkins bidness only." Gabe Hawkins wanted to cause trouble for the pap of that "pyert little gal" Charley had fought to protect, and he yearned with every fiber in his brawny body for the chance to get even with Charley Scott.

When Brewster started talking to the men, Gabe stopped his haranguing to listen. Charley told Deputy Sykes to stay where he was and to keep a sharp eye out for trouble, and he moved back and around to the group's left to come up closer behind Gabe and the few men he was with.

As soon as McGraw finished speaking and waited for responses to his invitation, Gabe roared, "McGraw, you lie! Ya don't kyere 'bout the men who work for ya. All yer innersted in is makin' more money. Ya far a man once and fer all fer no reason 'cept that ya don't like his looks."

Charley slipped nearer Gabe and his cohorts. They were all facing McGraw, so Gabe was now behind the men he had been talking to. Charley edged closer to Gabe.

Brewster responded, "Ah, Gabe Hawkins. That's you, I see. You know I won't fire a man for no reason, and I won't stand for my supers doing that either. And you also know that I continue to give a man chances time and again to straighten himself out. If he won't do that, and if he's a danger to himself and to other men who work for me, then you're mighty right, I'll fire him. And that's why I fired you."

Seeming to dismiss Gabe, McGraw continued, "Now, who of my miners have anything you want to tell me or ask me?"

Charley saw that Gabe's face was livid, his eyes blazed in fury; the deputy moved even closer to the angry man. Neither Gabe nor any of the men near him noticed the deputy. Gabe leaned over and quickly straightened up with a softball-size chunk of coal in each of his huge, grimy hands, and Charley knew what the frenzied man was going to do. As Charley sprang the few feet toward him, Gabe threw a lump of coal at McGraw, transferred the other lump from his left hand to his right, and drew his arm back to hurl it. But suddenly an arm went around Gabe's neck and pulled him backward until he was still standing only because whoever held him was keeping him from falling on his back.

Gabe cursed and struggled. He dropped the lump of coal and grasped at the arm that held his neck in a chokehold. The arm that held him seemed to be made of steel; it was unmoveable, unyielding to Gabe's grasping, clawing hands.

As he continued to curse and struggle, a voice behind the strong arm said, "Cool down, Gabe." By now, all the miners' eyes were on Gabe and the man holding him.

Gabe rasped, "Charley Scott, turn me aloose! I'll kill ya, sonny boy!"

Charley tightened his arm around the neck and said, "You're just making it harder on yourself, Gabe. Settle down."

Gabe became even more infuriated and struggled to get out of Charley's grasp. He tried to pull the deputy over his shoulder but couldn't get leverage in the position he was held. The chokehold Charley used was a carotid restraint or a sleeper hold. This sleeper hold could render a man unconscious in a matter of seconds. Charley had one arm around Gabe's neck with the crook of his elbow over the midline of the man's neck. By pinching his arm together while adding pressure with his free hand, the carotid arteries and jugular veins could be compressed on both sides of Gabe's neck, cutting off the flow of blood to his brain. Gabe wouldn't cease his straining and thrashing against the chokehold, so Charley increased his arm pressure until the violent man passed out and slumped to the ground.

Charley quickly turned the unmoving man over on his stomach, pulled his arms behind him, and handcuffed him. Gabe regained consciousness in a few seconds and immediately began fighting the cuffs. The deputy put his foot on the thrashing man's upper back, preventing him from rising.

By this time, Elwood was by Charley's side, and Brewster McGraw joined them. He put a hand on the deputy's shoulder and said, "Good job, Charley. You put a stop to something that might have grown into a bigger problem."

Gabe's throw at his former employer had been accurate. The piece of coal had grazed Brewster's head; it cut a small gash just to the outside of his left eyebrow. Although the other men made no moves or sounds to indicate they wanted to take up Gabe's cause or threaten the mine owner, the two supervisors and most of the men who worked at No. 1 formed a protective line in front of him and the deputies.

"Are you all right, Mr. McGraw?" Charley asked

Holding to his head a white handkerchief already spotted crimson, he responded, "I'm fine. Just a little cut."

Then Brewster turned his head from side to side, looking at the somber miners standing around him, and said, "Boys, what I said still goes. If any of you have complaints or questions about working in my mines, I'm here to listen."

Nobody commented or posed a question. One of the older miners finally spoke up, "Mr. McGraw, I feel you've always treated us fair, and I'm just sorry this meetin' ever happened hyere this mornin'. I b'lieve we've got people who come in hyere today just tryin' to stir up a stink for reasons of their own, whatever they might be."

Several of the No. 1 miners nodded in agreement. As Charley looked around, he saw that men who didn't work here were starting to drift off toward parked vehicles, and soon all of them had moved away from the group of No. 1 miners.

Charley said, "Well, I think this meeting is over," and pointing to Gabe still lying facedown on the gritty, coal-strewn ground, he added, "I'm taking this troublemaker to the county jail."

Brewster McGraw said, "I'm not going to press charges, Charley." Then to the handcuffed man he said, "Gabe Hawkins, this is the last time I'll ever cut you any slack. If I ever have any more trouble from you, I'll prosecute you to the limit of whatever the law allows."

Charley looked at his girlfriend's father and said, "Mr. McGraw, I think you're making a mistake in not prosecuting Gabe now, but I can't tell you what you ought to do. I'm still taking him in, and the sheriff or a judge will have to decide if he's to be charged with a crime." As the deputy said this, he thought, *If Brewster knew what this Hawkins said to and about his daughter four years ago, he would take a much different line now.*

After he rolled Gabe over on his back, Charley helped him to stand; and the two deputies, each with a firm hand on his handcuffed arms, led a pale and subdued man to the car. But the deputy knew Gabe was seething inside, dangerous and determined.

"Now, Gabe," Charley said, "if you sit quietly and cause us no more trouble, things will be easy for you. If you get rowdy, I'll have to put you to sleep again. It's up to you. Do you understand me, Gabe?"

The man just glowered at the deputy with a malicious sneer, but he didn't utter a sound. Elwood got in the backseat with Gabe. Charley got behind the wheel, started the engine, and drove away toward the county jail. As he drove, he knew that no matter what happened to Gabe because of today's events, he would have to deal with this Hawkins again sometime, somewhere. Gabe was now too filled with hate and was lusting for revenge too much to ever give up on maiming or killing Charley.

The next day, Sheriff Fielding made a point of being in Creedy, and he stopped by Brewster McGraw's office to see how he was doing. Deputies Scott and Sykes had reported to the sheriff the happenings at the mine. As Harg walked into his friend's office, he saw Brewster working at his desk with a small bandage taped beside his left eye, and he said, "Well, Brewster, you seem to be doin' right well today. But just a little worse for wear, I'd say."

"I'm fine, Harg. Thanks to your deputy, my daughter's boyfriend, things didn't get nearly as rough as they probably would have if he hadn't handled Gabe Hawkins the way he did."

The sheriff replied, "I'd like you to give me your version of what happened yesterday."

"Charley and Elwood told you, didn't they?"

"Oh, yes, they told me, but Elwood didn't see most of what happened between Charley and Hawkins, and Charley just gave me the bare bones about what he did."

Shaking his head, Brewster said, "I declare! The way Charley had Gabe down on the ground! I didn't see how he did it. I just saw Gabe face down with Charley putting cuffs on him. How did he do that to a man much heavier than he is?"

Harg answered, "He learned the chokehold at the state police training he took. They demonstrate it to all new deputies and sheriffs, but Charley is the only deputy or sheriff that I know who has used the hold. I'm just glad he learned it well enough to be able to use it when he needed to."

"Harg," Brewster said, "I think you've got a mighty fine deputy there," and he proceeded to give his friend an account of what happened.

Brewster ended his report by saying, "And I think that what Charley did when he did it kept the outsiders, the miners who don't work in Powell County, from getting out of hand and causing more mischief."

"I agree with you about Charley. I'm glad to have him as a deputy, but I'm concerned how the doin's yesterday with Gabe may play out down the road a while."

"What do you mean?"

"Well, we know Gabe is mean. And I think he's not one who's likely to forget that he lost face and was belittled by a smaller man in the presence of many miners. I'm afraid he'll be looking for a chance to get back at Charley and to hurt him bad. I've told Charley what I think and that he should always be on the alert for possible trouble from Gabe, and I hope you'll caution him too."

"I'll do that for sure."

"I've got to be on my way, Brewster. Take care. I'll see you," the sheriff said as he walked toward the door, then left the office.

CHAPTER 22

December 1943

Lucille Thacker died in May and Clarissa in September 1943. In the months that followed his wife's death, Verle visited Madeline Massey, and his visits grew in frequency after his mother died. He spent nights with Maddie only when both of her children were away for a night or weekend. The quality of his relationship with Maddie's son and daughter was mixed.

The daughter, Cecilia, accepted Verle as a friend and as a male figure in her family. Cecilia acknowledged to herself that she had feelings for Verle. But what kind of feelings? She wasn't sure. Was she feeling the attraction of a female to a male? Or the natural feelings toward a father figure now that she had no father? That's what she often told herself—she was attracted to Verle because she needed a male in her life that she could look up to, someone to fill the void in her life without a father.

Verle liked Cecilia—liked her a lot. But he didn't have any uncertainty about what his feelings were for her. He saw her as a nice, pretty, friendly, highly intelligent young lady who had no father and who seemed to get short shrift from her mother—little appreciation, respect, or love. He hinted to Maddie his concern that she seemed to give her daughter little attention, little nurturing, but the mother had brushed his hints aside and acted as though she didn't know what he was talking about.

Verle's relationship with fourteen-year-old Lucas was a polar opposite of that with his sister. Luke had always resented Verle. He didn't like the man to be around his mother or sister. He didn't want anybody, especially Verle Thacker, trying to be a father to him. And Luke despised Verle for taking more of his mother's attention away from him. Even though Luke was jealous of his sister—of her popularity, her outgoing personality, her outstanding school record—he was at the same time jealous of Verle for the attention Cecilia gave him. Luke was always trying to come up with something on Cecilia that he could report to their mother—something that would degrade her in her mother's eyes and thereby make him feel superior. He fantasized about what he would do to get Verle out of their lives, especially out of the lives of his mother and sister.

Because of the way Luke behaved toward him, Verle had little compassion for the fatherless boy. Luke took every opportunity he had or could devise to be resentful, disrespectful, insolent, and insulting toward Verle. So now Verle just tried to ignore him and stay away from him as much as possible. Maddie and Verle had talked about marriage, and he mentioned to her Luke's antagonism toward him. Maddie made light of that idea and said Luke would "come around" after they were married and he got to know Verle better. She said Verle just needed to be patient and give the boy time.

Verle accepted the idea that he and Maddie would marry, but he hadn't set that thinking into a time frame. He was very much in love with her, but at times terrible scenes replayed in his mind and in his dreams. He remembered Lucille as the young beauty he had married and the vows he made to her. He sometimes awakened from dreams covered with sweat, with his heart racing. He had dreams in which he watched Lucille in agony in the last days of her life, and he dreamed of dogs writhing among leaves and bushes as they whimpered and howled in pain. In response to Maddie's incessant urging that they marry, and in spite of how his conscience still afflicted him regarding Lucille's death, Verle finally agreed to a date for their marriage; they would wed on December 20, about seven months after Lucille died.

One evening in the first week of December, Verle was at the Massey house and Cecilia and Luke were at home. Maddie called them from their rooms into the front room and told them she had something important to tell them, something she believed they would be glad to hear. Verle and Maddie were in the room when the two children came in, and she asked them to sit.

Maddie got right to the point by saying, "Cecilia, Lucas, we, Verle and I, want you to be the first to know that we're getting married."

Luke shot up out of his chair and shouted, "What? You can't be serious, Mother." And pointing a finger at Verle, Luke continued, "Surely you're not going to marry him and bring him into our house and into your bed." The boy's face was beet red and contorted in rage.

His mother said, "Lucas, watch your tongue! That's no way to talk! You sit down and apologize to Verle."

Luke responded, "I won't sit, and I won't apologize. I don't want you to marry him. I don't want him trying to be my father. He'll never be my father."

And with that, Luke bolted for the front door, ran from the room and off the porch into the dark night, leaving the door open to the wintry air.

Cecilia said, "Verle, I'm sorry Luke acted like a horse's . . . like an idiot. Maybe he'll change his mind." She paused, rose from her seat, and said as she started toward her room, "You and Mother both lost your spouses, and I hope you'll be happy together."

Cecilia hurried to her room, closed the door, and fell on her bed. Tears flowed; she wasn't sure why. She just felt she had suffered some kind of loss tonight. What loss was she crying over? Had her feelings for Verle been more than what a daughter should feel toward a father figure? She knew now that the answer was yes. She had wanted his attentions toward her to be more than those of a father, to be different from those of a father toward his daughter.

But now she realized there could never be, and should never be, more than a father-daughter relationship between Verle and her. And she vowed to herself that she would be a good friend to him and to try to act toward him as a daughter might act. She heard Verle leave, and a few minutes later she heard Luke's bedroom door close; he had sneaked back into the house after the object of his outrage left.

After the death of his parents, Rafe had seemed to grow darker in his outlook and demeanor. He seldom laughed or smiled. He was quieter and moody. He became less willing to put up with the usual pestering expectations of Luke Massey, but he didn't want to end his association with the boy. He was afraid he would have fewer opportunities to be around Cecilia if he did that. So Rafe continued to associate with Luke and to do things with him, but what he was still most interested in was being near Cecilia. Cecilia still tried not to be rude to Rafe, but she also remained certain she did not want to do anything to suggest to him that she was inviting romantic overtures.

Rafe learned from Luke that Verle and Maddie were planning to marry, and he feared he might not be welcome at the Massey house after Verle came to be there full time. Rafe too had grown to resent Verle, and one reason for his resentment was Cecilia's obvious friendly actions toward the man. He resented their chummy actions, comments, and smiling exchanges with each other. *Or was it much more than just friendship?* Rafe wondered. If Verle moved to the Massey house, Cecilia would be around him more than she had been, and no telling what kind of feelings might develop between the two of them, if they hadn't already.

Only occasionally now did Rafe spend a night at the Massey's, but when he did, he slept on the front-room couch. A week after learning that Verle and Maddie were going to marry, Rafe spent Saturday night with Luke. They hunted rabbits and quail all day and came home tired and hungry but carrying three rabbits and four bob whites. After they cleaned their game and themselves and ate supper, they were ready for bed. Verle left early, and Maddie went to bed soon after. Luke went to his room, and Rafe got under his blanket and heavy quilt to sleep on the couch.

Cecilia had gone to her room before Verle left, and Rafe could see light shining through the crack between the bottom of the door and the floor. He assumed she was reading as usual. He wanted so much to be with Cecilia. She was the only girl he ever had strong feelings for, but she wouldn't give him an opportunity to explain or demonstrate his deep affection. As he thought of Cecilia, sleep moved further and further from him. He thought, *What does she look like in that room? Is she dressed? In what? I have to talk to her to let her know how I feel about her. There's no better time than tonight for me to tell and show her how much I love her.*

Rafe was wearing only his undershorts, so he pulled on his pants and walked softly down the hall to Cecilia's room where he stood by the door listening. No sounds came from inside the room, but the light was still on. He grasped the doorknob and slowly twisted it, but the knob didn't turn. Cecilia had flicked the latch after she closed the door. This made Rafe angry. He tapped lightly on the door. No response. He tapped again. Again he got no response from Cecilia.

He hissed, "Cecilia, answer me. I know you're not asleep."

A tremulous voice asked, "Rafe?"

"Yes, it's Rafe. Who else did you think it might be? I have to talk to you, so open the door."

"Go to bed, Rafe, and leave me alone."

"You open this door, and we'll both go to bed."

"Go away, Rafe, you're not getting in this room."

Rafe gave two hard raps on the door with the flat of his hand, saying, "Open up, Cecilia Massey!"

He heard a door opening at the far end of the hall and realized instantly that Maddie was coming out of her bedroom, so he quickly backed up several steps toward the front room. By the time Maddie was in the hallway, Rafe stood unmoving, looking toward her.

"What's going on, Rafe?' she asked.

Rafe answered, "I'm not sure, Miz Massey. I heard a noise like Cecilia was pounding on something in her room, so I was coming to see if anything was wrong."

"You go on back to bed. I'll check on Cecilia," Maddie said as she stopped in front of her daughter's room.

"Cecilia, girl, is something wrong?" No answer. "Cecilia, do you hear me?"

"Yes, Mother, I hear you. There's nothing wrong now. I'll tell you in the morning about the noise. Go on back to bed, Mother."

"I swan, sometimes I don't know what to think of that girl," Maddie said, shaking her head as she turned and moved back toward her own bedroom.

Fuming at his lack of success with Cecilia, Rafe went back to the couch. He had heard what Cecilia told her mother. *If she tells her mother what really happened, I may not be allowed to come here at all in spite of what Luke wants.*

What neither Rafe nor Maddie knew was that Luke had not been asleep. He had heard Rafe calling for Cecilia, so he got out of bed and barely opened his door. Through the small crack, Luke watched and heard Rafe's pleadings, or orders, for Cecilia to open her door. He had seen Rafe retreat back down the hall when Maddie came out of her room. Luke stored this event in his memory, thinking he ought to be able to use it to some advantage later.

The next morning when Cecilia got up and came toward the kitchen, she saw that Rafe was not on the couch. He had already left. *Good riddance!* she thought. She went on into the kitchen where her mother was preparing breakfast and told her what Rafe had done last night. Maddie wouldn't believe her, saying that she had to be mistaken, that Rafe wouldn't have done that. Or that if he did, it was because she had led him to believe she wanted him in her bedroom.

In exasperation and disbelief at her mother's response, Cecilia ran back to her room, slammed the door, and fell on her bed sobbing. Rafe was not at the Massey house for the next two weeks. He was afraid Mrs. Massey would not allow him in the house after he had tried to get in her daughter's room.

The wedding day for Verle and Maddie arrived. They went to the Baptist church where Reverend Harley Davenport would marry them. Only a few relatives had been invited. Cecilia was here, but Luke was not. His mother begged him to come, but he didn't—said he wanted nothing to do with Verle Thacker. Verle had invited Charley and Bonnie; Charley's father and mother, J. R. and Belle; and his former father- and mother-in-law, the Musicks. Bonnie, Charley, and his parents came to the ceremony.

The minister had a brief ceremony and quickly came to the "I do" part. As Verle uttered that short pledge, a scene from seventeen years earlier flashed through his consciousness. He remembered he made that same solemn vow to a beautiful, happy young woman with whom he had expected to spend his remaining days. He didn't hear Maddie make her pledge to him.

After the preacher pronounced them man and wife, Verle kissed his exciting new bride and memories of his vow to Lucille Musick slipped from his thoughts. With the wedding over, the couple hurried off for their two-day honeymoon at the Martha Washington Inn over in Abingdon. Maddie had asked that they go there, remembering she had suggested that she and Sol go there the last time he sat in their kitchen. She also hoped her new groom would take her to a performance at Barter Theater just up the street from the Inn.

After the wedding, Charley and Bonnie took Cecilia home. Since county schools were closed for the Christmas holidays, Cecilia and Luke would be out of school until after the beginning of the new year. Maddie had arranged for Demus Ferguson, her sharecropper, to look after the livestock on her farm, and she instructed Cecilia to look after her brother.

CHAPTER 23

When the happy newlyweds returned from their honeymoon, Verle brought a box of clothing and personal articles into the house and took most of them to the bedroom, which was not just Maddie's bedroom now; it was *their* bedroom. When Luke saw his mother and stepfather coming from their car, he stomped into his room and slammed the door.

The next morning, Verle and his new wife didn't hurry to get up for breakfast. The honeymoon was not yet over. When they came to the kitchen, the sun had been above the horizon more than two hours, and Cecilia was eating freshly cooked oatmeal and a thick slab of bread from a loaf Maddie baked before the wedding. The couple's happy state of mind was obvious to the girl, and she thought she knew why they were just now emerging from their bedroom. After greeting Cecilia, Maddie fixed breakfast for Verle and herself. She asked where Luke was, but his sister didn't know. She hadn't seen him that morning.

"Still in bed, I guess," Maddie concluded.

Cecilia said, "I'll get him up."

She went to Luke's room, knocked on his door, and called his name. No response. She tried again with the same result. She slowly opened the door and looked into the room. Luke was not there, so Cecilia told her mother. Maddie wondered where he could be. He wasn't usually up and gone before he ate breakfast, but the lack of dirty dishes indicated he had not eaten.

"Oh, well," Maddie said, "he'll be back soon, I reckon."

Just as Verle and Maddie sat down for their meal, Luke came through the kitchen door. He was red faced and appeared to be out of breath, and Maddie thought he had a scared look on his face. Or was it more of a guilty look? Luke stopped briefly beside the water bucket, got a dipperful, and drank thirstily as he took a furtive look out the window. He finished his drink, hung the dipper back on the nail in the wall, and, without a word, marched back to his bedroom and closed the door.

Maddie was puzzled. She muttered, "I don't know what's going on with that boy. I don't know if he's still mad about the wedding or what. But let's eat before our eggs and ham get any colder."

Just as Maddie and Verle finished their meal, a car pulled up near the house. "Who's that?" Maddie asked.

Cecilia looked out the window and said, "It looks like Mrs. Hess."

Molly Hess was a neighbor who lived about half a mile from the Massey house. As Molly came up on the back porch and was about to knock on the door, Verle opened the door and said, "Hello, Miz Hess, it's good to see you. Come on in."

She thanked him and entered the kitchen.

As Verle closed the door, she said, "Maddie, I want to wish the best for you and Verle. We heard about the wedding, and I hope both of you will be happy."

"Thank you, Molly. Won't you come on in the front room so we can sit and be more comfortable?"

Molly said, "No, I won't be long. I wish I didn't even have to be here, but I thought you had to know."

"Had to know what, Molly?"

"Oh, dear. There's no easy way to talk about it, and it's embarrassing to tell, but here it is. Just a little while ago I caught your son in the act of . . . of . . ."

"You caught Lucas? In the act of what?"

With a crimson face and eyes now ablaze in anger, Mrs. Hess said, "I caught Luke taking a pair of my panties and a brassiere off my clothesline!"

"Oh, no! Not Lucas. You must be mistaken, Molly."

"I wish I was, Maddie. But it's no mistake. I just happened to be looking out a window when I saw Luke scramble from the barn over to the smokehouse. From there, he hurried over to the clothesline and started taking clothespins loose. By the time I opened the door and got outside, he had a bra and my panties in his hand and was starting to put them under his coat. I yelled at him and told him to drop my clothes. He did that and took off like a scared hant."

"Mollie, I just can't believe this. Why would Lucas do such a thing?"

"Don't know why, but I'm pretty sure it's not the first time he's done this. I've lost underclothes before, and so have other women around here."

"Wait right here, Molly. I'll bring Lucas in here and we'll see what he has to say for himself."

Maddie hurried to the boy's room, and as she opened the door, she said, "Lucas Massey, you've got some . . ." but she stopped when she realized Luke wasn't in his room. The curtains at his window were moving, and cold air was coming through the open window.

Maddie closed the window and walked back to the kitchen and, with a pained expression on her face, said, "Lucas isn't in his room. He left through the window. So he wouldn't have to face you, I guess, Molly. I'm so embarrassed by this. I don't know what to think or to say. If Lucas did this, Molly, you can be sure it will never happen again."

"Maddie, don't you believe me? Are you still unwilling to believe your boy took my bloomers?"

"I believe you, Molly, and I'm so sorry it happened. It's just such a shock to me. Why would he do it?"

"I can't answer that, but I've got to go now. I'll see you, Maddie."

After Molly left, Maddie didn't know what to do, what to believe. Surely Lucas hadn't taken women's underwear! If Lucas had taken the garments, had he brought them home? Did he keep them? If so, where? She decided she had to look for them, to find them if he had them. She started searching in the boy's room. She looked in the wardrobe, on top of it, in its drawers, but found no bras or panties. Then she started going through Luke's chest of drawers. She had searched carefully through all of the drawers down to the bottom one when she found in the very back of that drawer a box that a pair of boots came in. The box was stashed under a folded sweater. Dreading to look in the box, she lifted it out of the drawer, placed it on the bed, and removed the top.

"Oh, no!" she murmured as a hand covered her mouth.

In the box were several brassieres and panties. She dumped them on the bed and saw that one pair of panties looked like ones she wore. And another pair and a bra were like Cecilia's, and they were the right size to fit the girl. Cecilia came into the room and saw the underclothes on Luke's bed.

"Mother!" she exclaimed, then looking more closely at the garments, she said, "Why, these are mine," as she picked up a pair of panties, "and this is one of my bras!"

Maddie said, "Cecilia, what's got into that boy? Why's he doing this?"

"I don't know, Mother, but I've been telling you about things Luke does that aren't normal. I've told you he's a Peeping Tom, and that I've caught him looking at me when I had no clothes, or almost none, on. You've never believed what I said, you always made excuses for Luke."

Maddie just stared back and forth between her daughter and the clothes from the box with a look of dismay and helplessness on her pale face. Finally she put the clothes back in the box, put the top on it, and carried it into the front room where she placed it on a table. Then she went to her bedroom and closed the door.

Verle had remained in the kitchen, and Cecilia came in and sat at the table. He said, "I guess that box must hold proof of what Miz Hess said."

"Yes, it does." Cecilia said, "Luke even has some of my underclothes in the box. Why does he do that, Verle?"

"I don't know why, but your mother is going to have to set the law down for that boy."

"That scares me. I'm scared in my own home, even more scared now than I had been."

"More than you had been? What were you afraid of before this?"

"I don't think I should talk about it," Cecilia said as she stared at the tabletop.

"If you're scared about something, you should talk about it."

"I've told Mother, but she refuses to believe me."

"Believe what, Cecilia?"

The girl sighed in resignation and began, "A little more than two weeks ago Rafe spent the night here after he and Luke had hunted all day. After everyone was in bed, he came to my door and tried to get me to let him in my room. He made enough noise that Mother got up, and Rafe lied to her about what he was doing. I told her the next morning what had really happened, but she didn't believe me."

Responding to Verle's persistent questioning, Cecilia told the whole story of how Rafe had tried to get in her room. Upon hearing details about the incident, Verle's anger flared. He sprang from his chair, and he paced from the kitchen to the front room, back and forth, red faced and tense as he curled his fingers into fists and flexed them straight again. Verle muttered to himself questions for which he had no answers.

"What the devil is wrong with that Hawkins boy?" Verle asked. "What's Maddie thinking that she won't believe her own daughter?"

He finally simmered down and sat again in his chair at the table. Verle told the girl he would have a talk with her mother and with Rafe.

He got up to leave, but Cecilia caught his sleeve and said, "Verle, there's more."

"About Rafe?"

"No, Luke."

And Cecilia told her stepfather about how Luke spied on her when she was partially or completely naked. Verle was stunned.

"Luke takes women's unmentionables and peeps too? The little pervert! I have to talk to Maddie."

He strode to the bedroom and found Maddie lying on her bed staring at the ceiling. He struggled to keep his anger under control as he sat on the bed beside her and took her hand in his. He said, "Maddie, honey, we have to talk—now."

Maddie looked surprised and a bit irritated at Verle's statement and asked, "What's this talk about, Verle?"

"It's about Cecilia, and it's about Rafe Hawkins, and it's about why you refuse to believe your daughter when she tells you about something bad that almost happened to her in her own bedroom."

"You mean what she told me about Rafe trying to get in her room?"

"That's what I mean, and I believe her. She's scared. She's not making up a story about Rafe Hawkins."

"Verle, I was sure my daughter was either imagining or exaggerating what happened. I can't believe Rafe would try to force his way into her room."

"Maddie, Cecilia doesn't want to do anything that would encourage him or cause him to think she welcomes his advances. And you must know that Rafe is obsessed with her even though she has never wanted to be anything but a friend to him. But that's not enough for Rafe. He can't stand not having her, and he wants her to be his girlfriend and his lover."

"Oh, Verle, you don't know Rafe like I do, and . . ."

Verle interrupted, "I know more than I want to know about him. And I can believe that Rafe would do what she said happened. Haven't you noticed how he is always trying to be near her, wanting to talk to her, trying to get her to date him? That boy is absolutely mad about her. He's like a male dog after a female in heat, and he's after Cecilia. I care for the girl like I would for my own daughter, and I'm proud to treat her like my own. And I don't want Rafe around Cecilia anymore. I'm afraid what he might do to her if he got half a chance."

For a few moments neither of them said anything, absorbed in their separate thoughts about Rafe and Cecilia. Then Verle said, "Let's not have Rafe around here for a while."

"I've already told Lucas that Rafe could be here for Christmas dinner. With both parents dead and with the kind of brothers he has, I feel sorry for the boy during the holiday season."

"Maddie, if Rafe comes here, I'm going to have to talk to him about his actions toward Cecilia. I think I owe that much to the girl."

Maddie thought for several seconds before she spoke. "Okay, Verle. You do what you think is best for Cecilia's sake. And I've got to deal with Lucas and his pilfering women's underclothes."

"Don't forget about him peeping at Cecilia when he shouldn't be."

"Oh, she told you those stories about Lucas looking at her when she was undressed?"

"She told me, but I don't think they're stories, and you shouldn't either after what you've found out about Luke today," Verle said as he went from the room.

Verle donned his hat and coat and left the house to go check with Demus about beef cows he and Maddie had decided they should buy. He also needed to pick up salt blocks for cattle, barbed wire, and staples at the farm supply store.

Maddie waited in the house, hoping Lucas would come back in shortly. In the middle of the afternoon, Luke came hesitantly onto the back porch and into the kitchen. He was embarrassed or angry or both, Maddie couldn't tell which.

He said, "I'm starving."

His mother replied, "Missed breakfast and dinner, didn't you?"

Luke was mute.

"Luke, you can wait until supper is ready and eat what I cook for us, or you can scrounge up something for yourself in a few minutes. But before you do anything, we're going to talk about women's underwear."

As she finished the sentence, she was moving toward the box in the front room that came from her son's dresser drawer. She picked it up, walked back to the kitchen, and placed the box on the table in front of him. Luke's face got redder, and his eyes wouldn't meet her piercing glare.

"So what do you have to say for yourself, young man?"

No response from Luke.

"Lucas, answer me. What do you have to say?"

"Nuthin'," he mumbled.

"Why have you pilfered women's underwear? I want an answer."

"I don't know."

Several more questions got nothing from Luke that shed light on why he took clothes off clotheslines. Luke just sat with a hangdog look and muttered one-syllable responses to his mother's questions.

Finally Maddie gave up on the questioning but said to her son, "You certainly must have too much free time since you're spending some of it lurking around other people's clotheslines, so I'm going to give you extra jobs that will take up some of that slack time."

In addition to the few chores Luke was already responsible for, his mother added several more demanding and time-consuming tasks. Luke's daily chores had been to carry in water from the spring, chop kindling, and carry in enough wood and coal for the heating stove and cook stove. Additional jobs his mother assigned him were to feed the horses their oats or corn and hay every day, milk at least one cow morning and night, feed the chickens every morning, and gather eggs every evening. Every Saturday, Luke must clean out the horses' stalls, put the manure and bedding straw in the manure spreader, and put down fresh bedding. And once a month he had to clean out the manure in the chicken house.

Maddie continued, "Since I've already told you that Rafe can be here Christmas day and eat dinner with us, I'll still allow that. But after Christmas, you can't have Rafe here until after the end of January. And, at least until the end of January, you will be allowed to be off this farm only to go to school or with Cecilia to church on Sundays. And I'm still working on how you will either return the underwear you've taken or pay the women for it. We'll talk more about that later. Now, do you understand what I'm telling you, Lucas?"

"Yeah, I get it. I'm going to be in prison for more than a month, and I'll have to work like a slave to boot," he said with a tremor in his voice, "and I bet you're doing this because it's what your new husband wants you to do. He don't like me, and he don't like Rafe."

"This is my decision," Maddie said, "and you brought it on yourself. And one more thing: we'll have another talk in a day or two. A talk about you peeping at Cecilia when she's not dressed."

Luke didn't look up, but his mother noticed that his neck and ears flushed red again.

Maddie proceeded, "Whatever you have to do, and whatever you're not allowed to do, it's all of your own making. So start doing some serious thinking about what you want in the future. For now, you can get a biscuit and a couple of slices of streaked meat to eat, or you can wait until supper to eat. Whether you eat now or later, you *will* be at the supper table with us."

Luke poured himself a glass of cold milk from the small covered bucket sitting on a back porch shelf, then he grabbed a cold biscuit, put some fried country bacon with it and hurried to his room with his milk and food.

After Verle discussed with Demus the cows he and Maddie planned to buy, he drove to Creedy to pick up supplies. As he loaded the last salt block into the back of his truck, he saw across the street a familiar figure and face. Rafe Hawkins was standing in front of the barbershop, where he apparently had just got his hair cut. *No time like the present,* Verle thought, and he trotted across the street toward Rafe. As he approached, he saw that Rafe was already scowling at him.

Verle said, "Rafe, we need to talk. Let's go sit in my truck."

"I don't know of anything we need to talk about, and I reckon I won't bother to set in your truck."

"All right. You don't have to talk, but by the saints, you are going to listen. And if you want to do it right here on the sidewalk, that's just dandy with me. So as not to waste your valuable time, here's what I have to say to you. If you ever try to get in Cecilia's room again, or if you ever try to force yourself on her in any way, you'll have me to reckon with. And you won't like one bit what I'll do to you. So leave the girl alone. And I think it would be better for Cecilia, and for you, if you didn't show up for our Christmas dinner. Do you understand me, Rafe?"

Rafe glared at Verle, his eyes fiery points of anger and hate. He started to walk away without answering, but Verle clamped a hard, strong hand on the young man's arm and repeated, "Do you hear me?"

Rafe tried to jerk his arm out of Verle's grasp, but it held him like a sprung trap. Verle's hard eyes bored into Rafe's.

Rafe finally snarled, "Yeah, I hear ya."

Verle relaxed his grip, and the furious young man stomped off down the street without looking back.

Rafe didn't come to share the Christmas dinner, and Luke knew why. Luke had talked with Rafe a day after his encounter with Verle, and now Luke had an additional reason not to like Verle—he had kept the boy's friend, Rafe, away from the farm and the special dinner. And a special dinner it was.

Maddie had boiled, then baked, a cured country ham; to go with it she had sweet potatoes, canned green beans, pinto beans, cole slaw, canned corn, stewed apples, homemade biscuits and cornbread with plenty of butter to slather on them, plus coffee, milk, and buttermilk. For dessert, Maddie had a luscious chocolate cream pie and eggy boiled custard, and Cecilia made a yellow cake with white icing. Everybody stuffed themselves until they couldn't hold another bite. For Maddie, Verle, and Cecilia, the meal was a happy occasion, but Luke appeared to be miserable and didn't try to hide his hostility toward Verle.

Another year had passed, and the wars in Europe and the Pacific still raged. Thousands more Americans died, and untold numbers were wounded or captured. Almost everyone in Creedy and throughout the county had lost a son or brother or cousin or friend or neighbor. Even American women were dying in the awful conflict—nurses in the armed forces, primarily U.S. Army nurses. Rationing continued, but most people accepted the shortages with understanding, good humor, and a feeling of helping out in the war against Hitler and Tojo.

A local character, Cecil Denton, wasn't one of the brighter stars in the firmament, and he could barely read and write. Cecil eked out an existence by doing odd jobs around town and by working for any farmer who needed an extra pair of hands and a strong back. Tucked back in a wooded cove at the foot of Powell Mountain, Cecil's home was a small cabin that most people would call a shack. Cecil often worked for Verle on either the Massey or Thacker farm; when he did, he spent his nights in the cottage where Verle's mother lived before she died.

Verle had put his truck's spare tire on a wheel hub to replace a tire that went flat. He patched the hole in the flat tire's tube and decided to fill it with air at the Charles Garage and Repair when he went to town for groceries, nails, and lumber Saturday morning. Cecil rode with Verle, and he wore an important piece of his Saturday attire. In his left breast shirt pocket, he carried for everyone to see a small writing tablet, a fountain pen he found that had no ink or point, and two or three sharpened pencils, one or more with the eraser end up and the others with the sharpened ends showing. Cecil was proud of his tablet and writing instruments, although it would have been an arduous task for him to write just his name. That Saturday morning, as Verle pulled his truck to a stop in front of the Free Air sign at the garage, Cecil asked, "How much does that free air cost?"

One morning on the farm as Verle and Cecil worked digging post holes to put in a new stretch of fence, they talked about a recent radio broadcast that told of heavy American losses in a battle against the Germans. Cecil told Verle he believed he had a way to get rid of Hitler.

Verle asked, "What's your idea, Cecil?"

Cecil stopped his work, leaned on the post hole diggers and said, "If I wuz over there where Hitler lives, hyere's what I'd do. I'd git me a good rifle, and I'd find me a hidin' place on the hill d'reckly across the holler from his house. A place where I could see the house and have a clear shot at 'im. Early one mornin', a long time afore daybreak, I'd sneak in to my hidin' place and git set up fer a shot. Then when daylight come and Hitler got out of bed and come out on the front porch to take a leak, I'd shoot that s.o.b."

Maddie and Verle agreed that for the year as a whole, 1943 had brought better news for Americans on how the war was going. In January, fifty bombers mounted the first all-American raid against Germany. The following month, General Dwight D. Eisenhower took command of Allied Armies in Europe. In April, the architect of Japanese naval strategy, Admiral Yamamoto, died when his plane was shot down.

From their farm, Verle and Maddie often saw and heard formations of airplanes drone high overhead as they winged their way to some point where they would be shipped or flown overseas. Usually flying west or southwest, some of the formations consisted of small fighter planes, and some were made up of larger bombers. New planes were on their way to becoming part of the action in the war.

The Allies made progress against Axis armed forces—the Germans, Italians, and Japanese. Italy surrendered to the Allies in September and one month later declared war on Germany. But in November, the residents of Powell County were horrified when they learned of the unthinkable numbers of U.S. Marines killed and injured in battles for small islands somewhere in the Pacific—islands that virtually none of them had even heard of before—Tarawa and Makin, atolls in the Gilbert Islands.

Early in December, Edward R. Murrow delivered his moving "Orchestrated Hell" broadcast on CBS radio, describing a Royal Air Force bombing raid on Berlin. On Christmas Eve, General Dwight D. Eisenhower was named supreme Allied commander in Europe.

CHAPTER 24

December 1943 into March 1944

The last days of 1943 slipped by for Charley and Bonnie and left them wondering how another year could be gone so quickly. They both were happy—with their work, with each other. They were thankful to be living where men and women were willing to devote their lives, to sacrifice their lives if necessary, to protect the rights and freedoms of family, friends, and neighbors as well as of future generations. They felt especially blessed to be living in the ancient mountains of Southwest Virginia with their abounding beauty. That beauty included a peaceful, clean river and small streams that hurried on their way to feed it, fertile fields of river-bottom lands, verdant valleys, sloping and rolling upland fields, and green pastures.

These majestic mountains that come to life in spring with their greening buds and leaves and with scattered bouquets of white dogwood, serviceberry, and sourwood blooms and pink redbud blossoms are clad in varying shades of green in summer. And they feel no shame at autumn's end when they stand stark and uncovered as their leaves drift silently to their earthen skin because they expect to soon be under their snug, gleaming white blankets. In the season between summer greens and winter snows, the mountains display the unmatched artistry of their Maker as they preen in their vibrant garments of fall—subdued bronze hues of oaks, blazing gold tones of poplar and hickory and sassafrass, fiery yellow and orange and red of maples, and dark crimson of blackgum and sweetgum, of dogwood and sumac. Charley and Bonnie knew they wanted to live out their lives in Powell County, the only home they knew or wanted.

While Bonnie was on her Christmas break, she and Charley were together for at least a few minutes every day and for as many longer periods as Charley could be off deputy duty. During their times together, they talked about Bonnie's work, about accomplishments and successes she had with students at Creedy High School, as well as what she viewed as failures or shortcomings on her part. She worried about a few students in particular, including Cecilia and Luke Massey, but her concerns for the sister and brother were vastly different. She feared the girl would not be allowed to become the person she had the potential to become and what she wanted to become. Bonnie's fear for Luke was that he might become what she was afraid he wanted to be.

Charley's work was satisfying. He felt good being able to protect Powell County residents from others who were not willing to abide by the rules of a civilized society or of human decency. In spite of accomplishments he recognized or that Bonnie pointed out to him, he also was troubled by events that fell within in his realm of responsibility. During the two years he had served as a deputy, four deaths occurred in his community, and two of these were mysterious deaths—Sol Massey and Aunt Luce. To Charley's mind, neither of these two deaths had been satisfactorily explained.

He knew how Sol had died, but he didn't know why, and he didn't know what caused Sol to be in the river. He also did not know what had taken his aunt's life. Charley still had vague feelings of unrest and the foreboding sense that something sinister had brought about these two deaths. He knew that if this sense was correct, justice had not yet been served.

The other two deaths were tragic. Tragic that a woman had been so mistreated over more than three decades by her husband that she could see no way to end her suffering other than to kill her abuser and take her own life. Tragic too that nobody in the community—not her three sons, not her neighbors, not church leaders or members, not the sheriff or his deputy—had done anything to prevent the deaths. Charley thought, *Shouldn't some of us have been able to see what was happening to Nettie Hawkins? Did we just turn a blind eye to a situation that claimed two lives?* Charley believed that Nettie had meted out justice to her husband only as a desperate last resort. Nettie's sons failed to protect her, and she was denied justice. *What was it Harg said about justice a few days after Sol Massey died? Oh, yeah, I remember. Justice is hardly ever simple, and almost never is it pure.*

During moments of free time on the job, Deputy Scott often pulled out notes he had made about the deaths, especially those relating to Sol and his aunt. He studied his notes and racked his brain, trying to see or realize something that had eluded his consciousness thus far.

For several days after Christmas, though, Charley and Bonnie had a topic of conversation that was happy. In early afternoon on December 24, he picked up his sweetheart and drove to Bristol where they went to a matinee moving picture show at the Paramount Theater on the Tennessee side of State Street. The show was a lighthearted musical comedy, *Coney Island*, starring Betty Grable, George Montgomery, and Cesar Romero. Bonnie especially enjoyed the music, and Charley was most appreciative of Ms. Grable's acting assets. Both were impressed with the theater itself—an art deco motion picture palace with an opulent, richly embellished interior that included colorful, artistic murals.

"I've never seen anything this fancy," Charley whispered before the show started. "Sure beats the cramped, dingy little theater we have in Creedy."

After the picture show, the couple walked to Trayer Restaurant for a delicious meal, seated at a corner table with few diners near them. They finished their meal and decided not to have dessert because the options were not very appealing. Rationing of sugar, flour, butter, and other food items had made it difficult for restaurants to produce many of their traditional tasty desserts. As they drained the last coffee from their cups, they were talking about the big Christmas Day dinner they would enjoy tomorrow at Charley's grandparents' home in River Mountain. Then their conversation switched to the upcoming new year and what it might bring for the country as a whole and for local families. Charley veered away from that topic by saying, "Before we go any further, I want to ask you something."

"Ask away," Bonnie said.

"Will you marry me?"

Bonnie watched her beau pull a small, blue, velvet-covered box out of his coat pocket. Her face flushed, and her eyes widened in surprise and wonder. He opened the box, and Bonnie saw a solitaire ring supporting a sparkling diamond. She clasped her hands to her face, and her mouth formed a rosy circle as she breathed a long "oh-h-h-h." Her happy face glowed, and she blinked dewy eyes, causing glistening drops to glide down her cheeks.

All she could say was, "Oh, Charley! Oh, Charley!" Then she just looked at him with ecstatic, adoring eyes.

He said, "Bonnie, honey, I asked you a question. Are you going to answer it or keep me in suspense all night?"

"Of course, I'm going to answer, and of course the answer is yes. I will marry you!"

Charley took her left hand in his and slipped the ring on her finger. Then he kissed her—a long, tender kiss—and Bonnie eagerly reciprocated. After a few more minutes of sweetheart talk, the happy pair left the restaurant and began their ride back home, discussing and making plans for their wedding. Charley wanted the wedding to be on Valentine's Day. Bonnie wanted it to be later, after her school year ended, so that she wouldn't have to be concerned with her work during the first few months of their marriage. So they finally agreed their wedding day would be a day in the first week of June 1944.

Charley saw Bonnie to her door and kissed her good night there; she was eager to tell her parents that they would soon have a son-in-law. They wouldn't be surprised because two days earlier Charley had asked her father for his daughter's hand in marriage. Brewster had been happy for both his daughter and Charley, was glad to give his blessing, and told Charley how glad he was that the young man would be his son-in-law.

The state of affairs at Verle and Maddie Thacker's home was not nearly so happy or cordial as at the Scott and McGraw homes. Luke didn't like Verle before he married Maddie, and he liked him even less after the marriage. Now the boy was more antagonistic toward his stepfather than ever. He blamed Verle for his mother's assignment of farm work and more chores just because he had a box of women's bras and panties in his dresser. Also, because of Verle's influence on his mother, she now seemed to believe Cecilia's claims that her brother was a Peeping Tom.

In addition, Luke knew Verle had been the reason Rafe was not at their Christmas dinner and the reason his mother had banned him from visiting at least through January. Luke now spent most of his waking hours trying to devise ways to embarrass, belittle, or hurt Verle in the eyes of his mother and thereby reduce the man's influence on his life.

Rafe Hawkins was more upset with Verle than was Luke. He was furious because of the way Verle had talked to him and even more incensed at being kept away from Cecilia. He could visualize Cecilia laughing and talking with Verle, could see them occasionally touch each other in seemingly innocent ways. Rafe was insanely jealous of Verle—of his closeness, his connection to Cecilia. Rafe, like his faux friend Luke, spent much time thinking of how he could get back at Verle Thacker.

During the early months of 1944, Maddie Thacker became anxious, edgy, and morose as she considered the embarrassing activities of her son and the charges against him by his sister. She believed her husband was even taking Cecilia's side against her, his new bride. Maddie's affection for Verle and her expression of that affection seemed to be waning. She wasn't nearly as affectionate toward him as she had been prior to their marriage. Their physical intimacy became less intense and less frequent. Verle assumed it was because of his wife's concerns about Luke.

One night, after an infrequent but unusually satisfying and exhilarating marital romp, they lay spent and relaxed in their bed. Abruptly, Maddie broached the subject of coal deposits on Massey property to which Verle owned the mineral rights.

Propped up on one elbow, Verle looked at his wife with uncomprehending eyes. "What are you talking about, hon?' he asked.

"You know what I'm talking about!" And she spat, "The mineral rights the Thackers cheated my father out of! Mother Massey told me about them."

Verle could hardly believe what he was hearing. After calming his distraught wife, he explained to her why he didn't grasp at first why she was upset about mineral rights that were worth nothing.

Apparently what Maddie's mother-in-law, Martha Massey, had never learned about the coal deposits on Massey property was that shortly before her husband, Thaddeus, died, he had brought in a mining engineer whose team sampled coal seams on both the Massey and Thacker properties. The engineer reported to both Mr. Massey and the Thackers that their coal deposits were too thin and of such quality that they could not be mined profitably. Verle explained to Maddie what the engineer had found and reported to the property owners.

Maddie commented, "If the mineral rights are worthless, as you say, Sol's father must not have told Mother Massey, because she appeared to be so certain that the coal deposits were of great value and that we had been cheated out of them."

Verle promised his wife he would look through his mother's old papers; he was sure she had kept a copy of the engineer's report. Maddie just nodded her head and stared with unseeing eyes, unable to fully comprehend that her plans and actions to get mineral rights to valuable coal deposits were dashed to extinction.

After learning this, she became more and more withdrawn from Verle—colder, less affectionate, less interested in lovemaking and more contentious, resentful, and accusing. The couple had a sharecropper and often hired additional hands to work the two farms they owned; they were making a good living, the kind of living that 98 percent of Powell County residents would have been overjoyed to make. But Maddie had been expecting much more money from coal mines that were never to be. All her scheming and manipulating had gained her little. One day, when Maddie needed to talk to someone, she broached the subject of the mines and mineral rights to Cecilia. She said, "Girl, we would be a lot better off if what my mother-in-law told me had been the truth."

"What are you talking about, Mother?"

"Your grandmother Massey told me that the Thacker and Massey properties had valuable coal deposits on them but that the Thackers owned the mineral rights to the coal on our land. Now that I'm married to a Thacker, I learn that the coal isn't worth mining. So what good do the mineral rights do me? I'm not going to get one red cent from coal on these lands. Just remember, Cecilia, sometimes things don't pan out no matter how much planning you do."

Cecilia wasn't sure what her mother meant, but Maddie was up and out of the room before the daughter could ask. Cecilia wondered, *What brought that on?*

As weeks passed, Cecilia saw clearly what was happening between Verle and her mother. Maddie was trying to push her husband further and further away. Cecilia entertained fantasies of Verle becoming her lover, but she realized that could never be—Verle would not do that and she could not allow it even if he wanted it. She had dreams—provocative dreams. During the dreams, they were pleasant or exciting; but when she recalled them after waking, they scared her. In these dreams, Verle was sometimes holding, hugging, kissing her as a lover might; at other times he was consoling, advising, or protecting her as a father would. A face in her dreams changed back and forth from that of her father to

Verle's. During her dreams, when she saw her father's face and when she thought of the dreams after waking, Cecilia continued to have a sense of foreboding. She sensed that something important was lurking at the edge of her memory, but she couldn't retrieve whatever it was.

CHAPTER 25

March and April 1944

Following the death of their parents, the two older Hawkins brothers, Gabe and Mike, became lazier, more destitute. They even lacked ambition enough to keep their pap's moonshine still going, even though legal production and sale of alcoholic beverages ceased so that more industrial-grade alcohol could be produced for the war effort. As a result, liquor could no longer be bought at Virginia Alcoholic Beverage Control stores. Lack of whiskey through legal channels resulted in greater demand for it from illegal sources—moonshiners or bootleggers of whiskey smuggled into the country from Canada and Caribbean islands. So at a time when the demand for moonshine was high, the Hawkins brothers were too shiftless to carry on the family tradition.

Gabe had been banned from working in Brewster McGraw's coal mines, so he and Mike got jobs working with teams of loggers who brought logs to the sawmill where the youngest Hawkins brother, Rafe, worked. The older brothers worked sporadically. Some days, if they didn't want to go to work, they just didn't show up on the job; and of what little money they earned, a sizeable portion of it went for whiskey if any was to be found.

After working most of the month of March, the two brothers decided they would find some whiskey and have themselves a good time for a few days before going back to work. The only possibility they had for finding liquor without traveling several miles from Creedy was the local taxi operator, Monroe Bowman. Monroe's taxi service was of no interest to Gabe and Mike Hawkins, but the other service he provided was of more interest to the brothers and more rewarding for Monroe. As the only bootlegger in town, he was the sole source of whiskey, illegal though it was. Moonshiners in the county and surrounding counties usually kept Monroe adequately supplied. In addition, he was able to get smuggled whiskey and rum.

Around noon on April 1, with brother Mike in the passenger seat, Gabe drove his truck to town and to Monroe Bowman's house on the eastern edge of Creedy. Monroe's taxi cab was parked at his house. The Hawkins pair got out of the truck, climbed the steps to the porch, and knocked on the door. They heard shuffling feet, and the door opened. Facing them was Monroe, a man with mostly gray hair, standing about five feet eight inches tall with a full, rounded, rosy face and carrying too much weight for his height. He looked to be in his late fifties or early sixties. His red veined nose attested to his consumption of the wares he also peddled to others. These were not new customers facing Monroe, and he knew why they were there. He said, "Come on in." They did and he closed the door as he asked, "What do you boys want? I've got a good batch of moonshine, 'bout as good as your pappy used to make."

"We'll take two pints," Gabe said.

Monroe stepped into the adjoining room and in a few seconds was back before his customers with two pint canning jars of crystal-clear liquid. He held out a pint to each of the men and said, "That's a dollar fifty each."

"Dollar fifty!" Mike howled. "That's mighty steep, ain't it, Monroe?"

"Boys, I ain't makin' much on it. Seems like moonshine costs me more ever time I buy a batch. You boys are missin' out on some real money by not runnin' your pap's still."

"Well, we ain't," Gabe groused, "an' I guess we'll have tuh pay yer price. Ya seem tuh be the only likker store nowadays."

They paid for the whiskey, went back to the truck, and drove to the beach near the swinging bridge. The April afternoon was sunny and pleasant, so they sat on sand beside the river and began enjoying their white lightning. About two hours later, the Hawkins duo was back at Mr. Bowman's distribution center for two more pints of his elixir, and they returned to the same spot by the river to consume it. By four thirty, their second purchase was gone, and the Hawkins brothers were drunk, but they wanted more whiskey. Mike whined about the high price Monroe was charging them, and Gabe said they should go back to Monroe's house and take whatever they wanted to drink. But Mike told his brother not to talk crazy like that. That they didn't need to cause trouble for Monroe because he always treated them square.

"I guess yer right," Gabe admitted, "so let's go buy us some whiskey."

As they drove back to Monroe's house, Gabe had difficulty keeping his truck between the ditches. As the truck rattled into a spot beside the Bowman house, Gabe hit the gate post, causing a loud noise. Before they were out of the truck, Monroe was peering from his open door trying to assess how much damage had been done to the gate post and the truck. Gabe and Mike walked on rubbery, unsteady legs to the porch and into the house. Monroe had been watching them carefully as they came from the truck, and he eyed them closely as they stood in his front room swaying on their feet.

"Boys," he said calmly, "both of you've had too much to drink to be out here runnin' around in that truck. Y'all just go on home and sleep it off. Or better yet, go 'round to that workroom behind the house"—as he pointed toward the back of his house—"and you can sleep on the two cots out there. I'll bring some blankets and quilts to keep you warm tonight."

"We don't want tuh sleep, Monroe, we want likker," Gabe said.

"Now, Gabe, I'm not goin' to sell you no more whiskey. You've already had too much to be drivin' on the roads. You're gonna kill yourselfs or somebody else."

Mike pleaded, "Come on, Monroe. We need more likker."

"No more tonight, boys. Go sleep it off. When you're in better shape to take care of yourselfs, I'll sell you more likker."

Monroe pushed the pair toward the door, and finally they moved out and on toward the truck.

As they reached their truck, Mike said, "What's wrong with Monroe that he won't sell us what we want?"

Gabe was glaring into the bed of his truck, and he was boiling mad. He was quiet for a few moments and then said, "I'm goin' back an' get us some likker," and he picked up a tire iron that was lying in the truck bed.

Seeing the look on Gabe's face and the tire iron in his hand, Mike pleaded, "No, Gabe. Don't go back in there." As he held on to one of Gabe's arms with both hands, he said, "We can get likker tomorrow. Monroe said he'd sell it to us later. Don't go back now."

Gabe shook his brother's hands off his arm and walked unsteadily but quickly back to Monroe's door. He rapped hard on the door, and Monroe opened it. When he saw who was back at his door, he said, "Gabe, I done told you I ain't sellin' you no more . . ." He stopped without finishing his sentence because a tire iron slammed him hard on the left side of his head with a thump and crunch. The bootlegger dropped like a stone and lay unmoving on his floor.

Gabe spoke to the unhearing figure, "We're goin' tuh get what we want. Ya shoulda sold it tuh us. Now yer gonna have a bad headache when ya wake up, and ya won't have any more of our money."

Gabe dropped the tire iron to the floor beside Monroe and looked at a terrified brother standing with his mouth agape and an incredulous look on his face as he stared back and forth between Gabe and the man on the floor. Gabe walked into the next room and saw there a stock of distillery whiskey that must have been smuggled into the U.S., plus a cache of moonshine. Gabe told Mike to get a box that contained eight pints of moonshine, and he picked up a box of fifths of the amber distillery booze. As they came through the front room where Monroe lay, Gabe stopped and said, "He must have some money on him. No need tuh leave it all with 'im.'"

So he set the box on the floor, felt over Monroe's pockets until he felt the man's wallet. He took it out of the pocket, opened it, and extracted a quarter-inch thick sheaf of green bills and stuffed them in his own pocket. Mike was already out of the house, almost to the truck.

As Gabe stooped to pick up the box of whiskey bottles, a frightened face in another adjoining room peeked around a door facing. Her eyes grew huge, and her mouth opened as if to scream, but she stifled the sound and put her hand over her mouth. Thelma Bowman saw her husband lying on the floor; he wasn't moving. She recognized Gabe Hawkins as he picked up some sort of metal rod and stuck it down in his box of likker; he picked up the box and headed for his truck.

The Hawkins brothers put the boxes in the truck bed and got in the truck. Gabe said, "Let's go home and have ourselfs a fine ole time on Monroe's likker. When he wakes up, he's gonna have a real bad hurtin' in his head, and he'll be mad as hell that we took his whiskey and his money. But he's not gonna report it to the law 'cause it ain't legal to bootleg likker. So we'll have enough likker to keep us happy for a while and some extry money that we didn' have to work like a horse fer. Mike, brother, this's been a good night fer us."

"I don't know, Gabe. I'm worried about ole Monroe. Ya hit 'im awful hard. And he hadn't moved atall afore we left."

"Don't worry about Monroe. He'll be okay, an' we'll be even better."

Charley had just finished his supper with his mom and pop. He planned to leave in a few minutes to spend some time with Bonnie at her parents' house, but the telephone rang. When he answered it, a frantic Thelma Bowman seized his full attention.

She asked, "Is this Deputy Scott?"

"Yes it is."

"I'm Thelma Bowman and my husband is hurt. He may be dead. Can you come to my house right now, Mr. Scott?"

"Yes, I can, Mrs. Bowman. Are you all right?"

"Other than just scared to death, I guess I'm okay, but can you hurry? You know where I live, don't you?"

"Yes, ma'am, I know, and I'll be there in a few minutes."

Before hanging up the telephone, he asked the operator to dial the McGraws' number. Bonnie answered, and Charley said, "Honey, I can't make it over there for a while, maybe not tonight at all. I've got a problem to deal with, and I don't know how long it will take. I'll see you or call you the first chance I have."

"Don't worry, Charley. Just be careful." They said their good-byes.

Charley called Sheriff Fielding and told him what Mrs. Bowman said. Harg said he was involved in a matter that would take a while to finish but that he would meet the deputy at the Bowman house.

The deputy drove to Mrs. Bowman's house. He had passed by the house many times but had never been inside it. Most people in the city knew that in addition to providing taxi service, Monroe also provided liquor. Since there had never been any problems involving Monroe, Sheriff Fielding and his deputies didn't bother to try to stop the bootlegging business. As Charley drove up to the Bowman house, the front door was open, and a scared, worried woman stood in the doorway. As Charley came up the porch steps, he saw that Mrs. Bowman was crying and had a handkerchief twisted around her hand.

"In here, deputy," Mrs. Bowman said.

Charley stepped into the room and was beside the crumpled figure lying facedown on the floor; it was Monroe. He stooped beside the figure and put his fingers on a wrist; no pulse. He checked for a pulse on a carotid artery; none. With a sigh, Charley stood and looked at the expectant face of the man's wife. "I'm so sorry, Mrs. Bowman. Monroe's dead."

"I thought as much," she said. "He hasn't moved a muscle since Gabe left."

"Gabe? Gabe Hawkins?" Charley blurted out.

"Yes, Gabe Hawkins."

Charley knelt beside the body and noticed a patch of bloody hair on the left side of his head. *He must have been hit right there with something.*

"Did you see Gabe hit him, Mrs. Bowman?"

"No, I just saw him as he went out the door carrying a box—probably a box of whiskey. But it looked like he picked up a rod or something from beside Monroe and put it in the box he carried out."

"Was anybody with him?

"I didn't see anybody, but someone knocked on the door and Monroe opened it. They exchanged a few words, but I couldn't understand what they were saying. Then I heard a kind of thump, then voices from that room," and she pointed to the room where her husband had kept his stock of liquor. "So somebody must have been with Gabe and had gone out before I looked in here and saw Gabe."

Charley looked at the unfolded wallet lying beside Monroe and asked Mrs. Bowman whether her husband kept much cash in his wallet. She told him that Monroe usually had a few hundred dollars in it and that she had checked it just before Charley arrived; there was no money in it then. The deputy asked more questions, and Mrs. Bowman seemed to be answering them as forthrightly as she could. She didn't try to hide the fact that her husband had sold bootleg whiskey. That was the least of her worries right now. Harg Fielding arrived soon, checked the body, and talked to Mrs. Bowman.

Next the sheriff gave Charley instructions to call the coroner to come for the body and to have Doc Easton check for cause of death, even though both Charley and Harg felt certain that a crushing blow to the head with some hard object not very big around was what had killed Bowman. The sheriff said, "Charley, I hate to ask you to bring in Gabe Hawkins without me, but I'm involved in a sticky mess over near the Scott County line. The state police are there, and they say I need to be there for another two or three more hours tonight. You can take

Elwood Sykes with you to see if you can find Gabe, or we can wait until tomorrow and all three of us can go looking for him. It's your choice. I don't want you to be in a situation where Gabe could do you harm."

Charley responded, "I think we should try to bring Gabe in as soon as we can. And whoever was with him, and my guess is that it was Mike."

"He has another brother, too, you know."

"Yeah, but I don't believe Rafe would be mixed up in something like this. I'll take Elwood and we'll see what we can find out." Before he turned to leave, Charley asked, "Harg, what in the world is going on around here? In less than two years now, we've had five deaths. Three of them have involved one family, the Hawkins clan, and the other two, Sol and Aunt Luce, are still suspicious in my mind."

The sheriff replied, "That's just how it happens, I guess. It's been a long time since we've had any criminal deaths in Powell County. I hope it's a long time again before we have any more."

Half an hour later, Charley had called Delbert Kent, the county coroner, and Doc Easton. Sheriff Fielding called Deputy Sykes and told him to meet Charley in town and told him the bare bones of what happened. The sheriff left to meet with the state police. Thelma Bowman's sister came to be with her for the night. When Elwood arrived, he got in Charley's car, and they decided Gabe would most likely be at the Hawkins farm. As they drove toward the farm, Charley filled Elwood in on the details of what he knew.

As they neared the Hawkins house, Charley turned his car lights off; he could still see well under the bright moon in a cloudless sky. He stopped almost a hundred yards from the truck parked in front of the house, and they exited the car quietly, carrying their flashlights but didn't turn them on. Light shone through a window—probably light from a kerosene lamp. Charley remembered from his visit here when Mr. and Mrs. Hawkins died that the lighted room was the kitchen. Someone must be in the room. The two deputies walked to the truck, looked in the bed, and saw two cardboard boxes. Charley flicked his flashlight on and saw what they assumed were whiskey bottles in the boxes. The box containing pint jars had two empty spots. The other box contained fifths of whiskey, eight of them, plus one other item—a tire iron. *That's the murder weapon*, Charley thought. Apparently Gabe and his cohort had taken two pints inside with them.

The deputies conferred in whispers, and Elwood moved around the end of the house to another door Charley remembered from his previous visit. Charley headed toward the kitchen, the same room in which he and the sheriff had beheld the shattered body of Willard Hawkins. Charley rapped on the door and said, "Gabe, this is Deputy Scott. I need to talk to you and whoever is with you. So come on out."

He heard someone shout, "What the hell!"

Another voice said, "Oh my god, Gabe! They've fount us aready."

The first voice, which Charley now recognized as Gabe's, yelled, "Shut up!" Charley heard nothing more for several seconds, then came sounds of feet scurrying; he was almost certain someone had moved out of the kitchen into another room.

"Come out, Gabe. We have to talk."

"Well, what do ya know. Here's dep-uh-dee Scott agin. At my house agin tellin' me what tuh do."

"Come on out."

"No, I don't think so, depuhdee."

"We have to talk about Monroe Bowman."

"What's ole Monroe been tellin' ya? That I owe him fer a taxi ride?"

"He's not telling us anything, Gabe. Monroe's dead."

"*What?*"

"He's dead. You come out, Gabe, or I'm coming in."

"Come ahead, but I know you're lyin' to me 'bout Monroe bein' daid."

Charley opened the door slowly and peered into the kitchen. Gabe was seated at the table, and in front of him was a pint jar about two-thirds full of clear liquid. *Monroe's moonshine, I'd wager*, thought the deputy. Another pint jar almost full sat at the table end opposite Gabe.

"Who's here with you?" Charley asked as he looked around the room.

"Nobody. Just me."

Charley looked carefully at Gabe. Though the man was just in his late twenties or early thirties, his hard, dissolute life of too much whiskey and poor nutrition made him look more than twice his age. His oily, stringy hair and hands and face had not been touched by soap or a razor for several days and were accompanied by dirty, worn clothing that matched his soiled person. Gabe returned the deputy's scrutiny with a sullen stare from beady, bloodshot eyes.

Charley said, "Get up, Gabe. I have to take you in. You have to answer some questions about what happened to Monroe Bowman."

"I ain't goin' nowhere with you, boy," Gabe growled.

"Oh yes you are. You can come the easy way or you can come the hard way. Whichever way it's got to be, you're going to come with me."

"Charley Scott, ya can't take me in by yersef, and ya ain't got nobody with ya."

"How can you be sure about that?"

Gabe appeared to be slightly flustered by this possibility as he glanced around quickly, then showed a crooked, sinister smile as he said, "If ya had anybody with ya, he'd be right hyere in this room. So now that we're hyere, just the two of us, I'm going tuh pound the life right outta you. I been itchin' fer the chance tuh git even with you fer what ya did tuh me down by the river that day and, most of all, fer how ya waylaid me at the mine. Now I reckon I've got ya where I can beat the livin' daylights outta ya."

With that, Gabe stood quickly, knocking backward the chair he had been sitting in. He crept around the table like a wild animal stalking its prey.

Charley moved to keep the table between Gabe and himself as he said, "Gabe, you don't have to do this."

"Won't do ya no good tuh beg, depuhdee."

"All right, have it your way. We'll do it the hard way," Charley said as he stopped circling the table.

Gabe appeared a bit surprised. "Goin' tuh take yer medicine, hunh?" With that he lunged at Charley with his huge right fist drawn back, then throwing it but finding only air as the deputy deftly sidestepped and the fist barely missed his jaw. Before his attacker could recover from his missed punch, Charley landed a solid right punch on Gabe's ear, tipping him off balance. As Gabe turned to face him, Charley's hard left hook to the side of his opponent's head jarred him. He was surprised that Charley Scott was still standing and punching him. Gabe came rushing at the deputy with his arms spread and head lowered, intending to get Charley in a bear hug and squeeze the breath and fight, and maybe even the life, out of him. Charley quickly stepped back, and as Gabe's charge took him past his intended prey, Charley gave him a hard push with his left foot, sending the man crashing headfirst into a wall.

Charley said, "Gabe, you can stop this nonsense anytime."

"I'll stop when I have ya layin' hyere on the floor beat tuh a bloody pulp," and he lunged again at his intended victim.

Charley faded back, blocking most of Gabe's flailing blows with his arms and shoulder. As the deputy began to step to his left, he tripped on the overturned chair from the table; then as he tried to regain his footing and keep from falling, Gabe landed a hard blow on Charley's jaw that sent him sprawling on the floor. Gabe hurried to pounce on the deputy with a kick at his head, but Charley rolled to one side, grabbed Gabe's foot and twisted it as he lifted it out from his attacker's side. Gabe went down, and Charley scrambled up.

Gabe rose, roaring as he came at Charley again. The deputy stood in place until Gabe was almost upon him, then he landed a hard left jab on Gabe's nose. Charley slipped to the side, and as Gabe twisted to follow him, Charley caught him with a one-two combo, a hard left jab, followed by a vicious right cross. Both blows landed squarely on Gabe's jaw and chin, sending him reeling. He shook his head, wiped a hand across the bloody nose, and felt the bleeding cut above his swelling left eye. The fight seemed to have gone out of Gabe.

With both palms resting on the tabletop and without looking up from the table, he yelled, "Now, Mike, cut 'im down!'"

Charley saw the door to the next room open a few inches and the muzzle of a double-barrel shotgun appeared, but not high enough to be aimed at him.

A voice behind the door said, "He's a daid man, Gabe," and the muzzle started upward but stopped when another voice behind the door said, "Move that gun barrel another inch and I'll splatter your brains on the door."

The gun muzzle stopped moving. The second voice then said, "Take your hand away from the triggers and use the other hand to lay the gun down on the floor very slow."

The man with the shotgun did as he was told. Then the door opened wider, and into the kitchen marched Mike Hawkins, who looked as if he was so scared he might faint. Behind him was Elwood Sykes holding his .38 revolver against Mike's head with one hand while he grasped Mike's belt securely with his left hand.

"Good timing, Elwood. I was wondering if you had been able to get in the house through the other door."

Then looking at the bloody Hawkins, Charley said, "Now, Gabe, we can continue with this little contest we were having, or you can get down on your knees and put your hands behind your back."

Gabe Hawkins glowered at the deputy and said, "Go tuh hell," but he knelt with his hands behind his back.

Charley handcuffed him, and Elwood did the same to Mike. Before moving any of the pieces of evidence, Charley took pictures of them and of the two Hawkins brothers. He searched Gabe's pockets and found a wad of money.

"Didn't have time to spend any of Monroe's money, hunh?"

No response from a surly Gabe. Charley spread the bills on the table and took pictures of the money. The deputies gathered the money, the shotgun, the partially consumed pints of moonshine, and the boxes of whiskey still in the truck, including the tire iron which appeared to have blood and hair sticking to it.

As they drove away from the Hawkins house with the two brothers handcuffed in the backseat, Elwood said, "Charley, you sure took care of Gabe."

Charley replied, "And your timing was mighty good with Mike. I don't think I'd be here now if you hadn't handled that problem."

Elwood said, "What an April Fool's Day this has been!"

CHAPTER 26

May and June 1944

Near the end of May, Cecilia Massey graduated from high school as valedictorian of her class. In her valedictory address, Cecilia challenged her classmates to be agents of progress while using their time and talents to help those around them have better, happier, and more productive, fulfilling lives. She urged all in her audience—fellow graduates, their families and friends, and the school faculty—to do this whether they continued to live here in Powell County or in faraway corners of the world. Her positive and enthusiastic message belied how she felt about her own future—at least for the coming school year.

Maddie, Verle, and Luke attended the ceremony, as did Charley and Bonnie. The five of them sat together. Verle, Charley, and Bonnie's faces beamed with pride and admiration as Cecilia spoke to the audience. Bonnie and Charley noticed that Cecilia's mother seemed not to be totally connected to what was going on; she appeared not to realize that her daughter was graduating from high school, had been honored for outstanding scholastic performance, and was the only student speaker for the graduation ceremony. Luke appeared to be in his usual surly, sulky mood.

After diplomas were distributed to the graduating students, Bonnie and Charley congratulated Cecilia, and each gave her a warm hug. As happy as the girl was to be graduating, she was greatly disappointed that her mother would not agree for her to go to college and would not help her financially, even though Cecilia had been offered an academic scholarship at East Tennessee State College that would cover most of her tuition and dorm costs. Bonnie had counseled the girl not to give up hope of going to college, if not this year maybe next. She also told Cecilia that her father, Brewster McGraw, might have an office job for her in which she could earn money to pay expenses for her first year at East Tennessee.

Verle and Cecilia continued to build stronger bonds as friends and as a father and daughter. He was glad he could help the young lady to be a little happier. She was the kind of daughter he would have been proud to have fathered. She was such a pretty, smart, and caring person who got scant attention, support, and love from her mother; her brother either ignored or tried to vilify her. Verle's relationship with Luke and Rafe had not improved. Both of them saw him as a big part of their problems, and they were also jealous of him. Luke was jealous of the attention Maddie gave Verle and of the time she spent with him. Luke spied on Verle and Cecilia anytime they talked or were alone with each other. To his disappointment, Luke never saw anything inappropriate take place between the two. Rafe was jealous of the time Cecilia spent with Verle, and he was furious that Cecilia would talk with Verle as they both laughed and enjoyed being together.

Maddie's ardor for Verle had cooled to the extent that they seldom had sexual relations. Learning that the Thackers' mineral rights her mother-in-law told her about were of no value had been a disappointment and shock to her. She had become more moody. She brooded over the lost opportunity for a good income from the coal deposits; in her mind, Verle was somehow the cause of that loss.

One night when he walked into his and Maddie's bedroom, he saw a small cot in one corner of the room. Maddie was already in bed and saw the look of surprise and fleeting anger on her husband's face.

She said, "Verle, I've not been sleeping well the last several nights. When I move around, I'm afraid I'll wake you, and sometimes you make noises and thrash around in your sleep. That makes it hard for me to sleep. So for my sake, let's try it for a few nights with you sleeping on the cot."

Obviously not happy with that sleeping arrangement, Verle said, "Okay, Maddie. We'll try it," and he proceeded to undress and stretch out on the cot.

Luke's devious, troubled mind came up with a scheme that he hoped would hurt Verle and Cecilia while getting him back in the good graces of his mother. He made up a story. He told his mother he had seen Verle sneaking out of Cecilia's bedroom in the wee hours one morning. He said Verle was acting as though he didn't want to be seen, was carrying his shoes and shirt, and his hair was all messed up and tangled. Maddie listened to her son without saying anything until he finished the story, but Luke could tell she was really angry.

When he finished his sordid little tale, Maddie said, "Just keep this between us. Don't tell anybody else. I'll handle this."

Luke nodded his head in agreement, but he told the same story to Rafe the next time he visited. Rafe and Luke were in his bedroom when Luke told him, and Cecilia heard Rafe ranting and raving.

A few minutes later, there was a knock on her door, and Rafe's oddly calm voice called, "Cecilia, will you come out. I have to talk to you. I'll wait in the front room."

Cecilia's first impulse was to ignore Rafe's request. But she decided that since Rafe seemed to be calm, she would listen to whatever he wanted to say, so she went to the front room and sat on the opposite end of the couch from Rafe. Rafe was red faced and agitated, and he looked at her with hurt, anger, and accusation in his eyes.

"What do you want to talk about, Rafe?" Cecilia asked.

"Luke told me all about it."

"All about what?"

"About Verle coming to your bedroom at night and sneaking out way up in the morning carrying his clothes, that's what."

"I don't know what you're talking about, Rafe Hawkins. Verle has never been in my bedroom, so nobody could have seen him sneaking out of it at any time, day or night."

"Luke was right. He said you'd deny it."

"Sure, I deny it because it never happened."

"Well, I believe Luke. What reason would he have to lie about that? I can't believe you would do something like this to me, as much as I have cared for you and wanted to be with you."

Cecilia tried to say something, but Rafe wouldn't stop talking. "You've never even allowed me the pleasure of being in your room, but you've taken that old man into your bed."

Cecilia stood up, now furious herself; as Rafe straightened up, she slapped him hard with her open hand and screamed at him, "Just shut up. If Luke told you that, he's lying. And if you can't believe me, I don't want to be around you at all. Just get out and don't come near me anymore. I've tried to be nice to you as one person to another. I didn't want to be your girlfriend, but I didn't want to be mean to you or hurt your feelings. But now I've had it with you. Just stay away from me, stay away from this house."

Then she ran to her bedroom and slammed the door, leaving a bewildered, angry Rafe rubbing his cheek.

Later in the day, Maddie tapped on her daughter's door and asked if she could come in. When she came in, she confronted Cecilia with the same story about Verle coming to her room that Rafe had related.

"Luke told you that, didn't he?" Cecilia shouted. "He lied to you just like he lied to Rafe."

Maddie didn't confirm or deny her statement. Cecilia continued to deny that such a meeting ever happened and that Verle had ever been in her room. After Cecilia's repeated denials, Maddie looked at her daughter with cold, hard eyes and said, "If I ever find you and Verle together that way, I'll kill him. Then I'll kick you out of the house, and you'll have to fend for yourself," and she stalked out of the room.

Cecilia couldn't believe what had happened. She was confused and hurt, but most of all, she was angrier at her brother than she had ever been before. *Why did that little scoundrel make up such a story about Verle and me?* Cecilia decided she wouldn't tell Verle about Luke's lies; she didn't want to cause Verle to be even more upset with Luke and Rafe—at least not now.

As the end of another school year drew closer, Bonnie and Charley finished plans for their wedding. Actually, Bonnie had to do most of the planning; most of Charley's contributions had been "That sounds good" or "Whatever you want, Bonnie" or "If you like it, that's fine with me." They planned a simple wedding in their church with an open invitation to the whole community. Reverend Davenport would officiate, Cecilia Massey would be Bonnie's maid of honor, and J. R. Scott would be his son's best man.

The wedding would be on Friday afternoon in the first week of June. Charley had requested and been given permission to be off duty for ten days. After the wedding, the newlyweds would drive to Gatlinburg, Tennessee for a week where they intended to enjoy each other, the little town, and the beautiful Great Smoky Mountains National Park.

On the night before the wedding, Charley and his parents were helping Bonnie and her mother decorate the church with hemlock and mountain laurel greenery and fern fronds they had gathered. Harley Davenport came to the church, and J. R. told him he wanted to tell him a preacher story that one of his co-workers at the rail yard in Norton had told him. The reverend said, "Uh oh, J. R., I'm not sure I want to hear this."

J. R. replied, "Why, I believe you'll think this is a right good story, preacher, but I doubt you'll want to repeat it from the pulpit."

"I'll bet you're right about that part for sure."

"Well, this is about a preacher at a church in Norton, but I'm not saying which one. I don't want to be accused of making light of another denomination. Anyway, this preacher was well into his sermon and was going to quote the scripture verse, 'On this rock I will build my church, and the gates of hell shall not prevail against it.' The preacher had said, 'On this rock I will build my church, and the gates of . . . ' when he saw a big rat run across the floor at the far end of the church. After only a slight pause, the preacher continued with, 'hell, what a rat!' Now, Brother Harley, you'll have to decide if you want to retell this one."

"I've already decided, J. R.," the pastor said as he headed toward the door smiling. At the door he stopped, looked back and said, "I'll see all of you tomorrow at the wedding."

The wedding day arrived. Charley was nervous, more nervous than he ever thought he would be on this day; Bonnie was all atwitter and giggly most of the morning. The ceremony began at 2:00 p.m. with family, friends, neighbors, and townspeople filling the little church. Charley's parents and grandparents and his uncles, Woody and Verle, were there. His brother Edwin, who lived in Roanoke with his wife and two young ones, couldn't be at the wedding. Verle said Maddie was feeling poorly and couldn't come, even though her daughter was the maid of honor. Bonnie's mother was there, shedding a few tears, mostly tears of happiness and pride; Brewster McGraw, proud but stern, gave Bonnie away to be married. Cecilia was happy, thrilled, all smiles; she was so honored that her favorite teacher, Ms. McGraw, had asked her former student to be in her wedding. In a gorgeous white gown with a train, Bonnie was a radiant, beautiful bride; and Charley was handsome in his new black suit, white shirt, and tie. They made their solemn vows to each other and kissed for the first time as husband and wife.

Downstairs after the ceremony, a brief reception was held in the gathering room. The bride and groom cut the cake, took the first bites of it, and spoke with well-wishers as everyone received cake and sampled punch, candy, cookies, and a nut mixture. Long minutes ticked by for

Charley; finally Bonnie changed out of her wedding gown into a pretty, short-sleeved dress she would wear to Gatlinburg. The couple exited the church under a hail of rice and good wishes and finally pulled away in Charley's car that bore various words and phrases written in soap and white shoe polish announcing to the world that Bonnie and Charley were married.

The couple arrived at the little tourist town of Gatlinburg shortly after nightfall and checked in at Ogle's Motel. Soon after they checked in, they went for dinner at a cafeteria operated by the motel owners in the next building. Neither of them felt much like eating, but each had a few bites before heading back to their room—to the pleasures they had anticipated for years.

When they awakened late the next morning, the lovebirds were eager to enjoy more of the sweet fruits of their marriage bed. Sometime past midmorning, Mr. and Mrs. Scott realized they were famished, so they showered, dressed, and paid another call on the cafeteria next door for hearty breakfasts. While at breakfast, they learned that yesterday was an important day for America and for other countries around the world. No, not because it had been their wedding day. It was what that day would come to be remembered as—D-Day. On June 6, 1944, the D-Day invasion against Hitler's Germans was launched. The assault included 24,000 British, Canadian, and American paratroopers. In the largest amphibious landing of all time, 155,000 Allied troups stormed ashore on the German-held beaches of Normandy in France. In addition, almost 196,000 naval and merchant marines personnel in over 5,000 ships were involved in that assault. Including 15,000 American paratroopers participating in the attack, 73,000 men in the U. S. First Army hit Omaha and Utah beaches.

After hearing so much news about D-Day and only partially grasping its magnitude and importance, the newlyweds were in awe of the scope of the invasion. Finally Bonnie said with a smile, "Sweetheart, you shouldn't have any trouble remembering when our wedding anniversary comes around each year."

The couple returned to Creedy on Friday, one week after the wedding, and went to the house Bonnie's father had given them as their wedding gift. A frisky, happy Little Handsome moved in with them.

Almost two weeks after D-Day, Lowell Thomas brought to radio listeners news of the beginning of the Battle of the Phillipines, the largest aircraft carrier battle in history. Large numbers of Japanese planes were destroyed and pilots shot down. The battle ended with three Japanese carriers sunk and three more damaged, forcing their fleet to withdraw.

Gabriel Hawkins was charged with the premeditated murder of Monroe Bowman in the commission of a robbery, a capital offense. Michael Hawkins was initially charged with robbery and as an accomplice to murder, but Gabe and Mike's state-appointed attorneys convinced the state commonwealth attorney that Mike had no part in Monroe's death and had tried to keep Gabe from going back into Monroe's house when he was killed. So the charge of accomplice to murder against Mike was dropped.

Attorneys for the defendants successfully argued for a change of venue, contending that their clients could not receive a fair trial in Powell County, and the trials of the Hawkins brothers were moved to Lebanon, the county seat of Russell County. One day into Gabe's trial, plea bargains for both defendants were agreed upon by prosecution and defense attorneys. Gabe's sentence was for ninety years in prison, but his attorney assured him that under current Virginia law, he could be out in fifteen years if he behaved himself. What the attorney didn't say was that, based on Gabe's record, he doubted the prisoner would do what was expected of him. Mike agreed to a five-year prison sentence with little assurance that he would serve fewer than the five years. Both men were transferred immediately to Powhatan Prison at State Farm, Virginia.

CHAPTER 27

July to October 1944

Charley still fished in Clinch River occasionally and usually looked forward to crossing the old swinging bridge to fish from a rock that jutted out into the river just above the bridge. The aged wood flooring had continued to deteriorate. Charley warned family, friends, and neighbors to be especially careful if they used the bridge.

Maddie Thacker's mental state continued to worsen. She was obsessed with the reality that the coal deposits for which Verle owned the mineral rights were of no value. She would never make the handsome profits she had envisioned when she started planning how to get control of the rights by causing Verle to want to marry her. While she had been physically attracted to Verle and enjoyed their premarital trysts and their early marriage-bed pleasures, she had grown less interested in affection and intimacy, especially after learning about the mineral rights. She began feeling that marrying Verle had been a mistake.

As Maddie's mental and emotional problems progressed, she sometimes felt as though something or someone was pulling her, compelling her back to the beach and swinging bridge where she and

Sol had spent happy times before and during the early years of their marriage and where, years later, she had last seen Sol alive. These feelings became intense enough that, without realizing where she was going, on several occasions she became aware that she was seated in the sand beside the river or was standing on the swinging bridge listening to the raging torrent of the Narrows. One late afternoon as she sat in the beach sand, she heard whistling. The tune was "Clementine." She thought, *It sounds like . . . no, it can't be him!*

As the weeks passed, the dog days of summer were soon but memories; and fall, with its cool, sunny, Indian summer days, greeted Powell County residents. Verle Thacker was puzzled by Maddie's lack of interest in him in general and in sexual activity in particular. He almost always slept on the cot in their bedroom; only occasionally did Maddie invite him, either directly or by innuendo and come-hither glances, to share her bed. He loved Maddie, but he wondered if she really loved him now. *Has she ever loved me? Were her early passionate responses to me just the result of going so long without satisfying sexual relations with Sol? Did she push me to cause Lucille's death just because she was greedy and wanted more money even at the cost of another woman's life?*

These kinds of questions now arose into Verle's thinking much more often than they had in the past four or five months. He had been hopeful that Maddie's depressed, sorrowful moods would disappear or at least become less severe, but he was afraid she was drifting further into gloom, remorse, and depression.

Cecilia Massey was working for Brewster McGraw as a bookkeeper, secretary, and general flunkie. She liked the variety of duties she was involved in and the responsibilities Mr. McGraw gave her, and she appreciated her regular paycheck, small as it was. Cecilia hoped to be able to begin her college education at East Tennessee State College next fall.

Ever since Clarissa Thacker had whispered several words to Doc Easton and told him to "tell Charley," Bonnie McGraw Scott had been trying to find something that would give a clue to the significance of those words. She had memorized the words: Verle . . . amnitas . . . caps . . . wild dogs . . . Harold's dog . . . Tell Charley. She had checked medical terms, dictionaries, and textbooks, but she found nothing helpful. School would be starting again in early September, and she was working on finding more material for several units of her biology classes, material that she could refer her students to for individual or group research on topics in the units. One of the areas she wanted her students to explore was fungi, so she began checking in the volumes of *Encyclopaedia Britannica* her father had bought for her classroom. In the section on fungi, Bonnie read about various mushrooms. She read about and saw pictures of morels, chanterelles, immature puff balls, and a few other edible varieties. Then she began reading about poisonous mushrooms and came across one that was said to be highly toxic. Its name was *amanita phalloides*. Bonnie stopped reading and wondered, *Amanita. Why does that seem familiar?* She bounced the term around in her memory, and she finally realized why it grabbed her attention! *Amnita, amanita. Was this what Clarissa Thacker was referring to in her final words to Doc Easton?* Excitedly, Bonnie hurried to learn more about the poisonous mushroom, and she became wide eyed as she read and re-read aloud, "They are often called death caps." *That's what Clarissa was talking about! Poisonous mushrooms! These are her amnitas, the caps!*

As Bonnie continued reading, she learned that *amanita phalloides* have been reported to have a pleasant taste. Symptoms of poisoning from them included abdominal pain, diarrhea, and vomiting. Then liver deterioration follows as evidenced by jaundice, delirium, seizures, coma, and may include kidney failure and cardiac arrest. Death normally occurs from six to sixteen days after ingesting the death caps. She was so excited with what she had found that she could hardly wait until Charley's patrol ended and he got home. But then she sobered a bit from her excitement, thinking, *Exactly what does this mean? It has to be about more than wild dogs. Clarissa mentioned Verle and Harold. What's their connection? "Tell Charley," she had said.* Bonnie brought home with her the volume from the encyclopedia set that contained the material about mushrooms.

When her husband's car pulled up to the house and stopped, she ran out the door, with Little Handsome scurrying along with her, and faced Charley as he got out of his car. He took her in his arms and kissed her soundly, wondering at her apparent excitement and eagerness to greet him.

The happy young deputy said, "Bonnie, you sure seemed to be in a awful hurry to see me. I know I've been away all day, but I'm away all day most work days. What's up?"

Bonnie explained as they walked hand in hand to their door. "Charley, I'm always glad to see you and to welcome you home, but I've found something related to the words Clarissa whispered to Doc Easton just before she died."

She told Charley what she had learned about poison mushrooms and names that matched two of Clarissa's final words. She explained what the symptoms of the poison were and summarized by saying, "These mushrooms cause a slow, painful death."

Then she asked, "But what does this mean? How are the mushrooms tied in with Verle and Harold Kegley and wild dogs?"

"Well, let's take it one step at a time, honey. Step one. Dogs had been killing sheep, and four or five farmers thought a pack of wild dogs was doing the killing."

"Step two. Verle and Harold Kegley and one or two others talked about putting out poison for the dogs. Harold said he didn't think Verle or anybody else actually got around to putting out poison. He said Verle told him he never bought any poison."

"Step three: one of Harold's dogs died. He didn't know what killed her, but he specified her symptoms. Bonnie, what did you say the symptoms of this mushroom poisoning are?"

Bonnie rattled off from memory the sequence of symptoms she had read. Charley thought for several seconds, then a horrified expression came over his face, "Oh, Lord, I hope this doesn't mean what I think it means!"

"What, Charley? What? You look like something has scared you half to death!"

Charley's face was ashen, his demeanor subdued and solemn as he asked, "What were Aunt Luce's symptoms leading up to her death?"

"Let's see, she was . . ." and Bonnie started listing Lucille's symptoms as she remembered them. After listing only four, she stopped with wide, round eyes reflecting dread and amazement. Then she said, "Honey, the symptoms Luce had are the very same symptoms that are caused by death cap poisoning."

"And they include the symptoms Harold's dog had before she died. You know what I think, Bonnie? I think Aunt Luce didn't die a natural death. She died from poison mushrooms. And remember the note left in my car—Lucille didn't die natural."

"No, Charley. Surely not! But if she was poisoned, how? How did she get the mushrooms?"

"Or, maybe the question should be, who got them? Who got her to eat them? How would someone get her to eat poison mushrooms? After she got sick, she never mentioned anything about mushrooms."

"What I read says these death caps have a good taste, even though they are poison."

"Well, I know Aunt Luce liked fried morels, and if the bad ones tasted good, she may have thought she was eating morels."

"Maybe they were mixed in with morels."

"Could be. But how? Aunt Luce certainly wouldn't have gathered mushrooms, edible or poison ones. So how did she get them? Who gathered them? And, if Mr. Kegley's dog died from poison toadstools, how did it get them? Somebody had to feed them to the dogs in something they would like and would eat. And how is Harold's dog connected to a pack of wild dogs that was killing sheep?"

"Charley, suppose somebody put out some kind of bait for the dog pack and had poisonous mushrooms mixed in it. The dogs probably would have eaten it. That might have happened, because the sheep killing stopped. Maybe the dogs all died."

"Yes, and maybe Harold's dog really was running with the dog pack and also ate some of the poison bait. Then an important question is, who put out the poisoned bait? And if the poison was mushrooms, who would have known which ones were poison and where to find them?"

Bonnie responded, "Clarissa is the one who left the clues, if that's what the mysterious words were. And she must have known about the bad mushrooms. She mentioned amnita and caps. She also mentioned her son's name. How is Verle connected to this mess?"

"Let's assume that Clarissa showed Verle how to identify the death caps and where they grew so he could get rid of the dogs. He then gathered the mushrooms, mixed them with some sort of bait, and the dogs ate it and died. Aunt Luce and Harold's dog suffered the same kind of symptoms before they died, and those symptoms are the ones you found in your reading about death cap poisoning. So it's logical to conclude that Harold's dog, the dog pack, and Aunt Luce died from the same kind of poison—mushroom poison."

"So then. Who most likely poisoned the dogs and your aunt?"

"What's your best guess?"

After thinking several seconds, Bonnie answered, "I hate to even think it. I hate even more to say it. But in my mind Verle is the only one that fits in with all the other pieces of the puzzle. Death caps are supposed to taste good, so he could have fed them to Lucille, maybe mixed with morels, without her knowing they were poison. And Clarissa whispered her son's name to Doc along with the other words."

"I don't want to believe it, but I think you must be right, Bonnie. Everything we've learned points to Uncle Verle being the one who killed the dogs and his wife. And I believe his mother either knew this or had a strong suspicion that he did it. Why else would she have left the clues for us?"

"What in the world could have gotten into Verle Thacker to cause him to stoop so low as to commit murder, especially of his wife?"

Charley sat silent for at least half a minute thinking, drumming his fingers on the tabletop, mulling over ideas, discarding some, but finally saying, "I think what got into him was an itch."

"An itch? Itch for what?"

"For a pretty widow."

"You mean Maddie Massey?"

"She's the one."

Bonnie and Charley talked about how soon after Lucille's death the couple were spending time with each other and then married. Charley told her he had heard a rumor even before his aunt died that Verle was spending time with widow Massey but that he had dismissed it as unfounded gossip. Bonnie asked what they should do with what they thought they knew about the cause of Lucille's death, and Charley told her he had to talk it over with Harg Fielding. The sheriff would have to decide what to do next.

One evening after supper, Maddie and Verle sipped coffee in their front room. Maddie wondered aloud why Rafe hadn't come to their Christmas dinner and hadn't been around the house at all recently. Verle said, "That suits me to a tee."

"Are you saying you don't want Rafe around our house at all anymore?"

"That's what I'm saying."

"But, Verle, Lucas thinks so much of Rafe, and Rafe has been a good friend to him."

"Rafe isn't Luke's friend, he's just using Luke, pretending to be his friend so he can be here close to Cecilia. I know Rafe has had a hard life growing up, has lost both parents, and has two worthless brothers in prison. It's been hard on him, but that doesn't change anything about the boy and why he wants to be here." The longer Verle talked about Rafe, the more agitated and louder he got. Both Luke and Cecilia had left their doors slightly ajar and heard clearly the last several of Verle's statements. Cecilia was glad to hear what Verle said, but Luke was furious.

After Verle's last statement, Maddie sat quietly for a while. She didn't say what she was thinking. If she had said what she thought, Verle would have been astonished. What she did say was, "All right, Verle, I'll have Lucas tell Rafe it would be better if he didn't come around."

"Luke had better tell him. If he doesn't, I will tell Rafe in no uncertain terms that he's not wanted near this house."

"I'll see that Lucas tells him, Verle."

Luke could contain himself no longer. He ran to the front room, looked at Verle, and spat out, "I hate you, Verle Thacker! Rafe is my friend, no matter what you say. You're just telling my mother that to get at me. I wish you had never come here!" Then he ran out the door, slamming it hard behind him.

Maddie said, "Now look what you've done, Verle. You've upset Lucas again. He says you're always trying to make him look bad and trying to turn me against him. He also says your interest in Cecilia is not just as a father for a daughter, if you know what I mean without spelling it out."

"Why, that spoiled brat! He's got you twisted around his little finger, and you can't see what a selfish little devil he is. Of course, a dirty mind like his might think I have some immoral interest in Cecilia, but I have never thought of Cecilia in any way but the way I would think of my own daughter. A brother who goes around spying on naked women, even on his sister, has something bad wrong with him."

"Verle, you're going too far! Lucas is my boy, and I won't have you making such untrue statements about him."

"They're true, and you know it. You also know about him stealing women's undergarments. Is that all right too?"

Verle's words caused Maddie to take in her breath sharply, and then she became quiet and still with hard, piercing eyes boring into her husband. She thought, *Do I really want Verle around me anymore?* What she said was, "Maybe you should watch your mouth, my husband. We're very much like each other, you know."

"We are? How's that?"

Her voice rose with her anger, and she almost shouted, "Well, we both got rid of an unwanted spouse! You got rid of Lucille but only because I kept pushing you to do it. You wouldn't have done what had to be done so that we could be together and marry unless I had been there to push you. But I got rid of Sol without any encouragement or help from you or anybody else."

Verle looked stunned. "You got rid of Sol?"

"Oh, the river killed him. I just helped by making sure he went into the river. I knew what the Narrows would do to him."

"Are you serious, Maddie? Did you really kill Sol?"

Maddie replied grimly, "I did. And I'll tell you what I did after he went into the river. Nobody even suspected me." And she proceeded to recount minute details of what she did at the river.

After finishing her account, Maddie said, "Verle, I do what I have to do. You'd best remember that, lover boy."

Then after a long, direct glare at Verle, she walked to their bedroom and closed the door. She sat on the edge of her bed thinking. Finally she said aloud, "I don't want Verle around here any longer."

She quickly undressed, got under her bedcovers, and was asleep within a few minutes. She slept, but it wasn't a restful sleep. It was a nightmare, a series of nightmares.

She and Sol were sitting on the beach at the river, and he was singing "Clementine." Next they were on the swinging bridge, and he was trying to throw her into the water. Then she was in the water, and Sol was on the bridge singing "Clementine" and laughing.

As Sol laughed, he sang, "Drove she ducklin's to the water, ev'ry mornin' just at nine, hit her foot against a splinter, fell into the foamin' brine. Oh my darlin', oh my darlin', oh my

darlin', Mad-uh-line. Thou are lost and gone forever, dreadful
sorry, Mad-uh-line."

Now Maddie was on the bridge, and Sol was in the water
screaming for her to help him. Then Lucille and Verle were
on the bridge looking down at her as Lucille smiled and Verle
stretched out his hand toward her. She heard the roar of the
Narrows, and she felt the cold water sucking her under.

Maddie awakened suppressing a scream; she was sweaty and shaking uncontrollably. This kind of dream was happening often now. *What's happening to me?* she wondered. *Am I losing my mind?*

After Maddie left the room, Verle sat in his chair hardly able to comprehend what his wife had told him. She killed Sol! Then it dawned on him. Maddie was right about them being alike. At Maddie's pushing and prodding, and because he wanted desperately to be with her, he had done what she urged. He poisoned Lucille. Verle puzzled over why Maddie told him about killing Sol and about what she meant by saying he should remember that she does what she has to do. Another troubling thought formed. *Maddie was threatening me!*

Verle was just now seeing Maddie for the selfish, cunning manipulator she was. Her attitude toward him changed dramatically when she learned the mineral rights he owned were to coal deposits that could not be mined profitably. So she had wanted to marry him just to get access to the coal and the money she thought it would bring them. Oh, both of them enjoyed their romps in bed, but he loved her. Maddie had loved only the possibility of more money. *What a blundering, murdering fool I've been*, Verle thought. Verle sat with his elbows on his knees and with his head hanging low in regret.

A gentle hand touched his shoulder, and he looked up. It was Cecilia. She looked at him with inquiring eyes, "Verle, are you all right?"

"Can't say that I am." Then Verle noticed that Cecilia had red-rimmed, tear-filled eyes and asked, "But what's bothering you, Cecilia?" He pulled another chair near, motioned for her to sit, and said, "Tell me."

The girl dabbed at her eyes and said, "I heard what you and Mother said about Lucille and Daddy's deaths and what she said she did that night after Daddy went into the river."

His face was ashen, and he couldn't look at the girl. "I wish you hadn't learned it that way, but I can't deny it, Cecilia. I had fallen so hard for your mother that I was willing to do anything to be with her. I'm so sorry and so ashamed of what I did to my wife. And I had no inkling that Maddie was responsible for your father's death. After I get a few things in order, I'll have to confess to what I've done."

"Do you have to?"

"Yes, honey, I must."

"Without you here, I don't think I can stay in this house with Mother and Luke. And Rafe will probably be welcomed back if you're not here, and I certainly couldn't stand that."

"Maybe with me gone, Luke will be easier to get along with."

"Maybe so, but I doubt it." She paused and thought for a few seconds, then continued, "Verle, there's something else Luke did that I have to tell you."

She then told about Luke lying to her mother and Rafe about seeing Verle coming out of her room one night with his shirt, shoes, and socks in his hands. She said that both Rafe and her mother believed the story even though she told them Luke was lying and that Verle had never been in her room.

Verle jumped to his feet and paced angrily in the room. "That blasted boy! I could wring his lying neck! That's one of the reasons your mother is so cold toward me now."

Cecilia said, "There's more, Verle."

"More? What?"

"Mother told me that if she caught you and me together in . . . you know . . . that way, she would kill you and kick me out of the house."

"What's wrong with her? She believes everything that deceitful Luke tells her. I've got to do some hard thinking about this mess. You go on back to bed and try to get some sleep. I'll sleep on the couch tonight."

Cecilia went back to her room, but she was still crying. Now she was crying because of what she was remembering. What her mother had said about causing Sol's death had brought memories flooding back that had been blocked from her consciousness. Cecilia now remembered clearly what she had seen the night her daddy had died; she knew who was responsible for his death.

Her mother had pushed her father into the river. Verle, with encouragement from her mother, had killed Lucille. She thought, *If I have to leave this house, so be it. I can support myself.* Verle had said he would confess to his crime. When he did, she would tell Charley Scott about what she saw the night Sol died. She couldn't protect even her mother from the consequences of murder.

CHAPTER 28

October and November 1944

The next morning, Maddie asked Luke to get word to Rafe Hawkins that she wanted to talk to him and that she would meet him in town. A day later, shortly before dark, as Maddie sat with Rafe in her car near the post office in Creedy, she spun a sinister lie. She told the boy that Cecilia was in love with Verle and that there was no chance that she would ever want to be with Rafe as long as Verle was around.

She asked, "Rafe, are you going to do anything to get Verle out of your and Cecilia's lives? Or do you just want to lose her forever?"

Rafe asked, "But what can I do?"

"Think about it. You'll find a way. As far as I'm concerned, you can come to our house, but make sure you come when Verle isn't there. And don't try to get near Cecilia for a while yet." After a short silence, she continued, "I'll be going. Just think about Cecilia and Verle."

Rafe got out of the car, and Maddie drove away smiling to herself. She left Rafe standing alone with his hands jammed in his front pants pockets and his shoulders sagging. His crestfallen face, listless stance, and sorrowful eyes told Maddie that Rafe believed her perverted story about Cecilia and Verle.

As Rafe thought again of what Luke had told him about seeing Verle coming out of Cecilia's bedroom one night and of what Maddie had just told him, he began to get angry. The more he thought about Cecilia, the more irate he became. He had to do something to stop Verle from having Cecilia. He didn't know what yet, but he resolved he would figure out something.

On November 6, 1944, Verle heard Gabriel Heatter's news broadcast as he began with, "There's good news tonight." That day, U.S. B-29 planes began pounding Tokyo, Japan with their cargos of bombs. And on the homefront, Franklin Delano Roosevelt was elected to his fourth term as president that same day.

During the last week of October and the first two weeks of November, Verle, Demus Ferguson, and Cecil Denton had worked in tobacco—grading, tying, and baling the cured burley crops on the Thacker and Massey farms. On the third Thursday in November, two days after Verle's upsetting discussions with Maddie and then with Cecilia, the men loaded the tobacco bales on a truck to take them to market at one of the warehouses in Abingdon. Tobacco companies bought burley at auctions there, primarily to make cigarettes and to blend into pipe tobacco. Late Friday morning, Verle left on his way to market with a truckload of almost a year's work in the form of tobacco bales. He would get the tobacco unloaded this afternoon, and it should sell the next day. He would sleep in the truck tonight, watch the auction of tobacco, including his, get their checks for it, and return home by Saturday night.

Knowing that Verle would be gone Friday night and most of the day Saturday, Luke saw Rafe in town and invited him to come to their house Saturday. Rafe said he would be there. That Friday night, Luke was sitting in the front room munching on a molasses cookie Cecilia had baked. As he read a *Field and Stream* magazine, he saw his mother go down the hall to the bedroom she and Verle shared.

Luke crept down the hall until he could see into the bedroom. He saw his mother's reflection in her dresser mirror as she opened a drawer in a chest where Verle kept his stuff. She lifted something out of the top drawer and slipped it under her sweater. Luke didn't see what she took from the drawer. As his mother started toward the hall, he sped back to his chair in the front room and picked up his magazine.

Maddie went into the kitchen, and Luke had a clear view of her as she opened a cabinet door, stood on her tiptoes, and moved whatever she had under her sweater up to the back of the cabinet's top shelf. Maddie's quick, furtive glance through the doorway into the front room told her that Lucas had been watching her. *Good,* she thought. *Now he'll have to satisfy his curiosity and find out what I put on the shelf, and I don't think he's going to keep quiet about what he finds.*

Later that night, after he decided everyone else was asleep, Luke slipped from his room into the kitchen, struck a kitchen match, lit a lamp, and quietly moved a chair over to the cabinet. Holding the lamp, he climbed up in the chair and looked on the cabinet shelf where his mother had placed the item she brought from Verle's chest. He saw a revolver. "His .38," Luke whispered to himself. He got down from the chair, blew out the lamp, and went back to bed wondering why his mother had moved the gun from Verle's chest to the kitchen cabinet.

The next morning, shortly after Maddie, Cecilia, and Luke had finished their breakfast in silence, there came a knock on the door. Cecilia went to the door and opened it; startled, she drew in a sharp breath and exclaimed, "Rafe."

Rafe said, "Mornin', Cecilia. It's good to see you."

Cecilia said, "I have nothing more to say to you, Rafe," and she turned and hurried to her room where she slammed the door shut.

Rafe glanced at Luke, then stared at Maddie. As if he didn't understand Cecilia's attitude toward him, he held both hands in front of his body with upturned palms. He hunched up his shoulders, raised his eyebrows, and with a questioning eye and perplexed facial expression, he murmured a barely audible, "What's the use?"

Maddie said, "Rafe, just give her some time. Stay away from her for now, and remember what we talked about a few days ago. I have to go to town for supplies, so you two stay out of trouble and stay away from Cecilia, both of you."

Maddie left, and as soon as Luke heard the car pull away, he whispered to Rafe that he wanted to show him something. He opened the cabinet door, got up on a chair, reached into the cabinet, and pulled out Verle's .38 Smith & Wesson pistol. Rafe held out his hand for the gun, and Luke handed it to him. Rafe examined the gun, swung the cylinder out, and noted that it was loaded with six bullets. He was holding the gun when Cecilia surprised them. She stopped when she saw Rafe holding the gun. "What are you doing with that pistol, Rafe Hawkins?"

Luke piped up, "I let him have it."

Cecilia walked over to Rafe, took the pistol in her hand, and pulled it out of Rafe's. She asked again, this time to Luke, "Why do you have this gun here in the kitchen?"

Grudgingly and sullenly, Luke explained how he had seen his mother bring the gun from Verle's chest to the kitchen and put it in the cabinet. Cecilia said, "So that shelf is where it's going to stay," as she placed it back on the shelf. "And don't either of you dare touch it again. You hear me?"

Luke and Rafe both nodded their reluctant assent. They spent the afternoon together—part of the time in the house and part outside. Before suppertime, Rafe and Luke gathered up leftovers for Rafe to have for his supper—beans, sauerkraut, cornbread, and a glass of milk. Rafe took the food and milk out to the barn. Luke wanted Rafe to wait around outside until after Verle got home and went to bed. Then they could talk in the front room until Rafe wanted to go home.

Verle got home from the tobacco market shortly after dark that day and was well pleased with the prices their crops brought. He told Maddie how much they got for their tobacco, and she was happy with their checks. Maddie and Cecilia cooked and served supper, and with Verle and Luke, they ate supper with scant conversation. When Verle finished his meal, he said he was really tired and ready for bed and that he had to get up early tomorrow morning. He and Cecil were going to round up some yearling calves that he would take to market in Spring City on Monday. He didn't want to feed them through the winter, and prices for feeder calves were pretty high right now, especially for this late in the year. Verle went to his and Maddie's bedroom, undressed, and got under the covers of his cot. Within a few minutes, he was sleeping soundly.

What neither Maddie or either of her children knew was that Verle had decided he was going to turn himself in to Charley and tell him that he had poisoned Lucille. Verle had made out a simple handwritten will leaving the Thacker farm, its equipment and cattle, to Charley and Bonnie Scott. He penned another note telling the Scotts and Musicks how sorry he was that he had caused them so much grief by poisoning Lucille. He put the will and note in an envelope on which he had written "for Charley Scott," and he placed the envelope in a drawer of his chest. He intended to hand the envelope to Charley when he confessed to his crime.

After Verle went to bed, Luke went outside, ostensibly to go to the outhouse. But he went out to talk to Rafe. He told Rafe that Verle would be getting up early tomorrow, gone most of the day, and gone again on Monday. Since Cecilia and Maddie hadn't gone to bed yet, the two boys couldn't go in the house, but Rafe said he would like to spend the night in the hay loft in the barn if Luke could get him two or three blankets or quilts for cover. The night was going to be cold. Luke said he had extras in his room and could hand them out the window to Rafe.

Later Rafe tossed and turned under his covers in the hay loft thinking of what Luke had told him about Cecilia and Verle and about what Maddie had told him just a few days ago about Cecilia thinking she was in love with Verle. He spent a good part of the night thinking about how he could keep Cecilia and Verle apart and considered several alternatives. He finally decided that only one of the actions he could take was sure to work.

Shortly after five o'clock Sunday morning, Rafe crawled out from under his covers, brushed most of the hay and chaff off his clothes, and climbed down the ladder to the hallway floor. He opened the barn door slightly and looked toward the house; all was dark there. Under a quarter moon that went in and out behind scattered, scurrying clouds, he walked to the kitchen door and tried the knob—it turned. Rafe opened the door slowly and moved silently into the kitchen.

Moonlight lit the room enough that he could make out the cabinets, table, chairs, and cook stove, so he didn't light a lamp or a match. As he moved toward the cabinet where he had seen Cecilia put Verle's pistol, he stumbled over a small stool, knocking it over and falling against the cabinet. He was afraid the noise had awakened everyone in the house, and he stood ready to run out the door if he heard footsteps, but he heard no indication that anybody was up. He opened the cabinet door and felt around on the shelf until his fingers met the cold steel of the revolver. Carefully he lifted it out of the cabinet, stuck it in a pocket of his coat, left the kitchen, and moved into the darkness of the shed near the toilet.

Luke also had been restless that night and did not sleep well. Sometime before daybreak, a noise in the kitchen roused him. He assumed that Verle was already up getting ready to round up the calves he planned to sell. Several minutes later, however, Luke heard Verle's bedroom door open and shut, and he recognized the man's footsteps as he walked down the hall and through the kitchen. He heard the kitchen door open and close. Luke got out from under his warm quilt covers, looked out his window, and could see the indistinct figure of Verle as he headed toward the toilet.

Just as a hint of daylight was beginning to show in the eastern sky, Rafe Hawkins saw a figure come out of the house and head toward the toilet. With the pistol held beside his thigh, Rafe followed the person quickly but soundlessly. As he closed the distance between them, he saw it was Verle. Verle was dressed in a heavy coat and a cap with thick ear flaps pulled down over his ears, and he heard no sounds behind him. As he opened the toilet door, he was looking toward the barn on his left and noticed that the barn door was slightly ajar. He wondered why.

Rafe was now an arm's length behind Verle. His hand was shaking as he held the .38 a few inches from Verle's head and pulled the trigger. The gun barked, and Verle fell to the ground without uttering a sound. As he fell, his left hand reached out and involuntarily grabbed Rafe's coat, clamped on a button, and pulled it off as he hit the ground. Verle Thacker slipped into his beginning of eternity. His hand relaxed, and the button fell from his downturned palm into the frosted grass. Rafe bent down, placed the gun near Verle's outstretched left hand, and waited a long minute to see if any activity in the house indicated somebody had heard the shot. Then in a cold sweat, sick at his stomach and shaking badly, Rafe began to run back to his room at the saw mill.

Luke had been about to turn and get back in bed when movement behind Verle caught his eye. A figure came up quickly behind Verle. Luke saw a flash between the two figures and heard the muffled sound of a shot. Verle fell to the ground. The other figure looked at Verle, stooped down beside him, got up, stood still for what seemed like a long time, and then took off running out of sight toward the road. Luke heard no other sounds in the house or outside. He got back in bed, pulled his quilts up over his head; he was shaking all over, even though he wasn't cold. Luke realized he had just witnessed the murder of Verle Thacker. But who had he seen?

Luke stayed in his bed until he heard his mother come out of her room and go to the kitchen. He got out of bed, and as he started dressing, he heard Cecilia come out of her room. He stuck his head out the door, beckoned with a finger and whispered, "Ceecee, come in here."

She turned around and asked, "Why do you want me in your room now? You've never wanted me in there."

"Just come on in. It's important."

Cecilia noted that he had an unusual expression on his face—fear. And he was pale as a flour sack. She came in the room and looked around, not seeing anything unusual or noteworthy. She started to ask Luke again why he wanted her in his room, but he moved over to his window and said, "Come over here."

She did as he asked, and he pointed out toward the toilet and said, "Look!"

Cecilia looked and she was shocked to see a form, what looked like a person, lying on the ground in front of the toilet. She stammered, "Is . . . is that somebody? Is it a . . . a person?"

"It is, Cecilia. It's Verle."

"Verle? Well, we have to help him. Let's go see what's wrong with him." And she started to dash out of the room.

Luke grabbed her arm and said, "I think he's dead."

"Dead? He can't be dead!"

Cecilia then rushed out of the room, on through the kitchen and outside. She ran to Verle's side and stooped to see what was wrong with him. She touched his hand; it was cold. She felt his face; it was cold too. She put a finger on an artery in his neck, but he had no pulse. The girl stood and screamed. By this time, Maddie and Luke were beside Cecilia.

Maddie checked the body and said, "He's dead, children."

They saw the .38 caliber pistol lying beside Verle's hand and knew it was his own gun.

Cecilia sobbed, "No, no. Not Verle. He can't be dead."

Maddie put her arms around the girl and tried to comfort her. The mother said, "Let's go to the house. Cecilia, it's too cold for you to be out here with no coat. We'll have to call the sheriff's office."

Cecilia was inconsolable and continued to weep. In less than a year after he married Maddie, Verle was dead. Maddie was stoic, shedding no tears, and she mused, *Well, I guess Rafe finally decided to do what he thought he had to do.*

Luke had despised Verle, but he certainly didn't wish him dead. He wondered if the lie he had told his mother and Rafe about seeing Verle come out of Cecilia's room had anything to do with Verle being killed.

Luke didn't mention that he had seen Verle get shot. He wondered if the figure he had seen could have been his mother. If so, she could be sent to prison or to the electric chair, and he didn't want that to happen no matter what she had done. Then he remembered that the figure he saw had run away toward the road.

CHAPTER 29

Novermber 1944

Deputy Charley Scott arrived at the Massey house about a half hour after Maddie called Sheriff Fielding. The sheriff had asked Charley to get to the scene as quickly as he could and said he would join the deputy as soon as possible. Maddie met him and led him to Verle's body. Charley was saddened that his uncle was dead, even though there was strong circumstantial evidence that Verle had poisoned Aunt Luce, and he was sorry that another death would affect his parents and grandparents as well as the Massey children.

Verle's body was sprawled in front of the toilet, and the toilet door stood open a few inches. His unseeing eyes were open wide as if registering shock. Blood had oozed from a hole just behind his left ear, but he had not lost much blood. The bullet that killed Verle was lodged just under the skin above the outer edge of his right eyebrow. A revolver lay on the ground about a foot from Verle's left hand. Maddie identified the gun as Verle's, and Charley knew it was his because he and Verle used to fire it in target practice. In the gun's cylinder were five .38 caliber bullets and one spent shell.

With Charley on the scene, Maddie acted as if she were devastated by her husband's death. She told Charley it was obvious he had killed himself, that he had been despondent for some reason. Cecilia *was* devastated and said Verle had not been despondent and that he would never have shot himself. She said he was supposed to pick up Cecil Denton and they were going to round up calves that Verle planned to take to market Monday. Harg Fielding arrived on the scene and asked Maddie, Luke, and Cecilia questions, some of which Charley had already asked, but the sheriff wanted to hear their responses.

Verle's death could have been a suicide. He was killed with his own gun. But the angle of the fatal bullet meant it would have been hard—not impossible, but hard—for Verle to have held the gun in the position necessary to shoot himself. Also, Verle was right handed, and he would have had to hold the gun in his left hand to shoot himself behind his left ear. The deputy took pictures of the body and the surrounding area, including the pistol and toilet.

Using a clean handkerchief wrapped around the barrel of the revolver, Charley picked it up carefully. Fingerprinting was now an accepted way of identifying individuals, but the Powell County Sheriff's office had no fingerprinting equipment. Anyway, Charley and Harg realized that various fingerprints would be found on the gun; from their questioning, they had learned that Cecilia, Luke, and Rafe Hawkins had all handled the pistol recently. Luke knew his mother had handled the gun, and he had told Cecilia that his mother brought the gun from the bedroom to the kitchen. But again he didn't mention this to the sheriff or his deputy, nor did he tell what he had seen from his bedroom window when Verle was shot.

Charley began searching for evidence in the area around the body, looked a few minutes, and found a large button in the grass under Verle's left hand; it looked like a coat button. It didn't match the buttons on Verle's coat, so where did the button come from? Harg said the death was probably a suicide; and Delbert Kent, the coroner, ruled it a death by gunshot, probably a suicide.

Charley felt that Verle might have been murdered, and he continued to think, search, and ask questions. All the Masseys, Maddie, Luke, and Cecilia, had the opportunity to shoot Verle, and they all knew the gun was in the kitchen cabinet. Maddie insisted that her husband had moved the pistol from his chest drawer to the cabinet. Luke wouldn't tell that he saw his mother sneak the gun from the bedroom to the kitchen.

When the deputy moved farther from Maddie, Cecilia walked over to him and said in a low voice, "Mr. Scott, Luke won't tell you something he knows. He saw Mother bring Verle's gun from their bedroom to the kitchen."

"Thank you, Cecilia. We need to know as many facts related to the shooting as we can, and if you think of anything else, let me or the sheriff know."

There was no question in the mind of either the sheriff or the deputy that a bullet fired from Verle's gun was what killed him. Harg returned the .38 to Maddie, telling her to keep it in a safe place, and she said she would return it to the shelf in the kitchen cabinet where Verle had put it. The sheriff told the coroner and undertaker, Delbert, to take the body.

As Charley continued to look around, he noticed that the barn door was open slightly. He asked Maddie if the door was usually kept shut, and she responded that it was. She didn't know why it wouldn't be closed.

Charley said to Harg, "I'll go look around in the barn."

Inside the barn, he saw nothing out of the ordinary. Everything seemed to look normal, but he decided to check the hay loft. He climbed up the ladder. As soon as he was high enough to see the loft area, he spotted items not normally found in a hay loft. Charley called out, "Harg, I think you should come look at something."

Charley climbed on up the ladder and stood in the loft area, and Harg soon joined him. Harg saw what had grabbed Charley's attention—quilts, an unwashed plate, a glass, and a spoon. From the depression in the hay beside where the quilts lay, it was obvious that someone had slept in the hay very recently, probably last night. Charley descended the ladder, retrieved his camera, and took pictures of the hay loft, including the quilts, the spot where somebody had lain, and the dishes.

Charley asked, "Whose quilts and dishes are these? If they're Maddie and Verle's, how did they get out here? Who brought them out here, and when?"

The sheriff said, "This is a mite peculiar, Charley. Somebody could've spent the night here and waylaid Verle this mornin'. But how did that person get Verle's gun without the family knowin' about it?"

"I don't know the answers to your questions, but I'm feeling more and more like Verle didn't kill himself."

"You may be right. I think we should look around some in the house."

So he asked Maddie if it was all right for them to look through Verle's belongings in the house. Maddie said that was fine and that Verle kept all his stuff either in the chest in the bedroom or under the cot. The sheriff and deputy began examining Verle's belongings, clothes, and papers in the bedroom. They found nothing of any apparent significance until the deputy found an envelope in the top chest drawer that had "For Charley Scott" written on it. He scowled at the envelope and looked questioningly at his boss.

Harg said, "Well, it says it's for you. Open it up and see what we have."

Charley pulled the contents out of the envelope as the sheriff stood at his shoulder. They saw the will and the note, and each of them read both. "Well, I don't know what to make of this," Charley said.

"You might make a case for this bein' the last message of a man plannin' to kill hisself."

"Yes, you might. But there just seems to be too many other parts of this mystery that don't fit into a suicide."

"I agree, Charley. I think we need to do some serious questionin' of Maddie and her children, one at a time and not in the presence of the other two. But let's hold off on that for a day or so. We'll leave the family to grieve or do whatever they need to do in gettin' ready for another funeral. We'll have to ask about Rafe too. When was he here last? We'll also need to question him. Lord, we sure have had more than our share of death investigations in the past several months."

The sheriff told Maddie they were taking an envelope that Verle had left in his chest drawer. Maddie asked, "What's in the envelope, sheriff? Is it a suicide note?"

"We'll talk about that in a few days. Now, is there anything Charley or I can do to help you and your children?"

"No, thank you, sheriff. We'll be all right."

"Well, we'll be goin' then, Miz Thacker. I sure am sorry that you've lost your second husband so soon after you all married."

After the lawmen left, Cecilia went to her room, grieving for Verle. She began to think back over the past several days to see if she could recall anything that might be connected to his death. She remembered her mother's admission that she caused Sol's death and that she goaded Verle to get rid of Lucille. Cecilia also recalled Maddie's threat to Verle. Then she remembered that Luke had told her that he had seen their mother sneak Verle's pistol from the bedroom to the kitchen cabinet shelf. *Rafe Hawkins was here yesterday, and he knew the gun was in the cabinet. Did he have anything to do with the murder?*

Cecilia decided to face her mother and ask questions. She strode to the front room where Maddie sat, apparently deep in thought and with a worried expression. Cecilia stood near Maddie and said, "Mother, I have to ask some questions."

Seemingly with great effort, Maddie responded, "Child, I have a lot on my mind right now. And I've got to make arrangements for Verle's funeral. We'll talk later."

In a loud, demanding tone, Cecilia said, "I have to know, Mother. Did you have anything to do with Verle's death?"

"Heavens no, Cecilia. Why would you ask a fool question like that?"

"Luke saw you sneak Verle's pistol from the bedroom to the kitchen."

"You don't know what you're talking about." Now both mother and daughter were yelling at each other.

"And why was Rafe Hawkins here yesterday? Did you arrange that?"

"You're crazy, young lady! What's got into you? I'm giving you fair warning. If you know what's good for you, you'll keep your mouth shut on things you have no business talking about. Bad things can happen to a person anytime. Remember that."

With that statement, Maddie rose and stomped down the hall and slammed her bedroom door shut. Cecilia sat on the couch with her shoulders slumped and began crying again. A few minutes later, she heard someone enter the room. She looked up and saw her brother. Luke had an expression and demeanor that his sister had not seen on him for several years. Was he afraid? Ashamed? Sorry? Maybe all of these.

He said, "Ceecee, I have to talk to you."

She wiped her eyes with a hankie and said, "Well, this is something new. You wanting to talk to me. What is it?"

He sat on the couch near her. "I heard what you and Mother just said. I have something I have to tell you." Looking down at his hands clasped in his lap, he said in a barely audible voice, "I lied about seeing Verle come out of your room."

"You think I don't know that?"

"Yes, I know you know it, but I wanted to tell you I'm sorry I lied. I'm ashamed I told that story to Mother and Rafe. And I'm wondering if that lie had anything to do with Verle getting shot. Do you think it does?"

"It may. I don't know. But you could tell Mother the truth. And Rafe. That won't change the damage the lie has caused, but at least they'll know the truth."

"I'll tell them. Ceecee, do you think Mother's been acting strange lately?"

"Yes, Luke, I think she has. Maybe she has some kind of mental problem. Or worry. Or, maybe memories that are bothering her. I don't know. Anyway, I'm glad you owned up to lying about Verle and me. And, Luke, whatever you know about Verle's death or about anything you think might be even remotely connected to it, I beg you to tell Mr. Scott or Sheriff Fielding. I know you didn't like Verle, but he should not have been shot down from behind, and whoever did it should have to answer to the law. I'm going to my room now."

Luke remained seated on the couch, thinking. He began itemizing in his mind what he knew that might be related in some way to Verle's death.

I saw Mother bring Verle's pistol to the kitchen.

Just a few days ago I told Rafe that Mother wanted to meet with him. I assume they met.

Cecilia, Mother, Rafe, and I knew where Verle's gun was kept in the kitchen. And I don't think Verle knew it had been moved from his chest drawer.

I know that last night Rafe ate supper in the barn and spent the night there.

I didn't hear anybody except Verle come in or leave the house this morning before he was shot. But . . . wait! I did hear some kind of noise in the kitchen several minutes before Verle left his bedroom.

I saw somebody shoot Verle. I thought it was a male figure, but I couldn't be sure. Was it Rafe I saw? Did Mother have any part in the shooting? Could that be why she wanted to meet with Rafe?

Luke worried about the quilts and dishes he had got for Rafe to have in the barn. He knew his sister and mother would know the quilts came from his room and that he must have got the food for whoever ate it. He wanted to tell Cecilia all that he knew, but he was too scared to tell anybody now. *Maybe in a few days.*

The next morning, Cecilia called Mr. McGraw and asked if she could be off from her job for a few days. Brewster had already heard of Verle's death, and he told her to take as much time off as she needed. At about the same time that Cecilia telephoned Mr. McGraw, Charley Scott stepped out of his office into the chilly, gusty, overcast November day in Creedy with the harsh reality of another violent death in Powell County foremost in his troubled mind. Brown leaves clinging to pin oaks along the street rustled and rattled in the wind. The deputy turned up his jacket collar and started up the street toward the post office. He saw coming toward him a man with his head down, not looking beyond his feet as he walked. It was Rafe Hawkins. As they neared each other, Charley spoke up, "Rafe, are you okay?"

As Rafe's head jerked up, his eyes were wide, and he appeared to be startled. Or was it fear showing in his expression? Rafe blurted, "What? Oh, yeah, I'm fine, Mr. Scott."

But you don't look fine, Charley thought. "I guess the sawmill's not working today since you're here in town."

"Oh, the mill's going today. I just decided to take a day off, that's all," Rafe replied as he pulled his coat collar tighter to his neck. "Got something I have to do."

Rafe's coat was buttoned against the cold, but Charley noticed that the second button from the top was missing. And Rafe's coat buttons looked to be exact matches to the one Charley had found beside Verle's body the day before. Same size, same color, similar markings.

Charley wondered, *Is it possible that button came off Rafe's coat? Even if it was a button from his coat, it could have come off anytime that Rafe had been at the Massey farm. But the button under Verle's hand had been lying on top of the grass. It hadn't been stepped on to press it closer to the ground. That button probably had not been lying in place very long.* Charley didn't want to believe that Rafe was involved in Verle's murder, but he couldn't be ruled out. *For what reason would Rafe shoot Verle?* Charley thought Rafe seemed ill at ease and eager to get away from him. Charley said, "I'll see you, Rafe."

"Yes, sir, Mr. Scott," Rafe replied, and each of them walked away, Rafe hurrying along at a faster pace than before they met.

As Rafe left, Bruce Charles, owner of Creedy's only automobile repair shop, was near Charley and stopped when they met. "That was Rafe Hawkins, wudden it?" Bruce asked.

"Yep, that was Rafe. Seemed a little edgy this morning."

"I saw 'im early yistadee mornin'."

"Yesterday morning? Where was he?"

"Well, I thought he must be agoin' to the room he stays in at the sawmill. He was aheadin' in that d'rection. Runnin' he was."

"Where was he exactly when you saw him, Bruce?"

"He was on River Road 'bout half a mile or so past the Massey house. Or the Thacker house, or whatever it's called now."

"When did you see Rafe?"

"It was barely after daybreak. I was headin' out to pull ole man Artrip's truck to the grahge. Had a broke axle. That's when I saw Rafe. I would've offered 'im a ride, but I was only goin' a few hunnerd yards futher to the Artrip place. As I was hookin' the truck to mine to pull it to the grahge, Rafe passed by without lookin' to his right or left. And he was still runnin' like a scared rabbit."

"See ya, Bruce," Charley said as he walked on toward the post office, thinking as he went. *Was Rafe running from the Massey place?*

Several hours after Charley Scott had met Rafe on the street in Creedy, Cecilia decided she needed to get out of the house for a while, so she slipped into her winter coat, put a scarf over her head, and laced her heavy shoes before heading out into the November afternoon. The sun was playing peek-a-boo through the clouds. As she sauntered upstream alongside a gurgling little branch, she noticed there was still tasty, succulent water cress, bright and green, growing in the water. *Water creases is what most everybody around here calls them. They sure would be good with some onions mixed in them and wilted with hot grease.* She followed the tiny stream up into the woods to a secluded small cove that had some grassy open spaces with large boulders scattered about.

Cecilia found a huge limestone boulder that rose several feet above the soil but had a nice bench about three feet high. She backed up to the rock, leveraged herself up with her arms, and sat. As she looked out from her perch, her face blanched and her eyes widened. Facing her about twenty feet away was Rafe Hawkins. He was still, just gazing at her, mute. Cecilia said irritably, "Rafe, you've been following me. For how long?"

"Hi, Cecilia. Since you left the house. And don't worry. I'm not going to bother you any. I just have to tell you some things. It's important. Will you let me talk to you? Please."

"I'll listen. Come a little closer and sit on that rock," Cecilia said, as she pointed to a rock about ten feet from her. "Now, talk."

"Cecilia, I've been crazy about you ever since I laid eyes on you that first day I saw you in Creedy. You may already know that. I know I've been wrong to try to force myself on you, like tryin' to get in your room that time. But two things happened that made me so jealous and so mad that finally I had to do something to keep from losing you."

Cecilia started to speak, but Rafe held up a hand and said, "No, let me have my say, then you can have yours if you want. The first thing that nearly killed my soul was when Luke told me he had seen Verle comin' out of your room late at night carryin' his clothes."

Cecilia tried to interrupt again, but Rafe said, "Not now. Let me finish what I have to tell you. The other thing was when your mother told me that you were in love with Verle and that, as long as he was around, I could never hope to get to be with you. The only way out that I could see was to get Verle Thacker out of the picture. So I shot him."

Rafe stopped talking and watched as the color drained from Cecilia's face, and she buried her face in her hands, sobbing and moaning, "Oh, no. No. No."

Then she raised her head as tears flooded down her cheeks and dropped on her lap. Cecilia looked at Rafe and said, "Oh, Rafe. You murdered Verle because of two lies."

"Sure," Rafe said derisively. "Both your brother and your mother lied to me about Verle? I don't believe it."

"It's true. Verle was never in my room. And I loved him, but like a daughter loves her father. He never thought of me as anything but a daughter. Until just recently, I've always tried to be nice to you, to treat you the way I would want to be treated. I've never been interested in you as a boyfriend, but you tried to force yourself into my life to become one. Now you've killed a man who was like a father to me because of lies you were eager to believe."

Rafe stared at Cecilia, and his look of disbelief slowly changed to a questioning, quizzical countenance. The reality of what Cecilia had just said slowly dawned on him. With a wretched expression on his face, he stammered, "Cecilia, I don't . . . I mean . . . But, Luke, Maddie . . . Oh, Cecilia."

Wiping her eyes and cheeks with the backs of her hands, she finally sighed and said, "Rafe, you have to tell Charley or Sheriff Fielding what you did. They're going to find out sooner or later that you killed Verle, and it'll make things easier on you if you confess to your crime."

"I don't know. I'll have to think about that."

"I won't tell Charley what you've told me for two or three days. If you haven't told him or the sheriff by then, I will. You go on your way now, Rafe."

Rafe looked at Cecilia with longing, aching, sad eyes but said nothing as a fat teardrop rolled down each cheek. Finally with a hopeless shrug he turned from her, and with his head drooping, he half stumbled, half ran out of sight. Cecilia bowed her head and cried again.

CHAPTER 30

Another funeral and burial service was over. A saddened community—neighbors, friends, and family—had paid their last respects to another of their own. Most could not grasp the reality of Verle's death, and most viewed it as a murder, although the sheriff and his deputies had never indicated that it was. Verle's death made the sixth in the community in a little over two years that had been either violent or mysterious or both. Bonnie and Charley felt especially sorry for Cecilia because the girl seemed so genuinely grieved by Verle's death, and they did all they could to support and encourage her. At the services, Maddie had appeared stoic, unmoved, uncomprehending, detached. Luke seemed apprehensive. Maybe guilty? Charley was looking forward to talking with, and asking more questions of, Maddie, Luke, and Cecilia, as well as Rafe Hawkins.

Early the morning after the funeral, Cecilia confronted her mother and told Maddie that she had witnessed what happened to Sol on the swinging bridge and had overheard Verle and her talk about getting Lucille out of their lives not long before Lucille died. Maddie appeared to be shocked by her daughter's statements, and she denied any wrongdoing in either case. She retreated to her bedroom.

Maddie's nightmares had become more frequent and scarier; they now featured Sol, Lucille, Verle, and Rafe. In her dreams, she always heard the roar of rushing water. When she was awake at night, she often heard, or thought she heard, whistling; it was the tune Sol had often sung and whistled—"Clementine." She became delusional and paranoid. Maddie was now convinced that Rafe, with Lucas and Cecilia's help, was going to kill her or that they were going to tell Charley that she had murdered Sol or Verle or both.

Later in the morning, after Cecilia confronted her mother about Sol and Lucille's deaths, Rafe paid a visit to the Massey house. He said he came to visit Luke, but he really wanted to talk with Cecilia again about what he should do. Both Luke and Maddie were in their bedrooms. Cecilia and Rafe sat in the front room—she in a chair facing the couch, Rafe on the couch. They talked about what Rafe should do, and he agreed to confess to shooting Verle, but he wanted Cecilia to tell Charley about it first. When Charley came to the Massey house, Rafe would go with him peaceably.

Cecilia telephoned Charley's office; he was there. Cecilia told him she had something important to talk to him about and asked if she could come to his office. He told her to come on as soon as possible. Luke was out of his room now, and Rafe said he would stay with Luke until Cecilia got back from her talk with Charley. Cecilia dressed warmly, got on their bicycle, and pedaled to Charley's office. School was out for the Thanksgiving break, and Charley thought Cecilia might feel more at ease talking about whatever she had in mind if Bonnie was there with them. So he called Bonnie at home, explained the situation, and Bonnie told him she would be there right away. She arrived a few minutes before Cecilia did.

At the deputy's office, Cecilia was pleased that Bonnie was there for her talk with Charley. She said, "Mr. Scott, first I need to tell you what I know about my daddy's death. It's something I must have blocked from my memory without knowing that I did. I only remembered what happened a few days ago when I overheard a conversation between Mother and Verle. Here's what I remember from that night when I last saw Daddy alive," and she began her story.

"On that Sunday night, Daddy came home after midnight. We hadn't seen him for several days. We were all in bed, and the first thing I remember hearing was him trying to sing 'Clementine.' He was really belting it out. That song was probably his favorite, and he liked to sing and whistle it. Maybe the sound of his truck or slamming the truck door was what woke me. I heard Mother tell you and the sheriff that she heard the slam of his truck door. Then Daddy was calling Mother's name as he opened the door and came into the kitchen." Cecilia paused and stared at her hands.

Charley asked, "What happened next, Cecilia?"

"Well, Mother went to the kitchen and I heard them. Daddy was still loud, but I couldn't make out the words when Mother spoke to him. So I got out of bed, crept down the hall, and peeked around the corner into the kitchen. Daddy could barely stand up, he was dirty and beardy, and his hair was a mess. Mother tried to calm him down but she couldn't. He yelled at her and tried to hit her, but she dodged his fist, and he almost fell. He called her a witch—I think that was the word—and he fussed some more. Then he tried to hit her again, and she dodged him again. But before she knew it, he was swinging with the other fist and smashed her on the face. Mother staggered back against the wall. Mother had this look of disbelief on her face. She said, 'Sol, what's wrong with you?' as she put her hand to her cheek." Looking at Charley, Cecilia said, "You probably saw that big bruise on her cheekbone."

Charley nodded, "I did. Go on."

"Then Daddy sat down in a chair by the table and just stared at nothing. Mother began talking to him again, saying they should do some things that they used to enjoy. Then she said, 'I know. We could go to Bristol and look around in some of the stores and go see a picture show. Or we could go to Abingdon and see a play at the Barter Theater and after that have a nice meal at the Martha Washington Inn.' Sol quickly replied, 'Don't want to go to Bristol, and don't like to eat at them fancy places like Martha Warshin'ton. Anyway, drivin' that far would use too much gas, and I'm 'bout out of gas ration stamps for this month.' Mother seemed surprised that Daddy was already out of gas ration stamps for the month and made some comment about it. He didn't respond but sat quietly for a minute or two. Mother stood up and said, 'Let's drive down to the river, look at the river in the moonlight, and recall good times we had there years ago.' Daddy thought for a little bit, then said, 'Let's go.'"

Charley interrupted with, "Wait a minute, Cecilia. Your mother told Harg and me that Sol suggested they go to the river. Are you sure your mother was the one to suggest going?"

"Yes, I'm sure. Mother helped him walk out the door. When the door closed, I went to the window and looked out. The moon was bright, and I saw Mother help him into the passenger seat, she went around the truck and got behind the wheel. She started the truck, the lights came on, and she drove away slowly. I hurried back to my room, jerked on some clothes and my shoes. I was afraid of what Daddy might do to Mother, so I decided to follow them. It wasn't far to the river, but it would take me several minutes to walk and run there, so I thought of our bicycle propped against the wall on the porch. I could get to the river on the bike real quick."

Bonnie asked, "So you followed your parents on a bicycle?"

"Yes, ma'am, I did. In a few minutes, I was near the river, and I saw the truck parked near the little beach just above the old swinging bridge. I pushed the bike into some willows behind the truck and looked toward the river. There, close to the water, were my parents sitting on the sand. They were there several minutes, and I could hear talking sounds but they weren't loud enough for me to understand what they were saying.

"I sneaked a little closer to them but stayed behind bushes. Then, as Mother pointed to the bridge, I heard her say, 'Let's walk out on the bridge so we can see the full moon's reflection in the water of Fugate Hole.' You know, the swimming hole a little way upstream from the beach. Daddy must have agreed because she helped him get up and helped support him as they walked to the bridge while he was trying to sing 'Clementine.'

"I moved out of the bushes and hid behind the truck. On the steps at the end of the bridge, they stopped, and Mother helped him take off his shoes and coat, saying that he would enjoy the fresh air more without them. Daddy didn't object. Mother laid his coat and shoes on a step at the bridge floor."

Cecilia stopped talking again. By now she was beginning to act nervous and her hands were trembling slightly. With her left hand, she clasped her right fist.

Bonnie said, "Honey, I know this is hard for you. But it'll be better for you to just get it all out in the open. What happened next?"

"They walked slowly to the middle of the bridge. It was swaying a little. Mother told him to look at the man in the moon showing himself in the still, calm water of the swimming hole, and Daddy just stared in the direction she pointed him. Then Mother turned him around and they looked over the lower side of the bridge, facing the roaring, foaming water as it started down the Narrows.

"Daddy started trying to sing 'Clementine' again as he stared toward the cascading water. Mother pulled something white from a pocket and dangled it over the side of the bridge and said, 'Look, Sol. Watch what happens to my hankie,' as she let it waft down to the water. The stream quickly took it out of sight, but Mother said, 'See how my hankie is just floating around under the bridge.' Daddy gazed glass eyed over the side of the bridge, but of course he couldn't see a handkerchief because it had already gone down the Narrows."

The girl stopped her story again. She was starting to breathe faster, she had turned a shade or two paler, and her mouth was dry. She licked her dry lips and said, "I don't think I can do this. I can't talk about it anymore."

Bonnie quickly brought Cecilia a glass of water and said, "Drink some." After several seconds, she pulled her chair over until it bumped into Cecilia's chair. Then she took one of the girl's hands and wrapped it in her own hands, and she said, "Now, take deep, slow breaths. Try to relax a little. You're going to be fine."

Cecilia nodded. She took another drink and seemed to be getting composed again.

Charley said, "Cecilia, we don't want you to talk more about this if it's too much for you to stand right now. It would be a big help to us to know the rest of what happened, but you have to decide whether you want to go on."

The girl sat silently for a full, long minute without saying any more. Charley and Bonnie looked at each other with strong empathy for the scared young Massey.

Cecilia sat more upright and said, "I know I've got to finish telling what I saw," and with a heavy sigh she began again. "That's when Mother said, 'Sol, lean way out and look back under the bridge so you can see my hankie.' Daddy seemed to be thinking for a few seconds, and then he leaned out as far as he could, looking into the water back under the bridge." Cecilia stopped again briefly, took some deep breaths, and said, "That's when it happened."

After a few seconds, Bonnie said, "Is that when Sol fell into the river?"

Cecilia replied, "That's when . . . That's . . . That's when Mother grabbed his ankles real quick, lifted them up, and the weight of Daddy's body leaning out over the side of the bridge pulled him over the side. As he began falling, I heard a hoarse scream, 'Maddie!' He hit the water, disappeared, and bobbed to the surface. I could see his white shirt clearly as he was sucked into the beginning of the Narrows. Then he was gone." With that Cecilia placed her arms on the table, laid her head on her arms, and sobbed.

Bonnie patted the girl's back as she hugged her gently. "It's okay, honey. It's okay. You're going to be fine. I know this is awful for you, but you're a strong young woman. And you're not alone. You have friends and neighbors who care for you and want the best for you, and I'll do anything in my power to help you, Cecilia. Do you understand that?"

Slowly Cecilia raised her head, wiped her eyes, looked at Bonnie, then at Charley, and back at Bonnie. She nodded, saying, "Yes, ma'am, I think I understand, and I thank you, both of you."

Charley asked gently, "Cecilia, have you never told anybody about what you saw that night?"

Bonny hurried to intercede, "Charley, maybe we shouldn't be asking her any more questions now. She's just had to relive a horrible experience. She can tell us more when she's ready, when she's feeling better."

Quickly Cecilia responded, "That's all right, Mrs. Scott. I need to finish the whole sorry tale of what happened." She heaved a long sigh and continued, "For months after that night I had been unable to face the reality of it. Then after I heard Mother tell Verle she was responsible for Daddy's death, I knew I had to admit to myself what I saw. When I did that, I knew I had to tell somebody."

"Did Maddie not know you saw her at the river?" asked the deputy.

"No, but she must have seen something to make her think somebody was around there. She looked behind trees and in the willow bushes. While she was looking, I ran to where I'd left the bike, got on it and rode like crazy back toward the house. I thought she would drive the truck back, but she didn't. Just a little ways from where I'd got back on the bike, I saw headlights coming toward me, so I got over to the side of the road, laid the bike in the ditch, and stretched out beside it. I'm sure whoever was in the car didn't see me. So after the car passed, I rode on home as fast as I could pedal.

"When I got home, I just let the bike fall to the ground near the porch, and I ran to my room. Mother thought both Luke and I were asleep when Daddy came home and when they left for the river, and I wanted her to think we were still asleep when she got back to the house. I thought she would be there anytime and thought I didn't have time to undress. I jumped in the bed and covered up, clothes, shoes, and all Several minutes later, I don't know how many exactly, I heard Mother come into the kitchen, then the living room. She went down the hall to Luke's room. I heard the door squeak a little, so I assume she looked in on him. Next she came to my door and opened it, and she could see by the moonlight that I was in bed. I thought I heard her sigh, and then she went out, thinking I had been in bed asleep all night.

"By this time, I guess I was reacting to what I had seen at the river. I was sad. I was scared. I was horrified. And I had started shivering and shaking, then I started crying, sobbing, trying not to make sounds that Mother would hear. I must have cried myself to sleep, for the next thing I remember was waking up to a bright sunshiny morning at about seven o'clock."

Charley slowly exhaled a long breath and said, "Well, Cecilia, I guess we've got the whole story now."

"Not quite."

"What do you mean not quite? Don't tell me there's more to this awful tale."

"It's not all if you want to know about what Mother did that I didn't see."

"How can you tell about something you didn't see?" Bonnie asked.

"I can tell you what Mother said she did, because she told Verle, and I overheard what she said."

Charley said, "Cecilia, I sure hate to ask you to talk more about this terrible time you've had, but I need to know everything you can tell me."

So she related what her mother had told Verle. She said her mother had watched Sol's body disappear down the Narrows. Maddie then walked back to the end of the bridge, stepped over Sol's coat and shoes on the steps, and looked toward the truck. Thinking she had seen some movement, her mother had hurried past the truck and looked around, peering into the willows, and behind the big tree, but she had seen nothing.

Maddie had said she began walking back toward her house. Before she was out of sight of the truck, she saw headlights of a vehicle coming toward her, so she scampered off the gravel road and got behind a thicket of elderberry bushes and blackberry briars. A car passed her and stopped near the truck. A man got out and looked around briefly, and her mother heard him say to whoever was still in the car, "Well, I guess we won't have this lovely spot all to ourselves tonight after all. We'll have to try for another spot to enjoy this moonlit night."

After the car pulled out and headed on down River Road, her mother had alternated walking and running toward home. In about fifteen minutes, she entered her kitchen, and she said she heard the mantel clock in the front room strike two times. Maddie had said she collapsed on the couch and was freezing even though the room was warm. Her mother had started shaking uncontrollably and made a mad dash for the front porch where she retched violently. She went down the hall to our bedrooms. Both of the children had been in bed, and she thought they were asleep. Cecilia finished with, "And *that's* the end of the story about Daddy's death as far as I know. But I have two more sad tales to tell you."

"Two more?"

"Yes, and here's one of them. A day or two before Lucille Thacker died, Verle came to our house. It was after dark. He and Mother were talking about getting rid of dogs that had been killing sheep. Mother said she was at the Kegley farm that day and Mr. Kegley thought Verle might have put out poison for the dogs. One of his dogs was sick, a female. Mr. Kegley told Mother the dog had seemed to be in pain. She was whimpering and thrashing around. She had diarrhea and vomited. Then after a while, she started having seizures. After the seizures stopped, Mr. Kegley said the dog lay without moving but was breathing for quite a while. Mother said she was sure the dog was dead when she saw it.

"After that, I could understand only a few words of what they were saying. I heard Verle say something about 'doing away with her' and 'will kill her.' Mother's response to him included only two phrases I could understand, and they were 'better off dead' and 'we'll be rid of her.' I thought they were still talking about Mr. Kegley's sick dog. After I heard that Doctor Easton didn't know exactly what killed Mrs. Thacker, I started to wonder if Verle and Mother had been talking about something or someone other than the dog. That's when I left that note on your car seat." Bonnie and Charley exchanged somber glances.

Cecilia went on, "Then recently I learned for sure that Verle, with encouragement and proddings from Mother, poisoned your aunt Lucille with mushrooms."

Charley said, "That's what Bonnie and I pretty well decided had happened. But why was Maddie so set on getting rid of Aunt Luce? Was she so madly in love with Verle that she couldn't live without him?"

Cecilia thought a few seconds and said, "Verle was madly in love with Mother, but I think the main reason she wanted him was the prospect of a whole lot more money than she would ever see otherwise."

"You mean money from the Thacker farm?"

"Not just from the farm itself, but from mineral rights the Thackers owned on their farm and on the Massey farm, our farm." Cecilia then told Charley and Bonnie that three or four months after Verle married her mother, Maddie told her that Verle owned the mineral rights to coal deposits on the two farms but that they had turned out to be worthless. The coal was not worth mining. She quoted her mother as saying, "Remember, Cecilia, sometimes things don't pan out no matter how much planning you do."

Bonnie said, "So greed, not love, was the main reason Maddie wanted Lucille out of the picture." She wanted to move the girl's thoughts away from her mother. So she continued, "But you mentioned another tale you have."

"This terrible, sad tale is about Verle's death. Rafe Hawkins shot him."

Bonnie exclaimed, "Oh, my Lord, honey! Are you sure?"

"I'm absolutely sure. And I'm absolutely ashamed."

Charley asked, "You're ashamed? Why should you be ashamed?"

Cecilia was slouched in her chair with her shoulders drooping and her eyes downcast as she replied, "Because my mother is involved in that death too. And my brother to some extent."

Charley sighed and said, "Good Lord, can this mess get any worse? Can you give me more details?"

Cecilia proceeded to tell about the lies Luke and her mother told a jealous Rafe; lies that had inflamed him to murder in hopes of gaining the affection of someone he loved. Charley told Cecilia and Bonnie that he had begun to suspect Rafe, and he told of Rafe's coat having a button missing and of Bruce Charles seeing him running along River Road away from the Massey place the morning Verle was shot.

Cecilia told Charley and Bonnie that Rafe had agreed to confess to the crime and that Charley could pick him up at her house. After Cecilia finished, Charley told her he would have to call Sheriff Fielding and tell him what she had told Bonnie and him. He expected that the sheriff would arrest Rafe for Verle's death and Maddie for Sol's.

CHAPTER 31

Cecilia left the deputy's office full of anxiety but relieved that she had told him all she knew about three deaths. Whatever happened next was in his and the sheriff's hands. She got on the bicycle and started for home. She rode to their house and went inside to the front room where Rafe and Luke were now seated. Before she could take her outdoor clothing off, Maddie came from her bedroom and saw the three of them together. Upon first seeing Rafe, she began to get more nervous and agitated.

Maddie said, "Well, look here. We have little Ms. Prim and Proper and Mr. Cowboy Hawkins and my big boy Lucas all close and cozy! What are you three doing? Hatching up some plan to try to do me harm, I'm sure."

"Mother, everything's not about you," Cecilia replied.

Rafe popped up with, "Mrs. Thacker, you're purty good yourself at hatching up stories, ain't you. Good at tellin' lies."

"You shut your mouth, you mealy mouthed excuse for a man."

Rafe started to respond, but Cecilia shook her head and wagged a finger at him, telling him not to speak.

Her mother looked at them with an expression of fury, with hatred blazing from her eyes. She seemed to lose all connection with reality. Suddenly she turned and ran into the kitchen. Cecilia heard a cabinet door close; in a few seconds her mother was back in the front room with them—brandishing Verle's pistol. She held it steady with both hands while her eyes still flamed.

Cecilia gasped and said, "Mother!"

"Shut up, girl," Maddie rasped as she thumbed back the hammer on the revolver. She now had the gun trained on Rafe. His gaze locked onto the dark, menacing hole of the gun muzzle ready to deliver its impending doom. Rafe recalled in a flash what that gun, when in his hands, had dealt Verle Thacker.

"Mrs. Thacker . . ."

"You shut up, too, Rafe," she yelled. "I know you came here to kill me, but I'm going to get you first." With that she pulled the trigger. Cecilia and the boys flinched at the loud click of the gun's hammer falling, but there was no explosive sound, no shot from the gun. Rafe was pale and wide eyed, as was Luke.

Maddie looked at the pistol puzzled as Cecilia ran to her, grabbed the gun, and jerked it out of her mother's grasp. Maddie asked, mostly to herself, "What happened?"

Cecilia said, "It didn't shoot, Mother, because I took the bullets out and threw them into the toilet pit."

Enraged more than ever, Maddie ran back into the kitchen; Luke ran to his room. Maddie emerged from the kitchen holding one of her long, sharp butcher knives, waving it in front of her as she walked slowly into the front room. She stopped and, staring at Rafe, said, "There's more than one way to skin a cat."

Then, as if she had made a good joke, Maddie laughed wildly and said, "And, Rafe, you ain't much of a tom cat, but this knife will do the job as good as a gun."

She started moving slowly again toward Rafe with the knife thrust out at arm's length.

Cecilia grabbed Rafe's arm with one hand and opened the door with the other as she whispered, "Come on, Rafe."

Rafe followed Cecilia quickly, and they were out the door, closing it behind them. She said, "Follow me," as she sprinted down the porch steps, out of the yard, and down the road toward the river.

Maddie watched the pair from a window and figured they would go as far as the river, probably to the sandy beach there. So she put on her heavy coat and shoes and followed them. Luke saw his mother leave the house with a determined, resolute look on her face; she was holding tightly to the knife. Maddie stepped quickly on the road toward the river. Her only thought was that she had to get rid of Rafe Hawkins because he was going to do something bad to her if she didn't.

Sheriff Fielding had sent Charley to the Massey house to arrest Rafe Hawkins and Maddie Thacker, both of whom would be charged with murder. When Charley arrived at the Massey place, Luke was on the front porch and told the deputy what had just happened involving his mother and sister and Rafe. He said they all left heading toward the river, so Charley hurried in the same direction.

As Maddie neared the river, she slowed her pace and began searching the shoreline and clumps of bushes along the river, but she expected them to be just around the bend in the road where it came closest to the river. Maddie rounded that bend and saw what she had thought she would: Cecilia and Rafe were on the sandy beach. Memories came flooding back. Some of them were of happy times when she and Sol used to come to the river. But sinister, disturbing feelings came with memory of being on the beach with Sol the night he died. She didn't want to relive that night at this moment. She heard Sol singing again, *Hit her foot against a splinter, fell into the foaming brine.*

"No, Sol, that can't be you singing," Maddie cried. *Ruby lips above the water, blowing bubbles soft and fine. But, alas, I was no swimmer, so I lost my Mad-uh-line.* "Stop, Sol!"

Anyway, there sat Rafe, and he was the one she had to shut up for good. From about twenty-five yards away from her daughter and her target, she screamed and began running toward them. Rafe and Cecilia jumped up, and Rafe ran toward the swinging bridge as the daughter moved toward her mother and pled, "Mother, please don't do this. Put the knife down, and we'll go home. Please, Mother!"

Charley came in sight of Maddie and Rafe as she chased him toward the bridge. The woman would not be diverted from her prey; she didn't even look at her daughter but ran on in pursuit of Rafe Hawkins as he scurried toward the swinging bridge. Cecilia ran behind her mother, still pleading for her to stop, for her to drop the knife; her frantic calls didn't register. Charley stopped his car and jumped out, watching Rafe and Maddie go onto the bridge. As Rafe ran up the steps to the bridge, he saw a sign painted on a wide board beside the last step up to the bridge.

By order of the sheriff, a sign had been posted at each end of the bridge that warned: DANGEROUS, DO NOT CROSS. Rafe read the sign and looked back to see Mrs. Thacker still running toward him with the big knife, screaming at him to stop. He had no choice but to start across the bridge. He remembered that just a few days ago he had crossed the bridge to fish and had to get past a large, gaping hole in the bridge floor that had only a narrow rotted board spanning the middle of the hole. Rafe jumped across a three-foot section of the bridge floor. The board his foot landed on bent and gave a cracking sound but did not break completely, and he continued to run awkwardly on the swaying bridge as he held out his hands to grasp the horizontal support cables.

A few seconds and twenty feet behind Rafe ran Maddie. She heard whistling again—"Clementine." She heard the roar of the Narrows. She came to the hole in the floor Rafe had jumped over; without pausing, she stepped onto the narrow board in the middle of the hole. The old, weathered board bent and crackled loudly. Maddie grasped the left horizontal supporting cable of the bridge but held firmly to the precious knife in her right hand. The board gave way completely, with two jagged pieces falling into the river. *Hit her foot against a splinter, fell into the foaming brine.*

Maddie slipped down through the hole until her knees were barely above the level of the bridge floor as she held on to the cable with her left hand. She struggled to get a leg up above floor level to support some of her weight, but she couldn't. *Thou are lost and gone forever, dreadful sorry Mad-uh-line.* As she tried in vain to get a leg above the floor, she called, "Help me, Cecilia! Rafe, help!"

Rafe stood at the far end of the bridge, staring at the woman who had been trying to kill him, not knowing what to do.

Cecilia was just coming up onto the bridge when she saw her mother break through the floor. Each step the daughter took on the bridge made it undulate, and that bouncing movement increased the load on Maddie's tiring left hand. Still unwilling to lose the knife in her right hand, Maddie struggled to hold on with her left, but her weight was too much for one hand to support. While she tried to muster strength to hang on, her fingers gradually straightened. Still grasping the knife, she fell through the hole screaming, "No, Sol! Sol! No!" Maddie was quickly drawn into the churning waters of the Narrows.

Cecilia stared in horror and disbelief at the chute of turbulent water where she had last seen her mother, and in her mind she saw her father as he had vanished in that same roaring mass of water a little more than two years ago. She sat on the bridge near the hole through which her mother plunged. Dazed, she couldn't even cry.

Charley had stood still until the board broke under Maddie, then he hurried toward the bridge to see if he could keep her from falling; but before he reached the steps, he saw her tumble and heard her screams. He stopped again, looking for her in the water but never saw her. He then went up the steps and started out to where Cecilia sat on the bridge. The grieving girl felt movement of the bridge and looked behind her. There came Deputy Charley Scott toward her. He came to her, squatted beside her and asked, "Are you okay, Cecilia?"

She nodded her head.

He said, "Let's get off this bridge. It's brought you too much pain and loss."

Cecilia let him help her stand. Then he took her hand and led her back to the end of the bridge and down the steps.

As they descended the steps, movement beside Charley's car caught Cecilia's eye. She spotted Luke getting off his bicycle. He appeared scared and bewildered. She ran to her brother. He had scanned the area for his mother but didn't see her. That fact and Cecilia's facial expression told him something bad had happened. Cecilia took his hands in hers and said, "Luke, Mother's gone, she was taken by the Narrows."

Luke glared angrily at his sister and responded, "No, that can't be true. You're just telling me that, Ceecee. Mother will be okay."

"I wish I were wrong this time, Luke, but it's true. Mother fell into the river and went down the Narrows. There's no way she could live through that stretch of water and rocks."

The awful truth dawned on Luke, and the grief-stricken boy clutched his sister while she hugged him and tried to console him. Cecilia wept with her brother as he sobbed uncontrollably; his body shook with spasms of anguish. Finally the siblings stopped crying, and Charley took the two Masseys and Rafe Hawkins away from the river—Cecilia and Luke to his and Bonnie's house and Rafe to jail at the county seat.

After filing the necessary paperwork for Rafe's incarceration, Charley asked the young man if he could do anything for him before he left and if he wanted Charley to get in touch with anyone for him. Rafe said there was nobody to tell anything for him. The deputy told Rafe an attorney would be appointed for him but that if he needed something to let him, Charley, know. Rafe thanked him.

A few minutes after sunset, Charley was back with Cecilia and Luke where he had left them with Bonnie. Almost as soon as the deputy walked through the door, Cecilia said, "Mr. Scott, Luke has some things to tell you."

"I'll be glad to listen," Charley said, thinking that he would rather be eating supper. Bonnie brought her tired husband a cup of hot coffee, and he sipped from it as Luke talked.

A contrite Luke told Charley everything he knew about events related to Verle's death, including the lie he told Rafe and Maddie about

Verle and Cecilia and about his feeding Rafe and giving him quilts to sleep under in the barn Saturday night. He ended his statement with a description of what he saw when Verle was shot. After a long silence, Luke asked Charley, "Am I in trouble because of the lie I told Rafe about Verle and for giving Rafe food and quilts?"

"I can't answer that, son. You may be, but Sheriff Fielding and the commonwealth attorney will be the ones to decide if what you did was a crime."

Charley paused, thought for a few seconds, and continued, "But I will tell you what I think about what you've done in general. You've made bad decisions and said and done things that hurt people, maybe even contributed to a death, and you should be ashamed of them. I hope that what has happened to Verle and to your mother will be a strong signal to you that you need to change your way of thinking and acting. You need to think of how others might be affected by what you say and do. Don't think just about what you can get for yourself. You have a wonderful sister. And she loves you. She's a fine young woman, and you should do everything you can to earn her respect and trust. Do you understand what I'm saying, Luke?

Solemnly, Luke replied, "Yes, I do, Mr. Scott."

Bonnie said supper would be ready in a few minutes and they would eat. She also told the Massey children that she hoped they would spend the night with her and Charley rather than going back to their house, and both Luke and Cecilia agreed. With supper over, everyone was tired and soon in bed, with Cecila and Luke each in a spare bedroom.

After a short discussion of the tragic events of the last few days with Bonnie, Charley's exhaustion caught up with him, and he drifted off to sleep. Bonnie lay awake pondering how a pretty, intelligent woman like Maddie Thacker could have been so greedy and uncaring for others that she caused the death of one person and was instrumental in bringing about the deaths of two others.

The next day, Deputy Scott found himself in a situation similar to what had faced him little more than two years ago. He led a group of volunteers as they scoured the banks of Clinch River searching for a body, and the body they were searching for now was the body of the person who had been responsible for the death of her husband in the river two years ago—Maddie Massey Thacker. As so often happened when Charley was near Clinch River, an old favorite hymn came to his mind, "Shall We Gather at the River." He knew the hymn didn't refer to a physical stream on this planet earth, but he thought the last verse and refrain were especially fitting for the serene, picturesque Clinch. The tune and words ran through his mind.

> *Soon we'll reach the shining river, soon our pilgrimage will cease; soon our happy hearts will quiver with the melody of peace.*

> *Yes, we'll gather at the river, the beautiful, the beautiful river; gather with the saints at the river that flows by the throne of God.*

The river was running at a much lower level and was clearer than it had been during the search for Sol Massey, so Charley hoped Maddie's body had not been carried as far downstream from the Narrows as Sol's had and that it would be easier to spot in the clear water. Both of Charley's hopes were realized. Shortly after ten o'clock, one of the searchers located Maddie's body about halfway between the Narrows and where Sol's body had been found. She no longer clutched the knife she had clung to so desperately on the bridge. The battered and torn body was retrieved and transported to the funeral home to be prepared for burial.

Another violent death had dismayed and unnerved many in Creedy and the surrounding countryside. As details of the deaths and what caused them became known, family, friends, and neighbors expressed their consternation, and they asked why. Why would a respected, capable, hardworking woman want to do away with two husbands? Was it greed that drove that woman to pressure her lover to kill his wife? Did her failure to get the money she expected drive her into insanity? Why would a husband kill his wife just to be with another woman? Why would a human crush the skull of another for a few pints of whiskey? Why would a husband physically and emotionally abuse his wife so severely and for so long that the wife saw no way out of her suffering other than the death of both of them? Why would a young man with many years ahead of him take the life of another man because of vile lies he was too ready to believe?

Finally Deputy Scott and Sheriff Fielding were satisfied that they knew how and why each of the seven mysterious, violent deaths in or near Creedy during the past twenty-six months had occurred. In addition to her own demise, Maddie Massey Thacker was directly responsible for Sol Massey's death, and she was the underlying cause of Lucille and Verle's deaths—she had maneuvered Verle into poisoning Lucille and Rafe Hawkins into shooting Verle. The killers of Sol Massey, Lucille Thacker, and Monroe Bowman were dead or in prison; and Rafe, the killer of one of the killers, was headed to prison.

Abused by her husband and neglected by her sons, Nettie Hawkins had not received justice while she lived. In Charley's opinion, she had probably meted out justice to her tormentor. Hawkins men were responsible for the deaths of Nettie and Willard Hawkins and Monroe Bowman. The first and the last of the seven deaths happened in the water below the swinging bridge, and Maddie Massey had been on the bridge in both instances. With the exception of the plight of battered and dispirited Nettie Hawkins, Charley was satisfied that at least some measure of justice had prevailed.

As Pa and Ma Jess, Belle, and J. R. gathered with Charley and Bonnie in their home, Pa Jess commented about Maddie amd Verle's deaths.

He said, "To me, her passing is the logical, natural outcome resulting from what she did over the last couple of years. Verle's death is tied to what he did to our Lucille. We reap what we sow! Now, that's a biblical principle, but it's also a natural principle. A farmer can't sow mustard seed and reap wheat. He can't plant corn and harvest beans. And a man, or woman, can't sow death and destruction and reap happiness and good fortune—at least, not in the end. Now, that was a long-winded sermon from me, but I'm finished." None of the other solemn family members disagreed.

EPILOGUE

Early 1945

The Christmas holidays and New Year's Day 1945 passed. The first month of the new year brought encouraging war news. The Battle of the Bulge had begun December 16, 1944. Hitler's armies launched a surprise counteroffensive; but after initial successes, the German attack resulted only in a large bulge in the Allied lines. By the end of January 1945, American units had retaken the ground they had lost but at terrible cost. Many, many thousands of American casualties resulted from the Battle of the Bulge, but the Germans lost significantly more than did American forces. The Allies dealt severe damage to German strength. Finally defeat of the German armies seemed to be only a matter of time.

In their original wills, Lucille and Verle Thacker had left all their possessions, including their farm, to the surviving spouse; at the death of the spouse, Charley Scott was to inherit their estate. In the handwritten will Verle prepared a few days before he was killed, he left his farm to Charley and Bonnie. In Maddie Massey Thacker's will, she bequeathed her estate to her two children. A lawyer for Cecilia pointed out that Maddie, as Verle's surviving spouse, had a legal claim to at least a share of the Thacker farm and that those rights passed on to Maddie's children. But Cecilia insisted that Verle had wanted Charley and Bonnie to have the farm. Cecilia appreciated so much the support and care from her former teacher and Charley, and she did not want to claim any part of the Thacker farm. So Charley and Bonnie became owners of that farm. Cecilia and Luke inherited the Massey farm and all their mother's other possessions, including several thousand dollars in her bank accounts.

The commonwealth attorney, with the agreement of Sheriff Fielding, declined to charge Luke with a crime, but they gave him a lecture similar to what Charley had given him. Luke appreciated the break they gave him and promised that he was determined to be a better brother and a more responsible person. It was not difficult for Cecilia, Charley, and Bonnie to convince Luke to enroll in Millersburg Military Institute at Millersburg, Kentucky to finish his high school education. They believed the strict discipline and rigorous academic structure at the school would help Luke change his careless, selfish, and unhealthy behaviors if he wanted to change; Luke now seemed to be genuinely committed to doing just that.

Rafe admitted killing Verle Thacker. Cecilia, Luke, and Bonnie gave depositions and urged the commonwealth attorney not to seek the death penalty for Rafe. The prosecutor's recommendation to the presiding judge was accepted. Rafe was not sentenced to death; the sentence was life imprisonment. Raphael Hawkins was assured by the commonwealth attorney and by his own court-appointed attorney that, under current Virginia law, he could be eligible for parole after serving twelve years. The bearer of Nettie Hawkins's last hope of having one of the three sons she named for angels live up to his name would soon be behind steel bars and walls topped with razor wire. Raphael was on his way to prison, perhaps to join his brothers Gabriel and Michael at Powhatan Prison.

Cecilia asked Charley to manage the Massey farm, oversee the sharecropper, and hire additional temporary farm hands as needed in exchange for one-fourth of the net farm profits, and he agreed to the request. Cecilia made plans to enroll at East Tennessee State College in Johnson City to earn a nursing degree. Or she might decide to go to medical school.

Harg Fielding was elected sheriff for another term. In spite of the series of deaths that occurred during Charley's watch as deputy, he had derived a great deal of satisfaction from his law enforcement work, but he decided he would not continue to serve as a deputy. He wanted to have a regular, more structured schedule to balance time between job demands and family activities. Bonnie was happy when Charley told her of his decision.

Then Brewster McGraw, Bonnie's father, asked his son-in-law to begin working with him to learn about the operation of his businesses, properties, and coal mines because one day Bonnie and Charley would own it all anyway. Bonnie had made clear to her father that she wasn't interested in running the family businesses; she wanted to continue working in the career she loved—teaching school. Charley accepted his father-in-law's offer.

Brewster told Charley he had an offer from Eastern Consolidated Energy, Incorporated to buy his mining operations. He didn't know yet whether he would sell, and he wanted the decision to be made only after he, Mrs. McGraw, Bonnie, and Charley had considered carefully all aspects of the matter and agreed on what they should do.

While Bonnie and Charley were happy about the upcoming changes in their lives, they were ecstatic when they learned they would be blessed with a baby in a little less than six months. The prospective McGraw and Scott grandparents and Musick great-grandparents were thrilled, of course, with the news of a coming little Scott. Charley was supremely thankful for the good life and bountiful blessings that were his—especially for Bonnie, for his family, for the prospect of a son or daughter, and for the freedoms and opportunities he had as an American.

Edwards Brothers Malloy
Thorofare, NJ USA
July 12, 2012